Bourbon Chase

The San Francisco Mystery Series, Book 1

ALEXI VENICE

Published by eBookIt.com

ISBN-13: 978-1-4566-2811-6

Also by Alexi Venice

The Pepper McCallan Series
Ebola Vaccine Wars
Svea's Sins
Victus – Margaret River Winery (Part I)
Margaret River Winery (Part II)
Loch Na Pollach – (Coming in 2017)

The Starr Series
Australia's Starr

Dedicated to my LGBTQ friends

Table of Contents

Carnal Catch — That exquisite, sweet moment when a woman is seized with passion in a romantic encounter and committed to fulfilling her sexual desire without turning back.

Chapter 1

San Francisco

Jen shivered in the damp morning air as she started her ancient Toyota that Tommy had named Aethenoth. She smiled, remembering the night they had parked on a cliff overlooking the Pacific Ocean at Half Moon Bay and made love in the back seat under the full moon. Tommy had said that the silver light shining off her pale skin reminded him of Lady Godiva riding her famous horse, Aethenoth. That night, he declared that Jen's car would henceforth be called Aethenoth the Ancient in honor of Jen's nakedness, just like Lady Godiva.

She adored Tommy for being a romantic, reciting literature and opera lines at intimate moments in their relationship. She, too, had adopted his name for her car, not only because it reminded her of their intimacy, but also because she had agreed with Lady Godiva's cause—forcing her husband to lower taxes. Jen wondered what would become of her if she decided to drive around San Francisco nude. Dangerous thinking. She snapped back to reality.

Aethenoth the Ancient had been a loyal companion, transporting Jen to college in Wisconsin, medical school in Los Angeles, a residency program in San Francisco, and now, three years later, to her position as an emergency room physician at San Francisco Community Hospital. The miles had taken a toll on Aethenoth, however, so as sentimental as Jen was about her, she was considering buying an SUV.

"Aethenoth, I'm sorry to break it to you, but the SUV I'm interested in has heated seats. I could use those about now," she said, revving Aethenoth to life, flipping the wipers to remove the ocean fog that had condensed on the windshield overnight. The sky was dusky pink, and Jen was groggy, just coming off the night shift and now working days. She sipped hot coffee from her Thermos as she began the thirty-minute drive to San Francisco Community Hospital. She lived a few blocks from the beach, and the hospital was on the other side of the city, so she had an easy commute in the morning, but a traffic-packed one in the evening.

Once the heat was pouring through the vents, she drove north on 46th Avenue, turned right onto Lincoln Parkway, followed Golden Gate Park to its panhandle, then crawled through the Haight Ashbury neighborhood with the other early morning commuters. Finally entering Highway 101, she had a clear shot to the hospital.

Despite Dr. Jen Dawson's minimalist appearance of a ponytail and no makeup, male patients would still hit on her while she cared for them in the emergency room. She was a classic Nordic beauty—high cheek bones, deep blue eyes, aquiline nose and a smile like California sunshine.

Addicted to the thrill of all things physical, Jen had a muscular figure, and was training for the Dolphin Club Escape from Alcatraz Triathlon, which was only a few months away. The physiology geek in her had prepared a calendar on poster-sized paper, then taped to the wall in her kitchen. On it, she penciled in her daily training stats of calorie and protein intake, as well as her time and distance for running, biking and swimming. Her chart kept her focused and on-track, notwithstanding her demanding work schedule. She was at the peak of her training, building muscle and endurance. Nothing would interfere with her goal. No partying with Tommy. No going out with people from work. No distractions. Just training for the big day.

She deliberately blinked her eyes as she drove, drinking more coffee and fighting her circadian rhythm to wake up for the day shift. There was a heaviness in her bones from flipping her sleep cycle from day to night. Today would feel like wading through waist-deep water, never making it to shore, but she would slog through. Tomorrow would be easier, and each day thereafter until she could catch up on sleep over her days off. In fact, the only thing that could tube her triathlon performance would be sleep deprivation, so she had carefully planned her work schedule around the big day.

Tommy joined her on runs and bike rides when he could, but he worked long hours as a detective in the homicide unit at SFPD.

Recently, he had baked a large pan of lasagna for Jen, freezing individual serving sizes in plastic containers for her evening meals. His Italian philosophy was that pasta was the best training food, and she couldn't argue with that, especially if he made it.

As she entered the neighborhood where the hospital was located, she found a parking spot a few blocks off Potrero Avenue. Leaving Aethenoth unlocked, Jen walked to the hospital campus in the dawn light with other employees. Pushing through the revolving doors, she greeted the staff at the main reception desk, then swiped her name badge to open a side-door into the Emergency Room. She skirted the Unit Station and walked down a long corridor to the physicians' locker room, where she changed into turquoise scrubs. Emerging seven minutes later, she was ready to work a ten-hour shift.

Jen joined the nurses and physicians who had congregated at the Unit Station, a long desk facing three banks of patient rooms, enclosed by a glass wall running from desktop to ceiling. The glass partition dampened the noise from nurses talking at the station. More importantly, however, it was a barrier between dysfunctional visitors and the staff behind it.

Jen's colleagues were huddled at the long desk, talking in hushed tones about something serious.

"Good morning. What are we talking about?" Jen asked.

"You haven't heard?" a nurse asked.

"I just woke up and came to work. I don't know anything."

"Oh. Horrible news. You know the ultrasound tech, Natasha Farber?"

"Yeah. The cute one who likes to chat?"

"Yes. She was found dead in her apartment yesterday afternoon."

"What? You have to be kidding me? From what?"

"They don't know. It might have been natural causes, but she was so young, and she never told any of us that she had a condition, like an arrhythmia or something."

"Maybe it was a pulmonary embolus or an aneurysm. You never know," Jen speculated. "Are they doing an autopsy?"

"I think they have to. It's a Medical Examiner case," the nurse said.

"That should yield some answers. Funeral arrangements?"

"Haven't heard anything yet. I'm sure her family is in shock right now."

"Does she have family in the area?"

"She was from Ohio and friends with Cheryl, her supervisor in Radiology. Cheryl will know."

"How sad. She was so young. Keep me posted on arrangements."

"My money says that her husband killed her," another nurse blurted.

They all stared at her.

"What do you mean?" Jen asked.

"I heard they were separated because he beat her. Cheryl told me that Natasha showed her bruising on her arms from him grabbing her. So, Cheryl connected Natasha with the Employee Assistance Program, then helped her file charges against her husband."

"Really? So, you think he actually killed her?" Jen asked.

"Yes. I think he was a vengeful bastard who was jealous of her."

"Why?"

"Because she was moving on from him. They were separated. Word on the street is that she was in a relationship with a new man."

"Anyone we know?"

The nurses shook their heads, then busied themselves with other duties as Dr. Lane Wallace, Jen's colleague, entered the station, maneuvering around the chairs with his cane, so he could sit at one of the computer screens designated for x-rays and other imaging tests.

"Good morning, Lane," Jen said.

"Not really," he said in disgust.

"I take it you heard the news about the ultrasound tech," Jen said, as the nurses scattered.

"Her name was Natasha Farber," he grumbled, staring at the computer screen and entering his password.

Jen heard his voice catch when he said Natasha's name. "Did you know her?"

"We all knew her. She did ultrasounds in the ER." Dr. Wallace stared hard at the X-ray on the flat screen, not making eye contact with Jen.

"Yes. Well, some better than others. I didn't interact with her much on day shifts."

"What's *that* supposed to mean?" he asked, whipping off his half glasses and staring at her.

She put her hands up in surprise. "Nothing! It's an expression—some better than others."

He continued to stare at Jen.

"Whoa, Lane. Did I stumble into something? Did I offend you?" She lay her hand on his shoulder.

He tried to talk, but couldn't, his face creasing and tears filling his eyes.

"Come on. Let's go in the back doc room," Jen said, referring to the physician work room. She led the way, and he grabbed his cane, following her into a small room with a conference table, three computers, and a mini fridge in the corner. When the physicians needed to review medical records, dictate notes, or otherwise get some quiet time during their shift, they used this room. Thus, its moniker—back doc room.

Jen spied a box of Kleenex and handed it to him. He grabbed a handful and fell into a chair, letting his cane fall to the floor. He sobbed uncontrollably, so Jen slid a chair next to him and rested her arm across his shoulders.

"Let it out, Lane. Let it all out." She sat silently while he shook in sorrow, doubled over, his face in his hands. Several minutes passed as they sat together.

She had no idea he was this close to the ultrasound tech, but her mind was racing with possibilities.

When he had gathered himself, he blew his nose and sat straight in his chair. "I'm sorry you had to witness that."

"Don't be. It's what friends are for. I'm here for you...and, I know you'd do the same for me."

"It's just that—she was so young. So beautiful—"

"I take it you knew her better than I did."

"I was in love with her."

Jen had no clue, believing he was happily married to Susie. They had a little girl, named Angelina, who Lane talked about frequently. "Care to talk about it?"

"It's all so confusing. I helped Natasha get rid of her asshole husband who abused her, and, in the process, we grew closer. Not at first. It was very professional at first. One colleague helping another. We met for lunch, then drinks and—"

"I understand," Jen said, resting a reassuring hand on his knee.

"She needed me, you know? More than Susie needs me. Natasha was vulnerable and scared. And with my military training, I thought I could protect her. I spent more and more time at her apartment—just in case her husband made a surprise visit. At first, it was platonic, but I think we both knew we wanted something more."

"What about Susie? Does she know?"

"No. God, no. She'd divorce me if she knew. I think she suspected I was going through something but assumed it had to do with baggage from serving in the desert. We've been through so much together that I think she sort of lost interest at some point along the way. She loves me. Don't get me wrong. She just has so many other things on her mind— her work at the gallery, functions at Angelina's elementary school."

"How old is Angelina now?"

"She's eight, and I'm worried about how this is going to impact her."

"She loves you, and knows you're a good father."

"I try. With Susie's mom in the nursing home now, Angie and I have more time alone together because Susie and her brothers are always taking care of her mother."

"I'm so sorry, Lane. You know I'm here for you."

He nodded, but his mind was elsewhere.

"Have you considered some counseling?"

"What? And make a formal medical record of my affair and how messed up I am? The hospital brass would probably use it against me."

"You know it doesn't work that way. It's confidential. Administration wouldn't see it."

"Don't you believe it," he sneered. "Hospital administration gets their hands on everything. They're like the fucking CIA."

Jen disagreed but didn't want to argue. He was prone to paranoia, which she assumed stemmed from his military experience. "You take some more time to gather yourself. I'm gonna start my shift."

"It might take a few minutes."

"That's okay." She picked up his cane from the floor and leaned it against his chair.

Jen left the room and quietly closed the door. As she walked out, the nurses who had previously scattered were reassembled at the desk, staring at her.

Why am I always the last to learn everything around here? she wondered.

***

Chapter 2

South of Market Street

George Banks, a plain clothes police officer, opened the rear door of District Attorney Amanda Hawthorne's Jaguar at the Hall of Justice at 850 Bryant Street, the large government building that housed law enforcement. She was met at the foot of the stone steps by a police escort who walked her from the curb into the lobby. She produced her identification badge and set her black leather briefcase and Chanel bag on a conveyer belt for scanning.

George, her driver, would park her car in a secured area behind the building, then occupy his cubicle in Amanda's suite of offices to do light desk work until she needed him to escort her outside the building. George had worked in law enforcement for thirty years and was spending the last few years of his career as her primary security detail. Her busy calendar was his work life.

Amanda rode the elevator to the third floor, exited and walked down the polished, green floor, her heels echoing off the marble wainscoting of the paint-chipped walls. She scanned her badge on the pad to enter the District Attorney's Office. As she strode through the private corridor, she was greeted by early-bird staff and the assistant DAs who were working at their desks, preparing their cases for court.

Amanda had been District Attorney for three years. At the age of thirty-five, was one of the youngest ever to be elected to the post. The Bay Area voters loved her. Not only was she a cunning professional with a proven trial record of putting away criminals, but she also was gay. Being active in the gay rights community, she had garnered most of the LGBT vote, a formidable coalition to have in San Francisco County.

Sylvia, Amanda's Press Secretary, fell into step beside her, reporting that the media was inquiring about the death of a twenty-eight-year-old ultrasound technologist named Natasha Farber who worked at San Francisco Community Hospital.

"Why? Someone dies in San Francisco every day," Amanda said.

"Mrs. Farber was married to an abusive husband, Mr. Blake Farber. It could have been an overdose, or any number of causes, but her father is a glass manufacturing tycoon in Ohio who has political connections. He's some billionaire immigrant from Russia, and he's already called the mayor's office and SFPD, alleging that Mr. Farber killed Mrs. Farber," Sylvia said.

"How did you find this out?" Amanda asked.

"I spoke to Ryan a few minutes ago," Sylvia said, referring to Detective Ryan Delmastro, the supervisor of the SFPD detectives.

"What did Ryan say?"

"He told me to tell you all of that. Oh, and he assigned the file to Detective Vietti."

"To the extent there is a file, I'm sure Tommy will be on top of it. I'll call him right away. He and I can call the Medical Examiner together. Given the optics and family connections, I'm going to oversee this file myself. Mayor Woo will probably be calling."

"Do you want me to disclose that to the media?"

"Sure. Tell them the District Attorney and a senior detective are looking into Mrs. Farber's death, but it would be premature to comment at this time. Thanks."

Amanda swiped her badge to enter her private office, flipping on the lights to her well-appointed government lair. Her dignified office was complete with the California state flag on one side of her picture window and the United States flag on the other, framing her million-dollar-view of the Bay Bridge.

She hung her black, Burberry raincoat on the back of her door and stowed her bag in a desk drawer, plugging her cell phone into a cord that lay on her desk.

Her calendar would be packed with a variety of matters today, but she personally wanted to oversee the Farber case because her gut told her it would be a challenging file, from both a political, as well as a legal, perspective. She would have to carve out time to think like a prosecutor instead of a manager, which she was required to be in her current post. As boss of the Assistant District Attorneys, she oversaw and was involved in the prosecution of a variety of cases, but hadn't personally taken one in a few years.

She was at the top of the pyramid in the criminal justice system for the County of San Francisco, and accountable to the voters for making decisions whether to prosecute, enter into a plea agreement or dismiss the charges of a crime. To keep her skills sharp and her credibility high with voters, she would dig into this file. Plus, she liked Tommy Vietti, as they had worked many cases together when she had been an ADA.

There weren't any political flare-ups at the moment, and she didn't have anyone at home waiting for her, so it was as good a time as any to take on work. Her last relationship had ended six months ago, and she hadn't thought about Elizabeth in a long time. They had enjoyed each other's company, but both quickly realized there wasn't long-term potential there. Elizabeth had called it and quietly removed herself from Amanda's life. For that, Amanda had been grateful. No drama. No media coverage.

The voters didn't seem to care about Amanda's lifestyle, but she didn't want to test the limits of her popularity by splashing the details of her personal life all over social media.

She powered up her computer and instant-messaged Detective Vietti, asking him if he had time to meet. He replied that he would come to her office right away, so she busied herself with emails while she waited.

"Good morning, Tommy!" she said a few minutes later when he knocked on her door. Amanda surprised Tommy by jumping up and hugging him.

"You look gorgeous, as always, Amanda," he said, returning the hug. "To what do I owe the pleasure?"

"I assigned myself to the Farber file."

"Any particular reason? It's probably going to be a nothing."

"I know, but apparently, her father is a glass manufacturing billionaire who lives in Ohio, and he's already called Ryan Delmastro and Mayor Woo. Plus, it's time for me to get back in the rotation." She returned to her chair and motioned for Tommy to sit as well.

"I heard. Ryan spoke to Mr. Dimitri Ivanov, the victim's father, late yesterday. The guy is connected, so Ryan asked me to babysit the file until the autopsy results come back."

"I'm sure the Ivanovs will fly into the city in the next few days."

"I can meet with them."

"Thanks. I'll call Mayor Woo and run interference."

"Better you than Ryan. They clash."

"Right. Not a good mix."

"It will be good having you on the front lines again, dealing with all the shit we have to every day. Just think, I can give you a hard time again," he teased.

"Trust me. I've missed it—more than you know. The ADAs are afraid of me, so don't hold back with your ideas," she challenged.

"I won't. Let me tell you what I've learned so far."

"I'm ready," she said, her pen hovering over a yellow legal pad.

"The victim worked as an ultrasound technologist at San Francisco Community Hospital. She was married, but separated from her husband, Mr. Blake Farber. More on him in a minute—"

"Tell me about the scene," Amanda interrupted.

"She died in her apartment. No signs of a struggle. No forced entry. She was found on the kitchen floor. An empty tumbler was on the white rug next to her, a stain of amber-colored liquid in a spray pattern next to where she lay. Probably from the tumbler. There were some dirty dishes and glasses in the sink and on the counter. Door was locked."

"Did you seize the tumbler and bottles?"

"The officers at the scene did. Let me find the evidence log." He flipped through the papers on his lap. "There were open bottles of several liquors, including bourbon, gin, vodka and wine. They dropped them at the crime lab for analysis."

"Is the lab any faster than when I was an ADA?"

"No. Hopefully, we'll get the results tomorrow. They expedited the request."

"Good. Next question—who found her?"

"Her supervisor at the hospital, Cheryl Gutierrez. When Mrs. Farber didn't report for work, Ms. Gutierrez tried texting and calling her. It wasn't like her to miss work, or not return texts, so Ms. Gutierrez called the police. She met an officer at the apartment complex, and the manager let them in."

"Did the officer interview Ms. Gutierrez?"

"Yes. He's finalizing his report, but I spoke to him already. He said Ms. Gutierrez told him the estranged husband had recently beat the victim. That's why they were separated, and the victim was living alone. Ms. Gutierrez said that Mrs. Farber told her on a number of occasions that Blake Farber had beaten her, and showed her bruising on her arms. The officer reported seeing bruising on the victim's arms at the scene."

"Whereabouts of the husband?"

"Lives in the city," Tommy said, referring to San Francisco.

"Has anyone spoken to him yet?"

"No. The officers were planning to last night, but didn't get to it. I can today."

"Track him down and invite him to meet here. Given Dimitri Ivanov's status, I think we should talk to Blake Farber in the interrogation room so we can record it."

"Will do. Blake's no stranger to visiting our fine establishment. He has several priors. Aside from traffic citations, he had a breaking-and-entering eight years ago, at the age of twenty-two. He entered into a deferred acceptance of guilty plea if he agreed to pay for the damage to the building and do community service. He completed both, and the charge was dropped a year later. That was followed by a sexual assault charge at a night club, which he denied, and that was later dropped, too. He had a disorderly conduct and domestic battery against the victim two months ago. The prosecutor dropped it when Blake agreed to move out of the apartment."

"What does he do for a living?"

"The file we have on him says construction work."

"Hmm. If she came from money, why did she marry such a loser?"

He shrugged. "Can't help who you fall in love with."

"True. Message me when he gets here. I'm curious about him."

"Will do."

"Which Medical Examiner is assigned to this case?"

"Steve Strumboldt."

"Have you spoken to him yet?"

"No."

"Let's call him together."

Tommy read the phone number to Amanda as she dialed it on her speaker phone.

"Strumboldt here," Steve answered.

"Hi Steve. It's Amanda Hawthorne and Tommy Vietti."

"Hi. Two senior people. To what do I owe the pleasure?"

"We're curious about the Natasha Farber death," Amanda said.

"The autopsy is underway. I was just planning to join it. My initial inspection of the apartment didn't reveal anything suspicious.

Could be natural causes. Could be anything from an anaphylactic reaction to sudden heart failure. Could be a drug overdose, which is my bet. No exterior signs of a struggle. It looks like she fell to the floor and perhaps hit her head on the counter on the way down. She has a bruise on her forehead about the size of a quarter. There were some older bruises on her arms. No needle marks, so the bruising wasn't related to drug abuse."

"You said there was a bruise on her forehead? Like a goose egg?" Amanda asked.

"Not that big. Could just be lividity from how she landed. I'll send photos of it with the autopsy report. Lots of possibilities. Like I said, she could've overdosed on something. Wait for the toxicology results to come back, and we'll know what drugs were in her system. I should join the pathologist now."

"Thanks, Steve. Call us if you and the pathologist find anything. Bye," Amanda said.

"Bye," Steve said, and ended the call.

"Overdosed?" Amanda asked, raising her eyebrows.

"Probably. Could have been natural causes, or an overdose—either accidental or intentional."

"I think you should question the victim's supervisor at the hospital, too, even though the duty officer did."

"Want me to bring her in so you can listen?"

"Absolutely."

"Will do. It feels good to be working with you again, Amanda."

"Likewise," she said, meeting his eyes. "Just like the good old days. I'm off."

Tommy left, and Amanda consulted her electronic calendar to see what the day held for her. Meetings, more meetings and a charity event at seven o'clock.

Terrific, another night standing at a fundraiser, she thought. She clicked open the event and saw that it was at the Moscone Center—dinner and silent auction for San Francisco Community Hospital. What a coincidence. Maybe the CEO of the hospital would be there, and she could do a little reconnaissance, perhaps asking him if he knew anything about Natasha Farber, and more realistically, who might.

***

Chapter 3

Hall of Justice

Tommy dialed the cell phone number listed in the police database for Blake Farber. The fact that Blake had a record, prints and contact information on file made Tommy's job much easier.

"Hello?" Blake answered.

"Is this Blake Farber?"

"Yeah. Who's this?"

"This is Detective Tommy Vietti, San Francisco Police Department."

"It's about time you called me."

"What's that supposed to mean?"

"My wife died yesterday, and San Francisco's finest waited until *today* to call?"

"In that case, want to talk in person?"

"Where?"

"Are you familiar with the Hall of Justice on Bryant Street?"

"Been there a few times."

"Come to the lobby and check in. I'll meet you. How many minutes away are you?"

"Thirty."

"See you in thirty. Bye."

Tommy clicked off his phone and dialed the cell phone number for Cheryl Gutierrez, Natasha's work supervisor at the hospital. She couldn't break away from the hospital today, so he arranged for her to come in for an interview the next morning.

He instant-messaged Amanda that Blake Farber was on his way, and that he would call her as soon as Blake arrived.

Tommy's cell phone beeped, indicating he had an incoming text.

Hey, ur still planning to take me to the hospital charity ball tonight, right? Jen asked.

Caught a case today, but I'll try.

Do I have to go alone? My attendance is mandatory. In and out—two hours—max.

I might have to meet you there. What time?

7pm. I'll be the sexy lady in the blue dress☺

Let's meet there. Work clothes ok?

No. Black tie. Is ur tux clean?

Hanging on the back of my office door.

Ur very handsome in it.

Anything for u.

Maybe you'll get lucky.

Maybe I should wear it more often.

Ha. See u there.

Tommy didn't much care for formal fundraisers, but he cared for Jen, so would dutifully stand by her side. This would be the second year he attended the hospital charity event. Or was it the third? Since they'd been together, anyway.

He returned his attention to reading Blake's police record until the lobby security called him, informing him that his visitor had passed through and was waiting to be collected. He IM'd Amanda, then took the stairwell to the lobby. Blake was an averaged-sized man, with brown scraggly hair and a soul patch on his chin. He came off as a bit defensive, his shoulders rounded and an ape-like walk.

They shook hands, and Blake followed Tommy to the elevator bank. The doors were covered with vertical corrugated sheet metal, a stark contrast to the caramel-colored marble walls flanking them. When the metal doors cracked open, Tommy and Blake entered the roughest looking elevator outside of a Third World country. The walls were adorned with brown-flecked Formica that resembled the countertops of a 1974 trailer home. The well-traveled floor was chipped and worn, a patina of grime built up from years of heavy traffic.

They rode the elevator to the third floor where the interrogation rooms were located. A singular fluorescent train of lighting in the middle of the ceiling illuminated their walk down a long hallway. The interior was ugly, by any measure of a government building, desperately in need of a multi-million-dollar remodel.

They turned right into the District Attorney Investigations Department, where Tommy scanned them through the glass door and into an area occupied by cubicles. They walked briskly past staff to a door jamb in the blue-painted wall at the far end of the space. They entered the interrogation room.

His home-away-from-home, Tommy was comfortable with the stark governmental surroundings of the small room. He loved the raw simplicity of it—two people having a conversation to see if one of them committed a crime. Or witnessed a crime. He sat on one side of the metal table and Blake on the other.

Amanda arrived in the hallway outside the room to listen and watch through the one-way glass. She had a microphone on a table in front of her, and Tommy had an ear bud in place, so she could whisper in his ear as he conducted the interview. The exchange between Tommy and Blake would be videotaped as well.

Even from several feet away, Amanda could see that Blake looked like he hadn't slept. His bloodshot eyes were puffy slits. He sat slumped in his chair, his elbows resting on the table. His right knee was bobbing up and down under the table, burning off excess energy, exposing his nervousness. Blake looked like one of many punks she had seen throughout her career. Sweatshirt and jeans. Expensive Air Jordan tennis shoes. A guy in his mid-thirties who was stuck living in his twenties.

"I'm sorry for your loss," Tommy said.

"Thanks," Blake said, staring at the metal table, his jaw set.

"Can you state your name, date of birth and address, please," Tommy asked.

"Why? It's not like I'm under arrest or anything," Blake said.

"No. You aren't. We're just investigating the death of your wife, Natasha Farber, and I need to do my job and make a record of it. It helps if I have to contact you for any reason."

"Fine," Blake said, providing his vitals.

"I noticed the address you gave is different from the deceased's apartment."

"That's right. I moved out about two months ago. Can you not call Natasha 'the deceased?' Her name was Natasha."

"Of course. How insensitive. Where do you live now?"

"With a friend. He let me crash in his extra bedroom, thinking it would be only a few nights. It turned into two months."

"What's his name?"

"Trevor Ross. Why?"

"Just for the sake of completeness. It's my job. Why did you move out two months ago?"

"I'm sure you've read the police report, so you know why. It's part of my plea agreement. I keep my distance from Natasha, and the charges get dropped," Blake said, indignation rising in his voice.

"I'd like you to tell me in your own words how that domestic battery charge came to be filed."

Blake sighed. "We drank too much, got in a fight, and I lost it. She called the police, and they arrested me. The prosecutor agreed to drop the charges if I moved out and had no further contact."

"Have you been back to the apartment since?"

"No. We just texted if we needed to communicate, because Natasha wanted 'a record' of everything I said," Blake said, using air quotes.

"Are you willing to turn over your cell phone today for us to verify your texts with her?"

"Absolutely. Here it is," Blake said, removing it from his sweatshirt pocket and sliding it across the table.

"What's the passcode?"

"fuckyounatasha. All lower case."

"Still harboring a little anger?"

"Well, she already started fucking another guy, and we'd only been apart two months. I'd like to see how you'd handle your woman fucking another guy."

Tommy sat back in his chair and studied Blake. Average height and weight. No distinguishing features. No visible tats with his sweatshirt on. No visible piercings. Anger burning in his bloodshot eyes.

"When was the last time you saw Natasha?" Tommy set Blake's phone aside.

Blake opened his mouth to answer, but no words came out. Tears filled his eyes, so Tommy gave him a minute to compose himself.

Blake wiped his blotchy cheeks with his sweatshirt sleeve.

"Try the passcode in the cell phone," Amanda said into Tommy's ear bud.

Tommy entered the passcode and the phone came to life. He thumbed his way into texts and read the last exchange between Natasha and Blake, which was on the night she died. She asked him if he had been in her apartment. He hadn't replied yet.

Tommy read it aloud. "'*Blake, have you been in my apartment?*' Did you receive that text from Natasha?"

"Yes," Blake said, rubbing his eyes.

"Did you reply?"

"No."

"Why not?"

"I thought I would talk to her about why she thought I'd been in her apartment—ask her what was going on."

"Makes sense," Tommy said, scrolling through their text exchanges. "She also texted you a few weeks ago, asking if you were following her."

"And, see, I wasn't. I wonder if someone else was, and she thought it was me."

"Okay. We're going to review all the texts on your cell phone, and I might have follow-up questions. Is it okay if I keep it for a few days?"

"Yeah. Like, two days. It's my brain, you know?"

"Thank you for the courtesy. About my last question, when was the last time you actually saw Natasha?"

"Within the last couple of weeks."

"Where?"

"On the street in front of her building."

"What for?"

"She was giving me some stuff from the apartment. Pots and pans. Picture frames. My stereo. Stuff like that."

"Did you enter the building?"

"Maybe the lobby to pick up the boxes. Check the security video from the lobby if you want. I'm sure I'm on there, picking up boxes."

"There's a security cam in the lobby?" Tommy made a written note.

"Yeah. Been there forever. I assume it works."

"Okay. Thanks for the tip. How do you think Natasha died?"

"I think the fucker she's sleeping with killed her." Blake's bloodshot eyes turned wild with fury.

"Who would that be?"

Amanda's ears perked up from the other side of the glass.

"She was having an affair with a doctor, Lane Wallace, from San Francisco Community Hospital. He was at our old apartment all the time—staying several hours," Blake said, again breaking down.

"How do you know? If you haven't been there in two months?"

"She told me. We talked, you know? She asked me for a divorce because she said she had—she said she had fallen in love with Wallace."

"Really? Did she text you asking for a divorce, or call you, or meet in person?"

"I don't remember. You can look through her texts to me."

"Tell me what you know about this Lane Wallace, and why you think he killed Natasha."

"Older than Natasha. In his forties. He's married, and I think he has a kid or two. He's an emergency room physician. Kinda ugly. Has a beard. Walks with a cane."

"Go on."

"I tried to tell her that he wouldn't leave his wife and family. That he was just using her, but she wouldn't believe me," Blake said, his face reddening.

"How long had this affair with Dr. Wallace been going on?"

"I don't know. Maybe a month. Maybe longer."

"Why do you think he'd kill Natasha?"

"The oldest reason ever—to keep his wife from finding out about his affair," Blake said, squinting at Tommy like he was dull.

"What makes you think the wife didn't already know?"

"Natasha told me when I said I wanted to meet him and check him out. She begged me not to bother him or make a big deal out of their relationship. They had to keep it a secret from work and his wife."

"And, you have reason to believe that Natasha threatened to make it public, so he killed her?"

"Yeah. That's what I think happened. Natasha was in love with him, and he didn't want her to mess up his perfect family life."

"What makes you think Dr. Wallace would be capable of murder?"

"He was in the Army—served in Iraq. I researched him. He has a record, too. Domestic battery charges himself a few months ago. You should look him up. Guys change when they serve in the Army. So yeah, I think he coulda killed her. He even texted me a few times, telling me to stay away from Natasha, 'or else.'"

"Or else what?"

"I have no idea. I took it as a threat. It should still be in my text messages on my phone. I put him in my contacts list."

"Have you met him?"

"No. But I've seen him going in and out of our old apartment building."

"Were you parked out front, keeping tabs on Natasha?"

"Maybe," Blake cleared his throat, recognizing this answer didn't jibe with his previous answer about not being at the apartment for two months. "I'm her husband, you know? I was worried about her."

"So, you *were* stalking her, huh?"

Blake sat for a minute, staring at the wall behind Tommy, his right leg bobbing at a higher rate of speed. "It's not stalking if I just sat in my car and watched who went in and out of a large apartment building."

"Judging by Natasha's text to you, she thought it was."

"Whatever. I still think he did it."

"I'll make a note. Do you have any other ideas?"

"I bet there are text messages between them on *her* phone, too. Do you have her phone?"

"Yes. I believe it was taken into evidence."

"You should check it."

"It's password-protected."

"Bring it to me. My thumbprint is in it. Or, at least it used to be."

"When did you put your thumbprint in it?"

"Long time ago. Before I moved out."

"In front of her?"

"No. She was probably in the shower or something. It was pretty obvious. I entered my thumb as number three. I think her thumb and forefinger were numbers one and two."

"Why did you do that?"

"To check up on stuff. Good thing I did, too, because it's going to help you in your investigation," Blake crossed his arms over his chest.

Amanda whispered to Tommy that they were retrieving Natasha's cell phone from the evidence room. They waited in silence for a few minutes.

"Do you want some water?" Tommy asked.

"Yeah. That'd be great," Blake said.

Tommy left the room in search of a bottle of water. He met up with the officer who was bringing Natasha's cell phone and returned to the interrogation room with both. Tommy sat, then slid the water and phone across the table to Blake. Blake turned it on, used his thumbprint, and unlocked it.

"Do you want me to program a new passcode for you?" Blake asked.

"Yes. Use SFPD. All caps," Tommy said.

Blake did as requested and handed the unlocked phone to Tommy.

"We're going to review all the information on both your phones. After that, I might have more questions. Do you have any suggestions about friends or relatives we should talk to?"

"No. Just the bastard she was dating." Blake guzzled his water.

"Got it. What about family?"

"I called Dimitri and Elena, even though they hate me. They're flying in on their private jet today. I'm sure they'll be on your door step as soon as they get here, wanting me hanged in the town square."

"Why?"

"They thought I was a loser from the beginning, because I wasn't some big fancy lawyer or something. I just work construction, usually commercial jobs."

"What do they do for work?"

"They're first-generation Russian and came with enough money to get into manufacturing. Natasha told me her father was running from Russian politics. He wanted to get out before he pissed off someone close to Putin. So, he bought a glass manufacturing plant, which was his business in the old country, and successfully expanded, going into different lines of business. He's done very well for himself. Natasha's mom, Elena, is a stay-at-home mom."

"Okay. Why don't they like you?"

"They never gave me a chance. Natasha and I fell in love, but they didn't buy it. They wanted her back in Ohio, but she fell in love with me and San Francisco, so they stopped sending her money. She rebelled, married me and started a job at the hospital. I was the guy who stole her from her family."

"Did they stay in touch?"

"Sometimes, but when they tried to control her with money, she drew the line. Money never meant that much to her. She sure as hell wasn't going to work in the glass manufacturing industry and live in Ohio, I can tell you that. Dimitri even tried to buy me off before I married her. Told me he'd give me fifty grand if I never saw her again. I guess that's the way they do it in the old country. Bastard."

"Harsh. What's your trade in construction, Blake?"

"General construction crew."

"Are you working now?"

"Yes." Blake gave Tommy the location on Potrero Hill.

"Okay. I'm instructing you not to leave the city. If I need you, how do I reach you, since you just gave me your phone?"

"How about I call you tomorrow to see if you're done with my phone?"

"That works," Tommy said. "Here's my business card with my direct line on it."

"Thank you for investigating this. I truly believe that bastard doctor killed her."

"I appreciate your candor," Tommy said, leading Blake out of the room and down to the lobby. He watched him walk out, memorizing his appearance.

***

After Tommy finished with Blake, he returned to Amanda's office. "What do you think?"

"Interesting story. He obviously didn't stay away from her apartment for two months, but he covered himself well. Interesting that Ms. Farber thought someone had been in her apartment."

"She didn't say why though."

"Makes you curious, doesn't it? Let's get Dr. Wallace in here, too."

"I plan on it."

She consulted her notes. "We need to transcribe all the texts between and amongst the three of them. We also need to download all the contacts in each of their phones."

"Yep. I'll ask the guys in Computer Forensics to get on it right away."

"And, Natasha's supervisor, Cheryl Gutierrez. When?"

"Tomorrow morning."

"Okay. You're on top of this, as per usual."

"Yeah. I can't stay late tonight, though. I have to leave around six to attend the Community Hospital charity ball with my girlfriend, who's a doctor there. Are you going?"

"I heard a rumor you were dating a doctor. Moving up in the world, huh?" she teased. "I have to attend as well. Maybe I'll get to meet your girlfriend."

"I hope so. You'll like her."

***

Chapter 4

Moscone Center

Amanda's Jaguar rolled along Howard Street, its five-hundred-fifty horsepower engine growling under the hood. As George drove it beneath the yellow lights of the Moscone Center entrance, the car's finish looked like a black vapor eddying in the shadows of a river bank. In direct sunlight, it was a rich burgundy, but in certain light, its patina turned darker. Like its owner, the car was powerful and possessed many shades.

George and Peter, the other security detail, were dressed in their tuxes for the event. Peter stopped the car next to the media's clicking cameras, the rear door poised over the red carpet for Amanda's entrance. George jumped out and opened Amanda's door, offering his hand. She took it and rose out of the back seat in her black dress and high heels, a red sole briefly showing, as she scooted out and onto the red carpet.

Amanda clutched her Hermès black box and confidently strode down the red carpet, George one step behind her, while the photographers from the local media snapped a thousand photos of her. Her jet black, naturally curly hair was swept up, save for a few corkscrew strands around her face, accentuating her long, slender neck. She wore a black cocktail dress, complemented by a modest amount of jewelry—dangle earrings and a diamond-ruby necklace.

She smiled demurely, not a limelight-seeker by nature. This amount of attention made her uncomfortable, although she concealed it well behind her confident, composed demeanor—a professional mask. A photographer snapped a close-up of her face, capturing the depth of her intelligent, brown eyes that angled up ever so slightly at the corners. The photo would be splashed over social media, alongside the celebrities and mega-rich who also attended that night.

The closer the lens, the more her unvarnished intelligence and compassion emerged. There wasn't always warmth, but her eyes conveyed understanding and knowledge. There was an intensity there, too, reflecting the importance of the work she did —overseeing the investigation of crimes, trying cases, and putting criminals behind bars. Amanda had as many layers of steel as a modern skyscraper, but withstood the earthquakes with more poise and grace.

She was stunning, but more than that, she was the living embodiment of how sophisticated and diverse the people in the Bay Area were. She represented their full potential, and her constituents adored her for it.

George guided her through the crowd to an escalator, and they ascended two floors to a magical ballroom, decorated in an aquarium theme for the entertainment of the high-rolling benefactors. Amanda worked her way around the room, easily conversing with the rich and powerful. Between promises for lunch dates and whispered support, she found time to bid on several items in the silent auction along the north wall. She took personal satisfaction in raising the stakes on the bids, prepared to pay the hefty dollar amounts she scribbled down for the items.

At the auction tables, she found herself next to the Chief Executive Officer of the Hospital, Mr. Harold Bertrand.

"Good evening, District Attorney Hawthorne. Thank you for attending," he said, admiring her figure.

"Please, call me Amanda. I wouldn't miss it. How are things at the hospital, given the death of one of your employees?"

"People are shocked and saddened. I'm relieved that SFPD is investigating it."

"Do you know anything about it?"

"No. I didn't know the deceased or any of her coworkers. Though I've been informed that her supervisor is Cheryl Gutierrez. You might want to talk to her."

"Thanks for the tip."

"Anytime." He was interrupted by other partygoers, so Amanda smiled and returned to bidding on select items.

***

Jen steered Aethenoth the Ancient into the Moscone Center parking ramp and grabbed the ticket the machine spit out. When the crossbar lifted, she drove in and found a spot on the second floor. She left the single key under the driver's seat, hoping someone would steal the car, and proceeded to the skyway toward the charity ball. Receiving several admiring glances as she entered the grand space, she decided she might have fun after all. Tommy would be late, which was no surprise, but it had been a few months since she had mingled with her colleagues, so she decided to enjoy herself.

She searched for table number twenty-three, where her group of emergency room physicians and their significant others would be situated. Over a hundred other physicians and significant others were in attendance. When she drew closer to her table, a passing waiter offered her a glass of champagne and she accepted it, her training protocol allowing only one for the evening.

As she greeted people, she wasn't surprised to see that Lane Wallace and his wife were absent. The hospital had scrounged up a replacement for them with an administrative fellow and his significant other. Jen introduced herself, chatting easily about biking and hiking in the Bay area.

Just as she was running out of small talk, she felt a strong arm encircle her almost bare back—the unmistakable arm of Tommy Vietti.

He kissed her neck. "Hello, gorgeous."

She leaned into him. "Hi Tommy. Let me introduce you to my colleagues."

As Jen had experienced on other occasions, the young couple was more enamored with Tommy's work as a detective than anything Jen had to say. She couldn't blame them. The gruesome work of a detective, fighting crime in a dangerous city, seemed much more intriguing than the patients Jen treated in the emergency room. Or, maybe it was the way Tommy told stories. In any event, after Tommy had regaled them with a few of his favorite stories, she pulled him over to the silent auction tables.

"Are you gonna bid on something?" he asked, glass of champagne in hand.

"Probably not. I'm just curious what the high rollers are bidding on these one-of-a-kind items. And, I want you to myself before we eat. You look handsome tonight, by the way."

He trailed his thumb down her bare back and planted a kiss on her temple, as she slowly moved along the tables of items.

"Tommy, look at this. The DA, Amanda Hawthorne, bid ten thousand dollars on this oil painting of Sausalito."

"I'm not surprised. It would be like her to increase the bidding, knowing full well she could afford it if no one bid above her. I admire her generosity."

"You know, I've heard you talk about her, but I've never met her. You seem to know her so well."

"I knew her better before she became DA three years ago. She's been busy managing her office and dealing with the press and politicians. She hasn't had time to work with the detectives. We're on a case together now, though, so we'll get reacquainted."

"I'd like to meet her."

"I'd like that, too," he said, kissing her cheek. "I told her you'd be here tonight."

"You talk about me at work?" Jen asked nonchalantly.

"Of course, baby. You're the most important part of my life."

She gave his hand a squeeze and scrutinized the next auction item until the flickering lights indicated the ten-minute warning that the auction would close.

***

When the lights flickered, it was Amanda's ten-minute warning to wrap up her socializing and find her table of eight Assistant District Attorneys. The celebration provided an opportunity for the assistant DAs to dine together since they were all so busy in court when they were at work.

"George, wait here," Amanda said, leaving his side. "I should use the ladies' room before I sit down."

"Take your time."

Amanda entered the posh ladies' room and turned the corner to use the lounge area for a hair and makeup check. She joined an attractive blonde woman at the mirror who was about the same age. They both leaned against the counter, reapplying lipstick and smoothing back runaway strands of their updos.

"I love your dress," Amanda said to the woman. "Navy is a fabulous color on you, and the design in back is gorgeous. I can never seem to find the right cut in an open-back style."

Jen looked at the compliment thrower in the mirror. She was taken aback, recognizing Amanda Hawthorne from extensive media coverage. "Thank you. Although I wish I were wearing your heels. I'm dying to know if they're Christian Louboutin," Jen asked, her voice somewhat husky from the champagne.

Amanda blushed and lifted her heel to reveal the tell-tale red sole. "I'm embarrassed to say they are. One of my few extravagances, I have to admit."

"Well, they're amazing. You're Amanda Hawthorne. I'm Dr. Jen Dawson," Jen said, extending her hand.

"Have we met before?" Amanda asked, training her sharp eyes on Jen.

"Ah, no," Jen said, smiling. "But my boyfriend, Tommy Vietti, seems to be making it his goal for us to meet tonight."

"You're Tommy's girlfriend? Finally, I get to meet you. It's my pleasure."

They shook hands, Amanda's grasp strong and warm on Jen's larger hand. Jen felt Amanda's assessing eyes travel quickly over and through her. She had never felt so exquisitely invaded in subsecond time. So disconcerting, it was as if she had just told Amanda her life story.

"You're very fit. How do you find the time to work out as a busy ER doctor?" Amanda asked.

"I'm training for a triathlon right now, so you pretty much struck gold with that compliment," Jen replied.

Their eyes met and Jen's heart flip-flopped. Her own passion for life was thrown right back at her, except with gold flecks dancing in brown eyes. If she weren't careful, she could get lost in those eyes. A stirring occurred. One that had lain dormant for over a decade. One that she hadn't experienced since college. One that she thought she would never experience again.

Jen broke eye contact and shook if off. "Well, it was nice meeting you. I should get back—"

"To Tommy," Amanda finished for her. "I hope we meet again."

Jen dropped her lipstick into her clutch, turned from the mirror and walked toward the door. With her fingers resting on the door handle, she stole a glance over her shoulder at Amanda in the mirror. As she expected, Amanda gave her a quick smile in the mirror. Was it seductive, or had Jen imagined it? She masked her response and slipped out the door to rejoin Tommy.

***

A few minutes later, Amanda exited the ladies' room to find George waiting for her, and they weaved their way to her table of colleagues. The ADAs were several drinks into the evening, laughing heartily. She accepted a glass of champagne from a waiter, and George slid out the only remaining chair at the table for her. She melded into work talk with her colleagues and ate the mediocre meal, while recalling the subtly-charged exchange she had experienced in the ladies' room.

She'd never been that attracted to a woman at first sight, and found the notion distracting. Jen had classic Nordic features, piercing, blue eyes and a tanned body. Her smooth back in that dress was positively kissable. Amanda had immediately picked up on Jen's strong hands— hands that were used for work as well as working out. An athlete's hands. The small veins over the top were visible as they ran up her forearms. Amanda chided herself for lapsing into a reverie about Jen's body. How schoolgirl. She dismissed Jen from her mind.

As the crowd finished their dinner, the Master of Ceremonies announced that a band would start at the other end of the room shortly. First, however, he had the honor of announcing the winning bidders in the silent auction who had overpaid for the items by thousands of dollars, knowing the money went to a good cause.

The hospital sponsored the ball to finance the needs of the bottom quartile of the city's socio-economic class. Located in the heart of the city and accepting everyone without regard to ability to pay, the hospital's frequent flyers included the homeless, the uninsured, those who couldn't afford to pay what their insurance didn't pay, and a variety of gang members who never planned on paying anyway.

After several items were bestowed on their new owners, the MC came to the oil painting of Sausalito that Amanda had bid on.

"And the top bidder for this oil painting of Sausalito is Amanda Hawthorne, our renowned District Attorney. Thank you, Amanda, for your generous bid of $10,000."

Amanda gracefully rose and walked to the podium, escorted by George, who looked distinguished with his thick grey hair combed straight back. When the MC presented her with the painting, George stepped forward and took it for her.

"Maybe District Attorney Hawthorne would like to say a few words about safety initiatives in our fair city. I don't know about you, but I've never felt safer walking around at night than I have since she took office," he said, abruptly handing the microphone to Amanda.

It was obvious that Amanda wasn't expecting to make a speech. Jen felt nervous for her, but simultaneously curious to see how she would handle herself.

Amanda deftly took the mic and comfortably addressed the audience. "Thank you, Dave. I appreciate your kind words. I wasn't planning to speak at this event, but when the cause is so important, it's easy to make a few extemporaneous remarks." She smiled, connecting immediately with everyone in her confident, reassuring voice.

"I, too, am grateful for the service of our men and women in law enforcement who patrol the city streets day and night. Reducing crime is really a multi-agency effort that involves much more than my office. Many of you in this room are involved in efforts to address mental health issues, teenage homelessness, drug addiction and the list goes on. This is one of the reasons tonight is so important. San Francisco Community Hospital serves some of the most vulnerable residents in our community, so it desperately needs financial support. We're all proud to donate to the hospital and we're very thankful to all of its staff for the care they provide. Thank you for your generosity in giving to the cause. I'm grateful for your efforts in working together to reduce crime."

Everyone broke into applause as she returned the mic to the MC. Amanda blushed as she returned to her table, stopping to shake hands with a few people on the way, George in tow with her painting.

Her team congratulated her with pats on the back, as George held her chair for her. Once she was seated again, the corners of her mouth turned up subtly as she sipped her champagne. Public speaking came easy for her even if being the center of attention didn't. When the auction items were fully distributed, the MC kicked off the live band and invited people to mingle and dance.

Amanda's boisterous table of attorneys accepted the invitation, dragging her over to the dance floor, even though she had no intention of joining. There were some things she just couldn't do as the DA, and one of them was make a fool out of herself on the dance floor. She considered herself a good dancer, but not to *this* music, and certainly not in front of the cameras. She stood at the edge and watched her table of lawyers tear up the floor.

"Amanda! There you are," Tommy Vietti said behind her.

She was relieved that someone was going to save her from feeling ill-at-ease by the dance floor. She turned to greet Tommy.

"Tommy, I'm so glad to see you," Amanda said, giving him a peck on the cheek.

"Me, too. I want you to meet my girlfriend, Jen. Jen, this is District Attorney Amanda Hawthorne. Amanda, this is Dr. Jen Dawson," Tommy said.

"We actually met before dinner in the ladies' room," Amanda said, making a note that Jen obviously hadn't relayed their encounter to Tommy.

"What? The mysterious powder room? I think more happens in there than men will ever know," Tommy said.

Amanda smiled, and Jen returned the favor of coolly assessing her this time. She immediately picked up on Amanda's discomfort about their previous exchange.

"Jen has practiced as a physician for three years in the emergency room at San Francisco Community Hospital," Tommy said.

"You mentioned that at work," Amanda said, raising an eyebrow and thinking about their new file. Their eyes met.

"Nice spontaneous speech," Tommy said.

"Thank you. If I'd known I was expected to make a few remarks, I wouldn't have imbibed. I'll have to make a note for next year."

"It was perfect," Jen said, smiling reassuringly. "Tommy tells me you two have worked together a long time."

"Oh yes. We go way back, but we haven't worked a case since I became DA. Tommy actually taught me how a detective puts the evidence together, then we collaborated on how to present the case to a jury. And, for that, I'll always be grateful," Amanda said, raising her glass to him.

"That's not true, and you know it. I'm just happy we get to work together again. It's been too long," he said.

They smiled at each other. Jen wondered what they were working on, finding herself a little jealous of their relationship, but from which angle, she wasn't sure.

"How are things at the hospital?" Amanda probed.

"Sad. We're all shocked and heartbroken that our colleague died suddenly. I hope the autopsy yields some answers," Jen said.

"It's troubling, isn't it? Please convey to your coworkers that we're going to do everything we can to rule out foul play."

"When is the autopsy?"

"We're not at liberty to discuss this, Jen," Tommy said, as if on script. "It's an on-going investigation."

"I thought we were talking as friends. I'm not the media, you know. I knew Natasha. Not well, but I knew her," Jen said.

"We understand. It's just that we're prohibited from discussing evidence or an investigation until there are formal charges. We have to be careful about not speculating or leaking anything. We've been burned in the past, so Tommy's right. It's probably best if we consider this topic off-limits for now," Amanda said.

"Good suggestion," Tommy said, swirling the whiskey in his glass. "Off-limits."

Jen gave them both an icy stare. "How condescending."

"Jen—" Tommy was surprised that Jen would say something like that to Amanda, of all people.

Amanda waved him off. "You're right, Dr. Dawson. It comes off as condescending, but we have certain rules—"

"I understand the concept of confidentiality. We're all professionals here," Jen said.

Amanda and Jen locked eyes for the second time that night, but this time it wasn't friendly. An arc of energy resonated between them—equals at an impasse. There was an awkward silence as Tommy looked from his girlfriend to his colleague, uncomfortable that the situation had taken such a strange turn.

"It was a pleasure meeting you," Amanda said, still holding eye contact with Jen. "I should say goodbye to a few people before I leave."

"Likewise," Jen said, finally blinking.

Amanda disappeared into the crowd, George in tow.

"Fuck me," Tommy said after Amanda left. "That was uncomfortable."

"Don't be so dramatic. I'm ready to leave," Jen said.

"Are you angry?" Tommy asked.

Jen didn't reply. She simply set her glass of water on a table and walked toward the door, Tommy trailing after her.

They rode the escalators in silence to the parking garage where Aethenoth the Ancient was parked.

"Did you drive?" Jen asked.

"No. One of the guys dropped me. I thought you'd have Aethenoth."

"I do."

"Can we go back to your place?"

"Yes."

***

Chapter 5

The tension in Aethenoth was palpable when Tommy and Jen settled in for the drive to her row house in the Sunset District.

"Baby, how many times do I have to tell you not to leave your keys under the seat of the car?" he reprimanded.

"I'm hoping someone will steal it."

"Insurance won't cover the loss if the keys are left in it."

"I don't believe that. Just because the keys are in it doesn't mean I don't own it. If someone steals it, it's still stealing. If I leave my house unlocked and someone comes in, it's still trespassing. Anyway, what business is it of yours?"

"Just trying to look out for the woman I love."

"Is that it?" she asked, as they wound down the ramp and paid at the window.

"Yeah. Why?"

"I'm not a teenager. I don't need you to look out for me. And, I sure as hell don't need to be told that certain topics are 'off limits' by you and your power-tripping prosecutor."

"Whoa. I didn't know our conversation upset you so much. I can't help that it's standard operating procedure."

"Fuck your SOP!" she snapped. "My coworker died. I tell you stuff about the hospital. You could at least reciprocate when one of your cases involves my world. God,

Tommy. We're not in front of your boss anymore."

"Technically, she's not my boss. Ryan Delmastro is my boss. She's the DA. Different department. Anyway, the problem is that you know some of the people I have to investigate. I don't want to find out information from you that I didn't get through the investigation. And, likewise, I don't want to put you in a position where you know more than your colleagues do."

"I never realized how paternalistic you were. Do you honestly believe I don't know how to compartmentalize?" she asked, exasperated.

"Of course, you do, but, I'd feel better about not forcing you to do that on this case."

"That's for me to decide. Not you. Quit trying to sell it like you're withholding for my benefit. You're withholding for *your* benefit. Period."

"I don't know why you're so pissed. It's a Department rule, like Amanda said. Especially when we don't even know if foul play was involved. The victim could have accidentally overdosed."

Jen didn't reply, silently vowing not to tell him anything she knew or learned in the future about his investigation. She was so angry that she was afraid she'd say something she regretted, so decided to remain silent for the remainder of the drive back to her place.

Tommy dropped her at her door, then went in search of a parking spot on her block. He figured this small gesture of gallantry would go a long way, but she didn't even say thank you as she got out and slammed the car door. Her mercurial nature was a mystery to him, but he had been raised in an Italian family with an explosive mother, so he was well-conditioned to handle Jen's emotions.

He drove down 46th Avenue, then turned right onto Judah Street, which was named after 'Crazy Theodore Judah,' a civil engineer who had a radical vision in the late nineteenth century to build a railroad over the Sierra Nevada mountain range. It worked, but he was later ostracized by the railroad barons.

By the time Tommy let himself into her house with the key on her ring, she already had shaken off her dress and removed her makeup.

"Hey baby, want something to drink? A nightcap?" he asked, the rich timbre of his voice filling her small kitchen.

"No. Just water. I'm tired." She padded to the kitchen in her slippers, pajama pants and a tank. Frost covered her entire body, the chill stinging Tommy in the small space.

Tommy leaned back against the counter, an adoring stare on his face. Jen poured herself a glass of water and leaned against the opposite counter, reluctantly admiring his rugged good looks. Her irritation dissipated as she let her eyes roam over his weathered face and hunky body. He had untied his bow tie, the loose ends now hanging down his simple, white dress shirt that was unbuttoned a few.

"You look good in that tux," she said, breaking the silence. There was something about him in a tux...

"Thanks. I'm glad you think so because I have something for you." He set his glass on the counter.

"Oh?"

He reached into his jacket pocket as he dropped to one knee in front of her.

"What are you doing?"

Tommy carefully opened the lid on a black velvet box, and held up a diamond engagement ring to her. His hands were shaking, jiggling the ring under Jen's eyes.

"Jen Dawson, will you marry me?" he asked, meeting her intense eyes.

Jen's hands flew to her mouth. "Oh God, Tommy. A ring? I didn't expect this so soon."

"Not the response I was hoping for." His Sicilian eyes transmitted the anticipation in his heart.

"I'm sorry. This is just such a surprise. We just argued—" she said, her hand still covering her mouth.

"Think about how long we've been together."

"Three years..." she whispered behind her hand. "I'm sorry."

"Is this *Tosca's kiss?* Are you going to stab me now, too?"

"What are you talking about?"

"Nothing important."

"Is it opera again?"

"Yes." He hoisted himself into a standing position and stared down at her, the ring box still in his palm. "Don't you love me?"

She focused on his chin, confused herself as to why she hadn't said yes. "I love you. I just don't know if I'm ready to take the leap, that's all."

"What the hell?! Is this because I won't break police protocol and tell you about the case?"

"Of course not! It's about my shortcomings. Nothing more. Can I sleep on it?"

"Seriously? I put myself out there, and you need to sleep on it? What have you been doing for the last two years?"

"We've been together three years."

"That's my point! Most women wouldn't have waited this long!"

She could see his thick neck straining as his voice rose.

"I think we both know that I'm not most women," she said, raising her chin to him.

"What the hell is *that* supposed to mean?"

"It means that you should know me well enough by now that my request to sleep on it shouldn't be surprising. Can you cut me some slack here?"

He ran his hand through his thinning, sandy-colored hair, then thrust the ring box at her, refusing to return it to his pocket. Draining his whiskey, he watched the love of his life stare blankly at the ring he had just offered her.

Jen couldn't bring herself to try it on, not wanting to send him mixed messages. In fact, she wasn't sure she even liked it. It was a simple platinum band with a traditional setting and a decently sized diamond. Too bad she didn't want a diamond. She just wanted a gold band, so she could wear it on a chain around her neck at work. She had to don and doff latex gloves a hundred times per shift, so rings were a nuisance. Moreover, she was into sports and CrossFit, and this fragile setting would break if she wore it while lifting weights. It was totally impractical. Not her. How could she tell him she hated the ring?

"What are you thinking?" he asked.

"That you went to a lot of trouble to buy a pretty ring. I'm sorry," she said, handing it back to him.

He snapped the lid shut and held it in his palm, which had stopped shaking. "Where do we go from here?"

"To the bedroom. Will you stay tonight?"

"Now you're amorous?"

"I just need some time." She leaned into him, twirling the end of his tie in her fingers.

"Let me convince you." He scooped her up and carried her to the bedroom.

***

The next day

Despite making love the night before, it was an uncomfortable ride to work in Aethenoth next morning. Tommy drove expertly through his native city. Like all cops and cabbies, he drove fast, taking shortcuts, timing the lights just right and sliding through stop signs.

They arrived at the Hall of Justice first. It was located South of Market, referring to the diagonal street layout south of Market Street. More recently, the district had been tagged SoMa, à la SoHo in Manhattan.

They both got out, meeting on the sidewalk next to her car.

"Thank you for last night," he said, engulfing her in a bear hug.

"Are you being sarcastic?" she asked against his neck.

"No. I meant for having sex with me, not for saying you needed more time."

"Oh. I liked that too." She ran her finger along his clean-shaven cheek.

"I left the ring in its box on your nightstand." His eyes were full of hope.

"I didn't notice."

"Well, think about it." He started to say something else, but stopped.

She waited a second, finally saying, "I will."

He gave her a hug and turned to jog up the stone steps.

Jen returned to her car, slid behind the wheel and drove over to Potrero Avenue, following it to the hospital.

Alone in Aethenoth, she reflected on Tommy's marriage proposal. *Why did I turn him down? Women have been falling all over him for years. He's dependable. Stable. At forty-two, he's ready to marry. He's good-looking. He treats me well. We have a lot in common. He wants kids. I want kids. He's lived in the city his entire life. I definitely want to stay here. My parents like him.*

She absent-mindedly kept up with traffic.

Why did I tell him I only liked sex last night instead of loved it? Why can't I bring myself to say yes? I love him, don't I? If I don't marry Tommy, how many more opportunities are realistically out there for me? I'm sure he'll get me another ring if I ask him to. A simple gold band. I hate that ring. It has a diamond in it. Sooo not me. But Tommy is for me, isn't he?

She pounded the steering wheel. *I might need more than one night's sleep on this.*

Completing her ten-minute drive from the Hall of Justice to the hospital, Jen turned off Potrero onto Hampshire, a residential side-street, and scored an unusually close parking spot for the day. She left Aethenoth unlocked and briskly walked a few blocks, then disappeared into the revolving Emergency Room doors.

***

Chapter 6

Hall of Justice

Tommy barely got to his desk and booted up his computer when an instant message popped up from Amanda, asking him to meet her as soon as possible.

He left the Investigations Unit and walked down the fluorescent-lit, public hallway to the District Attorney Office suite. He passed through the small waiting area, its dated furniture dismal and spartan, then scanned himself into Amanda's office corridor.

Her door was closed, but he could see her on the phone through her sidelight window. She spied him, waved him in, and watched as he quietly observed her expansive digs. She smiled inwardly at the detective in Tommy when he gave her the thumbs up on where she had hung the ten-thousand-dollar oil painting of Sausalito that she had purchased at the hospital auction. He didn't miss a trick. She recalled how he had long ago noticed the dragonfly theme on the Tiffany lamps in her old office, which she had brought to her new one.

"Very well, then. Goodbye," she said, ending her call. "Tommy. Good morning. You like where I hung my new painting?"

"It goes well in here. Too bad your view is of the Bay Bridge and not Sausalito, or you'd have the same view out the window as the painting hanging beside it."

"How true. Did you and Jen enjoy yourselves last night?" She remembered seeing him run his thumb across Jen's bare back, then lean in for a smooch.

"We did until we got back to her place."

She cocked her head.

"It's nothing."

"It doesn't sound like nothing."

"She's not like the other women I've had in my life, that's all."

"In what way?"

"The other ones—they all wanted to get married. Especially my ex-wife. Man, did she wanna get married fast." He shook his head.

"And Jen?"

"I can't figure her out."

"She doesn't want to get married?"

"I guess not. She turned down my marriage proposal last night."

Amanda's eyebrows shot up. "Are you serious?"

"Yes. I was down on one knee, holding a big diamond ring and everything, and she turned me down."

"I'm so sorry. How long have you two been dating?"

"Three years, she tells me. Seemed like only two to me."

"Did she give you a reason?"

"No—just that she needed to sleep on it. But, the look on her face this morning wasn't very promising. I left the ring on her nightstand. Maybe it will remind her that I still exist."

"Do you think it's because we wouldn't discuss the case with her last night?"

"I have no fuckin' clue, Amanda," he said, his voice rising. "I don't understand women. Maybe you could read the tea leaves and tell me what they mean."

"Ha. I doubt it. If it makes you feel any better, in matters of the heart, women aren't any better at reading each other than men are."

"Good to know. I'll give her some time. What else am I gonna do, right?"

"So true," she agreed, curious herself.

"You wanted to talk this morning?"

"Yes. I see on my calendar that Natasha Farber's supervisor, Cheryl Gutierrez, is coming in to meet with you."

"Yeah. At nine o'clock."

"I'm looking forward to hearing what she has to say."

"Me, too."

"On another topic, did you read these texts that the Computer Forensics guys assembled last night? The ones they removed from Natasha's cell phone between her and Dr. Wallace?" She gestured toward her flat screen.

"Haven't had a chance to." He wondered what time she got to the office if she had already hung a painting and read reports.

"Well, they definitely establish a relationship between Dr. Wallace and the victim, as Blake told you. At first, the texts are just friendly 'can-I-help-you' messages from him, referring to her abusive relationship with her husband."

Amanda sat behind her desk, reading the texts as she summarized them for Tommy. "They agreed to meet a few times in his office. There were also several emails about meeting in 'the rad room,' wherever that is. Probably their clandestine love nest at the hospital. Then, she told him she was anxious and wanted to see him as a patient. From what I can tell, he prescribed an anti-anxiety med for her—Xanax. We'll know more when we get her medical record, if he made a record of her patient visit, that is. I assume you've sent a subpoena over to the hospital for that?"

"Yesterday. Your paralegal prepared one for me. I spoke to a frosty lawyer in the hospital Legal Department, and she agreed to expedite our request. I told her I'd pick it up today—personally."

"Good. That will tell us when their doctor-patient relationship began. If he saw her as a patient first, then had sex with her, that could present a licensure issue for him. Although the texts seem to present the opposite picture, meaning sex first, then a patient."

"Regardless, if he isn't in prison for murder by the end of this, then he might have a licensure issue."

She nodded and continued. "The texting continued, and they met in-person, going out for coffee, then leaving the hospital campus. There are lots of messages back and forth about days and times when they could meet at her apartment. The sexting started after that, almost exclusively by her, though. He wasn't very chatty."

"So, Blake wasn't imagining that they were sleeping together."

"Oh no. Things burned hot and heavy for a good month between Natasha and Dr. Wallace. The tone soured, though, because she clearly wanted more. Probably got a little clingy from his perspective. He texted her that they needed to cool it because his wife was suspicious. That didn't sit well with her, though. Recently, her texts overtly suggested that Wallace tell his wife about the affair, then get a divorce so he could marry Natasha."

"No surprise. When will men figure out that their mistresses want the same thing as their wives—half. Half his time, his house, his cars, his money, everything." Tommy shook his head and threw up his hands.

"Male or female, it's the same. The reason you're in a relationship is to spend time with that person. Be together. Share everything." Amanda stared at her flat screen.

"Did Natasha threaten to out him?"

"She didn't by text, but the tone became more persistent that he needed to tell his wife. It appears that Natasha must have been delivering some ultimatums in person, because Dr. Wallace's texts turned cautious and guarded. He used phrases like, 'Give me some time...Stop pressuring me...We can't discuss this by text.'"

"Sounds like he's running, doesn't it? The big question is whether he threatened her."

"Let me see. I'm scanning. We're getting there...Here's one. 'Stop threatening to tell my wife. I won't see you any longer if you threaten me.'"

"Yeah, but does Wallace say, 'Stop threatening to tell my wife, or I'll kill you?'"

"No. It simply sets the stage for escalation, and what he might have said in person."

"Does it end there?"

"No. Here's something interesting to Dr. Wallace. It's the last text from her phone—the night she died. It says, "*I think someone has been in my apt.*"

"That was the second text she sent that night. She also sent one to Blake, asking him if he had been in her apartment. I wonder what made her think that?" Tommy asked.

"Equally as important, she didn't suspect Dr. Wallace. Instead, she conveyed her fear to him."

"Did he reply?"

"No. That's it," she said.

"Do you think they were emailing at work, too?"

"Good question. We have to check, don't we? I'll get a search warrant for both Natasha and Dr. Wallace's work computers, as well as their offices." Amanda scribbled a note to herself.

"Be sure to include the hospital computer system. There might not be any emails saved on their individual hard drives. They might all be stored on the hospital servers."

"Good point. I'll start drafting the warrant right away. We should present it to a duty Judge today. Let me see who's on." Amanda pulled up a calendar. "Good. It's Judge Grady. He likes me. The sooner you can grab those emails, the better. I wouldn't be surprised if Dr. Wallace already deleted them."

"I agree."

"When are you going to question Dr. Wallace?"

"I'd like to get the lab results on the liquid on the kitchen rug and what was in the liquor bottles, first. There might be something in the lab results that I need to ask him about."

"Will you goose the lab and tell them we want those results today?"

"Will do. We're also waiting on Natasha's autopsy toxicology results. The reference lab takes so long."

"As I recall, it took over a week on some of my cases when I was an ADA."

"That's too long for this case."

"Tell them it's high profile, and I'm personally requesting it."

Tommy made a note.

"Did you put a tail on Blake yesterday?" she asked.

"I ruled it out because I was still thinking this would be a big nothing. Why spend the resources, right? I'd better do that now." He made another note.

"You know how it is. Once they realize they're a suspect, they start destroying evidence. We need to keep close tabs on him for the next few days."

"Yeah. Got it. Anything else?"

"Did Natasha's parents contact you yet? Blake said they were on their way."

"It's seven-thirty in the morning, Amanda. They might not be awake."

"Right. Although, I bet they didn't sleep. Tell me as soon as you schedule a time to meet with them. I'll keep my calendar flexible."

"I figured as much," he said, itching to get out of her office.

"Okay. We both have things to do. Catch up later?" she asked, picking up on his impatience.

"Right. And, thanks for listening about Jen." He headed for the door.

"Any time." She stared at the door after he left. Tommy wasn't the only one who was confused about Jen. Her behavior didn't make sense to Amanda, either. The pretty doctor wasn't sure she wanted to marry a good guy like Tommy, yet she'd invested three years in him. That didn't make sense.

***

Chapter 7

Hall of Justice

Tommy returned to his desk and called his supervisor, Ryan Delmastro, to ask for more resources on the case.

"What can I do for you?" Ryan answered. He was Tommy's second cousin. Born and raised in the North Beach District of the city, Tommy was related to almost everyone in law enforcement.

"I need help on the Farber case. Amanda Hawthorne is busting my balls to get everything done ASAP, and I can't be everywhere all the time."

"She took the case? Did Dimitri Ivanov call her, too?" Ryan asked.

"Not that I know of, but he called Mayor Woo after he spoke to you, so she said she'd run interference with the mayor."

"The good news is that she's really good at handling rich, powerful men. The bad news is that you have to work this case with her."

"I've worked plenty of cases with her, and I'm sort of glad to have the head honcho. By the time Amanda and I finish this investigation, the Ivanovs and Mayor Woo will be satisfied that we did a thorough job."

"No doubt."

"Listen, if I'm gonna quarterback this thing, I need a team that can play fast."

"Fine. What do you need?"

"A tail on a suspect, Mr. Blake Farber, and someone to run over to the victim's apartment building to get the lobby security cam footage."

"I'm short-staffed, but maybe I could pull a couple of guys from the drug unit to surveil the suspect. A patrol officer assigned to the neighborhood where your apartment building is located could get the security cam footage."

"Perfect."

"If Amanda is personally on this case, then we'll give her everything she wants."

"I owe ya one."

"Just give me the addresses, you dumb fuck."

Tommy gave Ryan the addresses.

"Do we need a search warrant for the security cam footage?" Ryan asked.

"See if they'll release it voluntarily first. If not, I'm sure the DA's office would be happy to prepare one."

"Will do. Anything else, your highness?"

"Yeah. Could you ask the Computer Forensics guys to review the security cam footage when the patrol officer returns with it? That way, I don't have to be the middleman, and it won't sit on my desk if I'm out."

"What should I tell them to look for?"

"I'll email you a photo of Blake Farber."

"Just out of curiosity, how many hours are on the security cam footage."

"I don't know, because I don't know how far back they save footage."

"Okay. How long are we supposed to tail this Blake Farber?"

"Let's start with a couple of days and see what the reports look like."

"I can make that work, but you owe me."

"Thanks man," Tommy said, ending the call.

Tommy called the SFPD forensics lab and asked about their analysis of the liquor bottles in Natasha's apartment. *Nothing yet. Later today. Yes, they know it's a rush.*

Next, he called the reference lab located in South San Francisco about Natasha's toxicology results from her autopsy so he could learn what was in her system when she died. *They'd see what they could do.*

He called the Medical Examiner, Steve Strumboldt, about the final autopsy report. Steve told him it was on its way.

"Anything interesting?"

"Not really. Aside from the lividity in her forehead, the autopsy was normal. Heart and other organs looked healthy. No aneurysms. We were postulating that it looked like an overdose," Steve said.

"Overdose of what?"

"Only the toxicology results will determine that."

"Right. Tell me more about the arm bruises."

"They were fairly deep, which means a lot of pressure was applied. I'll send you the photos. It's difficult to tell whether she was grabbed from the front, with her arms at her sides, or whether her arms were being held above her head. With fresh bruises, you can tell by the thumb and finger mark distribution to determine that. These were faded, though, so we couldn't tell. Maybe you'll be able to from the autopsy photos. It would have taken a day for the bruises to appear, so you're looking at the incident taking place seven to ten days ago."

"I'm making a note. I'll have to correlate that information with the timing when the men in her life visited her. Thanks Steve."

"No problem. Bye."

Tommy remembered that Blake had told him he hadn't seen Natasha for two months. Maybe he was lying. Or, maybe the doctor bruised her while trying to convince her not to call his wife. The bruises were a prime subject area for the doctor's interview, so Tommy made a note to the list of questions he was starting for Dr. Wallace.

His cell phone rang.

"Hello?"

"Is this Detective Vietti?"

"Yes."

"This is Dimitri Ivanov. Natasha Farber's father."

"Mr. Ivanov. I'm so sorry for your loss. Are you and Mrs. Ivanov in San Francisco?"

"Yes. We'd like to talk to you if you have time."

"I'm planning on it. How about noon today?"

"That works for us. Where do we meet you?"

"The Hall of Justice, 850 Bryant Street."

"We'll be there."

"I'll meet you in the lobby."

After they hung up, Tommy IM'd Amanda that the Ivanovs were coming in at noon.

Let's have it in my conference room, she replied.

***

Chapter 8

San Francisco Community Hospital

A few hours into her shift, Jen was sitting at a computer in the back doc room, entering information into a patient's electronic medical record. The room was conveniently located behind the nurses' station, so the physicians were easily accessible if the nurses needed them, and it was a quiet place to work. A secret benefit was that the physicians could hide from patients and families for a few minutes if they needed to focus on something.

Lane Wallace opened the door and joined Jen. "How was the charity ball last night?" he asked.

"Sucked. How was your night?" she asked.

"Sucked even worse," he replied, closing the door. "I finally told Susie about my affair with Natasha. It hit her pretty hard. We had a big fight, and she doesn't know if she'll stay with me. It wasn't just the affair. It's Natasha's death, too. She's majorly freaked out, threatening to take Angelina and move out."

Jen looked up from reading a patient's chart. "Lane, I'm sorry." She regarded him more closely. There were large beads of sweat forming on his forehead, and his complexion was ashen. He was resting a lot of weight on his cane, struggling to breathe, and leaning like the Tower of Pisa. Leaning more, and more—

"Lane?" she asked.

"I don't blame her. I fooled around—" Wincing in pain, Lane didn't get the chance to finish his sentence. He put his right hand to his chest, dropped his cane with his other, and crashed into the table.

The force of his fall sent the other end of the table into the air. Computers and flat screens flew, as Lane bounced off the table and hit the floor with a loud thump. He rolled onto his back, semi-conscious.

Jen flew out of her chair and rounded the table, opening the door on her way over. "Code Blue!" she yelled to Cindy, the Health Unit Coordinator, who organized everyone and everything in the department. "Need some help in here! Call a Code Blue!"

Cindy had already heard the cacophony of crashing computers and jumped out of her chair. She ran to the doorway of the back doc room. Once she saw Lane on the floor, she returned and called the hospital operator to announce an overhead page for "Code Blue in the Administrative Conference Room, ER."

Within seconds, a team arrived with a crash cart equipped with medications and a defibrillator.

Jen kneeled at Lane's side. He was still awake, but struggling for air. She loosened his tie and leaned in close to talk. "Lane, talk to me. Are you on any meds?"

"No."

"Do you have any heart issues? Family history?"

"No."

"Where does it hurt?"

He lay his hand on his chest. "Tight."

He was in obvious pain and was cold and clammy to her touch. She removed her stethoscope from her white, jacket pocket and put the ear buds in. She inserted the diaphragm between the buttons on Lane's shirt and listened. He was in an arrhythmia. She felt his pulse. His heart rate was slow. The Code Team arrived, and Jen downloaded what he had just told her, as well as her findings.

They immediately transferred him to a bed that they wheeled into an available patient room. On the way to the room, Lane vomited, so they rolled him on his side to prevent aspiration.

Jen and the team attached electrodes to him, two at his wrists, two at his ankles, and six around his heart, to perform an electrocardiogram, or EKG. The overall magnitude of his heart's electrical activity would be measured from twelve different angles and be recorded over a ten-second period.

Jen ordered the resuscitation panel of blood work, so the phlebotomist drew several tubes of blood that would be analyzed in the lab for oxygen saturations, enzymes, ammonia, acetaminophen, electrolytes and a medication screening, among other things.

The team gained IV access and hung a bag of saline to hydrate him and prepare for any other meds that might need to be administered. They also inserted a straight catheter into his penis, all the way up to his bladder to collect urine for a toxicity screen for both legal and illegal drugs.

A nurse attached an oxygen mask to Lane and connected it to the oxygen outlet on the wall.

Jen read the computer display of the EKG. She frowned and read it again.

"That's strange," she said under her breath.

"What?" Lane asked, his voice muffled behind the mask.

"You have an atrioventricular block on your EKG. You know, the hockey stick pattern," Jen said, referring to an upward spike, followed by a dip. Also known as "Salvador Dali's Moustache," the pattern indicated an abnormal heartbeat, which could be caused by a number of factors, including a heart attack or medication toxicity.

"You're sure you're not taking any meds?"

"I'm sure."

"Well, you have an AV block. Your atrium is beating fast, but the bottom of your heart is slower than it should be. Any history of heart issues?"

"No. Help me."

"I will, Lane. Don't worry."

Her first priority was to treat his arrhythmic heart. She looked at the monitor and saw his heart rate was still very slow—at 38.

At the top of her differential was an MI, but she had to wait until the lab results came back. Medication toxicity (an overdose) was also in her differential, but he said he wasn't taking any meds, so that was confounding. Something niggled at the back of her mind that she couldn't rule it out. The fainting, nausea, EKG pattern and irregular heart beat were all indicative of a potential medication toxicity. She couldn't start a treatment regimen until his test results came back to prove it, however, and the phlebotomist had just left the room with his tubes of blood. It would still be a few minutes before the lab processed them.

Her mind raced with possibilities, analyzing his symptoms and EKG pattern, comparing them to her knowledge base and experience. It briefly occurred to her to discuss his condition with a cardiologist, but she didn't have the lab results yet, so that would be premature. She hated this part of medicine, seeing the symptoms, making a differential diagnosis, but waiting on a test. She felt so helpless, standing by his side, but not being able to cure him.

Normally, she would have left the room and attended to other patients, asking a nurse to track her down when the lab results came back. Since Lane was a colleague and friend, however, Jen remained by his side as the staff made him comfortable. After a few minutes, she picked up his hand and held it.

"We're going to figure this out."

He was too weak to speak, but he nodded slightly and looked at her, his eyes full of fear. She stayed with him for twenty minutes, occasionally being interrupted for questions on other patients who were in the ER. Jen told the nurses to consult the medical residents first, before coming to her in Lane's room, because she intended to stay by his side until she could provide a treatment.

After waiting as long as she could, Jen called the lab to see if they had analyzed his blood yet. They had. They reported a high concentration of a medication known as Digoxin, as well as hyperkalemia, which was increased extracellular potassium. Its presence was a strong indicator for Digoxin toxicity as well.

It wouldn't make sense that Lane would be on Digoxin. It was customarily used to treat the elderly, who were already *in* heart failure due to an irregular heartbeat. And even then, it wasn't used that often. It was considered a somewhat dated drug. The presence of Digoxin was a curious finding. She re-read the EKG and saw the hockey stick pattern— Salvador Dali's Moustache. It was clear as day.

"Lane, the lab says you have Digoxin toxicity. Does that make any sense to you?"

"No—not on Dig," he uttered.

"Well, with your EKG finding, slow heart rate and lab results, I have to treat you for Dig toxicity. Is there any way this could be in your system without you knowing about it?"

"I don't know."

"We can figure all that out later. Let's treat you first."

Jen called the pharmacy and discussed the appropriate dose of a reversal agent for Digoxin toxicity. She ordered a loading dose of Digibind to be administered to Lane right away.

Binding with the Digoxin in Lane's system, Digibind would stop, and reverse, the toxic effects of the Digoxin.

The pharmacy delivered the Digibind a few minutes later, and a nurse administered it directly into Lane's IV tube. When she finished, Jen stood by Lane's bed while they watched his heart rate on the monitor together. After about twenty minutes, his heart returned to a normal rate, so she did another EKG. Much better. Almost normal.

She studied his face and saw his color returning.

"Your heart is coming back around."

He nodded.

Jen walked over to the computer monitor and looked up the full panel of Lane's lab work, which the lab had just entered in his electronic medical record. She wanted to confirm what they had told her over the phone. Indeed, he had Digoxin in his blood. For someone who wasn't on the medication, it was out-of-the-question mysterious.

How can he have this on board without knowing? They would have much to discuss when he regained his strength. Jen scanned the remainder of his labs and saw that his opioid level also was elevated. He had denied being on any drugs when she questioned him in the back doc room, yet there was a small level of opioids in his system. *Had he self-prescribed?*

She made her own entries in his medical record, then returned to Lane's bedside. His eyes were open, and he was watching her and the nurses.

"Do you know why you would have both Digoxin and opioids in your system?"

"No," he said, shaking his head.

"Okay. We'll get to the bottom of this." Jen patted his hand and looked at the nurse across from her. They frequently encountered patients who took drugs and lied about it, but Lane didn't fit that profile—not by any stretch of the imagination.

"My wife. Can you call Susie?"

"Of course. Her cell number should be on the list in the doc room, right?"

He nodded.

"You should rest. I'll be back in a few minutes," Jen said, leaving the room.

Jen walked to the nurses' station and discovered them discussing Lane's condition in hushed voices. While it wasn't uncommon to work as a team, discussing the patients' care in the various ER rooms, there wasn't a reason to be gossiping about Lane's condition. There would be a formal avenue to debrief the Code Blue that had been called, which was standard operating procedure for the Code team. Gossiping wasn't debriefing, and Lane was a respected colleague.

"Just to be clear," Jen said. "We're not going to discuss Dr. Wallace's care and treatment. He's a patient here, so he deserves to be treated like any other patient. His healthcare is confidential. If I hear anyone talking about his condition to anyone who isn't on the care team, I'll report you for breaching confidentiality. Understand?"

Everyone nodded. "Good. Let's get back to work. We have other patients to see."

Jen went into the back doc room, which she recently learned Cindy had dubbed the shit show room, and saw that someone had already called the Technology Department to restore the computers and flat screens that Lane had broken with his fall. A young man from Technology was busy hooking up new monitors. Indeed, it had been a shit show today.

Jen picked up Lane's cane, then located the spouse list for contact information. She returned to his room, where he was dozing. Out of habit, she clinically assessed anyone in a bed as soon as she entered the patient room. His heart rate looked good. His color looked good. His chest was rising and falling with regular breaths.

She sat on a guest chair and dialed Susie Wallace.

"Hello?" Susie answered.

"Is this Susie Wallace?" Jen asked.

"Yes. Who's this?" Jen couldn't blame her for being terse, considering what she had been through with Lane's affair.

"This is Dr. Jen Dawson. I work with Lane."

"I remember you," Susie said cautiously. "We've met a few times."

"Likewise. Lane is doing all right at the present time, but he had a heart incident earlier. He's sleeping now, but he asked for you."

"What? A heart attack? Oh, my God!"

"Not an attack. More of a medication issue. His heart went into an abnormal rhythm and slowed down. We treated him, and I think he'll be fine. He did ask for you, though, if you'd like to come and see him. He's going to be here for the remainder of the day, so we can repeat tests and monitor him closely."

There was a long pause. "Yes. I'll come right away."

"I'll look for you when you arrive."

***

Chapter 9

San Francisco Community Hospital

Thirty minutes after Jen called Susie, Susie entered the trauma center, bustling through the rotating glass door, making a fuss as she passed through security, then bursting through the double-doors of the ER in her high heels, black dress and scarlet ruana wrap.

She was an attractive woman, her black hair in a bun and her makeup applied dramatically. Heaps of jewelry dangled and clanked as she sashayed across the clean, white floor. She was a Jackson Pollock painting—an irregularly shaped swirl of red paint splattered onto a white canvas. The erratic swirl was three-dimensional, however, loaded with energy, and now advancing on the nurses' station.

"I'm Susie Wallace, Dr. Lane Wallace's wife. Dr. Dawson called me."

"Hello, Mrs. Wallace. Let me get the nurse caring for him," Cindy said.

"Thank you." Susie surveyed the ER, taking in the controlled chaos and grim reality of the environment, the opposite of her art gallery. She immediately detested it.

A few minutes later, a young woman in blue scrubs introduced herself to Susie. "I'm Carly, the nurse taking care of Dr. Wallace."

"I'm Mrs. Wallace. It smells like vomit in here."

"Yes, ma'am. I believe a patient did vomit," Cindy said, actually referring to Dr. Wallace's spray of his stomach contents while being transported.

"You should get it cleaned up. It's making me sick."

Cindy stared pleasantly at Mrs. Wallace, conveying with her eyes that she didn't take orders from her.

"Please, follow me," Carly said, leading Susie to Lane's room.

Carly and Susie entered Lane's room to find Jen listening to his heart with her stethoscope. Jen maintained the round diaphragm on his chest for a few more seconds, made a note of her finding on an index card, and stuffed the card into the breast-pocket of her scrubs. She would enter the information into his medical record in a few minutes— after she spoke to Susie. Jen draped the stethoscope around her neck and turned to see who had entered. "I'm Dr. Jen Dawson."

"Nice to meet you," Susie said, shaking Jen's hand with a limp effort. Susie quickly focused her attention on Lane. He stared at her, as if he were seeing her for the first time in their marriage. Neither spoke, but much was exchanged in the first second.

Jen assumed Susie was in shock, grappling with the new knowledge of his affair while simultaneously processing his near-fatal heart episode. Lane looked scared, but that wasn't uncommon for someone who just experienced what he had. They were staring so intently at each other, Jen realized much more was passing between them than a simple greeting, making her feel like an intruder.

Susie momentarily dragged her eyes away from Lane, training them on Jen. "You said he had a heart issue?"

"Yes." Jen glanced at Lane's pale face. "His heart went into an arrhythmia, and he collapsed. We implemented emergency measures right away, hooking him up to diagnostic machines. His EKG had a classic pattern for Digoxin toxicity, a drug used to treat heart failure. His blood tests also came back positive for Digoxin and an opioid. I administered a reversal drug, and his heart converted to a better rhythm shortly after that. His heart rate also picked up again."

"I'm so sorry," Susie said, dismissing Jen again and moving to Lane's side. She started crying, crumpling on top of his arm and shoulder.

Lane stared at the ceiling, his expression a mixture of anguish and disappointment. After a few seconds, it softened, and he raised his hand to her head, stroking her hair. She straightened, bringing his hand to her heart and holding it there as she again searched his face, as if she were imploring him to get better. Jen decided it was time to leave. They had more than enough to discuss, and were perhaps reticent with her in the room.

She returned to the nurses' station and took report on several other patients in the ER. She had a busy day ahead of her, especially now that she was down a physician. She asked a nurse to contact the ER Department Director to explain that Dr. Wallace was sick, so they needed to start paging and calling another ER physician to come in. If they couldn't find anyone, then Jen suggested the hospital go on bypass, because she and the other two physicians couldn't treat the routine influx of patients themselves. They had twenty-eight rooms, and those were usually filled every day.

***

A few hours later

After attending to other patients, Jen circled back to Lane's room. Susie was still with him, sitting next to his bed and holding his hand. The room was a soupy milieu of turmoil and stress. Jen saw the remnants of tears staining their blotchy cheeks, and despite the heavy emotion churning in the stale air, she entered to do her job.

"I don't mean to interrupt, but I want to conduct another exam. Is now a good time?"

"Yes. Of course," Susie said, rising from the edge of the bed and walking to the far corner by the curtain.

Jen thought Lane looked stricken, almost as bad as he had before he had collapsed. She hoped he wasn't going into another arrhythmia.

"Lane, how are you feeling?"

"Tired. And emotional." He wiped his eyes with the back of his hand.

"That's understandable, considering what you've been through. I'm going to listen to your heart again." She inserted the stethoscope under Lane's hospital gown. After listening for several seconds in two different spots, she withdrew the stethoscope and draped it around her neck.

"Normal rhythm," she said to Lane.

He nodded.

"Let me check another EKG." Jen turned on the machine. The electrodes were still on Lane's body, so she activated it for another test.

She watched the monitor for a few minutes, then pressed a button that printed out a sheet of paper with the electrical waves inked on it. She studied it, noting there was improvement in Lane's rhythm, but it still wasn't perfectly normal yet. She held up the printout for Lane to see, and they studied the strip together, agreeing that it appeared that he still had traces of Digoxin in his system that were causing irregularities.

Susie watched from the corner as Lane and Jen read the strip, using technical terms and talking in hushed voices. She seemed detached and in shock, a common defense mechanism in reaction to an emergency condition in a loved one.

"I think it'd be best if you stayed for five or six more hours to allow the IV fluids to flush the Digoxin from your kidneys. I'll want to repeat the labs every two or three hours."

"Sounds good," Lane said.

Jen looked at Susie and smiled. "He should be ready for discharge this evening."

"In that case, if it's okay with you, I'm going to the cafeteria in search of a latte. I haven't eaten anything yet today. I'll have my cell with me," she said, holding it up.

"You can bring your food back here," Lane suggested.

"I have some calls to make on gallery business," she said, referring to her upscale art gallery in the Financial District. "I don't want to interrupt your care, so I'll make my calls in the cafeteria. Be back in thirty minutes or so."

Jen thought Susie's departure was rather abrupt, but, then again, she had just been through a lot.

***

Chapter 10

Hall of Justice

Tommy was working in his office when his desk phone rang. It was Security in the lobby, informing him that Cheryl Gutierrez was waiting for him. He told them he'd be right down, then he IM'd Amanda.

Cheryl Gutierrez is here

Same interrogation room?

Yes

See you there

Tommy rode the elevator to the lobby and introduced himself to Cheryl.

"I'm Detective Vietti. Thanks for coming in today, Ms. Gutierrez."

"It's the least I can do. She was a good person," Cheryl said.

"Let's go to a conference room," he said, attaching a less foreboding name to it.

They rode the third-world wonkavator to his floor and entered the Investigations Unit. Tommy showed Cheryl to the interrogation room and grabbed the electronic ear bud from his coat pocket, surreptitiously inserting it into his ear as he walked into the room.

He invited Ms. Gutierrez to sit while he appraised her appearance. She was in her late-forties, pleasant looking, and had quick brown eyes that scanned everything. Her hair was short and dyed brown, and she wore spectacles with brown rims. Her cherubic face was serious this morning, but she had laugh lines around her eyes. Her body was on the plump side—the kind Tommy knew was good for hugging, like his mother had. Ms. Gutierrez was dressed in nondescript blue slacks and a blousy top, with a minimalist floral pattern.

After establishing her address and telephone number for the record, Tommy asked her about her work responsibilities at the hospital.

"I'm a supervisor in the Radiology Department. I've been there for fifteen years. I started out as an ultrasound tech, just like Natasha."

"What is that, exactly?"

"We take images of densities in the body by using echoes of ultrasound pulses."

"Like babies in utero?"

"Yes. Some technologists are assigned to the Women's Health Clinic where they ultrasound pregnant women. In the ER, where Natasha worked, she took images of other organs like the spleen, gallbladder, aortas and veins."

"Okay. Was she physically located in the ER?"

"No. Natasha would transport the patient from the ER to the Radiology Department for ultrasound studies," Cheryl explained.

"Would Natasha wait in Radiology for the patient to be brought to her?"

"No. She'd go to the ER for the patient, then bring him or her back to the Radiology Department herself."

"How far away is the ER from Radiology?"

"Thirty yards. It's purposefully located close. After the test, Natasha would return the patient to the ER and give the attending physician her impression of the result. That wouldn't be official, though. The attending physician would wait for the radiologist report before making a definitive diagnosis."

"Did Natasha work on the day shift?"

"She was on a pattern of nights."

"Any particular reason?"

"I think it just fit her lifestyle. Some people prefer that. It's nice and quiet at the hospital at night. Less commotion."

"Did she ever talk about her husband, Blake Farber?"

"Oh yes. I heard all about him."

"What did you hear?"

"Are you asking me to tell you about him beating her? She told me on more than one occasion—showed me the bruises, too."

"She had bruises? Where?" Tommy asked, pretending he didn't know.

"Everywhere. Her arms most recently…"

"When was the last time you saw bruises on her?"

"In the last two weeks."

Amanda whispered into Tommy's earpiece. "Ask her who raised the topic first. Natasha or Cheryl."

"Did you see the bruises and ask Natasha about them? Or, did she come to you and raise the subject?" Tommy asked.

Cheryl stared at Tommy for a minute, then looked at the one-way glass. "Is someone whispering questions in your ear?"

Tommy was impressed. Over the course of his career, only a few witnesses had figured out that he had an ear bud in place. She didn't miss a trick. "Yes, Ms. Gutierrez, it's standard operating procedure. As I mentioned when we came in, this conversation is being audio and visually recorded. And, yes, there are people on the other side of the glass who might whisper questions in my ear."

"I thought so. You looked like you were listening to something," she said, moving out of her chair so she could look in his ear. After spying the earbud, she sat down.

"Did you raise the topic of bruises on Natasha's arms, or did she?" Tommy asked.

"Who?" she asked, looking at the glass again.

"You or Natasha?" Tommy asked.

"No. Who's whispering questions in your ear?" Cheryl insisted.

"I'm not at liberty to say," Tommy said.

"Then, I'm not at liberty to say. For all I know, Blake Farber is sitting on the other side of the glass."

"I can assure you that he's not."

"I'd like to see for myself before we continue."

"It doesn't work like that."

"It was nice meeting you. I'll be leaving now," she said, standing and walking toward the door.

Tommy rolled his eyes and looked at the glass.

"I'll come around and introduce myself," Amanda said into his earbud.

"Ms. Gutierrez. Please don't leave. I'll introduce you to the person on the other side of the glass."

Her hand was on the door knob. "I want to see for myself. Bring me back there."

"Of course, follow me," Tommy said, cursing in his mind.

Ms. Gutierrez opened the door and stepped out into the hallway. Tommy led her around the corner to the side of the interrogation room, where the table with the microphone was located below the one-way window. Amanda rose from the table and faced Ms. Gutierrez.

"Hi. I'm District Attorney Amanda Hawthorne."

Cheryl and Amanda shook hands.

"Why don't you just come into the conference room?" Cheryl asked.

"Good question," Amanda said. "Here's the reason. I'm the lawyer who's going to try this case in court. I can't be a witness if I'm the lawyer trying it. Tommy, as the investigating detective, on the other hand, will be a witness in court. That's why he conducts the interviews. So, he's on the video and his voice is recorded."

"So, you just stay in the background and whisper stuff?"

"Essentially, yes," Amanda said.

"I'm okay with that. Nice meeting you," Cheryl said, turning and walking back to the interrogation room.

Tommy made a face at Amanda, indicating Ms. Gutierrez was more observant than most, then followed her back into the room. Once they were settled again, Tommy picked up where he had left off. "Did you see the bruises and ask Natasha about them? Or, did she come to you and raise the subject?"

"We were working together, and I asked her first. Women who are abused don't always come forward, you know? So, I saw them, then grasped her hands and looked at her arms. I asked her who did that to her," Cheryl said.

"What did she say?"

"She cried for a few minutes, then admitted it was Blake."

"Did you have to drag it out of her?"

"No. I just waited patiently until she told me."

"How long did that take?"

"Not long. Couple of minutes."

"And she said it was Blake, huh?"

"Yes."

"Did it look like he grabbed her or hit her?"

"They were grabbing bruises, like he was holding her real tight, preventing her from getting away."

"Did she tell you what happened?"

"She said he surprised her at her apartment, and confronted her about her affair with Dr. Wallace."

"Did that surprise you?"

"What? That Blake confronted her at her apartment?"

"No. That she was having an affair with Dr. Wallace."

"No. Everyone knew they were an item."

"Since when?"

"Maybe a couple of months. I lose track of these things."

"Did the bruises look like he grabbed her from the front or from behind?"

"I have no idea. I just saw bruises."

"What did you say to her?"

"I told her to call the police and report Blake. He was supposed to stay away from her as a condition for not being prosecuted with domestic battery from the last time he beat her. It was appalling."

"How did you know about that domestic battery?"

"She told me."

"Recently? Or, when it happened."

"In real time. When it happened. I told her to call the police and go to counseling."

"Did you ever visit her at her apartment?"

"No. We weren't that close. We were just work acquaintances."

"Did you ever go out for drinks or dinner?"

"We had some work functions where we all socialized, celebrating someone's birthday or retirement, you know."

"What did she drink?"

"I don't remember. I guess I didn't pay any attention."

"Did you ever meet Blake?"

"Once or twice. Maybe at the hospital holiday party."

"Is there anything you'd like to tell me about Blake that you think might help?"

"Just that he did it. She said he was crazed with jealousy about her relationship with Dr. Wallace. I feel so guilty, because I should have done more. In retrospect, it was so obvious, like her wearing long sleeves in the summer. Now, I know it was to hide the bruises."

"People often feel guilty after the fact. The reality is that you didn't see this coming. Flush the guilt, Cheryl."

She nodded.

Amanda whispered, "Ask her if she's ever spoken to Dr. Wallace about Natasha."

"Did you ever talk to Dr. Wallace about Natasha?" Tommy asked.

"God no. I wasn't supposed to know they were having an affair. I heard he can be a real pill when he gets angry, so I wouldn't bring up their relationship to him," Cheryl said.

"What do you mean, 'when he gets angry?'" Tommy asked.

"He's got a bit of a reputation among the nursing staff for blowing up. If he's really busy in the ER, he can bite someone's head off. He's one of those."

"Has he ever been written up for it?"

"I have no idea. Not by me or my staff. You'd have to ask Administration if any nurses have written him up."

"Are you afraid of him?"

"Not in the least."

"Why?"

"He's always been polite to me. And, he helped Natasha when she needed it."

"What do you mean by that?"

"He helped her realize she was in an abusive relationship, and, like me, encouraged her to go to the hospital Employee Assistance Program for counseling. He stood by her when she pressed charges against Blake, and I respect him for that."

"I see. Is there anything else you think I should know?"

"No. I can't think of anything right now."

"Okay. Thank you for your time, Ms. Gutierrez. If you think of anything else, here's my business card. Thanks for coming in."

Tommy escorted Cheryl back down to the lobby.

Afterward, he immediately went to Amanda's office, where he found her on the phone again. It seemed to be permanently attached to her ear, but she waved him in.

"Yes Mayor Woo, Detective Vietti is assigned to this case. Uh-huh. One of the best. Yes, I know Mr. Ivanov is a rich, powerful man who has connections. I understand he called you. I'm sorry. I plan to meet with the Ivanovs personally. Today, in fact. I know you have an election around the corner. None of us want Ivanov as an enemy. I understand...Oh yes... Will do...Thanks. Goodbye," Amanda said, hanging up.

"Mayor Woo thinks Dimitri Ivanov is going to donate money to his re-election campaign?" Tommy asked.

"You know him. Money talks. Even the hint of money talks."

"Well," Tommy said, scratching his head, "I'll stick to what I know best. Investigating."

"Good thinking. Leave Woo to me. Say, Cheryl Gutierrez is sharp, isn't she? She made your earpiece."

"Yeah. Only a handful have busted me over the years. She definitely thinks Blake somehow killed Natasha, though."

"I know. Is it such an anathema to consider Dr. Wallace as equally suspect?"

"Right. Just because he's a doctor, doesn't mean he couldn't kill someone."

"Ms. Gutierrez was useful as a background witness, but I don't know if we'll need her beyond that."

"I agree."

***

Chapter 11

San Francisco Community Hospital

Jen was sitting in Lane's room, chatting, as she watched him pick at a tray of food positioned over his bed. At least he was upright, and his color was better.

Jen ate her yogurt and fruit snack that she had brought from home.

"Did you find someone to cover my shift?" Lane asked.

"Yes. Dr. Patel came in as soon as we called him."

"Good. Sorry to leave you in a lurch."

"God, Lane. Don't think twice about it! I'm just glad you were here when your heart flipped into the arrhythmia. If you'd been at home, I'm not so sure you would have survived."

"I agree. I've been refamiliarizing myself with Digoxin toxicity while lying here, and learned that quite a bit can build up in your system before the symptoms manifest. I think that's what happened to me. It was in my system for a few days, maybe even a week."

"Any guess as to how Dig and opioids found their way *into* your system?"

"You'll keep our conversation confidential?"

"Of course."

He took an unsteady breath. "I sure as hell didn't intentionally take Dig and opioids, but I wonder if someone poisoned me—and Natasha for that matter. My heart went into an arrhythmia, but hers stopped. It's the only way I can explain it. She weighed at least eighty pounds less than I do, and was also taking Xanax, which I prescribed for her. If she got the Dig and opioids, too, on top of her Xanax, the drug interaction was fatal for her." He pushed his tray table aside and cried again.

Jen sat in silence with him. "I'm so sorry, Lane. It's obvious that you cared deeply for her. Don't you think you should turn this information over to the police, so they can investigate *how* the drugs got into your and Natasha's systems?"

"At this point, we're just speculating that she died from that fatal mix. She could've had a PE or brain aneurysm for all we know. Let's see what her autopsy results say. Then I'll decide."

"We can wait, but it's more than a coincidence, don't you think?"

"I'm not sure. There might be a perfectly reasonable explanation for what happened."

"I call bullshit. Everyone thinks her husband was trying to kill her, so why wouldn't he want to kill you as well? This is kind of scary, Lane. You have a wife and daughter to protect, you know."

He sobbed again. When he was finished, he looked at Jen. "I know. Just give me some time to process it. I want to know more about how Natasha died. The police could be overreacting."

"That hasn't been my experience with Tommy."

"I just don't know if I want to become part of a formal police investigation. Susie is just coming to grips with the fact that I cheated on her, and I'm grieving the loss of Natasha. I think I loved her—" he cried, burying his face in his hands.

Jen sat in silence while he cried. After he had regained his composure, she said, "I'm so sorry, Lane. She was a pretty girl."

"She was, wasn't she? If you don't mind, I just don't want my health condition to become public information now. If the police investigation turns into something, I'll consider telling them."

"I won't say anything."

"Thanks. And, thanks for saving my life today."

"Well, I think the EKG saved your life. I just interpreted it."

They were interrupted by a firm knock on the door.

Jen and Lane both said "Come in," and the Chief of Staff for the hospital, Dr. José Cruz, entered, wearing his usual crisp, black suit.

"Hi Lane. How are you?" Dr. Cruz asked, approaching the bedside and shaking Lane's hand.

"Word travels fast, I see," Lane said.

"Your Department Director had to call in extra support, so official administrative channels were notified," Dr. Cruz said.

Lane nodded.

"Dr. Dawson, how are you today?" Dr. Cruz asked.

"Very well, thank you," Jen said.

"Will you excuse us, please?" Dr. Cruz asked.

"I'd like her to stay, if you don't mind," Lane said.

Dr. Cruz looked from Lane to Jen, then back again. "Very well."

"You can say whatever you have to in front of Jen. She's a colleague and a friend," Lane insisted.

"As you wish. First and foremost, I want to tell you how sorry I am that you had a health concern."

"Thanks. It was short-lived, so I should be ready to return to work tomorrow."

"Good to hear you'll be on the mend quickly. However, about returning tomorrow, hospital administration met and determined that it would be best if you went on a paid leave of absence for a few days."

"Leave of absence? But, I'll be ready to return—"

Dr. Cruz interrupted. "It's not about your health, Lane. It's about the police investigation into Natasha Farber's death. It's pretty widely known that you were seeing her."

"What the hell? Widely known?" Lane was shocked.

"Are you disputing that you were having an affair with her?"

"No. I'm just questioning how 'widely known' it was."

"That's not really the point, is it?" Dr. Cruz asked rhetorically. "You were having an affair with a woman who was found dead, and the police are investigating it. The optics of that aren't good for the hospital, so we're placing you on a temporary leave of absence. Once the investigation is concluded, which shouldn't be too long, you can return to work."

"After the investigation is concluded?"

"Well, unless there are charges and a trial. In that case, the hospital lawyers told me we'd have to keep you out on leave. But, we're getting ahead of ourselves. You know the lawyers, they overanalyze everything. Let's take it one step at a time. For now, you're on paid leave," Dr. Cruz said in rapid-fire fashion.

"What if I don't want to be on paid leave?"

"You don't really have a choice in the matter," Dr. Cruz said, then paused. "Cut me a break here, Lane. I'm just doing my job. Let's not make a big deal out of this. A few days away might do you good. Get some fresh air and sunshine. Everyone will assume you're just recovering from a health problem. On the other hand, if you fight this decision, everyone, including the police and media, will notice your situation. You don't want *that*, do you?"

"I guess not. Now that you put it that way. I don't like it, but I'll do what you want."

"Good. Dr. Dawson, do you have anything to add?" Dr. Cruz asked, turning on her.

"No," Jen said wisely.

Dr. Cruz wheeled back around to Lane. "And, I almost forgot. Since you're Chair of the Department, we've appointed someone else as interim Chair."

"For a short leave?" Lane asked, bewildered.

"Again, I hope it's short, but we don't know how long it will be. As such, Dr. Patel has agreed to serve as Chair."

"He'll do a good job," Lane said, deflated.

"We think so. I wish you a speedy recovery," Dr. Cruz said, shaking Lane's hand. "I'll be in touch."

"Bye," Lane said.

Dr. Cruz nodded to Jen and quickly departed.

"Administrative bastards," Lane growled after Cruz left.

Jen held her tongue regarding the Chief of Staff. "Listen, I should get back to my other patients. Catch you later."

"Thanks, Jen," Lane said.

As Jen walked to the nurses' station, she glanced toward the double-doors and saw Tommy entering. *Her* Tommy. She stopped cold. *He couldn't have heard about Lane's Digoxin episode, could he?* She plastered a fake smile on her face, hoping to hell she didn't look as duplicitous as she felt.

"Hi," she said, detouring to greet him. "What brings you here?"

"The investigation." He planted a kiss on her cheek. "I have to go to the Legal Department to pick up a medical record. I just wanted to say hi, and see if you could take a coffee break."

"Oh. That's sweet of you." She lay her hand on his lapel. "I'd love to, but we're short-staffed and getting slammed. I can't break away."

At that moment, Susie Wallace re-entered the ER from her business call in the cafeteria, and headed straight for Jen and Tommy.

"Talk to you later. Duty calls," Jen said, lightly pushing Tommy's arm, indicating he should leave. He didn't budge, though. She tried again as Susie joined them. This wasn't like Tommy—not to pick up on her social cues. She hoped he'd get the hint when Susie started asking her medical questions.

"Hi," Jen said to Susie, not intending to introduce Tommy, given the confidential nature of the circumstances.

Adding to the speed at which Jen's world was spinning out of control, Susie reached out her hand to Tommy when she joined them. "Tommy Vietti? Is that you?"

"Susie? Susie Sangiolo?" Tommy spread his arms wide in a big hug for the glamorous artsy lady. Susie was the type Jen had heard Tommy liked to date before he met Jen. The exact opposite of her.

Tommy and Susie hugged tightly, hanging on for a few extra seconds. Susie leaned back to look at Tommy's handsome face, her arms still around his body. Tears sprang to her eyes. "My husband is in the hospital. He had a heart attack this morning," she said in a thick Italian-American accent.

"Ahh—come here," Tommy said, falling into his baby-talk Italian accent as well, hugging her again.

What the hell is going on here?

Susie sniffled all over Tommy's lapel, prompting him to produce a handkerchief from inside his breast pocket. Jen had never seen him carry a handkerchief, and had no idea when he had become so gallant. She raised her eyebrow at him. He shrugged.

Susie drew back and wiped her tears, then blew.

"You keep that," Tommy said.

"Thank you, Tommy."

"So, you're married now?" Tommy asked.

"Yes. To a doctor—Lane Wallace. He works here, but he had a heart attack this morning, so he's a patient now. Dr. Dawson is caring for him." Susie motioned to Jen without looking at her.

Tommy did a double-take, looking back and forth between Susie and Jen. His mind was processing a million-bytes-per-second, catching up to what had just happened, and Jen's role in it. He squinted at Jen.

It was Jen's turn to shrug, as she watched him catch up to the present. She figured he'd have a ton of questions if he got her alone. *Maybe it was best to avoid each other entirely for the duration of this investigation*, she thought. *Note to self, do not invite Tommy over this week. No matter how desperate I get for sex, I cannot booty-call him.*

Tommy regained his composure. "I'm so sorry, Susie. Is there anything I can do?"

"No. He's in good hands. He should be ready to leave later today."

Jen nodded.

Susie refocused on Tommy, treating Jen like she was the hired help. "You look good. I heard you went to college and joined the force. Looks like you did okay for yourself."

"I can't complain," he said.

"I heard you got married, too."

"I did, but then divorced." He glanced nervously at Jen, who now thought his discomfort was damn amusing.

"You're a real catch, Tommy. I bet there's a long line at your door," Susie flirted.

For some reason, Tommy chose not to mention the fact that Jen was his girlfriend and would-be fiancée, which Jen found slightly offensive.

"My hands are currently full," he said diplomatically.

Susie laughed. "I'll bet they are."

"And, how's your family?" Tommy asked. "Your parents were so good to me."

"Well, daddy died a few years back, and mama is in the nursing home."

"I'm sorry to hear that. Give her my best, would you?"

"I will. She'll like that. And your parents?"

"Ma passed, but Pops is alive and well. Still living in the same house."

"Get out! On Vallejo?" Susie asked.

"The one and only. I bought one close by, so I could keep an eye on him."

"Good for you, Tommy, staying in the neighborhood," she said, referring to North Beach.

"Anything for Pops. Listen, I'm on the job, so I have to run. But, good seeing you."

"You, too. I'm off to Lane's room. Look me up sometime. I own the Sangiolo Art Gallery on Minna and Second Street."

"I can't place it off the top of my head."

"Between Mission and Howard."

"I know the neighborhood. Lots of galleries there. I don't get down there much."

"You need to come visit me. You'll like it. We have a coffee bar and a full liquor license."

Jen was impressed with Susie's audacity at inviting Tommy to her gallery, given that Lane had just suffered a major heart event and was lying in a room a mere thirty feet away.

"I will," Tommy promised. "Catch you later."

Even though Tommy had said he needed to get going, he still hadn't moved.

Susie turned to Jen. "Are you coming, Dr. Dawson?"

Jen refused to be bossed around by Susie Sangiolo Wallace. "I'll be along in a minute. I'm going to finish my business with Mr. Vietti."

"Oh, right," Susie said, surprised she wasn't the sole object of Tommy's attention. "I didn't mean to interrupt."

"See you in a few minutes," Jen hinted.

Jen and Tommy watched Susie strut across the ER to Lane's room. There was a distinctive swish to her hips that hadn't been there prior to Tommy's arrival.

"And?" Jen asked, after Susie disappeared.

"We dated in high school. Lived on the same block," he said.

"Haven't seen her since?"

"Absolutely not. She was a stick of dynamite back then, and it looks like she still is." He ran his hand through his hair.

"Good to know." Lane would have hell to pay by fooling around on Susie, Jen thought.

There was a brief silence.

"I should get back to work," Jen said.

"Yeah. Me, too."

"Good luck with your investigation."

"Which you're not helping me with."

"Not my job to help you. I have laws that apply to me, too." Lane had begged her to keep his Digoxin and opioid toxicity confidential, so she had called the hospital Legal Department and asked one of the lawyers whether she was required to report it to the police. The lawyer had advised that Jen was *not*, so she could respect Dr. Wallace's wishes to keep his information confidential, even though the police might find it useful in their homicide investigation.

"I guess I deserved that," he said.

"You and Amanda Hawthorne set the tone last night. In fact, maybe we shouldn't see each other at all during this investigation. It's hitting a little too close to my work and colleagues."

"Can we still—," he began, but then thought better of it. "No. You're right. Let's commit to not seeing each other while I investigate this case. It'll remove any temptation to tell each other something confidential."

"Be honest. You were never tempted. And now, neither am I. But, it will certainly remove the opportunity for you to quiz me."

"Ouch," he said, resting his hand on his heart. "Can you at least point me in the direction of the Legal Department?"

Jen gave him directions, but he still didn't move. She raised her eyebrow at him.

"Love you," he said, his brown eyes conveying it.

"Love you, too," she said, then watched him disappear behind the doors that led to the main part of the hospital.

My mind is going to explode, keeping all this shit straight, she thought. She was still standing in the middle of the ER, looking at the back of the door that Tommy had exited. She stretched her arms above her head, working out the kinks in her scapular muscles, wondering how this tangled mess would all unravel.

***

Chapter 12

Hall of Justice

Tommy returned from the hospital and carefully studied Natasha Farber's thin medical record at his desk. There was, indeed, an entry by Dr. Wallace dated six weeks ago. Wallace diagnosed her with situational anxiety due to 'circumstances surrounding her marriage,' and prescribed Xanax for her.

Tommy called Amanda. "Guess what?"

"You solved the case?"

"I'm further along, but no. Natasha Farber's medical record confirms what you saw in her text messages—Dr. Wallace prescribed Xanax for her six weeks ago."

"That would have been right after Blake was arrested for domestic battery, right?"

"A couple of weeks later. So, she was understandably upset."

"Do you think she and Wallace were having sex at the time?"

"I don't know."

"It just goes to his character. If she was a vulnerable coworker, then saw him as a patient, then became his lover, it tells me he might be predatory. At the very least, he's manipulative," she said.

"Well, if they were already having sex, it doesn't matter anyway. What matters is that he knew her medical history; and prescribed an anti-anxiety drug for her, so he was essentially in control of her moods."

"I agree. If she had Xanax on board at the time of her death, maybe it reacted to some type of toxin that he slipped into her favorite cocktail."

"I'll be sure to ask him about the Xanax script when I interview him."

"Are you keeping track of our list?"

"Of course, got it all in my head."

"That's what I'm afraid of."

"Don't be so stressed. It's just the first interview. I have to play it by ear, listen to his answers, and maybe have a second interview after I follow up on a few things."

Tommy's phone lit up, indicating he had another call coming in. "Listen, gotta go. I have another call."

"Okay, bye," she said.

Security in the lobby was on the other line, informing him that the Ivanovs were waiting for him.

Tommy told the officer he'd be right down, then IM'd Amanda that the Ivanovs were here. She asked him to bring them to her suite of offices.

***

Tommy collected the Ivanovs in the lobby and escorted them to Amanda's suite. She met them in the official District Attorney reception area, wearing her blue pinstriped suit.

"Mr. and Mrs. Ivanov, I'm District Attorney Amanda Hawthorne. I'm so sorry for your loss," Amanda said, extending her hand.

Dimitri and Elena nodded, shaking hands with Amanda and assessed her like they were fish.

"Follow me," Amanda said, leading them to a conference room where they all sat.

Mrs. Ivanov removed a wad of Kleenex from her purse and set it on her lap, peeling off one to wipe the tears from the dark circles under her eyes. She was a handsome woman, her grey hair pinned neatly into a bun, and her substantial girth covered by a black dress.

"Thank you for seeing us today," Dimitri said. "Do you think her bastard husband killed her?" His broad face was contorted in pain and his club-like hands were balled into fists. His large frame was draped in an expensive suit, and he was sitting on the edge of his chair, his belly spilling over his belt and elbows resting on the conference table.

"We don't know yet. We're investigating all aspects of her death, Mr. Ivanov. If there was foul play, we'll bring charges," Amanda said.

"What do you know so far?" Dimitri asked, his black eyes boring holes into Amanda, then Tommy. Clearly, he was a man accustomed to getting answers and directing the show. Anger, rather than sadness, poured off him.

"Well, we're in the middle of the investigation, so it's premature to conclude anything. Ethically, we're prohibited from discussing evidence, or the inferences we've drawn from the evidence, in the middle of an investigation," Tommy said.

"Are you giving us the brush off? We came here for answers, Ms. Hawthorne. She's our daughter! Our beautiful baby. If someone killed her, we deserve to know!" Elena burst into tears, covering her eyes with a Kleenex.

Amanda and Tommy exchanged looks. Unfortunately, they had met with too many family members on homicide cases over the years. The raw emotion that Dimitri and Elena were expressing was normal and part of the grief process, especially when there was a crime involved in the death. Usually, anger was at the top of the list for the sudden death of someone as young as Natasha, and, true to form, Dimitri was full of anger.

"We understand," Tommy said. "This is my case, and it's the only case I'm working on right now. I'm reviewing medical records, the autopsy report, the evidence we obtained from her apartment, and interviewing friends and coworkers. I've been doing this for over twenty years, and trust me, I know what I'm doing. I'll give this file my undivided attention, so that I can look you in the eye at the conclusion and tell you with confidence what my best assessment is."

"Do you have the results of the autopsy?" Dimitri asked, undeterred.

"Partially," Tommy said. "She had some bruising on her arms that was seven to ten days old. Her organs were normal. Frankly, she could've died from natural causes, but we're waiting on the toxicology results. Those usually take a few days."

"Toxicology means any drugs in her system, right?" Elena asked.

"Yes. We're still waiting on that," Tommy said.

"Do you think she overdosed on something?" Elena asked.

"I honestly don't know. What do you think?" Tommy asked.

"We don't know either. We haven't been on good terms for the last few years, but we spoke to her about a week ago, and she seemed happy. She was getting used to living without Blake, and she sounded normal. For the first time since she married him, she sounded truly settled. Ironic, considering they were living apart. She told us she was ready to move on, so we agreed to pay the legal fees for a divorce," Elena said.

"Which is probably why he killed her," Dimitri interjected, his face reddening again. "If only she'd moved back home."

"Tell us about Blake Farber," Amanda asked.

"We knew he wasn't good for her from the beginning—" Elena began.

"He's a punk!" Dimitri interjected. "Never held a solid job. Didn't have a long-term plan. I think he was sponging off my daughter. That's part of the reason I cut her off financially—so that punk would realize he wasn't getting a dime. She made a good salary at the hospital and had good benefits, so she was fine. I didn't respect him, though. Didn't like him. And he knew it. I told him if he ever laid a finger on her

—" Dimitri broke down, his angry face turning to anguish.

Tommy and Amanda waited patiently, watching the Ivanovs cry.

"We're so sorry," Amanda said. "I want to assure you that your daughter's case has our full attention, and we're committed to investigating it until we find some answers. Once we can come to a conclusion, we'll meet with you again and share our results with you."

"What do we do in the meantime?" Elena asked.

"We're going to introduce you to our Victim and Witness Coordinator, Marie. She's very good. She'll meet with you and communicate with you about the status of things as we move this investigation along. I'll bring her in now," Amanda said.

"One minute. Can we go over to Natasha's apartment? Pack up her things? We've been in contact with the apartment manager," Dimitri said.

"Not yet," Tommy said. "We put yellow tape around the door. It's a crime scene now, so it's vitally important that we not contaminate it with anyone or anything. If we have to go back in, and we find evidence, we need to establish a clear chain. If you were to go in there, then the defense could challenge the evidence based on the concept of tampering. Understand?"

"When will be able to?" Elena asked.

"When the investigation is concluded," Amanda said.

Dimitri and Elena nodded, finding each other's hands and holding on tight.

"One other thing," Dimitri said, his voice choking. "Her body. Where's her body? We need to make arrangements."

"Marie will go over that with you, but Natasha's body is currently at the county morgue. I can assure you that it's secure," Tommy said.

They both broke down again.

Amanda buzzed Marie, and she entered, introducing herself. Once she was settled with them, Amanda and Tommy left, returning to Amanda's office.

"So sad," Amanda said.

"I've seen it a hundred times. No matter how old they are, children never stop being their parents' babies. Natasha was their baby. I wish I could've told them more, but anything we say will be locked in their brains as absolute truth. If something contradictory surfaces later that causes us to change our opinion, they'll accuse us of lying to them. Or, worse, incompetency. As difficult as it is, the less information shared with the family, the better," Tommy said.

"I agree. It just feels worse in some circumstances than others. Marie will work her magic. You'd better contact the apartment manager and tell him not to let the Ivanovs, or anyone else, in Natasha's apartment."

"I was thinking the same thing."

"I want to know what was on her rug and in her liquor bottles."

"Me, too. The lab said they were working on it."

"Faster, Tommy. Faster."

"I feel the same way. Catch up with you later," he said, departing.

***

When Dimitri and Elena Ivanov left the Hall of Justice, they were met on the sidewalk by a reporter and a cameraman from a local T.V. station. "Mr. and Mrs. Ivanov? I'm Kip Moynihan from KPIX 5 News. Do you have a minute?"

"What? I suppose," Dimitri said, blinking at the bright light on the camera that was shining on him.

"Your daughter was Natasha Farber, right? Did you learn anything from visiting the Hall of Justice today?"

"Yes. We, ah—met with the District Attorney and a detective on the case. They were very helpful," Dimitri said. Elena cried by his side.

"What did they tell you?" Kip asked.

"They're investigating her death."

"Did they have any leads?"

"Not yet. They're looking at everyone, especially her estranged husband, Blake Farber."

"Do you think he murdered your daughter?" Kip asked.

"We think he could have, but it's in the hands of the police now," Dimitri said.

"Do you think other women are in danger of Blake Farber?"

"I have no idea."

"Do you have any knowledge of Blake Farber harming any other women before he met your daughter?"

"No. What are you talking about?"

"Just if you had any knowledge."

"No. That's a stupid question," Dimitri said, puffing out his chest and balling his hands into fists.

Kip took a different tack. "There's been speculation that she was seeing another man. A physician at the hospital. Were you aware of that?"

"What? The District Attorney didn't tell us that. I don't believe you!" Dimitri's hands clenched and released.

"Word is that the doctor is a suspect, too. He's the reason she was estranged from her husband," Kip said.

That was enough for Dimitri. He let loose with one punch, hitting Kip in the face, sending him to the pavement.

"Don't you dare accuse my daughter," Dimitri said, shaking with rage as he stood over Kip.

"Fuck! I think my nose is broken," Kip moaned, blood hemorrhaging into his hand. "I'm gonna file charges against you."

"The hell you will!" Dimitri booted Kip in the ribs, eliciting a yelp.

"You haven't seen the last of me," Kip moaned.

"If you stick your microphone in my face again, I'll kill you," Dimitri replied.

Elena pulled on his hand. "Dimitri, stop. Leave him alone. Let's go, come on!"

Rather than helping his coworker, the cameraman captured the entire exchange, including Elena pulling Dimitri down the sidewalk and around the corner.

***

Chapter 13

That afternoon

Superior Court

Tommy and Amanda met with the duty judge at Superior Court. The judges had a weekly rotation schedule for addressing urgent matters, such as search warrants and the like, and Judge Grady was on for the entire week. He was experienced and, more importantly, Tommy and Amanda were familiar with him, having appeared before him many times.

As a former prosecutor, Judge Grady was no-nonsense, and Amanda knew that he hated, absolutely hated, being overturned on appeal. Hence, he was very cautious about his rulings and decisions, taking care that they would be bullet-proof when reviewed by the appellate courts.

Among other things, Judge Grady saw his role in the criminal justice system as guaranteeing that the person who was charged with a crime received a fair and just trial, which started long before the jury was sworn. His analysis began with scrutinizing law enforcement's request for a search warrant, confirming there was probable cause for its issuance, and that it was narrow enough in scope to be relevant to the crime for which the perp was being investigated. If it were too expansive, it would violate the perp's Fourth Amendment Right against unreasonable search and seizure.

Tommy and Amanda were seated in Judge Grady's chambers, speaking off the record, meaning there wasn't a court reporter present. They all knew their roles, like jazz musicians occasionally playing a gig together. They performed the standard tunes, but for each gig, there was the opportunity for improvisation by a soloist. Sometimes, the facts of the investigation provided for a wild solo—Tommy usually doing the honors.

Tommy presented the facts of Natasha's Farber's case they had learned thus far, and Amanda argued that they had probable cause to search Natasha Farber's work computer, as well as her lover, Dr. Wallace's, both located at San Francisco Community Hospital. The law was well-established that employees like Farber and Wallace didn't have an expectation of privacy in their work emails.

During this meeting, Judge Grady was surprised at where Amanda was going with her argument. "You suspect that an emergency room physician killed his lover?"

"We can't rule it out, Judge," Amanda said. "The texts between the victim and Dr. Wallace really escalated toward the end, and we want to see if their emails at work are similar. We're concerned about spoliation of those emails if we wait any longer. The doctor is at work, so he could start permanently deleting emails if we don't intervene. In addition, we don't know how long the hospital computer system stores information like emails."

She continued, "As Tommy mentioned, Dr. Wallace isn't an angel. He was arrested last year on a disorderly and domestic battery. His wife, Susie, dropped the charges, but their altercation was violent enough for her to call the police. He's ex-Army, with time served in Iraq, so there might be some underlying PTSD there. We don't know. He's the central suspect in our investigation."

"Okay. You've made your case," Judge Grady said. "I'll sign the warrant. It's narrow enough that it should withstand challenge. You'd best make haste if you're going to execute it in 72 hours."

"Thank you, your Honor," Amanda said, and she and Tommy hustled out of the judge's chambers.

Tommy consulted his watch as they walked down the steps of Superior Court to Amanda's idling Jaguar. He held the door for Amanda, and followed her into the car. George drove them down Seventh Street, returning to the Hall of Justice.

"It's four o'clock already. In this traffic, it'll be twenty minutes before we get back to Justice," Tommy said.

"The hospital is open twenty-four hours a day, so it shouldn't be a problem executing the warrant after five o'clock," Amanda pointed out.

"I know. I just wanted to see if Jen would talk to me tonight—maybe have dinner together. I don't like the way we left things."

"What time does she get off work?"

"About now."

***

San Francisco Community Hospital

Jen gave report and handed off her patients to the ER physician who was coming on and taking over the block of rooms that she staffed.

After her report was complete, she ran down to the locker room, changed into her workout tights, a tank, and a hoodie, grabbed her gym bag, and ran back up the stairs to exit. If she hustled, she could still make the CrossFit class a mile away, and blow off all the stress that had imbedded itself in her.

She crossed Potrero Avenue, walked half a block, and turned right onto Hampshire Street. She hit the fob with her thumb to unlock Aethenoth the Ancient, but didn't hear a beep. She looked up and down the street. No car. No cars at all. Not a one. Wait a minute. Something wasn't right. Usually this street was packed with hospital employees' cars.

Am I on the right street? She looked at the sign. Hampshire Street. Let me think. I got here at quarter-to-seven this morning, after dropping Tommy at his work. I was lucky and got a sweet spot, close to the hospital. There were only a few cars. What am I missing? Was there no parking here today?

She checked the street for city signs, temporary or permanent. There were none that tipped her off that she shouldn't have parked there. On the other hand, there was orange spray paint on the street and flags on the berms, marking underground lines. It was clear that the city had started work on a project, and cars would be in the way.

Fucking figures. Now my car has been towed.

She Googled *car towed in San Francisco,* and found helpful city websites, suggesting she call the city service that coordinated towing, impound lots and car return, and ask them about her car. Fuck if she could remember her license plate number in the moment.

After spending an endless amount of time on the phone, she discovered her car was now downtown at an impound lot under the I-80 freeway. *Time to text Tommy. There goes my goal to stay away from him. I'm irrevocably attached to a man. Nice.*

***

Amanda's Jaguar

As if on cue, Tommy's cell phone chirped with an incoming text.

"See?" he said, holding it up to Amanda. "The after-work text has arrived."

She raised an eyebrow. "You know her well."

Tommy read Jen's text, and his face fell. "Shit!"

"What?"

"Jen's car was towed, and she's wondering if I can come and get her, then take her to the impound lot. How am I gonna tell her that I can't? She'll be royally pissed at me."

"Don't worry about it. Tell her I'll pick her up and drive her to the lot. We'll drop you at Justice first, then race over to the hospital and pick her up. See? Problem solved." Amanda smiled reassuringly.

"I can't ask you to do that."

"Nonsense. What am I gonna do while you execute the warrant? It would be my pleasure to help. Text her back," Amanda ordered. "Go on."

"Okay, but I doubt she'll agree."

They waited in silence for Jen's anticipated reply. When Tommy's phone beeped, he read Jen's text aloud.

Seriously? The same Amanda who didn't want to discuss the case last night? Fine. I'm desperate. "Oops. Guess I shouldn't have read that out loud."

Amanda laughed. "It'll give me a chance to put things right with her. No offense."

"Okay. I'll tell her you'll pick her up at the ER entrance in twenty minutes."

"Perfect."

Tommy texted Jen back with Amanda's message.

"Are you going to call the hospital Legal Department first to give them the heads-up about your search warrant?" Amanda asked.

"Hell no. They'd probably throw up obstacles to delay, delay, delay. I prefer the element of surprise," he said.

"Good plan."

They arrived at Justice and Tommy got out of the car so he could go in and assemble a team to execute the search warrant.

Amanda smiled. "Bye. Good luck. Text me if you need anything."

***

Chapter 14

SoMa

George drove Amanda toward the hospital. They were crawling in rush hour traffic on Potrero, so it was going to take the full twenty minutes that Tommy had predicted it would. When they entered the emergency room roundabout, Amanda spotted Jen. She was pacing, a frustrated look on her face, with no idea that the expensive car was her ride to the impound lot. George pulled alongside Jen, and Amanda rolled down her back window.

"Your ride is here," Amanda said with a smile.

"Oh. Hi. I didn't expect you to be in this car. For some reason, I thought it would be an unmarked police car," Jen said, opening the rear door and dropping into the back seat next to Amanda.

"Those are used only for police business. This is my car. Good to see you again," Amanda said, extending her hand.

Jen grasped Amanda's hand, appreciating that Amanda had a healthy grip and warm touch. Their eyes met, and Jen felt a connection. Again. She hadn't been wrong about her initial impression at the charity ball. "Thank you for doing this. It's kind of embarrassing to have the District Attorney collect me and bring me over to the impound lot for a presumed driving infraction. Honestly, I have no idea why my car was towed."

"Then, we shouldn't presume it was an infraction, should we?" Where were you parked?"

"On Hampshire Street, a block off Potrero and two blocks from the hospital. I don't usually park there, but I was a little late this morning, so I knew the spots on San Bruno, behind the hospital parking ramp, would be full."

"Did you notice any signs posted by the city for street repair or the like?"

"No, not until after work. They obviously started a project today."

"Maybe the city forgot to post the signs. Well, let's go get your car. Where's the impound lot?"

"I Googled it before you came, and it's over on seventh street, by the Hall of Justice."

"It's under the I-80 overpass," George said from the front. "I know where it is."

"Back to our neck of the woods," Amanda said, smiling.

Since George was experienced in such matters, he mansplained to Jen and Amanda. "You have to watch out for local residents pulling temporary 'no parking' signs after the city posts them. The residents resent the hospital employees taking spots on their streets, so they remove the temporary signs, resulting in the hospital employees being towed. I'll make a note to have patrol officers present next time the city posts 'no parking' signs in the neighborhood."

"Thank you for telling me that. It makes me feel a little better, knowing it might not have been my fault."

They rode in silence for a few minutes. "How were things at work today?" Amanda asked.

"Okay. Business as usual in the ER." Jen sure as hell wasn't going to mention Lane's heart episode to Amanda. Not after Amanda's lofty speech about confidentiality at the charity ball.

Jen's phone beeped, and she looked at it, reading the text silently. "No fucking way."

Amanda looked at her, arching her shapely eyebrow at Jen's expletive.

"Tommy's at the hospital with a search warrant for Lane Wallace's office?" Jen asked.

"Who texted you?" Amanda asked.

"Lane himself. Someone must have told him. What the hell difference does it make? You and Tommy think my colleague killed Natasha Farber?" Jen demanded.

Amanda blew out a long sigh. "Jen, you know I can't discuss this with you. I'm sorry that Tommy is your boyfriend and that Dr. Wallace is a colleague, but we have to do our jobs."

"You people are a shit show," Jen said, blowing up. "Was all this carefully orchestrated? To get me away from the hospital while Tommy did the dirty work, because he knew I'd go ape-shit if I were there right now?"

"What are you talking about?" Amanda said.

"You know. Tow my car, knowing I'd find that out when my shift ended. You take me away in your fancy car while Tommy searches Lane's office. Did you and Tommy plan this?" Jen knew it sounded farfetched as it fell out of her mouth, but she was pissed at them for suspecting Lane of murder.

"Whoa! God, no," Amanda said, putting her hand on Jen's arm and leaning around so they were face-to-face. "That would be waay too elaborate for us to orchestrate. Not only are we incapable of doing that, we *wouldn't* do that. Tommy is executing the warrant now because the duty judge couldn't see us until after three-thirty. That's the only reason it's so late."

"I don't believe you," Jen said, throwing up her arm and flicking Amanda's hand off.

Amanda calmly hit the button for the partition window, so George wouldn't hear what she was about to say to Jen.

"Jen, I didn't want George to overhear what I'm about to tell you. Can you please keep it in confidence?"

"Yes. It's about time you came clean with me."

"I can't come *totally* clean with you, because I'm bound by strict rules, but here's what I *can* tell you. We're obligated to investigate suspects. Since Natasha Farber and Dr. Wallace were having an extra-marital affair, we have to investigate him. I'm sorry he's your colleague, but we're just doing our jobs. If you had met with her parents today, the Ivanovs, you'd do the same thing."

Jen scrutinized Amanda, then leveled her eyes at her. "From what I hear, you and Tommy should be looking for Natasha's estranged husband, not at Dr. Wallace. You're going to ruin his career, you know. Hospital administration already put him on leave, and they're probably going to revoke his staff status."

"He's already on leave? Tommy must have served the warrant on hospital Administration rather than Dr. Wallace himself," Amanda pondered out loud, not realizing that Lane had suffered the heart incident.

"Whatever," Jen said. She shouldn't have told Amanda that Lane was on leave. "Maybe one of the staff texted him. Bad news travels fast, you know."

"Okay."

"Can you stop condescending to me like I'm some four-year-old? I'm a physician, Amanda. I deal with traumatic, and yes, confidential, situations every day. I know how to keep a confidence."

"I'm not being condescending. I told you. There are rules I have to follow. I don't expect you to be familiar with them, but you need to respect that, once you walk out of the hospital, you're no longer a physician. You're just a civilian, caught up in a criminal case. You might be entitled to know everything that happens in the hospital, but this isn't the hospital." Amanda's otherwise kind brown eyes drilled into Jen's, the color rising up her neck to her face.

"So, now you're personally offending me to make your point? That's rich." Jen turned and looked out the window.

"There are some paradigms that are out of your control, Doctor. If you find that personally offensive, then so be it," Amanda said, finally reacting to Jen's immaturity.

"Go to hell, Amanda. Let me out," Jen demanded.

George didn't hear Jen's request, so he continued driving toward the impound lot.

"If you want out, I'll ask George to pull over and let you out, but we're still ten minutes from the impound lot. Let me take you all the way. I owe you that much," Amanda said, forcing herself to use a calm voice.

"Fine." Jen sat back against her headrest and pressed her eyes shut. She felt her pulse on the inside of her wrist and realized her heart was racing.

Five excruciating minutes passed in silence. "I'm sorry," Amanda said, her voice returning to normal. "I'm sorry for insulting you and saying what I just said. I was out of line."

Jen opened her eyes and turned her head to Amanda. Amanda was looking at her with soft brown eyes once again, the tiny flecks of gold catching shafts of light through the sun roof. It was an authentic apology. God, Jen hated her in that moment, but admired her, too. Her ability to recognize her own role in a fight and take the initiative to apologize was so mature—in contrast to how Jen felt.

"I accept your apology. I'm sorry for being paranoid that you and Tommy purposefully towed my car. That was irrational. It's just that —I can't believe an ultrasound tech was murdered. And, on top of that, that my colleague is a suspect. It's insane." *And, I don't hate you. Quite the opposite, actually. You're stirring emotions I haven't felt since college.*

"I know," Amanda said, putting her hand on Jen's arm.

"I need a workout to clear my head. I was on my way to a CrossFit class after work, but with my car situation, I missed it. I really need to blow off some steam. I'm sorry I laid into you."

"No worries. Do you want me to go into the impound lot office with you?" Amanda asked, as they approached the ugly government building.

"Would you mind? I'm afraid I'll tell someone off and make a mess of it. I tend to lose it when I'm frustrated," Jen admitted.

"Not at all. Let me tell George."

Amanda powered down the privacy window, and explained to George that she would be accompanying Jen into the impound office.

"I'll park out front and wait for you," he said.

Amanda's hand remained on Jen's arm as she spoke to George, so Jen couldn't help but look at it. The first thing she noticed was a smooth lavender band on Amanda's right ring finger. It had a blue-striped glass hemisphere mounted to it that was hand-blown glass. It was very contemporary in design and smooth to the touch. Jen ran her finger over it, admiring how it caught the light.

"What a beautiful ring," Jen said, holding it between her thumb and forefinger.

"Thank you. It was a gift from a friend. We visited Australia together and happened upon this glass blowing shop on the beach.... The rest will have to wait. We should go in and get your car," Amanda said, as they arrived at the impound lot.

Jen dropped Amanda's hand. Interesting that just the way Jen touched her ring finger registered on Amanda's gaydar.

They entered the shabby government facility and stood in line, waiting for the only available person to wait on several people in front of them. When Jen finally made it to the window, she learned the towing fee was over four hundred dollars. She bit her tongue and reluctantly handed over her credit card. It was the exclamation point to a shitty day. After the paperwork was complete, the lady behind the window told Jen the number of the stall her car was parked in.

"Want me to walk with you?" Amanda asked.

"Sure. I feel like you're being too nice to me."

"What a strange thing to say. Why wouldn't I be nice to you?"

"Because I'm an arrogant physician who's full of herself," Jen quipped.

"That's not true. You're not full of yourself. Just arrogant."

"Likewise," Jen said.

They laughed as they counted the stalls and found Jen's car. The surroundings were pitiful, hemmed in by a chain link fence, the I-80 traffic buzzing above their heads and garbage strewn about from homeless people. Jen unlocked Aethenoth, and turned to thank Amanda.

She didn't know what to say with Amanda standing so close, so they unexpectedly fell into a hug, Jen feeling Amanda's intoxicating warmth.

"I'm sorry for what I said in the car," Amanda said.

"Me, too," Jen replied over Amanda's shoulder.

"Have a good night." Amanda dropped her arms first.

"You, too." Jen's eyes lingered a second too long.

Jen slipped into Aethenoth and cranked her to life. Amanda returned to her chauffeured car. She asked George to drive her back to Justice, where she'd wait until Tommy finished executing his warrant. She removed her cell phone from her bag and dialed the number for the forensics lab as George drove. To her surprise, they had finally finished analyzing the bottles of booze and the spray of amber liquid on the white kitchen rug.

The lab technician reported that both Digoxin and an opioid were found in the confiscated bottle of bourbon. The laced bourbon was also the liquid that had stained Natasha's kitchen rug. There wasn't anything in the other liquor bottles, including the open bottle of wine.

Amanda Googled Digoxin to learn what it was usually prescribed for, and what would happen if it were mixed with alcohol and an opioid. She discovered it most likely would result in a heart arrhythmia, due to Digoxin toxicity. She Googled Xanax and learned that it was potentially fatal if mixed with an opioid. So, if Natasha Farber was taking Xanax, then drank bourbon laced with Digoxin and an opioid, the combination could be deadly. Was deadly. Amanda deduced that Natasha died from the deadly combination of drugs and alcohol. The only question was, "*Who laced the bourbon?*"

***

Chapter 15

San Francisco Community Hospital

The receptionist at the main hospital entrance spied Tommy and his team of detectives entering the revolving doors, badges prominently displayed on their suitcoat pockets. She suddenly had a surge of anxiety about her unpaid parking tickets, as Tommy approached her desk.

"I'm Detective Tommy Vietti. How are you today?"

"I was good. I hope you're not gonna change that," she said cautiously.

He smiled. "I have a search warrant for a doctor's office. You might want to call the chief administrator of the hospital to meet with me right now."

"I can do that."

He watched her pick up her phone and dial a number. She was cool and professional as she spoke to someone on the other end.

A few minutes later, a man in a pinstripe suit introduced himself as a hospital administrator, and invited Tommy and his three detectives to follow him to a conference room to discuss the search warrant. They were met by two hospital attorneys who introduced themselves and shook hands with the detectives. Tommy recognized the female as the lawyer he met earlier in the day while picking up Natasha Farber's medical record.

The group of seven entered the conference room. Once they were all seated, Tommy pushed the search warrant across the table to the lead attorney, who quickly scanned it and handed it to her colleague.

Tommy couldn't help but smile at the in-house lawyers, who were probably shocked that their hospital was swept up in a murder investigation. They sat stick-straight in their expensive blue and grey suits, both wearing white shirts. The lead was an attractive woman in her mid-forties, with long, black hair. The second was a man of similar age, half-glasses perched on his nose as he read the search warrant. He whispered in her ear when he was finished reading.

"We'll cooperate with your warrant, and escort you to Dr. Wallace's office, where we'll remain and take notes and photos of anything you confiscate," she said.

"Sounds fine. Can we get started?" Tommy asked.

"One minute," she said. "I noticed your warrant says 'all emails of Dr. Wallace for the past twelve months.' You know those won't be on his computer in his office, right? We'll have to contact our Information Systems Department, so they can search the main server. We can request them to make a disk, or jump drive, whichever you prefer."

"Okay. How long will that take?" Tommy asked.

"I don't know if they can start tonight. It's after normal business hours. I'm sure they could start tomorrow morning, though. I'm guessing a couple of days. No more than a week."

"We don't have a week. This is a homicide investigation."

"We understand that," she said, smiling politely. "If you have a computer forensics expert, we can have that person talk to our computer people tomorrow to expedite the process as much as possible. If there's any patient information, however, we'll have to protect that."

"We're entitled to get all of Natasha Farber's patient information," Tommy reminded her.

"Of course. We went through that earlier today when you visited the Legal Department. I'm talking about other patient data. We have to protect the confidentiality of all other patient data. I'm not saying that there will be patient data on any emails from Dr. Wallace or Natasha Farber, but we have to look first."

"I just don't want this to drag out for days."

"Neither do we. Our interests are aligned, Detective Vietti. By the way, can you tell your partner to stop writing down everything I say? I don't want this in a police report. I'm obviously not a witness and not going to be a witness. I'm counsel for the hospital and trying to strategize with you about this investigation."

She waited with her eyebrow raised until the other detective set down his pen. "As I was saying, we want it wrapped up, too, so we'll do everything we can to cooperate with your request."

"Thank you for clarifying. Can we go to Dr. Wallace's office now?"

"Yes. We'll take the back stairwell, so we don't run into any patients or visitors. If you don't mind, I'd appreciate it if you removed your badges from the outside pocket of your coats and put them away. You're with us now, so no one is going to question who you are."

Tommy was amused. He respected that they had a job to do, protecting patient information and preventing damage to the hospital's reputation, but if they got in the way of the information he sought, he'd talk to Amanda about charging them with obstructing his investigation. He'd seen her deal with corporate attorneys before, and she could unleash a fury of legal threats that would make even the most experienced corporate attorney shrink in her chair.

They all trooped quietly through the hospital administrative area, down a back stairwell and to a labyrinth of hallways behind the ER. Tommy had never visited Jen's office in the three years they'd been together. He didn't even know she had one. He'd have to ask her more about her work life once this investigation was over—when she would see him again.

What shitty timing. She turned down his proposal on the night of this case breaking. Just when he wanted to spend more time with her, convincing her to marry him, she had declared a no-fly zone, ostensibly so they wouldn't fight about Lane Wallace's involvement in Natasha Farber's murder. Women were *so fucking unpredictable*, he thought, then snapped out of his reverie to refocus on the task at hand.

The hospital lawyers led Tommy and his team to a locked door with a nameplate next to it that said, 'Emergency Room Physician Chair.' The lead attorney swiped her name badge over the key pad and the door unlocked. She flipped the light switch and stood aside. The office was the size of a broom closet, allowing for only a small desk, a book shelf and two chairs. There was a framed nautical map of San Francisco Bay mounted on the wall above Dr. Wallace's desk.

"Not a very big office," Tommy said under his breath. He and the lead attorney were occupying the only standing space.

"We don't have a lot of room to spare in the hospital," she said. "Dr. Wallace has an office only because he's the Chair of his Department. Otherwise, physicians don't get offices."

"Interesting," Tommy said, learning that Jen didn't have an office after all. "Do you think you could step out so my team could join me in searching what we came for?"

"I'd be happy to, as long as you show me everything you seize. I need to take a photo and make a log," she said.

"Fine. I don't think we're required to under the law, but I'm happy to extend the courtesy."

"I'm pretty confident we're not obligated to provide our computer experts to talk to your computer guys either. But, I'm happy to extend the courtesy."

"Point taken," he said, and she stepped out.

One of the other detectives took her place in the office. Since there was room for only two people in Dr. Wallace's office, the other two detectives held up the walls on either side of the door jamb. Tommy donned his blue latex gloves, both to protect himself and to preserve any fingerprints that might be on objects he decided to seize for evidence.

Without further ado, they disconnected the hard drive and removed it to the hallway, where the lawyers photographed it and wrote down the inventory number off the sticker adhered to its side.

Tommy sat in Lane's desk chair and let his eyes roam over the desk, wall hangings and bookshelves. When searching someone's personal space, he liked to occupy the space as the owner would. This perspective allowed him the same feeling as the user, which was helpful in figuring out where the user would hide stuff.

As he sat, he let his vision sweep the surroundings, thinking about where he would stash stuff in the space if he occupied it. He started his search by rifling through the desk drawers. Nothing interesting. No little, black address book with names of prostitutes. No love letters from Natasha. No psychopathic shrine to Natasha.

Tommy turned his attention to the bookshelf. As expected, it was filled with text books and continuing education binders. There were framed photos on the second shelf—Wallace, Susie and their daughter hiking; Wallace's young daughter in a soccer uniform at a field; and one of Lane and Susie, sitting on a sailboat in the Bay. He picked it up, examining it closely. The boat was named *Sangiolo Sun*. Interesting that he used her maiden name for his boat. *Maybe she bought it for him. It looked expensive—a Beneteau.* He studied their facial expressions. They looked happy together, whenever it had been taken, which was most likely a few years ago, judging by Susie's younger appearance. Her face didn't look as strained as it had in the ER when he saw her.

"Let's take this," Tommy said, picking it up and handing it to the other detective, so the lawyers could log it.

The spine of a textbook on the top shelf caught his eye, <u>Tintinalli's Emergency Medicine.</u> *Written by an Italian, so it can't be all bad, huh?* he thought.

He opened it and fanned the pages. Much to his surprise, there was a five-by-seven photo of Natasha tucked in the book. She was lying in her bed, wearing a red negligée, with a come-and-get-me look on her face. Tommy guessed Lane had taken the photo, judging by the distance and angle. She was a pretty woman. On the back she had written, *Lane, Always Yours, Natasha,* encircled by a big, red heart.

"Take this hidden treasure," Tommy said to the other detective.

The hospital lawyers' eyebrows shot up when they read it.

Tommy painstakingly opened all the other books on the shelves, but he knew there wouldn't be anything else in them. No cash. No alias passports.

"I think we can leave," he said.

The other detective departed the office, and, to be thorough, Tommy closed the door but remained in the office, so he could see if there was anything behind, or hanging on, the back of the door. There was a white physician coat hanging on the sole hook, so he grabbed it and opened the door again. He showed the others while he searched the pockets of the coat.

There was a stethoscope in the left pocket, which he set aside. In the right pocket, he felt the cold, hard shape of a small, glass vial. He removed it and read the label. "Narcan," he said to the group.

The lead hospital lawyer rolled her eyes.

"Why are you rolling your eyes?"

"Because staff aren't supposed to have meds in their pockets. It's against hospital policy. On the other hand, we know that in certain care areas, like the ER, staff frequently have emergency meds handy so they can administer them fast. Or, the doctor may have already used it on a patient, but forgot to discard it pursuant to policy. Hard to say," she said.

"What's Narcan?" Tommy asked, inspecting the half-empty vial.

"I'm not an expert, but my understanding is that it's used to reverse an opioid overdose. I don't think it has any other use. That's why we're not concerned from a drug diversion perspective. In other words, you can't get high by taking Narcan. In fact, I'm not surprised an ER physician would have that in his coat pocket. If he gave a patient too much pain killer, like morphine or something, having Narcan within a second's reach could save a life."

"Very helpful to know. Take your photos and log it. We're taking this as evidence, too."

"The coat, too?" the other detective asked.

"Yes. The coat, too," Tommy said, removing his latex gloves and stuffing them in his pocket. Mission accomplished.

***

Tommy called Amanda from the unmarked police car on their drive back to the Hall of Justice. She said she would meet him in his office to discuss what he had learned.

When Tommy returned to his office, he took a pic of the framed photo of Lane and Susie, as well as both sides of Natasha's photo to Lane. He sent the originals to the Evidence Room for chain-of-custody safekeeping. He also photographed the vial of Narcan and sent it to the lab to see if they could lift fingerprints from it.

Amanda arrived, and Tommy downloaded the results of his search.

"Narcan and a photo of his lover. Not bad," she said. "I've been researching Digoxin, which is what the lab said was in the bottle of bourbon, in addition to opioids. Digoxin is used to treat congestive heart failure, usually in elderly patients. Of course, opioids will slow your respiratory rate. So, combined, they could really mess with your heart. Add Xanax to the mix and it could be deadly, according to the two-minute web search I did."

"When did you get lab results?" he asked.

"I called after I dropped Jen at the impound lot. There was Digoxin and an opioid in the bourbon bottle as well as on the kitchen rug."

"That tells us a lot. How was Jen, by the way?"

"She was fine," Amanda said, electing not to share their fight.

"And she got her car back?"

"Yes. No worries."

"Good to hear. So, Natasha was prescribed Xanax by Dr. Wallace. Then probably, and I stress probably, drank bourbon laced with Digoxin and an opioid. We won't know for sure what was inside of her until we get the toxicology results back, but that's what it looks like."

"Yes. Once we get those results, I plan to call one of our expert physicians and ask if that combination could kill her."

"We can also try to get Wallace's fingerprints off the Narcan vial so we can compare them to prints on the bottle of bourbon."

"His prints probably *are* on the bourbon bottle if he was her lover, spending time in her apartment. What man doesn't like a little bourbon before sex?" she asked.

He raised his eyebrows at her.

"You're right. I wouldn't know. Never been there."

"Never?"

"Never. I'm a gold star."

He smiled, recognizing the reference. "You've obviously never seen an Italian man naked."

She smirked. "It doesn't work like that, you know."

"I know. In any event, it'd be nice to see if there's a match from the vial to the bourbon bottle before I interview him," Tommy said.

"I agree. We're not even close to having enough evidence to arrest him."

"Speaking of which, I have Natasha's medical record here. I reviewed it, but why don't you look through it while I order us some Chinese?"

"Chicken and broccoli for me," she said, grabbing the small stack of papers from his desk that comprised Natasha's medical record.

Amanda kicked off her heels and curled up on Tommy's only guest chair in his small office. She had spent many evenings working cases with him in the old days, and actually welcomed the opportunity to solve a mystery together, late into the night. She texted George that he could go home, and she'd text him when she needed a ride, but it wouldn't be before ten o'clock.

Amanda studied Natasha's record, seeing the expected annual exams, interspersed with sinus infections. Not surprisingly, Natasha was on birth control pills.

As Tommy said, Natasha was seen by Dr. Lane Wallace six weeks ago, shortly after Blake was arrested and charged with domestic battery. Amanda flagged the page. Dr. Wallace formalized the visit in a physician's note, indicating her chief complaint was 'anxiety.' The note indicated he performed a cursory medical exam, then diagnosed her with 'situational anxiety due to personal stressors with her estranged husband.' He prescribed her Xanax.

Tommy busied himself with emails while Amanda studied pharmacology websites that warned against taking opioids while on Xanax. That much was clear. She also looked up the side effects of Digoxin, and learned that there were multiple warnings when taking it while on other drugs. She did the same with the birth control pills, but nothing populated except smoking.

"Tommy, it appears from my brief research that the combo of Xanax, Digoxin, opioids and alcohol could have killed Natasha," Amanda said.

He peered around his flat screen at her. "That's what we suspected."

"According to a pharmacology site, it can be fatal to mix Xanax and opioids. If she drank bourbon with Digoxin in it—which it appears she did because there was a tumbler on the floor next to her—you've got a lethal cocktail."

"I'm sure her toxicology results will confirm that theory."

"Who put the Digoxin and opioids in the bourbon?"

"Oh. That reminds me. I forgot to tell you something," Tommy said.

***

Chapter 16

Sea Cliff

Jen swung the steering wheel hard to the left, turning off El Camino Del Mar onto Sea Cliff Avenue, the Golden Gate bridge peeking through the fog on her right. She drove into the China Beach parking lot, where she found an open stall, intentionally reading the parking sign to confirm it said what she thought it said. She had read it ages ago, the first time she had parked here, but the towing incident had left her skittish.

She consulted her watch, calculating that she had at least ninety minutes of daylight for an open-ocean swim. She made haste to the trunk of her car, where she kept her wetsuit and other swim gear. Stripping down to a tank and bikini bottoms, she began the laborious task of pulling on her full-length wetsuit. It was like a sausage casing—except not as pliant. She pulled on the neoprene. It resisted. She pulled again, and it reluctantly slid across her skin, hugging and molding tightly as it slid up her body.

As she hopped around on one foot at the back of her car, she saw several others doing the same thing, in various stages of pulling on or peeling off. Most were surfers, but she spied another swimmer, his goggles hanging around his neck. They acknowledged each other, welcoming the thought of a swimming companion. Once she was snug in her black sausage casing, she reached behind herself for the long zip cord and pulled the zipper from her tailbone to her neck, where she covered it with the Velcro clasp.

She grabbed her bright orange swim buoy and put on her yellow Tyra swim cap. She didn't worry about locking her car because there weren't any valuables in it—her cell phone remaining on the kitchen counter at home. She tossed the keys on her floor mat and slammed the door.

She proceeded down the stairs to the concrete pathway that serpentined around the ugly concrete building, opening on the beach. As she stepped onto the cool sand, she saw several people out for their evening walks.

Book-ended by mammoth boulders spilling into the ocean on each side, China Beach was a picturesque cove nestled into the Sea Cliff neighborhood. Only a few hundred yards long, it provided its residents with a sense of privacy and exclusivity, affording them a majestic view of the Golden Gate channel and the infamous bridge spanning it. The beach was named after an encampment of Chinese fisherman who had lived there at the turn of the twentieth century, before being swept away by the wealthy land owners. It was rumored to be inhabited by Chinese spirits.

The cold waves splashed over her feet as she waded steadily into the turbulent ocean, acclimating to the frigid water. It was a steep incline, the water not only slamming the shore from the Pacific, but also churning against the tide flowing in and out of the bay through the narrow Golden Gate channel.

She raised her swim goggles to her eyes, feeling how strong the undertow was. It was close to low tide, so the Bay had almost finished emptying itself of trillions of gallons of water. During the ebbing tide, the rip currents were strongest, so she preferred to swim her laps parallel to the shore. She anticipated getting roughed up a little as the tide turned, but knew she could handle it. She breathed in the pungent, salty air and dove in, the orange buoy dangling from her waist. Her muscles tensed as the fifty-nine-degree water seeped into her wetsuit over the back collar, streaming down her back like ice cubes. Once the water was trapped inside the wetsuit though, its warmth provided the insulative effect the suit was designed to deliver.

She did the breast stroke a few yards out to where the depth plummeted, then converted to a front crawl. She was only thirty yards from shore, but it seemed a lot further when she was alone. The surfers had paddled to her left from shore, preferring the breaking waves that slammed into the rocks southwest of China Beach.

She started her routine, warming up her shoulders and kicking her legs, seeking the warmth that only a solid effort would give her against the pinpricks of penetrating cold.

Swimming along this stretch of coast always held risk, as the great white sharks were common in the Bay Area, preying on seals and sea lions for miles, including all the way out to the Farallon Islands. She was committed to her training, however, so wouldn't let a tiny thing like an eighteen-foot shark stand in her way.

She consulted her Garmin triathlon watch, which had a bright digital readout on a black face that was easy to see in the greenish water. Its comfortable rubber wristband hugged tightly, preventing salt from grinding against her sensitive skin. It tracked her distance and time by GPS monitoring, so she'd know when she had logged 1.5 miles, which was the length of the Dolphin Club triathlon swim from Alcatraz.

Jen came upon the other swimmer who had been changing in the parking lot. He was a few feet further out than she was, and likewise doing the front crawl. He, too, had a swim buoy trailing alongside. They nodded at each other as she passed, grateful for the comradery in dangerous currents.

She could complete her swim in about thirty minutes, but felt a little doggy today, given the amount of energy she had expended during her shift at the hospital—both mental and physical.

As she coordinated her arms and legs in a graceful motion, she let her mind turn over the events in her life, like a mixer automatically blending bread dough—flipping and twisting, turning it inside and out, revealing all sides of the substance as the flour, egg and water blended. This free-flowing thought, unspoiled by a disciplined analysis like practicing medicine, was her way of assimilating new information. There was no protocol or decision-tree to follow, just relaxation and abstract review, taking random thoughts as they occurred to her. The faces of friends and colleagues popped into her mind, as if they were floating up from the bottom of the ocean.

She saw Tommy's earnest expression as he proposed marriage to her on bended knee, holding the diamond ring. There was undaunted commitment in his earnest Italian eyes; followed by confusion and hurt when she told him she wasn't ready to accept. He had been a faithful boyfriend, and she loved him for that. The problem was that she didn't feel an abiding, burning love for him—one that would last a lifetime.

His image drifted away and was replaced by Lane's face, pale and stippled with beads of sweat, pleading with her to help him as he crashed into the table in the doc room. Even though he was successfully treated, she would never forget the panicked look that engulfed him in that moment.

Why didn't he want to tell the police about the Digoxin and opioids in his system? Was he paranoid that he'd be investigated by the hospital—that administration wouldn't believe him? Jen would keep his secret confidential, but she was perplexed about his decision.

Lane reminded Jen of his wife, Susie, and her red lipstick and bouffant hair, teased and sprayed like cotton candy on a stick at the fair. Her presence had dominated the entire ER, standing in the center, gesticulating as she spoke passionately, her long, red nails emphasizing her points. She had been so icy, except when she was around Tommy. *We dated in high school,* Tommy had told her. *Why didn't I feel jealous when Susie flirted with Tommy? Why didn't I care in the least when they hugged? What's wrong with me? Shouldn't I have blurted out that I was Tommy's girlfriend, at the very least, or even his fiancée? Instead, I stood there like a spectator, not feeling any emotion at all.*

Next, Amanda's image, naturally curly hair to pedicured-toe, permeated Jen's thoughts. Jen saw Amanda at the ball in her slinky, black cocktail dress and red-soled high heels. The charge that had passed between them in the ladies' room had been undeniably carnal, popping off fireworks in Jen's brain.

That image faded, and Jen saw herself seated next to Amanda in the back of her expensive car. Amanda's apology floated between them, her deep-set eyes genuine with emotion. Amanda was authentic. Confident. Self-assured. Jen thought Amanda had been an ass, but in retrospect, she simply may have been reacting to Jen's attack. She couldn't blame Amanda, since Jen had been slightly irrational herself, come to think of it. She knew she had a temper, and sometimes got emotional over things, but Amanda had been the better person, apologizing right away.

Should I have apologized? Did I?

Jen recalled Amanda's shaky smile as she apologized, framed by full, red lips—not lipstick red, like Susie's were—but healthy red. Lickable red. Enticing. Jen found Amanda's sheepishness attractive. Amanda's cool, powerful exterior apparently slipped in Jen's presence.

And Amanda's touch—firm, yet gentle. The sensation floated into Jen's mind, like the swells she was swimming through. She wanted to swim to Amanda, immerse herself in her, and become part of her world. That's how charismatic Amanda was, making Jen want all of her. She was consumed with wanting to possess Amanda. She had never felt this way about Tommy, and her feelings for Amanda were exposing the absence of deep passion for Tommy.

Jen was swimming as fast as she ever had. Swimming harder now, pumping her legs, swinging her arms, feeling the burn in her shoulders, she examined her deepest desires. She was filled with the fragrance, sight and touch of Amanda, her senses coming alive. Mid-stroke, she realized the alarm on her watch was buzzing repeatedly. She had met her goal of one-point-five miles, and it was time to swim back to shore. She flipped around and swam toward shore.

She was proud to achieve her goal, even though she felt more confused than when she had entered the water. She had sifted and sorted through the tangle of new information in her life, but inconvenient truths had emerged that would set her on a course she hadn't anticipated. A course that would upset her world as she knew it. As Tommy knew it. As her family knew it. Amanda was the disturbance in Jen's life, shattering her ordinary and predictable route.

As the ebbing tide turned, Jen was propelled easily back to shore. Once she touched bottom, she waded back up the steep incline, the undertow pushing against her legs.

Contrary to her usual routine, she plopped down on the coarse, amber-colored sand, gazing at the serene scape before her, her ankles still in the surf. The Marin Headlands stared at her from across the channel, and the Golden Gate Bridge dominated the skyline to her right. She was lucky to have such a picturesque workout space, nestled in her cove under the cliffs. She breathed hard as the waves swept in, eroding away the sand under her buttocks.

The realization that she was leaving Tommy finally hit her, and she started crying. Pulling her knees up to her chin, wrapping her arms around her shins, she quietly sobbed, the tears flowing onto her wetsuit, then dropping into the surf to be carried back out to the Farallon Islands. She convulsed with silent sobs, her back to the beachcombers.

As she unearthed her true feelings, she knew it wasn't meant to be—marrying Tommy. Until Amanda had stormed into her life, she thought he might be the one. Now, she knew he'd never complete her. It wouldn't be right to mislead him, and she'd be damned if she would deceive him. No, it was better to break his heart before they got engaged, than do it slowly over the course of a tormented marriage.

Her epiphany morphed into a fully-formed belief, becoming part of the fabric of her conscious thought, causing her to cry some more.

As much as she had hated Amanda in the car, Jen had Amanda to thank for her revelation. Amanda had ignited Jen's true inclinations. Inclinations she hadn't felt since a college romance. She had been too young to understand. Too young to figure out how to incorporate being gay into a successful academic and medical career. Too terrified of what people might think. Professors, colleagues, doctors, nurses, her friends, and most importantly, her family. It was all too much to navigate in her early twenties, especially since the zeitgeist of her Wisconsin college experience was being straight. If she had looked, she would have found support, but she had been too busy denying her true identity back then, so she had taken a decade-long detour.

Now, she found herself in her early thirties, sitting on a beach, rediscovering her sexuality —and she had Amanda to thank for it. She had stormed into Jen's life. Not quietly. Not anonymously, but with purpose and intention, as only Amanda could.

Jen was terrified. She was about to throw away a loving relationship with Tommy for a chance with Amanda. A chance to find herself. She knew it was only a chance—one that might not materialize. Poor Tommy. She would break his heart, and a piece of her own, in the process, but she had to be true to herself and pursue Amanda. In the meantime, she refused to betray Tommy. He deserved better, and she wouldn't reduce herself to skulking around behind his back.

As Jen's tears ran dry, they were replaced by resolve. Her new course wouldn't be easy. There were words that needed to be said. Emotions that needed to be felt. Plans that needed to be changed. A relationship that needed to end. It was going to get messy; maybe even ugly. However, she was determined to take the steps toward the happiness she deserved. Or, at least a shot at happiness.

She was finally ready to go, her soul dredging now complete.

The Asian man with whom she had been swimming waded out of the water toward her.

"Thanks for staying and watching me. It's nice to know that someone is waiting for you," he said.

Jen blinked up at him, wiping her tears away. "I know how you feel."

He patted her on the shoulder as he walked passed her to the steps that led to the parking lot.

She rose and ascended the steps a few yards behind him. When she emerged through the cypress and eucalyptus trees at the top however, he wasn't there. Her eyes followed his expected trajectory to his car, which had been across the lot from her own. Neither he nor his car was there. He couldn't have changed out of his wetsuit and driven away that fast! She had been only a few steps behind him. She spun around, looking for him in the lot, but there was no sign of him. *Had he been there at all?*

***

Chapter 17

Hall of Justice

Tommy's Office

"Okay, what did you learn today that's so important?" Amanda asked Tommy.

"It's both interesting and troubling," Tommy said.

"Ominous. What?"

"When I went over to the hospital earlier today, the first time to get Natasha's medical record, I bumped into an old high school flame in the ER."

"Really? Does Dr. Jen Dawson know about this?"

"Actually, Jen was standing there, so she met her as well—Susie Sangiolo."

"That's really fascinating. You were quite the Romeo, huh?" Amanda asked sarcastically.

"Well, not really, but Susie was really hot in high school. And she still is, sort of, but in an over-the-top way. If you know what I mean."

"We won't let Jen hear you say that."

"Jen's got nothing to worry about. Anyway, guess who Susie married?"

"The captain of the football team?"

"You're not going to believe it—Dr. Lane Wallace."

"No kidding. Small world, huh? Did Susie tell you anything interesting?"

"Very."

"What?"

"That Lane Wallace had a heart attack this morning at work, and was being treated by Jen, *my* Jen, that is."

Amanda stared at him, her wheels turning. "A heart attack, huh?"

"Yep."

"Isn't he a little young for that? Isn't he in his mid-forties."

"Yup."

"Stress?" she asked, knowing that wasn't the answer.

"Could be, but I doubt it."

"You're thinking he was taking Digoxin for an underlying heart condition, aren't you?"

"Yup."

"Which would mean he had Digoxin in his possession, and could just dump a little into the bourbon for Natasha to drink."

"Yup."

Tommy's phone rang. It was Security in the lobby, relaying that his food had arrived. "I'll be right back. The food is here."

When he returned, they moved to his small conference table and opened the white containers of rice and main entrées, both digging in.

"So, Wallace was possibly taking Digoxin himself and had easy access to opioids. And we know he had a Narcan vial in his pocket, so he could've stolen opioids just as easily. He had the knowledge, opportunity and means to kill Natasha with a drug overdose." Amanda delicately worked the chopsticks, eating.

"Yup," Tommy agreed around a bite.

"We need to figure out if she was a bourbon drinker."

"What difference does it make? She was obviously holding a glass of it when she died because it sprayed on her kitchen rug when the glass fell to the floor."

"I guess you're right. She probably was drinking it. The toxicology report will be definitive."

"That's right. I'll make a note to question Wallace about it when I interview him."

"She didn't weigh all that much," Amanda said, picking up Dr. Wallace's note of his examination of Natasha. "Only one-hundred-thirteen pounds."

"If Dr. Wallace wanted to kill her to prevent her from telling his wife, he sure chose an obvious way to do it. I mean, seriously, didn't he think we'd figure out a toxic booze-medication mixture? It just seems too simple to me," Tommy said.

"Some murders *are* easy to solve."

"I know, but I give Dr. Wallace more credit. He couldn't have been this stupid."

"How about Blake Farber? He easily could've bought the meds on the street, not knowing what they were for, or could do, and dropped them into the bottle of bourbon."

Tommy and Amanda ate in silence for a minute, each considering the likelihood of who got the Digoxin and opioids and dropped them into the bourbon. *Which man killed Natasha? Her estranged husband or her new lover?*

"I just thought of something," Tommy said, hopping up and moving to his desk computer. "I should email Computer Forensics before I forget. We want to know not only whether Blake is on the security cam footage of Natasha's apartment building, but also get the exact dates and times that Dr. Wallace visited her. We know he was there, but I want to know when. I should've thought of this yesterday. I can pull a photo of Dr. Wallace off the hospital website for them."

"Good plan," she said, scraping the bottom of her white carton.

"Here's one of Wallace on the hospital website," Tommy mumbled, staring at his flat screen. "Beard. Glasses. Shouldn't be too difficult to match in the security cam footage."

"If Blake knew about Dr. Wallace and Natasha," Amanda said, "maybe he wasn't trying to kill Natasha at all. Maybe he was trying to kill *Dr. Wallace.* Blake would have been knowledgeable about what Natasha drank, like wine, so *maybe* the bottle of bourbon was Dr. Wallace's drink of choice, and Blake didn't expect Natasha to drink *any* of it. After all, there wasn't any poison in the open bottle of wine, which adds credibility to my theory."

"I like the way you think," Tommy said, returning to the conference table.

"I don't know too many women who drink bourbon on the rocks. However, unbeknownst to Blake, maybe Natasha decided to dip into the bourbon because that's what her lover drank. And bingo, the laced bourbon interacted with the Xanax and killed her."

"That's actually not bad. Blake had a motive to kill Dr. Wallace—jealousy. He might have had the opportunity if we catch him on the apartment security cam footage. And, a medication poison mixture would be an easy means for anyone who knew how to buy drugs on the street. It makes sense that he was surprised and devastated by Natasha's death, because he actually was trying to kill Dr. Wallace."

"He was almost too cooperative with you in his interview, handing over his cell phone and unlocking Natasha's phone. He pointed us in Wallace's direction while simultaneously appearing genuinely heartbroken."

"I agree on both accounts," Tommy said. "That's why I'm having all the lobby video footage reviewed. Blake told us he hadn't been back to the apartment since the night of his arrest. I want to see if he's lying about that. If he is, he certainly could've poisoned the bourbon, intending to kill Dr. Wallace."

"And, if Wallace had a pre-existing heart condition, the Digoxin and opioids could've caused the heart attack he had this morning. Or, maybe he didn't have a heart condition at all, and I incorrectly assumed that."

"The poisoned bourbon could've been deadly to both Wallace and Natasha, but he weighs more than she did, so it didn't kill him." Tommy sat back in his desk chair and stared at Amanda. They both rolled that theory over in their minds, as well as the evidence that would be required to charge Blake.

Amanda packaged up the empty cartons and dropped them into the paper bag. "Did Jen say anything about Wallace's heart condition when you saw her at the hospital today?"

"No. She was quite clear that she planned to keep everything confidential about her new patient, even though Susie blurted out that Jen was Wallace's doctor.".

"Jen's a witness now, you know."

"I know, and it pisses me off because she's smart enough to know better. After Susie left to visit Lane, I pointed that out to Jen. She got angry and told me we shouldn't even talk to each other while I'm investigating this case."

Amanda's eyes flashed in reaction to Jen's new rule with Tommy. First, Jen turned down Tommy's marriage proposal. Now, she told him they couldn't even talk during the case. "But, you can still see each other, right?"

"No. She said we shouldn't even see each other because it might be too tempting to talk."

"That had to hit hard."

"It did. I'm worried about her. She really believes in Dr. Wallace. I think she resents that we're investigating him because we consider him a suspect. I'm concerned that she'll become more involved in the case, expanding her role as a witness."

"Someone needs to warn her off," Amanda suggested.

Tommy stared hard at her.

"Oh no," Amanda said, putting up her hands. "Not me. You saw her text today when you suggested I give her a lift to the impound lot. She doesn't care for me."

"So? She doesn't have to for this. You're the DA, and you're trying to warn her to stay away from an investigation. Use your official lawyer-speak."

"Why can't you do it?"

"I just told you. She won't talk to me about the case, or even see me for that matter. It's gotta be you."

"Couldn't one of the other detectives do it? Why do I always have to be the bad guy?" Amanda was recalling her earlier fight with Jen in the car, and how they apologized, then parted on a relatively good note. She didn't want to fight with Jen again. It was too upsetting.

"No. Jen wouldn't give a damn what any of the guys told her. She has to respect who the message is coming from, and I'm sure she respects you, Amanda. Pleeeease," he whined, imploring her with puppy dog eyes.

"Fine. For the good of the investigation, I will. But she won't like me, you know— probably for a long time. Years from now, when you wonder why she doesn't like me, I'll remind you of this conversation."

"Duly noted. I'll text her right now."

"Why don't you let me do it. Give me her phone number."

Tommy handed Amanda his cell phone, displaying his contact info for Jen. He cleared their empty cartons while Amanda composed a text to Jen.

Hi Jen. It's Amanda. Tommy gave me your number. I have to talk to you about something important. Can you meet for drinks tomorrow after work?

Amanda hit send and returned to the tasks before Tommy and her. "Alright. What else should we go over tonight?"

Tommy's phone beeped, indicating an incoming text. He picked it up and read it aloud, a dangerous habit in front of Amanda. It was from Jen. *R u working late with Amanda?*

Amanda smiled. "I admire her savvy."

"What should I reply?" he asked.

"The truth."

Yes, he replied to Jen.

They sat in silence, waiting for Jen to text one of them.

Amanda's phone beeped. "Guess I'm up next." She read the text silently before sharing it with Tommy. *"What time and where?"*

Amanda replied, *Boulevard, whenever you get off work.*

Jen responded, *See you there at 5:30.*

Amanda replied, *Looking forward to it.*

"Okay, I'm all set to deliver a speech to Jen tomorrow at five-thirty at Boulevard," she said.

"Perfect," Tommy said.

***

Sunset District

Across town, Jen ate her bowl of pasta with a strip of grilled salmon on top, pondering the text exchange with Amanda. She was wrapped in her favorite robe, having taken a hot shower. Swimming and soul searching had exhausted her.

Tommy and Amanda are working late, so it's obviously about the case. They discussed something involving me and decided it was best for Amanda to meet with me. That means Tommy probably told Amanda I put a moratorium on our relationship while he works the case. Tommy also most likely told Amanda that Lane was a patient today, and I was his doctor. Since that's my only involvement, that's probably what she wants to discuss.

Well, I'm sure they'll both appreciate that I can't talk about my care and treatment of Lane. They'll have to subpoena his medical record, just like they got a search warrant for his office. Why don't they just talk directly to Lane?

These two. No wonder it takes so long to solve a case if they're more concerned about my role than finding evidence that Natasha's estranged husband killed her.

More importantly, what should I wear to my meeting with Amanda? Boulevard is nice. A dress might be appropriate. Or would that be overdoing it? We're just talking. Considering what's transpired between us, I don't want to appear interested. But I am interested, and I want to look my best. What if she thinks I'm an over-eager school girl if I wear a dress? Shit. I'm sure I only imagined that she's interested, anyway.

***

Chapter 18

The Next Day

Sunset District

The sun had been up for an hour, steadily burning off the seaside fog, blazing the way for another blue sky in the city. Jen's shift started at seven o'clock, and it was already past six. She had to dash or she'd be late.

After sorting her thoughts and emotions on her swim, she had slept soundly. It was amazing what exercise and some solitude could do for her. Sure, she had a lot of work to do on two relationships, but she was confident she would succeed. It was all part of embracing her new feelings. She could no longer place other peoples' needs and expectations ahead of her own. Well, mostly Tommy's needs and expectations ahead of her own.

The decision confronting her momentarily was what to wear for her evening meeting with Amanda. It was eleven hours away, but Jen planned to bring an outfit to work, then change out of her scrubs and into her new life in the women's locker room.

She stared at her limited wardrobe in her cramped closet. Nothing jumped out at her at six in the morning. Black pants and a white blouse? No, she'd look like the wait staff, even though the black, wide-leg pants made her ass look fabulous. Tommy had told her many times and took great pleasure in possessively resting his hand there when she was in them.

A black cocktail dress? No, too dressy. Her favorite red wrap dress that always turned on Tommy? Maybe, although it reminded her of Tommy. He liked the way it accentuated her chest and narrow hips. And, it was comfortable. She had a pair of black shoes that looked good with it, and they didn't hurt her feet. Bonus. It was easy, and it was hanging in front of her. Done.

She threw a dry cleaner bag over it, folded the dress end-over-end on the hanger and placed it on the bottom of her duffle bag. She tossed in her undergarments, shoes and a makeup bag and zipped it closed. Standing lengthwise, the bag would fit neatly in her hospital locker.

She couldn't contain her inchoate excitement at the prospect of a romance with Amanda. They were only meeting for drinks to discuss business, but that's how relationships began wasn't it? She wasn't imagining this, was she? It was too early to think such thoughts. After all, she had a full day of work awaiting her in the ER, and God only knew what was in store at vomitville. And, she was simply guessing that Amanda felt the same way. A novice at female romance, Jen hoped that Amanda was interested in her.

Jen made it to the front door of her apartment, car keys in hand, then turned around. Back to the closet she went, grabbing the ass-pants and a tight, sheer white blouse that accentuated her toned body. She looked *good* in that outfit, and she hadn't fully decided what to wear. How could she at six in the morning? She rolled the pants and blouse over themselves on their hangers and placed them in the bag, too. Zipping it closed, she was ready to leave a second time.

***

Sea Cliff

Amanda completed her yoga routine in her basement workout room, her cat, Zumba, circling her and purring. She ascended her narrow, winding staircase that was hand-carved in a mission design, and padded down the hall to the kitchen, Zumba trailing after her. She fed Zumba, refilled her coffee and quickly ate some yogurt. She hadn't left much time to shower and dress.

After toweling off, she found herself staring at her expansive wardrobe in her walk-in closet, wondering what to wear. She consulted her iPhone calendar and saw a meeting had been scheduled with Mayor Woo—about the Farber case, no doubt. Otherwise, it was an ordinary day at the office. No press conferences.

Mayor Woo would probably want a photo with her in front of her office, so he could demonstrate to the voters that he cared about the Farber investigation, but that was a ho-hum moment for which a suit would suffice. Like herself, Mayor Woo was a tireless advocate for the residents of the city, so would want answers about the progress of the investigation. Amanda would tell him she couldn't disclose facts from the investigation due to strict ethical rules. He would promise to keep them confidential, but she would decline, and he would leave frustrated. At least, he would feign frustration. He knew damn well she couldn't release any info to him.

Early in her career, Amanda had seen a colleague make the mistake of inadvertently leaking some information to the Mayor's office, which ended up on the front page of *The Chronicle*. Since prosecutors were prohibited from speaking about the evidence or charges until they were made public in a charging document, her colleague was charged with an ethical violation by the State Bar and suspended from practice for a month. The rest of the ADAs learned quickly not to leak important info on a case—to anyone, much less a politician.

Amanda scrolled down to her five o'clock meeting with Jen at Boulevard. *Was it a meeting, or something else?* She pushed aside the eagerness her body felt whenever she thought of Jen. Not only was Jen straight, but she also was in a committed relationship with Tommy. Amanda's undeniable feelings simply required mind over matter. She was a professional who had long ago trained herself to control her emotions in a variety of settings. Controlling them around Jen couldn't be any different. Resolve.

Mind yourself, she told her body, looking down at her perfect shape, standing in her bra and panties in front of her closet.

She selected her black suit and threw it on, adding conservative jewelry and a scant amount of makeup. She left her bedroom and walked to the kitchen to collect her briefcase. George would be arriving shortly at the front gate with her car.

"Fuck it," she muttered to Zumba, dropping her briefcase on the counter and returning to her bedroom. She grabbed a small, black bag from the floor of her closet and hurriedly stuffed one of her many black cocktail dresses into it. She found a colorful wrap to spice it up, hastily stuffing that in as well. Her Christian Louboutin heels, which Jen had complimented at the charity ball, would complete the look. They were Amanda's favorites, too.

The exchange they had shared in the back seat of her car replayed in her mind. Whenever their eyes met, there was a connection. Amanda knew it. And the way Jen had toyed with Amanda's ring. She had felt not only a curiosity in Jen's touch, but also affection. She had experience in these matters, so it was silly to deny it. She would look forward to their meeting all day, hoping the message she had to deliver didn't piss off Jen too badly, because Amanda desperately wanted to know her better.

***

North Beach

Tommy finished his ten-mile run from his row house on Kearny and Vallejo to the Presidio and back, and trotted up the steps of his white and green Victorian. His narrow house was nestled between two other Italian families.

As he showered for work, he thought about Jen. They were having a horseshit week in their relationship. The problem was that he loved her, and missed her, and desperately needed to get laid while he investigated the case. Any case. Sex helped him solve crimes. Period.

He also was determined to have her as his wife. When this investigation was over, he'd take her up the coast for a long weekend to relax. She had loved a romantic weekend on the beach the few times they had gone.

She said she needed time to consider marriage, but they'd been together for three years already. And he had undershot it, which was good, right? The point was that he'd been with her longer than he'd been with any other girlfriend, but she didn't seem to care about that milestone.

He suspected Jen was simply afraid of marriage. He understood, because he'd been there many times, before meeting her. After all, he was divorced. He'd show her how good it could be, being married to him and part of his big Italian family.

Maybe he'd suggest that they live together, so she could make that adjustment first. He owned his house, which was more square feet than hers, so he decided they'd live together here, in his neighborhood. She had told him she liked North Beach, so he assumed she'd be happy here.

Tommy continued to make plans for Jen and himself as he changed into his detective attire—a clean shirt, tie, blazer and nice pair of jeans. Before he got in his car, he trotted down the hill to the corner of Vallejo and Grant, where his beloved Caffé Trieste was located.

The coffee shop had been there since he could remember, and, as far as he was concerned, made the best coffee in town. When he walked through the door, he was greeted by the barista and the old timers in the back, who were reading newspapers and talking politics. Politically, they were left of left, engaging in their endless debate over who was the best elected official in the city.

Tommy got in line at the counter, lusting after the chocolate croissant in the display case as he shuffled along with the others. Jen would discourage him from buying it, insisting that he was throwing away the benefits of his ten-mile run, but screw that. He didn't have to listen to a woman who had rejected his marriage proposal. He brushed the miniature Jen off his shoulder, dispensing with her advice.

In fact, instead of getting his usual to go, he ordered it to stay, and joined the retired old timers in the back to savor his croissant and cuppa. He pulled out a heavy wooden chair and joined the men at the big table littered with papers and dishes.

"Tommy, you have time for us this morning?" Cy, a large-nosed Italian septuagenarian asked.

"Yeah. I need to know what's really goin' on in the world, and I figure you guys are the most knowledgeable," Tommy said sarcastically.

"Whaddayaknow about that girl who worked at the hospital and was found dead in her apartment?" Cy asked.

Tommy had just shoved half his croissant in his mouth, so begged off on answering. He wasn't surprised, though, that the neighborhood was following the case. The local media kept the story alive, and repeatedly mentioned that Amanda wouldn't give a press conference or interview.

Without even picking up the scattered sections of the newspaper on the table, Tommy could spot the askew headlines and photos of Natasha. He scanned them as he ate and drank, the group discussing their perception of the investigation, each man with his own opinion:

Her husband did it because she left him. He has a record, you know.

Her lover did it because she threatened to tell his wife. He's a doctor, you know.

She overdosed because she couldn't take the pressure at work. She worked at the hospital, you know.

It was natural causes. Can't anyone die in peace anymore? She probably had a heart condition.

Did you see her Russian parents on the news—shocked to learn she had a lover? The parents are always last to learn, you know.

I personally liked that he clocked Kip Moynihan. He deserved it!

I heard her father is a big shot Russian who lives in Ohio. Rich people think they're above the law, you know.

That's what Tommy loved about these guys. No matter what the topic, if they weren't spot on, they were pretty damn close. And, more importantly, they loved seeing him. When he wasn't in the mood to talk, they didn't press. He was family no matter what—just to sit and eat his breakfast.

"You're not gonna tell us nothin', are you Tommy?" Cy asked.

"Pop, you know I would if I knew anything. I don't know everything that goes on down at the station. Don't you remember from when you were on the force?" Tommy asked, giving his father the signal. *Remember when you couldn't talk either?*

"I remember, I remember. Back when we used to wear suits, not jeans," Cy admonished.

"Okay. Time for me to go," Tommy said, draining his cuppa.

"Watch yourself out there."

"I always do."

"Come over here and give me a kiss before you leave."

"I'm forty-two years old, Pop."

Cy gave him the penetrating Sicilian death stare, so Tommy rounded the table, giving Cy a peck on the top of his forehead. "Love you."

"Love you, too. Say hi to Jennifer from me."

"I will. Goodbye everyone." Tommy set his dishes on the high counter by the glass display on his way out.

He walked back up the hill to his garage and drove to work, thinking he should host a big family picnic this month. Pops wasn't getting any younger, and he hadn't seen his sister, Tina, in a few weeks. It was summer, after all. Even though Jen had met his immediate family, she might not have met all the cousins and second cousins. She seemed to like his family, so maybe a family reunion would encourage her to feel like she was a part of it, too.

He arrived at the Hall of Justice, parked in the designated lot for detectives, a real perk from being a patrol officer, and passed through the layers of security to his office on the third floor. He powered up his computer and entered his password. There was a message from the outside lab regarding the toxicology results for Natasha Farber. This was a big moment in cracking the case. He clicked open the attachment and reviewed it.

Positive for Xanax. *No surprise. That was in her medical record. Dr. Wallace prescribed it to her six weeks ago.*

Positive for Digoxin. *Big news. It was in the bottle of bourbon, too. It wasn't in her medical record, so she either intentionally overdosed or someone slipped it to her.*

Positive for opioids. *Another development. It was also in the bourbon, again indicating she either overdosed or was poisoned.*

Blood alcohol level of .08, the legal limit in most states. *Not a huge surprise, considering she was drinking the bourbon.*

A fatal cocktail. *She died from the mix in the bourbon, combined with her Xanax. She either did it to herself, or didn't see it coming.*

If she wasn't trying to kill herself, then both Blake and Dr. Wallace had a motive to poison her. They both had the means, Wallace more than Blake. Arguably, only Wallace had the opportunity since Blake was barred from Natasha's apartment. But Tommy knew firsthand that no-contact orders weren't worth the paper they were written on.

However, something didn't feel right, and Tommy didn't like it when clues didn't feel right. He was still waiting for fingerprints on the bottle and security cam footage of who had visited the apartment in the last two weeks.

He expected both Natasha and Dr. Wallace's prints to be on the bottle. It was in her apartment and probably Dr. Wallace's drink of choice. There wouldn't be anything incriminating about that.

If Blake's prints were on the bottle, however, that would be a problem for him because he wasn't supposed to be in Natasha's apartment at all. Blake could argue the bourbon was old, from when he lived there, but Tommy was guessing Dr. Wallace had brought it to the party when he started his relationship with Natasha. Thus, if both Wallace's and Blake's prints were on the bottle, that would indicate Blake had entered the apartment *after* Wallace began his affair with Natasha. Thus, the presence of Blake's prints would be incriminating for Blake.

Tommy made a note to ask Dr. Wallace about the bourbon when he interviewed him. In fact, Tommy was accumulating quite a list of notes for his Wallace interview. There was no way he was going to cover everything he needed to know in one visit, so it was time to call Wallace and ask him if he'd come in voluntarily. As was Tommy's historical practice, he would track down Wallace later with follow-up questions after the first interview.

Tommy IM'd Amanda and told her about the toxicology report. She agreed it was time to interview Wallace as well, and asked Tommy to alert her as soon as Tommy scheduled a time with the doctor.

Tommy found Dr. Wallace's name and phone number in the police database from Wallace's domestic battery charges several months ago. He read the report, and reflected on how a marital dispute could have escalated into Susie calling the police.

Susie had a temper, and Tommy was sure she wouldn't take any shit from her husband. But, something had scared her. Enough so that she had called the police, which was a big step when a couple was fighting. Maybe there was some PTSD from time served. Combat trauma, combined with Susie's Italian temper, could be an explosive mix. Tommy planned to delve into it when he interviewed Wallace.

He dialed the phone number in the police report.

"Hello?" a male voice answered.

"This is Detective Tommy Vietti, San Francisco Police Department. Is this Dr. Lane Wallace?"

"What? Ah, no. This is Susie Wallace's phone. Wait a sec, I'll get her," the male said.

What? A guy is answering Susie's phone? I thought this was Wallace's phone number. He scanned the police report info again as he waited for Susie to come on the line. He discovered his error. There were two phone numbers listed for Wallace, and one of them must have been Susie's cell phone.

He listened as the male tracked down Susie. It was taking forever, and he swore he heard a shower running in the background. *Is she not at home? Is she hooking up with a guy? Does Wallace know? What about her daughter? Wouldn't she want to be at home with her daughter? Are they still together?*

"Hello?" Susie answered, sounding flustered and preoccupied.

"Hi Susie. It's Tommy Vietti."

"Oh, Tommy. Mike said it was a police detective. I didn't think it would be you."

"Well, that's how I introduced myself. I'm working on a case that involves your husband."

"Is anything wrong?"

"I'm looking for Dr. Wallace, and this was the number I was given. Evidently, it's your number. Can you give me his number?"

"What for?"

"I need to chat with him about the case I'm working on."

"The Natasha Farber case? *You're* investigating the Farber case? Is that why you were at the hospital yesterday?"

Shit. He should've known she'd be sharp and inquisitive.

"Yes. Just doing my job, Susie. I don't want to intrude into your life any more than I have to."

"I get it. No worries. If you need to talk to me, too, that's fine. Anything for people from the neighborhood, you know?"

"Thanks. Can I have Dr. Wallace's phone number?"

"Sure. Here it is."

"Thanks. You take care."

"You, too. Bye."

There was more to Susie Sangiolo Wallace than he originally thought. As he remembered her from high school, she was always working several angles at once. And, her loyalty to Italians from the North Beach neighborhood came across loud and clear. She was attempting to create a bond between them. Apparently, she still weaved quite a complicated social web. *Maybe Wallace was justified in stepping out on her...*

Tommy took a deep breath and dialed the number Susie had provided him.

"Hello?" a male voice answered.

"This is Detective Tommy Vietti, San Francisco Police Department. Is this Dr. Lane Wallace?"

"Yes, it is."

"Great. How are you feeling today?"

"Like new. And yourself?"

"Well. Thank you. I'd like to chat with you today about Natasha Farber. Would you have time this morning?"

"Yes, of course. When and where?"

"How about my office—the Hall of Justice, in thirty minutes?"

"I have to drop my daughter at school first. Give me one hour."

"That sounds perfect. Just say my name in the lobby, and they'll call me."

"Right. Detective Vietti. Will do."

They ended their call.

***

Chapter 19

Hall of Justice

Tommy was busy watching the clip of Natasha's apartment security cam footage that the computer guys had just emailed him. Dr. Wallace was on the video quite a few times, walking through the lobby and getting in the elevator. There weren't any other cameras in her building—only the one in the lobby.

Tommy's phone rang. Security relayed that Dr. Wallace was waiting for him downstairs. Tommy IM'd Amanda that he would bring Wallace to their favorite interrogation room on the third floor. He had already emailed Amanda his outline of questions for Wallace, so she would be fully prepped on where Tommy intended to go with the interview.

He went down to the first floor to collect Wallace. Exiting the elevator, Tommy observed Wallace's appearance like any detective worth his salt would. Wallace was wearing a ball cap, plain rain jacket, jeans and black walking shoes. He had a neatly trimmed beard and wore spectacles. He used a cane in his left hand and had a very distinctive gait, favoring his right leg. Tommy guessed it was a war injury from time served in the desert.

They shook hands and rode the elevator to the third floor, where Amanda was waiting in the back hallway, behind the one-way glass of the interrogation room.

Once Dr. Wallace was settled in his chair, cane resting against the table, Tommy began.

"I like your hat," Tommy said, referring to Dr. Wallace's sweat-stained, Giants ball cap.

"Oh, this." Wallace removed it and rolled it around in his hands. "Doesn't look like much, but my dad gave it to me for my sixteenth birthday. He passed on, so it's pretty sentimental. I wear it to games when I go."

"I regularly go myself," Tommy said, bonding over his beloved Giants.

Dr. Wallace replaced his cap and stared at Tommy. He had a neutral look on his face, exuding a relaxed demeanor. Despite appearances, however, when a person-of-interest was sitting in this chair, in this room, he was nervous as hell. Tommy leveraged their fear as he questioned them. Some recognized the room for what it was, others not so much.

Tommy assumed that Wallace was astute enough to know that this was a formal interrogation and what was at stake. He was a smarter beast than the average criminal—highly educated, worked in a noble profession and experienced in combat. Tommy wouldn't be able to interrogate him hard like he could some witnesses. He planned to take a friendly approach during this interview—at least at the beginning.

"I see you use a cane. How did you come by that?" Tommy asked.

"The cane or my limp?" Dr. Wallace asked.

"Fair question. Both."

"I was shot in the right thigh while serving in the desert. I've used a cane since I completed physical therapy and was discharged. I bought this hand-carved one from a woodworker in Mendocino. I liked the inlaid, rosewood shaft and the offset design. It allows the handle to be over the shaft, rather than behind it, changing the way you use the cane. Personal preference." Dr. Wallace shrugged his shoulders.

"Very clever design. I'd never thought about it before, but now that you mention it, the s-shape does place the handle above the shaft."

Dr. Wallace waited patiently for Tommy to ask the next question. He didn't appear to be a chatty man by nature, and he sure as hell didn't look like he was going to run at the mouth during this interview. Another sign of intelligence.

"Please state your full name, address and date of birth for me, Doctor."

Dr. Wallace recited them.

"Who lives at that address with you?"

"My wife, Susie, and my eight-year-old daughter, Angelina."

"Do you have any other homes or condos?"

"No. Just the one."

"Did your wife sleep at home last night?"

Wallace's face twitched in surprise. "Of course. Why do you ask?"

"I accidentally called her cell phone number this morning because it was listed first in our police database. It was early, like before eight. A male answered, and I'm pretty sure I heard a shower in the background. The male told me to wait a second while he went and got her." Tommy watched Wallace very carefully.

Wallace smiled for the first time, softening his serious features. "Yeah, that makes sense."

"Where was she?"

"Almost every morning, she meets one of her brothers at the nursing home where her mother is a resident. They help her mother with morning cares and stay to make sure she eats breakfast. I suspect you spoke to one of Susie's brothers, and Susie was helping her mother in or out of the shower."

"Oh." Tommy's Susie-having-an-affair theory went up in smoke. "What's her mother's name?" Tommy already knew this, of course, but it was good to ask questions to which he already knew the answer, to gauge what kind of witness Wallace would be. Truthful, hedging the truth, or a flat-out liar.

"Maria Sangiolo."

"What nursing home is she in?"

"Legacy by the Marina. It's across from Fort Mason, with a pretty view of the Bay and a baseball field across the street. The benefit is that it's only a few minutes from our house in North Beach."

Tommy wondered whether he should tell Dr. Wallace that he remembered Maria Sangiolo from his high school days, but that would entail disclosing that he knew Susie as well, and might change the entire tone of the interview. Best to withhold that unless it would be useful.

"Okay. That's a relief. You can imagine what my initial thought was this morning," Tommy said.

"I can. Although, I wouldn't blame her. I cheated on her with Natasha Farber, so she'll probably want to settle the score at some point."

"Tell me about Natasha Farber and how you came to know her."

Wallace scratched his forehead under his cap. "We met in the ER. She was an ultrasound tech. We talked easily, and then one night, I noticed she was upset. I asked her about it, and she told me about her abusive husband, Blake."

Dr. Wallace stopped there, as if that were the entire story.

"Then what happened?"

Wallace sighed again, as if being forced to lift a barbell loaded with weights. "I helped her with some resources to get away from Blake. We became closer, and we began an intimate relationship."

"When did you first go over to her apartment?"

Wallace stared at Tommy, his mind at work. "I don't know. Not very long ago. A month, maybe."

"Did you sleep with her?"

"Yes."

"Did you spend the night?"

"Probably the day, if we were coming off a night shift."

"Right. She worked nights. What kind of sex did you have?"

"What the hell kind of question is that?"

"She had bruises on her arms, Doctor. I need to know if you put them there."

"Oh, that. I did, and I can explain why."

"Please do," Tommy said, pushing back in his chair.

"She liked it when I held her arms above her head in bed. She wanted me to tie her up, but I told her I wasn't into that. So, she convinced me to pin her arms up forcefully, so I did, but I ended up falling into her because I couldn't hold my weight with my bad leg. It was too much pressure for too long, so my fingers left bruises."

"So, you're admitting to hurting her during sex?"

"I wouldn't call it 'hurting her.' She liked it, so I did it. I wouldn't hurt her."

"How long ago?"

"Recently. Within the past couple of weeks."

"Why would she tell her supervisor that her estranged husband left the bruises?"

"I don't know. Probably to protect me and my reputation at the hospital."

"Did Natasha tell you that she told Cheryl Gutierrez that Blake left the bruises?" Tommy asked.

"No, but I'm not surprised that's what she said."

"Did you ever talk to Ms. Gutierrez about your relationship with Natasha?"

"God, no. I didn't mention it to anyone at the hospital."

"Yet, people seemed to know about it?" Tommy confirmed.

"Amazing how that works, isn't it?"

"Okay. Let's return to Natasha's apartment. Did you have cocktails while there?"

"Yes. We would have a drink now and then."

"What was Natasha's drink of choice?"

Wallace paused. "Usually wine. Both red and white."

"What did you drink?"

"Bourbon."

"Did Natasha stock the bourbon, or did you buy it?"

"She didn't, so I bought a bottle at the liquor store across from her apartment building."

"Do you still have the receipt?"

"Of course not. I'm not even sure I *got* a receipt," Wallace said.

"Did you pay with cash or credit card?"

"Probably credit card."

"Can you get a printout of your statement and provide it to me, please?"

"I'd be happy to. Do you have a pencil and paper so I can make a note to myself?"

Tommy tore a piece of paper from his notepad and pushed it across the table with a pencil. He watched as Wallace scribbled a sentence.

"Do you always drink bourbon?"

"Yes. Unless I'm at a ball game. Then I'll have a beer.

"Did Natasha try your bourbon? Maybe join you in a drink now and then?"

"She might have had a sip, but she said she didn't care for it."

"Let me move to a different topic, Dr. Wallace. Did you see Natasha as a patient *before* or *after* you had sex with her?"

Wallace didn't flinch, apparently expecting this question. "After. She insisted. I told her to see someone else, but she wanted me to see her."

"If that's the case, then you were sleeping together shortly after Blake moved out, which was two months ago. You saw her as a patient six weeks ago. Here, look at your note." Tommy slid a copy of Dr. Wallace's note over to him.

"Okay, we slept together earlier than I remembered," Dr. Wallace said, a look of indignation on his face.

"When she was still with Blake?"

"Maybe. He was crazy, though. I wouldn't go over there if they were still together."

"Did you sleep together somewhere else?"

"Maybe."

"Where?"

"The hospital."

"Your office?"

"No."

"Where?"

"There was a small Radiology room close to the ER."

"You had sex in there?"

"Yes."

"Did anyone ever catch you?"

"No."

"Is the note in front of you the only note of your exam of Natasha?" Tommy asked.

"This is the only note of her visit, yes," Wallace said.

"You prescribed Xanax?"

"Yes."

"For what?"

"It's an anti-anxiety medication."

"Why did you prescribe it for her?"

"She was anxious."

"From what?"

"From dealing with the stress of an abusive husband and all that was entailed in pressing charges against him." Wallace sounded exasperated.

"How would this help?"

"It calmed her down."

"Was she on any other medication?"

"Yes. Birth control pills."

"Is Xanax okay to take while you're on the pill?"

"Yes."

"Is it okay if it's mixed with alcohol?"

"It's not recommended, but a small amount of alcohol, consumed with food, shouldn't hurt."

"Is it okay if it's mixed with opioids?"

Wallace stared at Tommy. He didn't answer, but he didn't look surprised by the question either.

Tommy crossed his arms over his chest and stared.

"Why are you asking me? She wasn't on opioids," Wallace finally said.

"Fair enough. Is it okay to mix Xanax and opioids?"

"No."

"So, you wouldn't have prescribed it to her if you had known she was taking opioids?"

"Correct. I wouldn't have prescribed it to her."

"How about Digoxin? Is it okay to mix Digoxin and Xanax?"

"Theoretically? Because Natasha wasn't on Digoxin, either. It probably wouldn't be a good idea. But, if you mixed alcohol, opioids, Digoxin and Xanax, it could be fatal."

"Is that what you think killed Natasha?"

"I don't know what she died from. I'm a scientist, Detective Vietti. I would read the autopsy and toxicology results before I drew a conclusion."

"What do you *think* killed her?"

"What or who?"

"Let's start with *what*?"

"I think a fatal cocktail of alcohol, Digoxin, opioids and Xanax killed her."

"Why?"

"Because I almost died from the same thing, so I'm not surprised that you asked."

Tommy let his chair fall forward, scooting back up to the table. "Is that why you were in the hospital yesterday?"

"How did you know?" Wallace asked.

Tommy was afraid that Wallace might think Jen told him, since he probably knew she was

Tommy's girl, so he decided to drop the Susie bomb. "Susie told me."

"When? Where?" Wallace asked, flustered. A lot of information had just been dropped in his lap.

"At the ER. I stopped by to pick up some records. Susie came over because she recognized me from high school. She told me you were there and had suffered a heart attack."

"Oh. She was half right. My heart went into an abnormal rhythm, and my respirations slowed. It was from the same thing that probably killed Natasha. But, unlike Natasha, I wasn't taking Xanax, and I weigh more, so I tolerated it better."

Wallace's voice caught, and he buried his face in his hands, fighting against crying.

Tommy reviewed his notes while he waited for Wallace to regain composure. Tommy had seen many men break down in that chair over his twenty-year career. Hell, he had caused most of the breakdowns himself.

"Why do you expect me to believe your story that you received the same combo of fatal cocktail as Natasha, and that you weren't already taking Digoxin for a heart condition?" Tommy asked.

"Because I have proof," Wallace said, producing a folded sheet of paper from his breast pocket. "These are my lab results from yesterday. They're exactly as you described a minute ago. I'm guessing you know Natasha's toxicology results, and that's why you asked me those questions. I'd like to see Natasha's toxicology results, if you don't mind."

"I don't have them with me, but I can assure you that they look very similar to your lab results, with Xanax added, of course."

"Of course."

"Still, this nags at me, how do I know you weren't on Digoxin to begin with?"

"Look at the medication list on my physician note. It says 'daily aspirin,' and that's it. No Digoxin."

"Let me ask you a different way. Why did you kill her, Dr. Wallace?"

"What? You son-of-a-bitch. I didn't kill her. Her husband, Blake, killed her!" Wallace yelled.

"Wasn't she threatening to tell your wife about your affair?"

"Yes, but that didn't matter. I told Natasha I was going to tell Susie myself. It wasn't fair to keep lying to her. I couldn't go on like that."

"Did you tell Susie?"

"Wait a minute. How did you know Natasha was threatening to tell Susie?"

"We have her cell phone. We've read all the texts between you and Natasha."

"Who gave you that?" Wallace asked, knocked off-balance.

"We confiscated her phone as evidence from the scene of her death. Her estranged husband unlocked it for us."

Wallace considered that piece of information for a minute. He removed his phone from his pocket and slid it across the table. "Every text between Natasha and me is on there. I've read them a thousand times. Toward the end, I told her I was planning to tell Susie myself."

"Did you?"

"Yes, but not until this week—after Natasha was found dead," Wallace broke down, burying his face in his hands again.

Tommy absorbed that statement. *Susie didn't know about the affair until Wallace told her?* For some reason, he found that hard to believe. *A woman always knows.* "What was Susie's reaction?"

"What do you think it was? She was furious. Then scared. Wondering if I was a suspect, which I suppose I am now. She threatened to divorce me. Our marriage is fucked," Wallace said, unable to stop himself from sobbing into his hands.

"I'll give you a minute. Want some water?"

"Yes, please."

Tommy left the room and met Amanda half way around the corner.

"Hey," Tommy said.

"I think you should ask him about his own domestic battery charges," she said.

"I plan to. Anything else?"

She shook her head no.

He grabbed a bottle of water and re-entered the conference room.

"A couple more questions, Dr. Wallace, then we're done." Tommy handed the water to Wallace.

"Thanks. You know you're barking up the wrong tree, right? It was her bastard husband who killed her."

"How can you be so sure?"

"He abused her. He was insanely jealous of her affair with me. He's a clever psychopath, Detective. He lives with a guy who sells drugs, and easily could have purchased the Digoxin and opioids from him. It all came together when he mixed them together and dumped them in a bottle. I'm guessing it was in the bottle of bourbon, since you asked me about it."

Tommy was impressed with Wallace's deduction. "Guys who sell drugs don't sell Digoxin."

"You're assuming I killed my lover because I have access to Digoxin?" Wallace asked, aghast.

"You had the motive to shut her up, so your wife wouldn't discover your affair. You had the means and knowledge at your disposal. The apartment video will show you had the opportunity. You were, in fact, in her apartment plenty."

"Then, why the hell would I drink my own poison and almost die myself?"

"Good cover?"

"Nice try. I'd be better off playing Russian Roulette with a loaded gun."

"She wasn't a bourbon drinker."

"Just because she told me she didn't like it doesn't mean she couldn't have sampled it when I wasn't there. Are you qualified to investigate this case?"

Tommy laughed. "If it was your go-to drink, then wouldn't it make more sense that Blake Farber was trying to kill *you,* Dr. Wallace; not his beloved Natasha?"

Wallace's eyes widened. He stared at Tommy, looking through him, his mind processing and catching up to Tommy's theory. "How would Blake know I drank bourbon?"

"Blake was married to her. If he decided to enter the apartment when she wasn't there, he'd notice the new bottle of bourbon and assume it was yours. If he dumped a mix of drugs into it, he probably intended to kill you."

"I think you're onto something there. Instead, he ended up killing the woman he loved."

"You were charged with domestic battery yourself. Tell me about that."

Wallace blinked several times, switching gears. "It was a one-time fight. I was drunk. She's Italian. We took it too far, and I'm the first to admit it."

"Why were you fighting?"

"Respect. She doesn't respect my opinion on anything anymore. She does her own thing at her gallery and raises Angelina how she sees fit. She shut me out. Doesn't need me anymore."

"Is that what drove you to Natasha?"

"Maybe."

"Did you prescribe Xanax for your own wife after you were charged with domestic battery?"

"What? Of course not. I'm not her physician. And, to my knowledge, she's not taking any Xanax."

"Well, why did you agree to be Natasha's physician if you wouldn't see your own wife?"

"Because Natasha asked me to see her. There's no chance in hell Susie would ask me to see her in a professional capacity."

"Uh-huh. One more question. Did you send a text to Blake Farber, telling him to stay away from Natasha, 'or else?'"

"It sounds like something I would've done early in my relationship with Natasha, but I can't remember the exact words I used."

"All right. I don't have any more questions today, Dr. Wallace. I need to instruct you to stay in the city and not travel anywhere until this investigation is closed. Understand?"

"I wasn't planning to. I'm on paid administrative leave, so I guess it's a good opportunity to putz around on my sailboat. She needs some work."

"Where's your boat?"

"St. Francis Yacht Club."

"What's her name?"

"Sangiolo Sun."

"How long is she?"

"Thirty-one-foot Beneteau."

"Nice boat. I'd appreciate it if you stayed in the Bay if you go sailing."

"No worries. When can I get my phone back?"

"Call me later today. I'm sure we'll have the information copied by then."

Tommy escorted Dr. Wallace back down to the lobby, the march for truth and justice well underway. They shook hands and Tommy watched Wallace walk out the doors and down the steps, expertly using his cane.

***

Chapter 20

Hall of Justice

Tommy went directly to the Computer Forensics Department and gave them Dr. Wallace's cell phone, including the passcode Wallace told him on his way out. Tommy requested the guys to copy all the information on the phone, but especially wanted them to isolate all text messages between Dr. Wallace and Natasha, as well as between Dr. Wallace and his wife, Susie. He had already requested all texts between Blake and Natasha from both of their phones.

Engaging in twenty-first-century wiretapping, he also asked them to sync Wallace's phone to the police computers, so after Wallace picked it up, they'd be able to read his text messages, record his conversations and locate precisely where he was on GPS. It was an invasion of the good doctor's privacy, but it would be legal when Tommy demonstrated probable cause for a search warrant. Technically, he didn't have the warrant yet, but time was of the essence, so he would ask Amanda to prepare one today.

Tommy suspected Susie was an emotional wreck. She had just learned that Wallace was having an affair, and that information alone was usually crushing to a wife, much less realizing that Dr. Wallace was a suspect in Natasha's murder. If Susie was anything like she had been in high school, she would soon be spewing forth fury and vitriol at Wallace, perhaps by phone or text. Tommy hoped Wallace would say something helpful in reaction to Susie's anticipated outbursts, pointing the investigation in one direction or the other.

First things first, though, Tommy had to catch up with Amanda. He exited Computer Forensics and ran up a flight of stairs to the third floor, where he walked down the long, public hallway to the DA's office. He passed through the small waiting area and scanned himself into Amanda's office corridor. Knocking lightly on her open door, he received her nod to enter.

"Some interview," she said.

"Wallace seemed genuinely sad about Natasha's death. He's either a good con man, or we're looking for someone else," Tommy said.

"He seemed surprised by my theory that Blake was probably trying to kill *him*, but accidentally killed Natasha."

"Or, he's just confused—grieving the loss of his young lover."

"Well, my money says Blake was trying to kill Wallace and accidentally killed Natasha."

"And, see, I'm not convinced yet."

"Would you care to wager?"

"Sure. I'll take your money any time. How much?"

"Twenty bucks?"

"Sure. Just to be clear, you think Blake was trying to kill Wallace, and I don't."

"Do you think Blake was trying to kill Natasha instead?"

"Maybe. Maybe not."

"Okay. Are you betting against Blake altogether? Or against his targeting Wallace?"

"My gut tells me Blake didn't do this, but that doesn't mean he can't be useful."

"Even though it sounds like you have something up your sleeve, I'll lay my money on Blake. Specifically, that he was targeting Wallace. Nice job getting Wallace's phone, by the way. I think we should put a wiretap on it."

"Great minds think alike. I just dropped it off in Computer Forensics. I asked the guys to tap it. In fact, I need a search warrant for taps on both Blake and Wallace's cell phones, so we need to schedule a hearing with Judge Grady right away."

"Will do. Maybe we'll get lucky with a confession from one of them."

"Even if we don't get a confession, I think we might get a text or phone call that reveals a major clue, especially after they've been interviewed. There's always a sense of relief after the first interview."

"A useful text could certainly declare one man over the other."

"Or shake loose another apple from the tree."

She looked at him quizzically. "I'll prepare an affidavit and warrant."

"Thanks. I'm gonna chase down Blake's roommate, Trevor, then watch more apartment lobby security cam footage. I want to pursue a couple of other ideas, too—in the field. I'll circle back with you this afternoon."

"I have a meeting with Mayor Woo in an hour. Anything I can tell him?"

"Not yet."

"That's what I thought, too. He's just angling for a donation to his campaign from Ivanov."

"Politics," Tommy said, leaving Amanda's office and returning to his own. He looked up Blake's roommate, Trevor Ross, in the SFPD database. If Trevor was a drug dealer, then Blake easily could have purchased the fatal cocktail mix from him. Or, Trevor might know who.

Trevor had a list of prior arrests, including drug dealing, disorderlies and theft. He was a chronic bad boy, living on the edge. Tommy guessed Trevor was probably still dealing, so he decided it was time to pay him a visit. He wrote down Trevor's cell phone number and printed a photo of Trevor to bring along for good measure. He copied the address where Trevor had last been apprehended for drug dealing and decided he'd start there.

Tommy needed to get out of the office and drive, and now was as good a time as any to do it. There were some nagging themes from Wallace's interview that Tommy needed to process mentally, and driving was the next best thing to running.

Something didn't fit with Wallace's story, but Tommy couldn't put his finger on it. There was a fragment of information orbiting around his head, confounding, but critical, and within his reach if he could just get a fresh perspective. In the past, a couple of good nights' sleep and getting laid would have teased out the critical fragment, helping it fall into place. But this investigation was moving along at such a quick pace, he had to let his subconscious work on clues while he was awake, performing mundane tasks like driving.

He drove to Seward Street between The Castro and Delores Heights Districts. Tommy drove slowly down the street, keeping a lookout for a guy who resembled Trevor's photo.

He had driven for about thirty minutes, circling a park and cruising a busy commercial street, when his efforts paid off. He passed a basketball court enclosed by a chain link fence, and thought he spotted Trevor hanging out on a concrete wall, feet dangling, talking on his cell phone as he watched a pick-up game.

Tommy parked and walked over to the court, ambling alongside the waist-high concrete wall. The players made him, each glancing in his direction. The way he was dressed and carried himself screamed 'I'm a cop!' Trevor was sitting on the concrete wall, staring into space while concentrating on a phone call, his cell to his ear. He didn't see Tommy.

Tommy hoisted himself up on the wall, sitting next to Trevor, eavesdropping. Once Trevor sized up Tommy, he ended his phone call without saying goodbye.

"Hello, officer. How can I help you today?" Trevor asked, staring straight ahead.

"I'm a detective, actually. Detective Vietti. Are you Trevor Ross?"

"Fuck me. I knew letting Blake stay with me would bite me in the ass."

"Indeed. I'm investigating the Natasha Farber homicide. I have a few questions for you."

"I don't know nothin'."

Tommy smiled. "I'm sure you don't. But selling drugs to Blake will make you an accessory to murder."

"I didn't sell drugs to Blake. Be damn sure about that."

"You're a drug dealer. You sell drugs to everyone. Come on, what did you sell him? I need you to talk to me about this, Trevor. You tell me what you sold him, and I'll owe you a favor, which you might need some day. Like in the very near future."

"I told you. Nothin'. He was staying clean because of his plea agreement. I even offered him some weed after she died, just to deal with the pain, ya know? He didn't take it."

"If I discover you're lying to me, I'll make sure you get busted soon—on felony charges this time."

"I swear to God," Trevor said, holding up his hands.

"Okay. Answer me this. If I wanted to buy some Digoxin, could you get it?"

"Never heard of it. Don't ask me about medical shit that I don't recognize."

"Never heard of it?"

"That's what I said. My specialty is weed, brown sugar and blow."

"It's a heart medication. Does it have a street name?"

"Like I said, man. I don't get involved in medical shit."

"If you hear of anyone who sold Digoxin to Blake, or who can get Digoxin, I want you to call me. Here's my card. Again, I'd owe you if you come up with some info."

"Okay. I'll take your card, but you need to shove off. You're bad for business."

"Thanks for the chat. See you around." Tommy slid off the wall and walked back to his car.

"Mother fuckin' detective crawlin' up my ass," Trevor whispered as Tommy walked away.

Shit. Dead end, Tommy thought. *Back to the office.*

***

A few hours later, Amanda asked George to bring her car around. She and Tommy met in the third-floor hall, and they rode the elevator down to the lobby, where they rushed by the security apparatus and ran down the steps to her waiting car. George drove them to Superior Court, where Judge Grady said he could work in a short meeting during a break in a trial over which he was presiding. They waited in the small reception area until the judge was ready to see them.

The receptionist ushered them into his chambers. Amanda gave Judge Grady the paperwork, then she and Tommy sat across from him, facing his oversized desk.

"So, you want me to grant a motion for a wiretap on two cell phones to further the Natasha Farber homicide investigation?" Judge Grady inquired.

"Yes, your honor," Amanda answered. "Detective Vietti has formally interviewed both Blake Farber and Dr. Lane Wallace, and they each willingly turned over their cell phones. They're equally suspect in this case, as you can see by the evidence set forth in Detective Vietti's affidavit."

"Didn't I just sign a search warrant for Dr. Wallace's work computer? Didn't you find anything on there?" Judge Grady asked.

"The Computer Forensics guys are still analyzing it, your Honor. They're working with the hospital computer experts, so it's slow-going. We're looking for communications not only between the victim and the doctor, but also between the doctor and his wife. We'd like to focus our efforts on future communications on both cell phones," Amanda said.

"I thought you said you already had his phone. You should be able to copy all the messages between Dr. Wallace and the victim without a search warrant," Judge Grady said, turning to Tommy, "Your investigation is only two or three days old."

"We did do that—copy the existing texts, I mean. That's why both Dr. Wallace and Blake Farber remain at the top of our list."

"So the wiretap isn't going to provide anything new?"

"We've reached a point in the investigation where we know the victim was poisoned by a fatal drug mixture in a bottle of bourbon. Both her estranged husband, Blake Farber, and her lover, Dr. Wallace, had motive, means and opportunity to poison her. We're still accumulating fingerprint, video and other evidence, but the timing is critical to tap their cell phones, because I promised to return them to each man today."

"Do you think one of them is going to call someone and confess to killing her?" Judge Grady asked.

"Maybe, your Honor. But in this day and age of texting, we think the killer will *text* something incriminating, especially now that both men have been interviewed. They're both avid texters, as we've learned from reviewing their phones so far. I think one of them will text enough information for us to arrest him. It might be a confession. It might be talking about his interview with me. I've learned over the years that there are an infinite number of ways a suspect can incriminate himself," Tommy explained.

"You're dancing on thin ice, Vietti. How will you limit the scope of what you see and hear to only relevant evidence needed for this homicide investigation?"

"If it doesn't relate to the homicide, the officers in the Computer Forensics lab have been, excuse me, will be instructed not to record the conversation or save the text, thus protecting both suspects' privacy," Tommy said.

"How long do you want to run the tap?"

"Thirty days," Amanda said.

The judge's eyebrows shot up. "I'll grant your tap for two weeks, Ms. Hawthorne."

"Thank you, your Honor. This is a critical information gathering technique to solve this case," Amanda said.

"Very well, then. The motion to wiretap both Blake Farber and Dr. Lane Wallace's cell phones for two weeks in the homicide investigation of Natasha Farber is hereby granted," Judge Grady ordered.

"Thank you," Amanda said, and she and Tommy exited.

Once Tommy and Amanda were safely ensconced in her car on their way back to the Hall of Justice, they spoke freely.

"I think we pushed the limits of Judge Grady's willingness to let us snoop," Tommy said.

"No doubt. If he didn't know us, and how trustworthy we are, I'm not so sure he would have granted our request. I'm just hoping either Blake or Wallace comes through with a text in the next few days, so we can button up this investigation."

"One of them will. Murderers can never keep it contained, unless they're professionals, which neither of these guys is. The enormity of what one of them knows will come out."

"I hope you're right. The mayor really rode my ass earlier today," she said, changing the subject.

"What did you tell him?"

"The usual. 'We have our best detective working on it... I can't talk about the details... We're aware of how important this is to the family and the community... Blah, blah, blah.'"

"Did he accept that?"

"He'll have to, won't he?"

"Are you still meeting Jen after work today to talk about her clinical role, and staying out of Dr. Wallace's life?"

"Yes. We're scheduled to meet at five-thirty. Don't worry. I have the situation well in hand."

"You haven't dealt with Jen."

"What's that supposed to mean?"

"Just that she's a woman with strong convictions, and she can be a little—ah—emotional sometimes. So, I'm glad it's you and not me."

Amanda raised her eyebrow. "Emotional, huh?"

He looked out the window, avoiding her eyes.

***

Chapter 21

San Francisco Community Hospital

Jen was mid-shift during a busy day in the ER. She was hustling from room-to-room, treating everything from broken arms to inflamed gallbladders. By late afternoon, she had the chance to wolf down some yogurt and a banana in the back doc room, as she mindlessly scrolled through her emails. Her business meeting with Amanda was in two hours—too far away to get excited, but soon enough to think about what she was going to wear.

I'm not gonna wear my red dress. That would be totally immature, coming across as anxious. She knows I'm working in the ER all day, so I'd look like this was my big night out. Talk about looking desperate, especially at a business meeting. Nothing about this—this situation with Amanda—is a date. I have to play it cool, come across as the professional I am, not some sex-starved newbie.

No dress. I'll wear the black slacks. My ass looks hot in those pants, and the blouse accentuates my body. I'm sure Amanda will still be in her work clothes. She's probably working with Tommy right now on the murder investigation.

They could be interviewing Lane. He said he thought they'd want to talk to him today, and he welcomed it. He has to share his own lab results with them, though. They're so exonerating. He obviously wouldn't poison himself, so someone else had to have done it. Why the hesitation to share them in the first place? What the hell is wrong with him? Maybe he wasn't thinking clearly after the heart episode.

There was a knock at the door, and a nurse popped her head around the edge. "Dr. Dawson, the family in room ten is asking to see you."

"Be right there," Jen replied, hopping up.

***

Hall of Justice

The timing of the wiretap order was perfect because when Tommy sat down at his desk, there was a message in his voicemail box from Blake, "Hey man, you dissed me by talking to Trevor. He thinks I killed Natasha now. I told you that *Wallace* killed Natasha. Not me. I can't believe you did that—behind my back and everything. I'm coming over to get my cell. You better have it ready."

Tommy was amused. He liked it better when suspects were defensive and surly, rather than boring and cooperative. Anger meant they were more likely to make a mistake. Slip up. Leave a clue for Tommy to find. Surly suspects made the investigation more fun, energizing him for the hunt.

He IM'd the computer guys, confirming they had synched up their computers to both cell phones, telling them Blake was on his way.

Tommy turned to his emails and saw that the computer guys had sent him another clip of Natasha's apartment security cam footage. He clicked it open and watched.

This clip was labeled "Dr. Wallace," so he expected it to be a montage of the dates and times that Wallace had entered her apartment building. As he watched, Tommy saw Wallace come into view, walking through the lobby and entering the elevator. Baseball cap. Rain jacket. Cane in hand. The elevator door closed.

Tommy was on the fourth clip of Wallace doing the same routine through the lobby and into the elevator, when something caught his eye. Tommy saw the baseball cap, the rain jacket and black tennis shoes, then the elevator door closed. However, this time, Wallace had switched the cane to his opposite hand. He was using the cane in his *right* hand rather than his left.

What the hell? Wallace told me he took a bullet to his right thigh, thus used the cane in his left hand. Opposite side. He explained it to me.

Tommy replayed the clip, pausing and stopping. The cane was definitely in his right hand this time. And it was stick-straight, not s-shaped like Wallace had described was his preference.

So, who the hell is this? Someone masquerading as Dr. Wallace. I have to call Amanda and get her down here.

"Amanda," she answered.

"It's Tommy. I just figured out something that's interesting."

"What's that?" Her stomach lurched, as he had busted her daydreaming about her upcoming meeting with Jen. Was it a bad omen? Or, a reality check? What was it about Jen that excited Amanda in the first place?

"I need you to come down to my office and look at these video clips of Dr. Wallace entering Natasha's apartment building."

"On my way." Amanda glanced at the clock. She had an hour before she met Jen for drinks, and the electricity was already pumping through her veins. She recalled the soft, yet strong feel of Jen's fingers, rolling her ring in the back seat of her car last night. Amanda had to shake off her anticipation as she entered Tommy's office, the guilt in his presence threatening to eclipse her composure.

"Hey," Tommy said, as she knocked on his door jam and entered.

"Got something exciting?"

"Yeah. Listen to this. The prints on the booze bottles came back from Natasha's apartment. Both the red and white bottles of wine had Natasha's prints and the good doctor's prints. No surprises there," he said.

She nodded. "That means we lifted a clean set of prints from the Narcan vial in Dr. Wallace's coat pocket?

"Yes. Now listen to this. The bottle of bourbon had three sets of prints on it. Guess who?"

"Natasha, Wallace and Blake, which tells us that Blake violated his plea agreement and indeed made a visit to Natasha's apartment."

"Precisely. Wallace introduced to the apartment after Blake moved out."

"That doesn't look good for Blake."

"It gets worse. Despite telling me he hadn't been in the apartment for two months, he returned multiple times."

"I thought you and the computer guys already concluded there wasn't any surveillance video of Blake in the lobby."

"There wasn't when the computer guys used Blake's photo to look for Blake. They came up dry, which corroborates his story."

"Okay...."

"Last night, I asked the guys to look for Dr. Wallace, based on that photo of him I grabbed off the hospital website, remember?"

She nodded.

"As expected, there were several clips of Dr. Wallace walking through the lobby and entering the elevator. On the fourth one, however, something caught my eye. Wallace's cane. He was using it in the opposite hand, which didn't make sense to me."

"Can I see it?" She circled his desk to view his flat screen, and was knocked off balance by a framed photo of Jen. Jen was on the beach in a bikini, posing for Tommy. She was tanned and gorgeous, her hair wet from a swim. *No wonder he wants to marry her.*

"Watch this." Tommy clicked play on the video.

Amanda tore her eyes away from Jen's half-naked body and watched as Dr. Wallace came into view by the lobby desk, his back to the camera. He was wearing a baseball cap and a rain jacket, his tell-tale cane in hand.

Tommy paused the video. "Look at the cane."

"What of it?"

"Is it straight or curved at the handle?"

"It's straight."

"Dr. Wallace uses an offset cane, which means it has an s-shaped curve in it, right below the handle. Remember? He explained all that at the beginning of his interview."

"Does he always use the same one?"

"We don't know, but we could ask him. We do know that he always uses it in his left hand, and that's the giveaway that this isn't Wallace in the video."

"Yeah, I remember. Right leg injured, so use the cane in the left hand."

"Bingo."

They watched as *Dr. Wallace* walked into the open elevator and turned to face the open door, in full view of the camera. Tommy paused it and enlarged the image.

"Check out the sunglasses. I don't think they're prescription, and Dr. Wallace wears prescription glasses."

"Uh-huh," she said, squinting. The video was grainy when enlarged, as it was located several feet away.

"Look at his ball cap," Tommy said.

"It's a Giants cap, which is what he was wearing when you interviewed him."

"Right. But he was wearing a *vintage* cap that his father gave him twenty-plus years ago. The cap on the guy in the video is NOT vintage. It's a modern Giants cap. You can tell by the Giants logo and bill shape."

"I see. Flat bill. So, someone is masquerading as Dr. Wallace to gain access to Natasha's apartment. Is it Blake?"

"The video is crappy, but it looks like Blake to me. Right height. Right body build."

"It's obviously a male, and who else would have a motive?"

"No one that we know of."

"It's gotta be Blake. How many times did he enter masquerading as Dr. Wallace?"

"There are at least two more times that I've seen today, the last of which was a few days before she died, which puts Blake at the scene at an opportune time to poison the bourbon," Tommy said.

"Combined with his fingerprints on the bottle, it looks like I'm gonna win this bet."

"There's more. He was even wearing his own tennis shoes—Air Jordan's. I crosschecked and confirmed that I have him on video in the interrogation room wearing those very same shoes."

"What shoes did Wallace wear?"

"Keen walking shoes, which have a very distinctive toe box."

"Brilliant," Amanda congratulated. "We need a search warrant for Blake's apartment to search for the cane, ball cap and shoes."

"He's probably ditched the cane by now, but I agree with you. I'll bet you anything he's wearing the Giants cap around town."

"Sloppy is right. Has he called you about getting his cell phone back?"

"Yes. He was pissed that I spoke to his roommate. He'll be by any minute."

"Then you'll have an opportunity to see what he's wearing on his head. I'm going to draft your affidavit and warrant for the search of his apartment. Do you mind if an ADA accompanies you to Judge Grady's chambers? I have to meet Dr. Dawson for drinks to discuss her role as a witness."

"No worries. Meeting with Jen is more important. Assign that Jeremy guy. I like working with him."

"I can't. He's in a trial right now. I'm sure someone else can do it."

"Okay. Any ADA will be fine. I'll be ready to go as soon as the paperwork is done."

"I'll let him know."

"Good luck with Jen. She can be a pistol."

"I've dealt with pistols before."

"Not one as beautiful as Jen."

"I'll give you that. Great detective work, Tommy," she tossed over her shoulder as she left. She was so proud to work with Tommy. He was an outstanding detective. Having a small crush on his girlfriend made Amanda feel horrible. She had designs on his would-be fiancée. How had she allowed herself to even entertain the idea? It wasn't fair to Tommy, or to Jen for that matter. She would erase her feelings and keep the meeting all business tonight. She needed to use her brain, not her desire.

***

San Francisco Community Hospital

A few miles away, Jen stared at her reflection in the bathroom mirror of the physicians' locker room. Bracing her hands on the counter, she assessed herself. She was at a critical juncture in her life—admit to the world that she was attracted to another woman, or forget it and accept Tommy's marriage proposal. She couldn't handle both possibilities co-existing in her body.

Her eyes were bright and clear, and she was firmly grounded in reality. She wasn't fooling herself or anyone else. It was time to make a decision. Her mind was sharp and buzzing with energy, and she was thinking rationally, not emotionally. Tommy or a new romance? Which would it be?

She loved him. She was sure part of her always would. He had been unbelievably good to her. They had shared their lives for three years—all the intimacy and laughter that two people in love sought. Yet, it hadn't fulfilled her. *He* wasn't fulfilling her. Something was missing —her innermost desires.

I need to be who I really am. I won't live a lie. I'm a successful professional who deserves to be happy. I'm simply going to see where things go with Amanda and tell Tommy at the earliest opportunity. In the meantime, I'll just have to keep my body under control, not acting on any emotions I might feel. No impulse behavior...

She pushed away from the counter, stuffed her bag back in the locker, and left for her meeting with Amanda.

***

Chapter 22

Boulevard Restaurant

Jen entered Amanda's restaurant choice on Mission Street. She was greeted by a refined hostess who led her to a high table in the bar by the window. Even the bar tables were covered with white linen in this upscale culinary icon. Jen could see why Amanda had wanted to meet here. It was dark and cozy, a domed brick ceiling providing character in the bar area. There were charcoal-colored wood beams running throughout the establishment and an ornate, stained glass window accentuating one wall. The floor was a mottled orange and brown tile, reminiscent of nineteen-seventies' décor.

Jen took in her surroundings at a glance, letting her eyes adjust to the dark corners, illuminated only by the dim glow of wall sconces. She didn't see any sign of Amanda, and was sure that if Amanda were there, Jen would know. Recent media coverage conveyed that Amanda caused a minor stir wherever she went. In addition to her natural beauty, she occupied a visible post, traveling with at least one security detail, thus turning heads in any venue.

Jen recalled that Tommy was friends with the guys who rotated through Amanda's security shifts, especially George, and he liked Amanda. She was polite and lived a low drama life, which they appreciated. They had run security for other dignitaries who liked to party and bask in media attention, resulting in late nights and big crowds. Amanda was easy in comparison, and for that, they were grateful.

Jen wondered if there was really an imminent threat to Amanda's safety necessitating a constant security presence. Would someone really do harm to her? Wasn't she just a cog in the wheel of justice that incarcerated the bad guys? Why single out any specific cop, detective, district attorney or judge? They were all just doing their jobs. On the other hand, Amanda was the face of the DA's office, so she probably was a target for that reason alone.

Jen decided that if security detail were required for a job, it would be a deal killer for her. It looked like a major hassle, even without considering the palpable threat.

A server appeared at Jen's elbow, taking her order for a Blue Sapphire gin and tonic. Jen inhaled deeply and smoothed her blouse over her front. It accentuated every curve and muscle on her body, for which she had labored extensively, thus was proud to flaunt. The blouse was sexy sheer, but tailored and classy. She was wearing a black, lacy camisole underneath that was the latest design from Victoria's Secret. Tommy said she looked hot in it, and he loved to unbutton it, one button at a time... *Would a woman like the same things that Tommy liked?* She had to stop comparing.

Feeling hot in her white blouse and ass-hugging slacks, she was buoyed about her decision to pursue Amanda. It was odd to be waiting for a woman, experiencing these sensations, including confusion, but it was a reality that she was determined to embrace. Enough pretending for the straight world.

From here on out, Jen would stop feeling so intimidated in the presence of Amanda. So what if Amanda was the DA? So what if Amanda was smart and rich? So what if she was one of the most powerful women in the city? So what if she was beautiful, charismatic and articulate? So what if her hands were soft and warm...

Jen had graduated from U.C.L.A. Medical School, which everyone knew was legions more difficult than a three-year degree from a law school. Yet, lawyers seemed to have all the power, especially when they became judges. Lowly ER physicians like herself were relegated to slogging away at the county hospital, saving one patient at a time, without any appreciation or acknowledgement from society. Her pay even sucked. It was probably less than Amanda's.

Tommy understood the professional side of Jen's life and respected how hard she worked. That was one of the things she loved about him—how he respected her intelligence and work. He was a good guy, and she was afraid she was going to break his heart when she broke up with him. More than that, she was afraid she'd miss him. She couldn't do both though, pursue her true desires and stay with

Tommy. It would be a devastating loss—for both of them.

The server delivered Jen's cocktail, and she sipped the delicious first sip, scanning the people at the bar. A handsome man in a suit raised his glass with a nod. Mid-thirties. Professionally dressed. Probably had women hitting on him all the time. Jen gave him a disinterested, polite smile and turned back toward the window. Nothing outside. Nothing inside. *If he only knew. I've decided to play for the other team, and I'm waiting for the young, powerful DA, who isn't the only woman in town who has her shit together.*

At that moment, she watched a burgundy Jaguar pull up in front of the restaurant. Or maybe it was black. It looked like Amanda's. The valet made a move to open the back door, but it was locked, surprising him.

The front passenger door opened and George got out, his waist holster visible through his parted blazer. He said something to the valet, who backed off, recognizing a cop when he saw one.

George opened the back door, and Amanda's shapely leg emerged in black heels, but not before Jen caught a glimpse of the tell-tale red soles. *Ah, the Christian Louboutin shoes that Amanda wore to the hospital charity ball.* George offered his hand, and Amanda stepped onto the curb. When she stood to full height, several heads turned.

She is one gorgeous bitch, Jen thought. *If she weren't gay, I'd be worried to death about*

*Tommy spending so much time with her. Then
again, I'm gay, so why would I be jealous of
Tommy falling for a woman? Wouldn't I really
be jealous if Amanda fell for Tommy, because
I'm attracted to her?*

Not only gorgeous, but also apparently
capable of mental telepathy, Amanda looked
directly through the restaurant window, finding
Jen in a heartbeat. It was as if Amanda had
expected Jen to be sitting at that very table.

Through the glass, their eyes managed to
find each other. Amanda smiled, and it melted
Jen's heart. She found herself smiling back,
even though she hadn't planned to. Amanda's
genuine pleasure at seeing Jen excited her
beyond measure. Even from inside the bar,
Jen could practically see the gold flecks
shimmering in Amanda's eyes.

George opened the restaurant door for
Amanda, and she confidently entered, turning
heads as she strode into the center of the
space, George clearing a path for her to Jen's
table. Always a politician, Amanda smiled and
nodded, but not in a self-aggrandizing way.
San Francisco residents couldn't stand overt
displays by politicians, and that type of
behavior wasn't what got Amanda elected in
the first place. She smiled discreetly and
nodded at those who recognized her, shaking
a few hands.

She was a local celebrity in professional
circles. Respected. Liked. Admired. And, here
to meet with Jen. Amanda made her way to
Jen's table and set her expensive bag on a

wooden stool. She shed her raincoat and stood before Jen in a cocktail dress rather than a work suit.

Funny, Jen thought, *I assumed she would be in work clothes. She looks fucking hot. Hotter than I do. God, look at how the neckline dips perfectly in front. Not too dramatic, but enough to let me know she has breasts, the tops of which are fantastic—smooth, pale skin and perfectly shaped...*

As Jen's eyes floated from Amanda's body to her eyes, she realized that Amanda was still waiting for some type of greeting. Jen slid off her chair and stood toe-to-toe with Amanda. Jen was a few inches taller and had a broader frame, but they were very close in stature.

"Hello, Dr. Dawson," Amanda said softly, very measured in her cadence, tilting her head back slightly. "You look like you have a lot on your mind."

"Hi Amanda. It's good to see you," Jen said, blushing.

Rather than engage in a phony hug, followed by air kisses, Amanda held out both of her hands, and Jen found herself placing her hands in them. This was a new twist. Jen had never engaged in a double handshake. She was once again reassured by how warm Amanda's hands were. Welcoming, steady and strong. She glanced down and a zing of reality hit her. Her somewhat larger hands were resting in Amanda Hawthorne's grasp. Amanda's touch confirmed the initial sensations that Jen had experienced in the back of her car on their trip to the impound lot.

She found Amanda's eyes again, seeing a genuine look of pleasure suffuse her face. Her eyebrows crinkled upward, suggesting vulnerability while questioning Jen's reaction. Amanda had disarmingly long, brown lashes. No mascara. Usually, only men were blessed with lashes like that, but gold dust must have been sprinkled over Amanda at birth.

"Thank you for agreeing to meet me. I've been looking forward to it all day," Amanda ventured.

"Me, too," Jen confessed. "You look beautiful in that dress."

Amanda inclined her head. "Thank you. Shall we sit?"

"Yes," Jen said, sliding back onto her chair. "I'm sorry. I already ordered a gin and tonic. I didn't know how long you'd be."

"No worries. I wish I could have a cocktail, but I recognized some politicos and media in here. I better stick to a conspicuous sparkling water."

"Politicos?"

"Powerful government officials and businessmen who are always looking for a vulnerability they can exploit in the next election."

"Oh." Jen was unaccustomed to viewing the world through this lens.

The server re-appeared, and Amanda ordered a Pellegrino, requesting that he bring the bottle and a plate of lemons, so if photos were taken, it would be obvious she wasn't drinking alcohol.

"I wasn't always so preoccupied with who's who, but after three years on the job, and my share of battles, I've become more attuned to my surroundings. And more importantly, who's lurking within them."

"In that case, I'm honored to be seen with you."

"Some people might assume we're on a date. I hope you're not offended by that."

"Maybe a drink would do you some good— to settle down that mind of yours."

"A drink might move it in a new direction. That's for sure," Amanda said, raising her glass. "Cheers."

They clinked and drank.

It was Amanda's turn to take in all of Jen. Unfortunately, Amanda's initial attraction hadn't subsided. What had she been thinking? Her gaydar was usually spot-on, but Jen was confounding her. She was straight and in a relationship with a colleague. Forbidden on two fronts. Yet, here she was, feeling what there was to feel, the electricity from their touch still pinging around in her body like a pinball machine.

Moreover, Jen was giving off an enormous amount of sexual energy. Amanda was quite certain that Jen hadn't worn her current outfit to work, which meant that Jen had purposefully chosen to wear a sheer blouse with a beautiful camisole underneath. It was very flattering. Sexy. Enticing. Even seductive. Jen's toned body was barely visible underneath, and it was all Amanda could do not to stare.

Jen looked at Amanda. "It's my turn to say that *you* look like a woman with a lot on her mind."

Amanda met Jen's eyes. "How true. I should've known that you'd be observant."

Amanda clearly had something to get off her chest, so Jen waited. She wasn't afraid to look Amanda in the eye, nodding subtle encouragement.

"There *is* something I have to discuss with you. I wouldn't usually meet with a potential witness in a criminal investigation, but, as a favor to Tommy, I agreed to."

"Favor to Tommy?"

"That came out wrong. Sorry. Not a *favor*-favor. More like we just talked about it, and I volunteered."

"You two talk about me at work?"

Amanda sighed. "No, but this investigation touched your world, so we had to. He didn't want to mix work with his personal life. That's the reason I volunteered."

Heat crept up Jen's neck, infusing her cheeks. She set her jaw. "Perhaps you should just say what you came to. I can see it's making you uncomfortable."

"You're right. Here it is. By seeing Lane Wallace as a patient, you became a witness in the Farber investigation."

"I'm not surprised. I've had to testify in criminal proceedings before on behalf of the victim."

"This is different, Jen. Tommy and I were surprised that you agreed to treat Dr. Wallace. We thought you'd steer clear of this."

"Steer clear?" Jen asked, her voice squeaking. "Steer clear of treating a patient while he's in acute heart failure? I'm an ER physician, Amanda. When someone collapses in front of me, I treat him." *How dare Amanda and Tommy second-guess my judgment as a physician. They may not like Lane Wallace, but that doesn't give them the right—*

Jen stared hard at Amanda, challenging her to explain. In return, Amanda held Jen's gaze, but didn't look angry. She was so damn calm that Jen found her infuriating.

"We're just saying, if this investigation leads to charges, you'll surely be a witness. We're worried that you might have a larger role than you intended, so we just wanted to tell you to be careful."

"I'm *always* careful," Jen said between terse lips. "Don't make it sound like I'm a reckless teenager. I'm a physician witness. Deal with it."

"I didn't mean to imply that you were anything other than professional and thoughtful." Amanda smiled, attempting to soften the harsh message.

"We both know what this is about. You may not believe in Lane, but I do. He's my friend and colleague."

"There are ways to support someone without becoming a witness in a murder trial."

Amanda was surprised at how angry Jen was getting. Tommy was right. She had a temper.

"Don't fucking lecture me. I know Lane, and I know he didn't murder Natasha Farber. Just because you view the world through suspicious lenses doesn't mean the rest of us do."

Amanda actually smiled, surprising Jen. "Got me there. Valid point." Amanda raised her glass to her lips and drank. She was very slow and deliberate in her movements, maintaining a calm exterior.

"I hate it when people underreact to a huge issue," Jen blurted.

Amanda cocked her head and squinted.

"What?" Jen asked.

"I just realized it's been over three years since someone spoke their mind to me—to my face. It's so refreshing. Everyone at work is afraid of me, so would never talk to me the way you just did."

Jen wasn't amused. "Then you've surrounded yourself with the wrong people. I hope you don't hold my directness against Tommy."

"Now you've gone too far," Amanda leveled, her voice lower. "I knew Tommy before I met you. I respect him, and we work well together. Trust me, there's nothing you could do to jeopardize my relationship with Tommy."

"That's reassuring." Jen thought how ironic Amanda's statement really was, because the reverse wasn't true.

Amanda wasn't finished with her message, but needed to let the air simmer down before she stirred it up again. She noticed that the veins in Jen's neck were pulsing, indicating she was pretty pumped up over this. The pulsation was sort of mesmerizing, as Amanda admired Jen's healthy, strong neck. A desire to graze Jen's neck with her tongue gripped her.

Jen clenched her jaw and looked around the bar—anywhere but at Amanda. Agreeing to this meeting had been a mistake. They hadn't gotten along during their last interaction, so why did she think this would be any different? She put her finger on the inside of her wrist and took her pulse, watching the seconds pass on her digital watch. Her heart was racing. She counted sixty-eight beats per minute. Considering her resting pulse was thirty-nine, Amanda really had her churned up. Why was she so emotional around her?

Amanda observed what Jen was doing, and found it attractive, in a scientific, geeky sort of way. *Taking her pulse when she's in the heat of an argument. How cardiac-centric.* She waited for Jen to look up before she spoke again.

"I hope I'm not making your heart race." Amanda nodded at Jen's wrist.

"You have no idea," Jen mumbled.

"In matters of the heart? I might."

There was a short silence as they looked at each other, feeling the attraction build again, but also the weight of other entanglements and unspoken words.

"I really admire you, Jen. People usually don't stand up to me—and you have. I'm sorry if I gave you the impression that I want to micromanage your medical practice. I don't. Truth be told—I want to micromanage this investigation so we can resolve it properly. The Ivanovs and the public deserve peace of mind. That's what Tommy and I are trying to give them."

"I believe you. I don't see how my treating a patient and ordering labs on him interferes with your investigation. Maybe you've just got the wrong guy in your sights. If you didn't suspect Lane, we wouldn't be sitting here."

"We're sitting here because Tommy and I wanted to make sure you see all the angles. I'm trying to warn you that becoming a witness in a criminal investigation is a complicated, emotional affair. But this conversation isn't going as I planned."

Jen noticed that Amanda's lips were thinning as she delivered her friendly warning. "Well, you said what you came to say. Maybe one woman's warning is another's meddling. I should leave now."

Amanda was stunned that Jen suddenly decided to pull the plug. She watched her slide off her chair and throw on her black leather jacket.

"Goodbye," Jen snapped, and walked away.

Less than twenty seconds later, Jen returned. She leaned across Amanda and tossed a ten-dollar-bill on the table. Their shoulders brushed, and Amanda caught Jen's scent. It was natural—and sexy as hell. There was no way she was letting Jen out of her sight.

"I've got this one." Amanda picked up the bill and tried handing it back to Jen, who was already three-people deep into the crowd, her sexy butt heading for the door.

Amanda quickly tossed another ten on the table and followed suit. She raised her eyebrows at George, and he broke up the bar crowd so they could pass through more quickly.

***

Chapter 23

Hall of Justice

Tommy and one of Amanda's ADA's were meeting with Judge Grady in his chambers for the second time that day. Tommy explained why he needed a search warrant for Trevor Ross' apartment, where Blake Farber was currently residing. He played the security cam clips for Judge Grady, so he could appreciate Blake's impersonation of Dr. Wallace, and the need to search Blake's half of Trevor Ross's apartment for evidence of the costume.

"This is an affront to Mr. Ross's privacy," Judge Grady warned, always a fierce advocate of the right against unreasonable search and seizure. "Even though the law permits you to act on evidence of a crime that's in plain view, Mr. Ross is not under investigation, so don't threaten him to get what you want."

"I understand, Judge."

"I mean it, Vietti. This warrant is limited to Blake Farber's room and any common areas. You don't have a warrant to go into Trevor Ross' room."

"I won't, your Honor," Tommy promised.

"Now get out of my chambers so I can go home." Tommy and the ADA skedaddled, warrant in hand.

They returned to the Hall of Justice and Tommy assembled a small team of officers to help him execute the search warrant, when he was interrupted by a phone call from Security in the lobby. Dr. Lane Wallace had arrived to pick up his cell phone.

"Shit. Bad timing. Send him up." Tommy met Wallace at the glass door entrance to the Investigations Unit and let him in. They remained standing, and Tommy returned Wallace's cell phone to him.

"Thank you for your cooperation, Dr. Wallace. I appreciate it."

"My pleasure. I hope you wrap up this investigation soon, so I can get back to work."

"I'll try my best." Tommy opened the door for Wallace to leave.

As soon as Tommy returned to his desk, he called the computer guys and told them to start monitoring and recording all of Dr. Wallace's phone calls and texts.

It was after regular business hours, so Blake was shit-out-of-luck today for picking up *his* phone today. It would have to wait until tomorrow. If Blake was at his apartment when Tommy and his team arrived, Tommy would remind Blake about his cell. He actually wanted him to pick it up so they could tap his communications, hoping to gather incriminating evidence.

***

After Tommy assembled his team, he and four officers rode in a squad car on a silent drive over to Blake and Trevor's apartment.

Tommy buzzed, and Blake let them in. Tommy flashed the warrant in Blake's face.

"What the fuck?!" You're still hassling me when I told you her doctor-lover killed her? What do you hope to find here?" Blake asked.

"The ball cap, cane, sunglasses, and tennis shoes you wore when you impersonated Dr. Wallace while gaining entry to Natasha's apartment building," Tommy explained, signaling his team to start the search.

"Bull-fucking-shit! You're high. I didn't impersonate no one! I told you. I haven't been back to our apartment since the night I was arrested."

"Yeah? Well, the videos belie your alibi, pal. Step aside so we can do our jobs. Which room is yours?"

Blake pointed to the second bedroom, and the officers entered it, turning everything upside down, looking for the items on their list.

Blake went to the kitchen, grabbed a beer from the fridge, and drank it as he leaned against the counter, tapping his foot and swearing under his breath.

The officer posted at the main entrance yelled "incoming" to Tommy, who came out into the living room to greet a very upset Trevor Ross.

"What the fuck are your doin' in my apartment?" Ross demanded.

"Executing this search warrant of Blake Farber's space." Tommy handed the warrant to Trevor.

Trevor grabbed it, crumpled it up and tossed it aside. "Get your fuckboys outta here, or I'm gonna sue the city."

"You'll do no such thing. I saw the shit you got going on in your room. Cash, guns and drugs. Keep your mouth shut, or I'll confiscate all of it and ring you up on felony charges."

Trevor stared at Tommy, but remained silent while Tommy and the officers finished their search. After an hour of coming up empty, Tommy declared the search a bust and suggested they leave.

"Fuck you," Blake said, as Tommy passed him.

"Lucky I don't arrest you right now for the murder of your wife. I have you on video violating your plea agreement by going into her apartment."

"That's a lie! And, even if you had me on video in the lobby, it doesn't mean I entered her apartment." Blake punctuated his statement with his middle finger.

"Fuck you," Tommy said as he closed the door behind him.

A defeated Tommy and team returned to the station. Tommy thanked them, and decided to visit Computer Forensics to see if they had anything interesting from Wallace's phone.

He entered their high-tech area to find the night shift settling in.

"Have anything on Wallace's phone?" Tommy asked.

"Just some texting banter between his wife and him," the analyst said.

"Like what?"

"Here, you can read it." The analyst turned the screen for Tommy to see.

Wallace had texted Susie a short time ago, *Got my phone back. When will you be home?*

Late. Meeting with a dealer at the gallery, then have a band coming in for a big party.

I'll make dinner for Angie and me.

Don't wait up for me.

Okay.

Tommy re-read the exchange. It was appropriately cold, considering their marital situation. Susie was running her business and didn't look very excited about eating dinner with her husband. End of story. Predictable. She'd be missing out on spending time with her daughter, though.

Maybe it's time I follow my gut, Tommy thought.

"Thanks guys." He raced down to his unmarked Charger in the parking lot.

***

Sangiolo Gallery on Minna Street

Tommy sat silently in his unmarked car on Minna Street, parked across from the Sangiolo Gallery. Susie had done well for herself. Her swanky art gallery was in the middle of the high rent district, nestled among other upscale galleries and design studios. The brick building was period, circa 1920s, built after the 1906 earthquake and fires had destroyed most of the city.

Caramel-colored granite adorned the gallery's front entry, accented by a red door and a green awning imprinted with the Sangiolo name. The gallery was double the size of most, with picture windows running the length of it. From his angle across the street, Tommy could see massive paintings on white walls and a long bar with liquor bottles and mirrors. If Susie had a liquor license, she could draw in a bigger and more diverse crowd than simply art aficionados. Art galleries were a dying breed, so to offset slumping sales, galleries that could market themselves as event spaces, hosting everything from book signings to wedding receptions, could break even on rent by selling liquor.

Given the size of Susie's extended family and connections, Tommy was sure that she booked several events throughout the year. As he recalled, she had three or four siblings, most of whom were brothers, and they were tough. He hoped they weren't involved in her business.

He was debating whether he should go in, introduce himself to her staff and request to chat with her, when he saw her exit. She was stylishly dressed in black boots, a black skirt and top, and a red wrap around her shoulders. She had a pair of designer sunglasses perched on top of her head and a black bag tucked under her arm.

Susie clicked her key fob, and Tommy watched the tail lights on a black Lexus coupe flash. Perfect. She was parked across the street and in front of him on a one-way, so he'd be able to pull out of his spot to follow her. She backed out of her tight space and drove slowly down the one-way, keeping a lookout. Tommy fired up his Charger and watched another car pull out behind her before he did. He tailed her, being careful to stay a few car lengths back.

He followed her out of the Financial District, down Columbus Avenue toward North Beach, then over to the Marina District by Fort Mason. She turned on Laguna Street and found parking alongside a stately brick building with a large sign out front that said, *Legacy Manor Nursing Home.*

Tommy assumed this was the facility Dr. Wallace had mentioned during his interview, where Susie's mother, Maria Sangiolo, resided. It was a large building, occupying almost an entire block. A tall, black wrought iron fence defined its perimeter.

Unlike other properties in the area, it had an expansive green lawn and a lovely view of the Bay. There was a baseball field across the street, which had to be entertaining for the residents when kids were playing. Legacy Manor looked expensive. He assumed that Medicare wasn't paying for Mrs. Sangiolo's residency, but the Sangiolos had money. He found a spot to park and got out to stretch his legs. A black sedan drove by him and parked around the corner from the Manor, which caught Tommy's attention. He made a mental note as he walked in the opposite direction.

There was no need to remain sitting in the car like an old-fashioned stakeout. Susie would be preoccupied in the large building, visiting her mother, so he just had to wait until she came out. He had time to kill, and the ball field across the street was a perfect place to do that. He entered the field across from the nursing home and walked the bases, assessing the upkeep. The gravel-sand mixture was freshly raked, and the white bags for the bases were new. A groundskeeper was chalking the baselines.

"Can I help you?" the groundskeeper asked when Tommy was within earshot.

Tommy walked over and showed him his identification. "Just killing a little time while keeping an eye on someone across the street."

"Oh. Stay on the field as long as you like, but an intramural game is scheduled to start soon."

"Good to know. Thanks." Tommy turned and made his way to the outfield.

It was a clear evening, and the air was fresh on this side of the city, away from the traffic and congestion of the Financial District. This side had a different feel and vibe— the warmth of the Bay as well as the fresh breeze off the Pacific. The air temp was also a few degrees warmer than where Tommy lived in North Beach. Keeping an eye on the front door of the manor, he enjoyed the balmy temp while he walked the perimeter of the outfield.

He mulled over the evidence that had surfaced thus far. The fatal mix of drugs in the booze bottle. Blake masquerading as Dr. Wallace. Blake's prints on the booze bottle. However, no evidence of the costume in Blake's apartment.

On the other hand, Wallace had been to Natasha's apartment in close proximity to her poisoning as well. He also had access to the type of drugs used to poison Natasha. He admitted to having an affair with her and dominating her during sex. *Was Wallace really that afraid of Susie finding out he was having an affair?* Tommy didn't buy it.

Something was missing. Right in the center of the investigation, there was a black hole. Tommy could see the hole, but he hadn't figured out what was in it. He knew that neither Blake nor Wallace filled the hole. *There's more. Someone else.* As he paced around the field, another possibility took shape in his mind.

Ball players began showing up for their pregame warmups, so it was time for Tommy to leave. He took a seat on the bleachers and watched the young men stretch, run and throw. He gauged various players' abilities as his subconscious considered the Farber case. He also noticed that the black sedan that had parked on the other side of the Manor was still there, the driver still in it. He saw the glowing end of a lit cigarette in the driver's mouth.

Just as the game was getting underway, Tommy saw Susie leave the facility and drive away in her expensive car. He watched her from the bleachers, blending into the fans, certain that she hadn't seen him. He quickly glanced at the black sedan. It pulled out behind Susie's car, following her. After they left, he sauntered across the street to the nursing home, unlatched the black gate and took the steps two-at-a-time up the grand entrance.

He hit the buzzer and announced who he was. They let him in, and he was met by a receptionist.

He flashed his identification for her. "I'm Detective Tommy Vietti. Can I speak with the Director of Legacy Manor, please?"

The middle-aged woman assured him she would retrieve the Director right away and invited Tommy to have a seat. A few minutes later, a woman in a dark pantsuit presented herself in the waiting area and introduced herself as Karen. Tommy showed her his identification as well.

"How can I help you?" Karen asked.

"I'm investigating a homicide, and some evidence has led me to your facility."

"How curious. I can't imagine why."

"Quite simple, actually. Have you had any incidents of theft of the residents' medications by staff or family members?"

She sighed. "Occasionally, but that's why we have very strict policies in place—to secure the medications. Would you like to see them?"

"Not the policies. I'm interested in one resident in particular—Mrs. Maria Sangiolo. Have any medications been stolen from her room?"

"I'm sorry, Detective, but the law won't allow me to discuss a specific patient with you unless you have a subpoena or an authorization signed by the resident. You understand, I'm sure."

"I do. I can get a subpoena signed by Judge Grady. Before I go to all the trouble of asking the District Attorney to prepare it, and bothering the judge with it, I'd just like to know whether it would be worth my while. Time is of the essence in a homicide investigation, so if my efforts aren't going to pay off, I don't want to waste your time and the court's time."

"I don't know how I can help you without a subpoena." She had a polite, but firm, smile on her face.

"Maybe we could approach it this way," he said, imploring her with his Italian eyes. "Could you ask the staff caring for Mrs. Sangiolo if any of her meds, specifically Digoxin or opioids, have gone missing in the last few months? If they give you any indication that the answer is yes, then I'll go get a subpoena for Mrs. Sangiolo's medical record."

"I'm not sure that's permissible," she said, hedging.

"It's a *homicide* investigation. I think the family of the victim would appreciate your making a general inquiry into missing meds, without disclosing anything about Mrs. Sangiolo's personal health to me."

He could see the scales of justice being weighed in her mind. Patient privacy being paramount in her world, she balanced that against helping the cute detective solve a homicide.

"I'll go chat with the staff to see what I can find out. Wait here."

She scanned herself through a locked double-door and disappeared down the hallway. Tommy busied himself by fixing a cup of coffee from the complimentary station in the corner of the waiting area.

He had finished his coffee by the time he heard the double-doors open and saw Karen approaching him. He rose to meet her.

Speaking in hushed tones, a sad look on her face, she told him what he needed to know.

"I'm sorry. I had no idea, but about four weeks ago, Mrs. Sangiolo's Digoxin went missing. The staff had to get another order from her physician for it. They didn't think much of it at the time because it's not a narcotic. However, as we looked at the record, we saw that Mrs. Sangiolo was in more pain recently, so they increased her fentanyl dosages for additional lozenges each day. In retrospect, someone may have been taking those as well."

"Lozenges?" he asked.

"Yes. The patient sucks on them like a cough drop."

"I'll bet those can be melted down into a liquid pretty easily."

"I've never tried, but I'm sure it's possible."

"I'm hearing that it would be worthwhile for me to get that subpoena."

"Yes, Detective, I think it would," she said, realizing the gravity of the situation herself.

"Thank you for your time. I owe you one." He shook her hand.

Tommy nodded to the receptionist as he left, hurrying down the steps to his car. The fragmented information that had been plaguing him came together. Even though he was energized by solving a crime, this one saddened him.

He couldn't choose the suspects he had to investigate, however, and he was long past being surprised by what ordinary people could do when they experienced betrayal and rage. Matters of the heart could ruin a person's judgment, leading to a crime of passion they later regretted. Usually, there was little or no premeditation, so the charges were manslaughter, rather than premeditated murder. That charge might not fit his current scenario, however, one that he was duty-bound to solve no matter how close it hit home.

***

Chapter 24

SoMa

Amanda and George exited Boulevard Restaurant into a light mist. Amanda scanned the street in both directions, catching Jen's flowing blonde hair and black leather jacket disappear around the corner down Steuart Street.

"Follow Jen," Amanda told George, who held the rear door for her. After she slid in, he shut her door and got in the driver's side. Neither he, nor the other security detail, was expecting such a hasty departure. George pulled a U-turn on Mission and gunned it. They turned right onto Steuart and quickly caught up to Jen, who had walked almost three blocks.

"Slow down, so I can talk to her," Amanda ordered from the back seat, admiring the way Jen's black slacks hugged her Beyoncé.

George pulled alongside Jen, who was storming at a quick pace, her long stride and determined face a prelude to war.

Amanda rolled down her window. "Jen, can I offer you a lift?"

Jen ignored her.

"Seriously, Jen. Get in the car so we can talk."

Jen ignored her.

"Jen, you're being childish. Can you just get in the car? The guys think you should, too."

Jen stopped and leaned her head back, stifling a scream and looking at the night sky. It threw the orange city glow back at her. The *guys*, who were Tommy's friends, probably hadn't said a word to Amanda. However, they *would* tell Tommy about this fight if Jen continued to make them follow her. *They had no idea. Tommy had no idea.* She shook her head and turned toward the car. Amanda opened the back door, and Jen got in beside her.

"The Curtain Call," Amanda said quickly to George.

Jen again found herself in the back of Amanda's car, seated next to the control freak. Worse—a beautiful control freak. Worse yet—a control freak who was wearing a fantastic fragrance. Under any normal circumstance, Jen would have asked what it was, but she'd be damned if she would give Amanda the satisfaction. Amanda's ego might explode into stratospheric proportions at the slightest bit of encouragement.

Amanda rolled up the privacy glass between the front and back seats. No need for the guys to overhear *this* conversation. There was a code of loyalty among the force, and Amanda correctly assumed they would relay the entire evening to Tommy. She preferred to give Tommy a version of her own making.

She moved her long hair over her shoulder and looked seriously at Jen, gently laying her hand on Jen's, beneath the view of the rearview mirror from the front seat. Jen's piercing blue eyes searched Amanda's face.

An intellectual with working hands, thought Amanda. She liked the feel. Soft exterior; strong underneath. A jolt of lightning shot from Amanda's fingertips to her belly. What was it with Jen that set her on fire? She touched her *here*, and it set her on fire *there*. *It's been so long since I've felt this way. I'm so fucked.*

Jen's world was spinning, too. The events from the past few days swirled in her mind like a kaleidoscope of images—Amanda in a slinky dress at the charity dinner; then rescuing Jen and walking in with her to the impound lot; then removing her raincoat at Boulevard, standing before her in her sexy cocktail dress. Now, Amanda here, next to her again, setting her world on fire with a mere touch of her hand.

No matter how many miles Jen ran, swam or biked, she couldn't keep up with everything that was happening in her life this week. It was too fast. Her world was simply moving too fast. She needed to slow down, so she wouldn't do anything she later regretted. The anger that had consumed her earlier was subsiding to the point where she had lost track of the precise reason she had become angry. It seemed as if Amanda's hand was pulling all the anger out of her body. Amanda had said she respected Jen's work. It was over.

Amanda's touch was warm and soft, yet reassuring. Distinctly feminine, it felt right to Jen. If anyone had asked Jen a month ago if she would have been comfortable with another woman's hand resting on top of hers, she would have laughed. She honestly believed that

Tommy could fulfill her. She realized she had been lying to herself.

Amanda leaned in and whispered into Jen's ear. "I was only trying to look out for you."

Jen felt Amanda's hot breath against her ear and a spike of pleasure hit her at the back of her neck, sending shivers down her spine. Jen knew Amanda wasn't playing fair, but it didn't bother her. Quite the contrary, actually.

Amanda noticed Jen's shiver, then smiled as she scooted back to her side.

Jen *for sure* didn't want to talk about the investigation again, wanting to avoid some lofty speech about the criminal justice system. She had heard Tommy's speech many times, a speech designed to justify whatever action the police wanted to take. Amanda's speech was probably more polished than Tommy's, but she was sure Amanda had one on the tip of her tongue.

As far as Jen was concerned, Tommy and Amanda could do whatever they wanted, suspecting Lane of murder like a couple of misguided delusionals. Jen believed in Lane, and would continue to follow her own moral compass, doing what she thought was right, treating colleagues as patients if they sought her out. *And where was Tommy in all of this anyway? He didn't have the guts to tell me what Amanda just did? Is Amanda that much stronger than he is?*

Jen lay her head back on the cushy headrest and closed her eyes, enjoying the smooth feel of the ride. Her anger dissipated with Amanda's hand still on hers, resting, but not caressing. It was *almost* a platonic touch, left open to interpretation. If she wanted to read more into it, she could. Right now, however, she was content to consider it an olive branch. She inhaled deeply and exhaled slowly, commanding her nerves to settle down.

They had been driving for ten minutes in rush hour traffic, rolling along with the other cars, heading toward Union Street in the Cow Hollow District. Jen kept her eyes pressed shut, and Amanda turned on some music—a French woman singing sultry lounge tunes. Amanda probably spoke French, too, just to add to her upper crust image.

Jen couldn't settle her mind. *This was the second time tonight Amanda initiated hand contact. She's a very touchy person. Maybe it's a by-product of those elections, glad-handing strangers, trying to win their votes.*

"Do you mind if we go to a favorite place of mine, so I can get a drink in private?" Amanda asked.

Jen still didn't open her eyes. "A drink?"

"Yes, I'd love a drink right now. I'm a ball of nerves."

Jen opened her eyes and squinted at Amanda. "So, the ice queen has nerves, does she?"

"Ice queen?" A flash of hurt crossed Amanda's face.

"Just joking. I thought you'd take it as a compliment. You're not icy. In fact, your hand is quite warm." Jen turned her own hand palm-up and twined her fingers through Amanda's. She surprised herself by taking the initiative, but it felt so natural with Amanda. She wasn't thinking, just doing. Doing what felt right in the moment. She examined Amanda's hand, unaware of what she was looking for, but it felt right to touch and look, keeping her warm hand on her lap.

"I'm sorry," they both said at the same time.

The sound of Jen's voice stirred passion in Amanda like no other. Lovely sensations were traveling from Amanda's heart to her toes, then back up again. She hadn't felt those in a long time—six months to be exact. Her last relationship had withered as quickly as it had blossomed, and she was ready for another. Beyond ready, in fact. Jen was a new mystery, and Amanda was bursting with optimism at the prospect of solving her. If only Jen weren't romantically involved with Tommy. He had been both a friend and a colleague to Amanda for ten years. *Am I luring Jen into a relationship behind Tommy's back? Could I even stop myself from being attracted to her?*

"I appreciate your looking out for me." Jen rubbed circles on the top of Amanda's hand as she continued to stare at it. Amanda was wearing the smooth, glass ring that Jen had noticed on their way to the impound lot. Jen liked the feel of it, again rolling it between her fingers.

"I'm nothing, if not well-intentioned," Amanda rasped, her voice catching at Jen's touch. This was an unexpected turn of events.

The way Jen rubbed, with just the right amount of pressure, caressing while she stared at Amanda's hand. It wasn't platonic.

Jen looked up to see tears spring to Amanda's eyes. *Oh God, she actually has feelings.* "Come here. You look like you need a hug."

Amanda hesitated only a second, so Jen pulled Amanda's hand around her back and placed it there.

Amanda scooted in closer, and they looked at each other, both realizing that this hug would be more than one woman consoling another. It was their first intimate embrace.

Amanda already knew that touching Jen drove her wild, igniting her carnal instincts. She had tried to restrain herself, sending semi-platonic signals, but Jen had responded immediately to Amanda's light touch with overtures of her own. *She seems like she's been here before,* Amanda thought.

Seeing tears spring to Amanda's eyes undid Jen. She was genuinely concerned that she had offended her and had to clear the air before they ended the night. She leaned in and hugged Amanda tightly, their fronts colliding for the first time. Their breasts crushed into each other, melding perfectly. It was fleeting, but, for the first time since college, a mere hug felt like a lover's embrace, like the two of them were meant to be.

Amanda immediately knew they felt good together. She wanted to stay curled in Jen's arms for the remainder of the night. Maybe longer. She had landed, and it was with Jen.

She just knew. When Jen pulled back, it required all of Amanda's control not to snuggle into her neck and kiss her.

Jen absorbed Amanda's warm embrace, once again aware of how exciting hugging another woman could be. Or, hugging Amanda, that was. In that two seconds, her sexuality sprang back to life—stronger than it had been with Tommy. She was surprised, but not really, to learn how hot she felt after denying it for over a decade.

Jen slid her hand from Amanda's back, trailing it along Amanda's ribs, and up to her shoulder, giving it a little squeeze. "Better?" she asked, looking into Amanda's warm eyes.

"Thank you," Amanda whispered, reading Jen's mind. Her eyes had turned a deeper shade of blue. *You're as turned on as I am.*

As they separated, George pulled up to the curb in front of the Curtain Call, their first intimate experience coming to an end out of necessity.

The guys did their drill, opening the curbside car door for the ladies. Jen scooted out first, and Amanda watched. Amanda again admired Jen's smooth, athletic slide, made possible by the nicest ass she had ever seen on a woman. Her insides did a back flip as she scooted out herself. She took Jen by the hand and led the way into her haunt.

Jen entered the dim, red club as a newcomer, surprised to see a live performer singing show tunes at a grand piano. There were several people around the piano singing backup. A few nodded and waved to Amanda, who was a regular. She led Jen to her favorite booth to the side of the entertainment area.

Amanda motioned for Jen to go into the booth first, whispering that her security detail liked her on the edge for a quick escape, if needed.

Jen rolled her eyes at yet another set of *cop* rules, but complied. She had had enough of cops recently. Enough safety. Enough of *for your own good*. Enough of controlling everything and everyone. She wanted freedom. Freedom from the law. From Tommy. From her job. From social convention. From her parents' expectations. She wanted Amanda and that possibility had just materialized in the car. Her heart was springing back to life.

The officer who accompanied them in walked to the bar and sat, affording him a full view of both the front and back entries. He ordered a soda while George was out driving around the block, looking for a suitable parking spot.

A server materialized out of thin air and asked Amanda if she wanted her usual.

Amanda turned to Jen. "What are you in the mood for?"

"Anything. What about you?"

"Sparkling wine?"

"Sure."

Amanda ordered a bottle of Sonoma sparkling wine. Once they had full glasses in their hands, Amanda tapped hers against Jen's, and they sipped.

"These singers are good," Jen whispered.

"They're professionals. They come here to unwind and practice. Most are in shows or bands."

"No wonder."

"I get to sample shows without the hassle of buying tickets and going. And, they're a very accepting crowd."

"I suppose." Jen studied them.

They listened for a while, and the waiter came around to refill their glasses.

"You know I'm going to do whatever you tell me to, right?" Jen said, fully loading her declaration.

"I'm honored." Amanda rested her hand on Jen's thigh, appreciating how toned it was. The wine was going to her head faster than she had anticipated.

The corner of Jen's mouth curved up in approval, and she put her own hand on top of Amanda's.

Invitation accepted. *Definitely experienced in being with a woman,* Amanda thought. *Perhaps a bit rusty, but nonetheless.*

There was a short break in the music, as the performers laughed and negotiated with each other the song they would sing next. One of the singers spied Amanda and came over to their table. "Hey Amanda! How the hell are ya?"

"Good Sugar. I'd like you to meet a friend of mine. This is Jen Dawson," Amanda said.

"Hi Sugar," Jen extended her hand.

Sugar shook Jen's hand and lingered for a few minutes, catching up on club gossip with Amanda.

As they conversed, Jen's gaze wandered back to the performers gathered around the piano. In the middle of the pack, there were two women with their arms loosely around each other. One caressed the other's back. The recipient slid her arm around the other and nuzzled her neck. Soon, they were lip deep in a juicy exchange as the pianist played again.

Sugar said goodbye to Amanda and rejoined her friends at the piano.

Amanda looked at Jen, following her gaze to the two women kissing at the piano, then turned back to read her reaction. Jen was really into it; mouth open, observing everything about them. Amanda saw raw lust building in Jen's eyes.

Jen was transfixed on the femme couple. She remembered the taste—the sensation. It was distant, but calling.

"I have to use the restroom. Be right back." Amanda patted Jen on the leg and slid out of the booth. Perhaps it was best to give Jen some space, Amanda thought. Jen needed to assimilate to her new surroundings as well as Amanda's overtures. There was still plenty of time for Jen to turn back. The night was early. A few touches. A hug. It was still in the harmless phase. Amanda passed her security at the bar, tapped him on the shoulder, and disappeared down the hallway to the restrooms.

***

Chapter 25

North Beach

When Tommy slid behind the wheel of his Charger, his stomach growled, reminding him that he needed to eat dinner soon, even though he was immersed in an investigation.

He removed his cell phone from his coat pocket and composed a text to Jen, then remembered he wasn't supposed to talk to her. *Shit.* He missed her, and he was curious about how well she had received Amanda's warning to stay away from this case. If she were angry at Amanda, maybe he could smooth it over. He just wanted to see her. *What was wrong with that? Was it too much to ask for a quick dinner together?*

He texted. *Hey. I know we can't talk, but do you want to eat dinner together?*

He waited for a reply, but none was forthcoming. Her radio silence made him wonder whether there was more to her request of not seeing each other than merely the investigation.

He started the Charger and drove down Columbus Avenue, heading in the direction of his Italian neighborhood, where he was born, went to school and now lived. If Jen didn't have the decency to reply to a text, then he'd ignore her. After all, he had his Italian pride. *I had a good life before I met you. I can pick up where I left off.*

Once Tommy was back in North Beach, he drove to a corner restaurant and peeked inside as he drove by, deciding whether to go in. Perfect, the usual gang was there, occupying their usual table on a weeknight. He found a parking spot a few blocks away and quickly walked to *Mama Mia's,* where there was a line stretching out the front door. Tommy bypassed the line and went to a side door around the corner. He snuck into the kitchen and was met by busy cooks in the food preparation line.

"Who do you think you are, walking through my kitchen on a busy night?" an attractive woman in a chef hat yelled at him.

"Your twin brother, that's who." He gave her a peck on the cheek.

"It's been too long. Where's Jen?"

"Doin' her own thing. You look beautiful tonight, Sis." He looked at the female version of himself.

"She finally dropped you, huh? Tell her I said hi. Go join Pops at the table, and I'll bring you a bowl of spaghetti—with a bill."

"Love you, too."

Tommy pushed through the swinging doors into the restaurant, barely missing a bustling waiter. He was pleased to see the restaurant was at full capacity. His sister, Tina, had owned it for five years now, and it was popular, drawing in the locals as well as tourists seeking authentic Italian in North Beach.

He squeezed in next to Cy, who was seated in a crowded booth filled with the same gentlemen with whom Tommy had eaten breakfast that morning at Caffé Trieste. They were all wearing collared shirts and blazers for their evening meal.

"Tommy!" Cy gave him a kiss on the cheek. "My boy is here!"

The other three men smiled and greeted Tommy, happy for the youthful company.

"Hey, Pops. What's new?"

"The Giants are losing to the D-backs, that's what," Cy lamented.

"It's early in the season." He ordered a beer from their server.

"Where's your beautiful Jen tonight?" Cy asked.

"I don't know. Probably working late or something."

"She doesn't fix you dinner?"

"No, Pops. She's a doctor, remember? She has to work. And we don't spend every night of the week together."

"Sounds to me like you got girl problems," Saul said.

"What would you know about girls?" Tommy laughed.

"I was quite a Romeo in my day," Saul said.

"I'll bet," Tommy said.

"Had a couple of women makin' dinner for me during the week," he continued.

"Yeah, who?" Tommy asked.

"Well, there was—" Saul began, but was interrupted by the server delivering their meals.

Tommy admired his large bowl of spaghetti, on which Tina had made the shape of a heart with sprinkles of parmesan cheese. Her sisterly love brought a smile to his face, as the heart melted into the sauce.

After a few bites, Cy picked up where he had left off that morning, inquiring about police business. "How's the investigation going?"

"You know I can't talk about it." Tommy twirled the noodles around his fork and stuffed them into his mouth.

"I know, but how's it *going*?" Cy insisted.

Tommy chewed and stared into space for a second. "You ever been in a situation where the pieces of the puzzle are all in place, except for a black hole in the middle?"

Cy drank some wine. "Is it because you don't know what piece belongs in the middle, or that you're unwilling to *admit* what belongs there?"

Tommy snapped his head up from twirling pasta and looked at Cy, struck by how sharp his old man was at the age of seventy-four.

"The latter, I see," Cy said.

"How did you know?"

"I've been there. You can't control who commits the crimes, Tommy. You have to investigate and charge based on the evidence, not your heart."

Tommy stared at his bowl as he chewed on what his father had said. Still insightful and full of good advice after all these years, Cy knew how to get to the heart of the matter, especially when it came to solving hard-hitting crimes.

Half way through his meal, Saul droned on again about all the women who had made him dinner while the guys razzed him. Tommy thought about his approach for gathering the final pieces of evidence he needed to complete the puzzle. He ate his dinner and rolled over the evidence in his mind, eager to bring resolution to any homicide investigation. Natasha Farber deserved that. So did her parents.

After recharging with dinner, Tommy received his bill, which was for one million dollars, signed personally by Tina. He broke into laughter, and showed it to Cy, who was tickled that his children still loved each other.

"Thanks for the advice, Pops."

"Anytime. Leaving so soon?"

"Yeah. I got some things I need to check out."

"Watch yourself."

"I will." Tommy threw a twenty on the table.

The gentlemen bid him ado, and Tommy retreated behind the swinging kitchen doors, where he waved his one-million-dollar dinner bill at his sister as he left. She laughed and returned to checking plates as they came off the line. Ever the sentimental, Tommy tucked the bill into his breast pocket as a keepsake.

Once he was back in his car, he checked his cell phone to see if Jen had replied to his text about dinner. Nothing. *She's really giving me the cold shoulder.* Swearing under his breath, he called her. After a few rings, it went to her voicemail. He was offended by her deliberate brush off, but had to dismiss it, determined to work this case until he solved it. There would be time for Jen after.

If it had been earlier in the day, he would've returned to the office and worked with the DA's office to get a subpoena for Maria Sangiolo's medical record at Legacy Manor. However, the ADAs and Judge Grady had gone home for the night, so that task would have to wait until tomorrow.

There was still investigative work he could do tonight, however. He drove back down to the Financial District and parked close to the Sangiolo Gallery on Minna Street. He sat in his car, mulling over his approach, watching the tourists who were attending conferences at the large hotels.

They were so easy to spot, dressed in business casual, some still wearing their conference ID badges on lanyards around their necks, even out to dinner and bars. They may as well have attached a neon sign to their body that said, "Rip me off. I'm a tourist attending a conference."

He watched as a scruffy young man with dreadlocks came cruising down the street on a skateboard and tucked into an entryway, where he removed his backpack. There was a bedroll and four pair of shoes tied to the backpack, along with a yoga mat and other household bits and pieces. He unrolled a cardboard barrier, and created a bed in the entryway. He obviously was planning to stay for the night. Tommy thought the kid looked too young to be homeless, but he wasn't surprised, given the city's burgeoning population of young people who found themselves on the street. It wasn't

Tommy's job to interfere with the goings-on of this neighborhood, however. The local officers would keep tabs on everyone. They probably already knew the kid's name. *There just weren't enough resources...*

Tommy popped a breath mint in his mouth, got out of his car and locked it with the fob as he walked toward Susie's gallery.

Rather than flashing his credentials at the door, thereby alerting everyone to his status, he paid the twenty-dollar cover charge and entered the space, which was now multi-colored from track lighting, casting the colors of the rainbow on the otherwise white walls. There was an all-female band on the stage covering Led Zeppelin tunes. They weren't half bad, the drummer being the real star. Tommy stood three people deep at the bar and received a generous pour of whiskey on the rocks.

He squeezed between people until he made it over to a wall he could hold up, affording him a view of the entire space. He was a little out of place, wearing his blazer and tie, quite sure his jeans weren't as expensive as the other patrons' clothes. Everyone else was wearing black, or designer jeans with hip shirts and leather jackets. He assessed the crowd as urban, polished and moneyed. The prevailing demographic was mid-thirties, so they had careers and disposable income, which Susie would help them part with at her gallery. The art on the wall to the right of

Tommy's shoulder was priced at twenty-thousand dollars. *Not bad.*

He scanned the crowd, looking for Susie, and spotted her on the dance floor. He hadn't expected to see her there, but she had always been fun-spirited. As the band pounded out a strong beat, Susie threw her arms around the neck of her dance companion, a swarthy looking gentleman who was at least ten years' her senior. She wasn't holding back, melding her voluptuous body in her red and black dress against his front. He whispered something in her ear, which brought laughter and her hand to his jaw. Tommy watched as she coaxed the man's face down for a kiss. It wasn't a business peck on the cheek. Rather, they canoodled in the center of the dance floor, getting into each other as people gyrated around them.

So, Susie has a man on the side. Did this guy predate Wallace's affair with Natasha, or is he her revenge fuck? Tommy wondered. Judging by how practiced their intimate movements were on the dance floor, Tommy guessed this guy predated Wallace's affair with Natasha.

Susie nestled into her lover's shoulder as he moved to the right, allowing her to sweep the patrons with her eyes. Her sexually energized eyes scanned the crowd, then came back to focus on Tommy. The dance spell was shattered as she snapped her head up and met Tommy's eyes.

Tommy appreciated her initial surprise, which was followed by a flicker of fear. She found her composure, masking her expression into one of pleasant surprise at seeing an old friend. Susie tapped her dance partner on the shoulder and led him off the floor, making a bee line for Tommy.

Tommy plastered a neutral look on his face as he scrutinized Susie. She was flushed, but that could have been from dancing in the center of the crowd. She looked guilty, but that could have been from being busted with her lover. Ever the hostess, she brightened with a smile as she drew near.

"Tommy! How good to see you," she yelled over the band.

They hugged. "Quite a place you've got here."

"Thanks. This band always draws a crowd. There's someone I'd like you to meet. This is Nick Nutini."

Tommy and Nick shook hands. With a practiced eye, Nick saw Tommy's holster as his blazer opened for the handshake.

"In law enforcement?" Nick asked.

"Yes. I'm a detective." Tommy didn't say, *my specialty is homicides.* "What do you do, Mr. Nutini?"

"Please, call me Nick. I own beer distributorships and some other businesses."

"Nick is my liquor supplier. What brings you here, Tommy?" Susie asked.

"I was hoping to chat with you in private."

"We can go to my office. Nick, you don't mind, do you?"

"Not at all. Nice meeting you Tommy." Nick lifted the door in the counter and let himself behind the bar. He was of average height and Tommy noticed he was wearing black Keen shoes—with the distinctive toe box. What a coincidence.

Susie led Tommy through the crowd to the opposite end of the gallery, where she pressed a security code into a pad next to a substantial metal door. She opened it, and they walked down a hallway, passing a storage room full of liquor and arriving at another door at the end. She pressed in a second security code, then opened the door into her plush office.

Tommy noticed security cameras placed in the corners of the hallway and her office. As expected, Susie's office was tastefully furnished with fancy pieces of art and several sculptures. Tommy appreciated fine art, but now wasn't the time. One wall, however, was devoted to flat screens with video of every angle of the gallery, including behind the bar and the hallway they had just passed through. He was impressed.

"Please, sit." She motioned for him to take a chair across from her, where she sat on the sofa. "I'd offer you a drink, but I see you already have one."

"Thanks. Please get yourself something."

"I'm fine. It's so good to see you again. I hope this isn't awkward for you."

"Not at all. Just doing my job, and that's never awkward for me."

He had set the tone. This wasn't a social call, and he wasn't going to go easy on her. He was about to shake up her world to see if his hunch would play out the way he thought it would.

Never a fool, she waited patiently for him to speak.

"Did you ever meet Natasha Farber?"

"Seriously, Tommy? Do we have to discuss this tonight? I've been drinking, and I'm trying to manage my gallery on a busy night. I'm distracted—"

"If you'd prefer to wait until tomorrow, we can arrange to meet in the interrogation room at police headquarters, where there will be several sets of eyes and ears on you, and we'll be recording every word." He gave her the impression that their chat in her office was going to be off-the-record.

She thought a moment about the picture he painted. "What do you need to know?"

"Who killed Natasha Farber?"

"Whoa! You drove all the way over here to ask me why the whore who was trying to steal my husband is dead?"

"Was she trying to steal your husband?" he asked, momentarily ignoring that Susie reframed his question of "who" to "why."

"Of course," she laughed sarcastically. "She told him she was in love with him and wanted him to divorce me."

"How do you know?"

"He told me." She exhaled, then stared blankly into a corner of her office.

"Why not divorce him? I mean, it looks like you and Nick are pretty close."

She flicked her hand in the direction of the door. "Nick's new. But, as soon as this investigation is over, I'm divorcing Lane."

"Don't want to try to patch it up?"

"Fuck no. He fooled around on me! Not like a one-night stand, or an indiscretion, mind you, but several times over the course of a few months. Why would I take him back?"

"Because you love him?"

"I may have at one time, but not anymore. I think he loved her," she said, tears forming now.

Per Tommy's recollection, Susie was practiced in theatrics and could turn on tears, anger, or flirtation at a moment's notice. He was sure she had honed her skills over the years, making him suspect whether he was getting genuine emotion or an act. She was probably confident she could paint an innocent silhouette of herself, one that Tommy would buy like an expensive painting off her gallery wall.

"I'm sorry, Susie. Did you ever meet Natasha?"

She stared at him. "Maybe once or twice."

"Where?"

"At hospital functions."

"When?" he asked.

"I can't remember. Maybe in the last six months."

"When did they start having an affair?"

"I don't know. You'll have to ask Lane that."

"When did you notice?" he asked.

"A couple of months ago, when he wasn't around as much, and he didn't want sex anymore. It probably took me a few weeks because I'm so busy here at the gallery and at Angie's school."

"How old is Angie now?"

"She's eight. Old enough to know something is amiss."

"Did you confront him?" There was a long silence as Tommy watched Susie consider her possible responses and the ramifications of each. He'd love to know what she was thinking. He inclined his head at her, signaling that he was still waiting for her answer to whether she confronted Wallace.

"Yes," she finally said. No tears. No theatrics. Just matter-of-fact.

"When?"

"About a month ago, or so."

"What did he say?"

"He denied it at first, but I didn't back down. I told him I followed him to her apartment and saw him go into the building."

"That had to have surprised him," Tommy said, encouraging her to spill more.

"It did. He blew up at me, threatening to ring my neck—so I let it drop. I was this close to calling the police again because I was scared, Tommy. Really scared. You don't know what it's like, living with an ex-soldier with PTSD."

The faucet turned on now, and she cried, working herself into small sobs. She reached for the tissue box on the coffee table and dabbed carefully around her eyes so as not to smear her mascara.

So, she knew two months ago, and she confronted Wallace one month ago. That doesn't mesh with Wallace's story. Tommy had what he needed and had accomplished what he came to do. It was time to go.

"I'm sorry, Susie. I don't have any more questions for you. I appreciate your seeing me tonight. I'll be in touch if I need anything else," he said, standing.

She stood, too, circling the chairs to hug him. "Thank you, Tommy. I really feel like I can trust you, you know? Being from the same neighborhood and our families going way back and everything."

He pulled her close and ran his hand over the back of her head. "I know, Susie. I know." As he had suspected, she had answered his "who" question by throwing Dr. Wallace under the bus. *Really scared...Living with an ex-soldier with PTSD.* It was enough for now.

***

Chapter 26

The Curtain Call

After Amanda left for the restroom, the female couple at the piano got lost in passion, until one of their friends nudged them to unglue their lips and start singing again. They reluctantly did, the shorter woman leaning against her lover's arm as they sang and swayed. So swept up. So accepted among their friends.

Jen sat alone for a few seconds, realized she was staring, then scooted out of the booth. She nodded to the security detail at the bar and followed the sign to the restrooms. On a mission, she pushed through the bathroom door and found herself in a pink lounge with a velvet settee.

Amanda was around the corner, washing her hands. She turned to see who had entered.

"Hi." Amanda threw her paper towel in the trash.

Jen stayed in the pink anteroom. "Hi," she said, barely above a whisper.

Except for the muted sound of the singers, they were enveloped in silence. Time slowed as Jen worked up the courage to act on her desire. She advanced on Amanda with purpose, planting her hands on Amanda's shoulders and pushing her against the wall. Ignoring the shocked look on Amanda's face, Jen leaned down and found Amanda's mouth with her own. Tentative at first, Jen quickly deepened the kiss, moaning when Amanda parted her lips. A tsunami of pleasure washed over Jen as she lost herself in Amanda's warm mouth.

Amanda, surprised that Jen was so brazen, couldn't recall ever being kissed by a woman with such strength and determination. Apparently, Jen had unleashed her carnal desire, and it was bearing down on Amanda with a crushing force. She met Jen's kiss with her own unbridled passion, instinctively rising into Jen's body, running her fingers through Jen's hair, then circling her tongue as a crescendo of craving overtook her.

They fell into an eternal embrace, one that had been waiting for them to discover, welcoming them home. They relished full lips and beating hearts, falling deeper and deeper, losing track of time and place. Their hands were buried deep into each other's hair, then moved to caress soft necks.

"So soft," Jen whispered against Amanda's lips. "I knew you would be."

"Are you sure?" Amanda asked, nibbling Jen's lower lip.

"Yes. I'm sure I want you...Need you."

"God, you turn me on," Amanda whispered, resting her hands on each side of Jen's face, exploring her lips and mouth like she had wanted to since they first met. Jen was slightly taller, and much stronger than Amanda, her fit body so powerful under her sheer, fitted blouse. She was driving Amanda over the edge with lust.

Amanda's breasts snugged up under Jen's, and the heat pouring off Jen engulfed her. She hadn't been this sexually charged in ages, throwing herself into their kiss with every ounce of energy she had. For the first time in her life, her legs felt weak, and her world spun. She was lost—unexpectedly lost in Jen. Tommy's Jen. Straight Jen. Dr. Jen Dawson. Whoever she was, Amanda wanted her. All of her.

Jen's straight world unraveled quickly in Amanda's arms. She had never felt this hot when making love with Tommy. Nothing about Amanda was the same as him. Amanda's skin was soft instead of rough. Her mouth was substantially smaller than Tommy's. Her lips fuller. Her tongue warmer. In fact, everything about Amanda was warmer. For an ice queen on the exterior, she burned hot as hell underneath.

Jen felt Amanda's breasts mashed against the underside of her own, and the sensation sent fireworks down to her toes. Or maybe it was the way Amanda was circling her tongue, then plundering her mouth. Jen looped her arms under Amanda's and wrapped them around her back. She lifted slightly, and Amanda's feet came off the floor. She was suspended, pinned to Jen in the heat of passion.

Amanda squealed with delight.

At that moment, the bathroom door opened, and Amanda's friend, Sugar, entered. "Uh-huh, ladies! It's gettin' hot in here."

Jen let Amanda drop to her feet, and they stopped, both panting and surprised.

"Y'all don't have to quit on my account. I'm just here to tinkle," Sugar said.

Amanda lay her forehead against Jen's chin. "You're something else. Not your first rodeo?"

Jen kept her arms tightly wrapped around Amanda's back, then pressed her lips to Amanda's forehead. "No. But it's been over a decade. I'd forgotten."

"Are you sure?"

"Yes."

"I was attracted to you the first night I met you—at the charity ball."

"Really? Because I was totally intimidated by you."

"Nonsense." Amanda ran her finger along Jen's jawline.

"That feels so—" Jen said, leaning into Amanda's touch.

"What would you like to do?"

"This minute, or in the future?"

"Both. You're dating a man who happens to be my work colleague and a friend. I've never been the 'other woman' in a relationship, and I've never, ever broken up an engagement."

Jen groaned, releasing Amanda when Sugar exited the stall to wash and dry her hands. Neither spoke until Sugar left.

"I'm not engaged to Tommy. And, this," Jen said, gesturing between them, "just confirmed that I can't continue to be with him, can I?"

Amanda was shocked at Jen's sudden decision, raising her hand to cup Jen's chin. "Don't make any decisions tonight. You're probably experiencing emotions you thought you left behind."

"Trust me, I didn't make this decision tonight. It will never be the same with Tommy. And, I refuse to cheat on him behind his back. For God's sake, I don't want him to hear it from someone else. I have to break it off."

"Think about it. He's a good guy," Amanda said, her eyes conveying she really meant it. "Speaking of someone else, we better go back out there. The guys will wonder what happened to us in the bathroom."

"Good idea. I'd already forgotten about them. See what you do to me?"

Amanda affectionately caressed Jen's chin with her thumb, then dropped her hand. "Okay, no PDA in front of the guys. Back to our booth —acting as platonic as possible."

"But, you rekindled something that was dormant for a long time. Can we touch each other?"

Amanda groaned in response, rolling her eyes, and they exited the restroom, walking single-file down the hall toward their booth. She swung by the bar, where the guys were eating a pizza and chatting with the bartender.

"Hey," Amanda said.

"Hi. Ready to go?" George asked.

"No. Just checking in. I see you got a pizza from Luigi's."

"Yeah. Want one?"

"Yes. I'm starved. A small pepperoni. Thanks."

"I'll take care of it."

"I'll get you some cash."

She purposefully looked over to the booth from George's angle. She could see the back, and it was high enough so that she couldn't see Jen at all.

Amanda returned to the booth, grabbed her purse, and dug out some cash for George to pay for the pizza. After giving it to him, she returned to the booth to find a very eager Jen waiting for her.

The performers were mid-song, singing seductive lyrics, really getting into it.

Amanda slid in, leg-to-leg with Jen. Jen's right hand flew to Amanda's leg, where she drew tiny circles on Amanda's thigh while listening to the music. Jen had come alive with desire and was filled with energy, so physical in every aspect of her life that wanting Amanda was no different. She wanted all of her—now.

Amanda leaned in close to Jen's ear, and whispered through her hair, "Thank you for pinning me up against the wall in the ladies' room. I've never been possessed like that before. You're very physical."

Jen squeezed Amanda's thigh. "I can't stop myself around you. Get used to it."

Amanda turned to face Jen, reaching around to smooth her blonde hair back, curling it around her ear. She ran the back of her hand down Jen's neck, admiring her tanned skin and sculpted strength. She wanted to trail her fingers across the top of Jen's breast, but that would be too much in public.

"You have beautiful skin," Amanda said.

"You have no idea how exhilarating that feels."

"I might. Not to be trite, but you just tossed napalm into my world."

Jen absorbed what Amanda was saying and doing. "Me, too. We need to slow down."

"Especially you, if for no other reason, for Tommy."

Jen sighed. "I know. A part of me still loves him, and probably always will. I just can't lie to him. About myself. About you. About anything. He deserves the truth."

"Wanting a new relationship is a huge change, much less with a woman."

"It is, but I've always known. When did you first realize you were gay?"

"When did you first realize you were smart?"

"Since birth, then?" Jen laughed, stroking Amanda's leg. "Seriously. High school?"

"No. Much earlier. I knew I wasn't interested in boys at a young age. In junior high, when all my girlfriends were excited about flirting and their first kiss with a boy, I wasn't intrigued at all. I didn't know I was attracted to girls, exactly, but I knew that boys didn't excite me."

"Hmm. Boys sort of excited me. When was it definitive?"

"It just built from there. There was never a conscious decision to move from men to women. I've never been with a man, in fact."

"Really? Isn't there a special lesbian term for that?"

Amanda laughed. "Yes. There's a lesbian term for everything. I believe you're referring to a gold star lesbian—one who's never been with a man."

"How fantastic. When did you go public with your sexual preference?"

"I think you're trying to ask me about my coming out story."

"And?" Jen sipped some wine.

Amanda ignored her, instead placing her hand on Jen's chest, sliding her fingers under the white shirt, atop Jen's lacy bra. "Your heart is beating really fast. Do you feel that?"

"Absolutely. It started at Boulevard when you were remonstrating me, and it hasn't stopped since. I think you're giving me a heart attack."

"I'm sorry." Amanda leaned in close and lightly licked Jen's neck and the underside of her chin.

Jen shivered with pleasure.

Amanda pulled back and smiled, unable to contain her excitement, despite the public setting.

"More," Jen said.

"God, you're on fire. You really *are* hot. I hope I can handle all of your energy."

"Let's get outta here."

"Slow down. We need to talk."

"About what?"

Amanda smiled. "Everything. Anything. I was going to tell you my coming out story. It's sort of boring, so maybe your heart rate will slow down. No drama or theatrics."

"I'm ready." Jen tried to blink away the sparks so she could focus.

"I was a senior in high school. My friends already knew, but my parents didn't. I'd confided in my brother shortly before, but he told me he had already figured it out. He encouraged me to tell our parents as soon as possible."

"Older or younger brother?"

"Older. Nate. Anyway, he was away at college, but he told me to tell them before they heard it from someone else."

Amanda drank some wine as Jen trailed her fingers up and down her thigh.

"I unceremoniously told them over the dinner table," Amanda recalled.

"What did they say?"

"They were stunned. It took them by surprise. They stared at each other, wondering what to do or say. What they didn't realize is that their hesitation really hurt. I guess I expected them to respond right away that they were happy for me and loved me. So, when they didn't, it hurt. They were very progressive in their thinking about everything else. And everyone else. They used to go on endlessly about young people they worked with, and how exceptional they were in this respect or that. I was never on the receiving end of that praise or admiration, though, so it hurt," Amanda said, staring at her glass, running her finger around the rim.

"I'm so sorry." Jen leaned over and kissed Amanda's temple, hoping to pull some of Amanda's disappointment out.

"As coming out stories go, mine is benign. I have plenty of friends who had it much worse. Mine is colored by layers of other feelings about my parents being so distant. They were more into each other, and their professional lives, than they were my brother and me. It seems like a family life just didn't fulfill them."

"That's so sad. I loved my family life."

"I want that someday. I plan to throw myself into it one-hundred-percent."

The bar tender appeared with their pizza, plates and napkins.

"Thanks," Amanda said.

"What's this?" Jen asked.

"Oh. I ordered a pizza from Luigi's. The guys were eating one, and it made me hungry. Are you hungry?"

"Starved. Always. What do I owe you?"

"I've got this. You can treat next time."

They dug into the pizza, silently eating for a few minutes.

"So, have your parents come around since that time?" Jen asked.

"Jack and Chloe? Not so much. Don't get me wrong. They love me, and they'd do anything for me. It's just that I see a look of sympathy on my mom's face at times. I think she feels sorry for me that I won't have a heterosexual life that's modeled after hers. As a result, she assumes I'm unhappy. What she doesn't realize is that I'd never model my life after hers anyway. I'm a warmer person than she is." Amanda wiped pizza sauce from Jen's cheek.

"I guess you'll have to *show* her that you're happy and well-adjusted. Isn't she proud of you for becoming DA?"

"Yes, of course. They're thrilled with my professional accomplishments. Don't get me wrong. They love me, and I love them. It's just that I can tell they wanted me to be heterosexual, and they don't have the emotional depth to deal with those feelings of loss."

"How many kids does Nate have?"

"Nate and Heidi have three."

"Do you get to see them often?"

"Oh yes. They live in Palo Alto, just a stone's throw from my parents' house."

"What do they do for a living?"

"Nate's a dermatologist, and Heidi is at home with the kids right now."

"Your mom can be fulfilled with grandchildren by them, I would think."

"It's more than her fulfillment. She thinks I need to have a husband and children to be fulfilled," Amanda said, eating her pizza.

"And do you? Do you want to become pregnant and give birth someday?"

Amanda turned and looked into Jen's eyes. "Yes."

Jen wasn't expecting such an emphatic response. However, she recognized Amanda's answer as a significant declaration. Jen's reaction would be remembered by Amanda for a long time, most likely defining the emotional contours of Amanda's long-term feelings for her. Jen set her pizza down and cupped Amanda's face.

"Perfect. I do, too." She smiled, searching Amanda's gold-flecked eyes for acceptance.

Tears sprang to Amanda's eyes, and she tried to blink them off, but it was too late. Jen leaned in and kissed Amanda's cheek.

"This is getting waay too heavy for an impromptu night out," Amanda whispered.

"What did you expect? We're both professionals who deal with serious stuff all day. Part of going out with someone is getting to know her better, and I feel like I know you a whole lot better. Who you really are in here," Jen said, touching Amanda's heart.

Amanda's lower lip twitched. She raised her eyes to Jen's, and there was passion behind the tears. "I never get this emotional. I must be tipsier than I thought."

"Or, I brought it out in you. Come to think of it, in all the times I've been out drinking, listening to music and eating pizza in San Francisco, I've never kissed a woman. So, it's a first for both of us."

"You *have* kissed a woman before, though, right?"

"Yes. In college. It was a brief affair, one that I was too young to understand and too scared to pursue. We never even had sex. I just didn't see myself as gay, as I understood that term back then. I was so misguided."

"I knew it. You emit a pretty strong gay signal. I picked up on it right away, so you can imagine how shocked I was when Tommy introduced you as his girl."

"At the charity ball in the ladies' room—I knew how you were looking at me, and I returned it. The first time our eyes met in the mirror, it felt right. Natural."

They finished eating, and continued listening to the music, casually holding hands under the table. The lounge began filling, however, which created too visible of an atmosphere for Amanda. Everyone had a cell phone and loved to snap pics, and she wasn't fond of seeing photos of herself on social media, cavorting at a club. More than that, it would be a disaster for Jen and Tommy.

"We should go. It's getting a little crowded in here," Amanda said.

"I agree."

As they slid out, two men in business suits walked up to them. "Hey ladies, can we buy you a drink?"

"Not tonight. Thanks," Amanda replied, heading toward George at the bar.

"Are you sure? The night is still young," one of the suits said, putting his hand over his heart and bowing.

Amanda waved over her shoulder as she walked away, Jen trailing behind her.

George and the other officer at the bar had seen it, and they smiled. They slid off their stools and greeted Amanda and Jen. "Time to go?"

"Yes. We're tired," Amanda said.

Feeling no pain, the two guys in suits followed Amanda and Jen to the bar. They watched them talk to the officers and misinterpreted the conversation as Amanda and Jen picking them up.

"Hey, what do these guys have that we don't?" the larger of the two suits slurred.

George quickly removed his bi-fold wallet and held it up to the drunk man's face. "Badges, pal. Time to back off."

The drunk man thrust his hands up in the air, and George led Amanda and Jen down the hallway to the back door. The second officer brought up the rear, glancing back at the drunk men to make sure they didn't follow.

***

Chapter 27

Hall of Justice

Tommy left Susie's office and walked through the main gallery. He squinted toward the bar, catching Nick's observant eyes. Tommy nodded goodbye, and Nick reciprocated, then busied himself making a drink. Tommy was sure that Nick would rush back to Susie's office after he left. Tommy pictured Susie watching Nick on the flat screens in her office from the security cams perched high in the corners of her gallery—Nick leaving the bar, walking through the gallery, proceeding through the locked door and coming down the long hallway to her office. *Nick on security cam video. Wouldn't that be something? Perhaps another visitor to Natasha's apartment building?* Tommy had to get a recent photo of Nick for the Computer Forensics guys.

He exited into the cool night air to a line of customers waiting to get in. This was a big night for Susie's gallery, indeed. The band was obviously popular, but Tommy found it too loud for his taste.

He walked down the street, replaying his conversation with Susie, analyzing the nuances in her clever replies. While not forthcoming, she had certainly implied that Wallace was more than capable of killing Natasha because he couldn't control his PTSD anger.

Tommy hadn't expected Susie to confess to murdering Natasha. Far from it. Rather, he had intended on sparking a conversation between Susie and Wallace by agitating her. Even though she had played it cool in her office, he hoped she was angry at Wallace, which would lead to texting or calling him. In turn, the Computer Forensics guys would record the calls and print out the texts, which might be incriminating.

He walked past the skate-boarder, who was tucked into his hidden entryway, his flimsy barricade the only shelter against the weather and passers-by. The young man was sitting on the step, a blanket around his shoulders and a lit cigarette hanging out of his mouth. He gave Tommy a menacing glare. Tommy made a mental note to talk to the patrol officers of this neighborhood to see if they were familiar with the skateboarder.

He continued down the block and crossed the street. He walked the opposite direction of his car, then circled back and walked up the sidewalk, across the street from Susie's gallery. He quickly crept up to the black sedan that had followed Susie to Legacy Manor. The unsuspecting driver was watching the art gallery entrance. Tommy opened his door and pulled the bulky man out, throwing him down on the sidewalk and planting his knee on the man's throat.

Tommy withdrew his nine-millimeter and pointed it at the man's face. "Name?"

"Albert," the man wheezed.

"Albert who?" Tommy eased up the throat pressure, so the man could talk.

"Petrov," the man choked, a Russian accent emerging.

"Albert Petro?"

"Petrov," the man said, emphasizing the "v."

"Why the fuck are you following me?"

"I'm not."

"Then who?"

"Susie. Susie Wallace."

"Why?"

"Because Mr. Ivanov asked me to investigate his daughter's death."

"Private investigator?"

"Sort of. I work for Mr. Ivanov. On private matters."

"Yeah? Where?"

"Usually in Ohio. Sometimes New York and D.C.."

"Why Susie Wallace?"

"Her husband was having affair with Natasha."

"So?"

"So, that makes her suspect in my book."

"Do whatever you want. But get in my way, and I'll arrest you for obstruction. Lay a hand on Susie Wallace, or anyone else, and I'll personally kill you," Tommy warned.

"Understood," Albert said.

Tommy jumped up and holstered his gun. He nodded goodbye to Albert and walked up the street, clicking his key fob to unlock his Charger. Once he was behind the wheel, he checked his cell phone for any messages from

Jen. None. He shook his head at her stubbornness and drove back to the Hall of Justice, scanning himself in the night entrance at the back of the building. He ran up to the second floor and scanned himself into the suite where Computer Forensics was located.

The guys working the night shift were each staring at their flat screens.

"Hi guys," Tommy said.

"Hi Tommy. What brings you in so late?"

"I'd like to see if you can pull up the cell phone of Dr. Lane Wallace. I just poked the hornet's nest of his marriage, and I'm betting he and his wife either spoke by phone or texted after I left her."

"No problem." One of the guys clicked a few buttons and pulled up a different screen. Tommy wheeled a chair over so he could see the screen.

"Let me just pull up Dr. Wallace's phone. Okay, we're going into text messages. Is there a specific person you want me to look for?"

"Yes. Susie Wallace. The wife," Tommy said.

The computer guy clicked through a couple of screens, then zeroed in on a string of texts.

"This just came through ten minutes ago. Is it what you're looking for?"

Tommy read it. "Yes."

Susie started the conversation. *WTF did you tell Tommy Vietti when you met with him?*
Where r u? I'm in bed
I told you. I have a live band at the gallery
Goodnight then

WTF did you tell Tommy?
Why?
Because he just visited me.
What did he want?
To know who killed Natasha
What did you tell him?
Nothing, but he's smart
Relax. He's just covering all his bases
I didn't get that feeling

"Perfect," Tommy said. "It worked. She's worried. I love it when a strategy works. Kindly email this chain to me, and continue to keep tabs on the conversations between Susie and Lane Wallace. Thanks man."

"No problem. Anything else?"

"Yeah. Pull up Nick Nutini in the police database."

The officer did and found several photos of him.

"Can you run these photos against the security cam footage from Natasha Farber's apartment building?"

"Sure. Might take a while."

"That's fine. I figured it would. Thanks for your help on this. Have a nice night." For the first time in this investigation, Tommy felt like he was really onto something. He left the guys to their work and drove home. It was past ten o'clock by the time he walked in the door, so he thought he'd have a night cap and catch the news.

***

The Next Day

Hall of Justice

Amanda was horrified that Tommy had IM'd her and asked that she come to his office as soon as she got to work. Visions of Jen taking charge and pushing her against the wall in the Curtain Call ladies' room kept replaying in her mind. The smell of Jen's hair. The taste of her lips. Jen's sinewy body beneath her soft blouse. The feel of Jen's breasts pressed against Amanda's own chest. The full sensation of their intimate encounter made Amanda's insides clench with desire. *Why does she have to be Tommy's girlfriend when I have this insatiable need to touch her?*

She knocked on Tommy's door and entered. "Good morning."

"Hi Amanda. Did you give it to Jen last night?" he asked.

Amanda choked and started coughing. She cleared her throat and shuffled her feet, holding up her hand for him to wait a minute. "Swallowed wrong. Sorry."

"Take your time." He gave her a quizzical look.

Amanda tried to look nonchalant. "Yes. We discussed her treatment of Dr. Wallace, and she promised she wouldn't do it again."

"I'm shocked she agreed so readily. Did she get pissed at you?"

"Initially." Amanda paced his office, unable to sit. "She stormed out of the bar and walked down the street. George and I got back in my car, and we followed her until she agreed to get in."

Tommy laughed, slapping his leg. "I *knew* it. I knew she'd think we were interfering in her physician practice. I'm glad it was you and not me. No wonder she didn't return my text or phone call last night."

"I'm sorry." Amanda felt even more guilty, if that was possible.

"Where did you go once she got in the car?"

"I took her for a little ride to my favorite bar, bought her some wine and pizza, and we hashed it out." Amanda was trying to keep the color from rising to her face, the memory of what actually transpired running like a movie clip through her mind.

"Not bad. Wine and pizza, huh? That's my go-to for calming Jen down, too."

"Oh really? Well, ahh—she agreed not to see Dr. Wallace as a patient again. And, she understood that if this case goes to trial, she'll probably have to testify."

"Was she mad about that?" Tommy asked, smiling.

Amanda was surprised that this was so entertaining for him, considering she was very carefully crafting a story that steered clear from Jen manhandling her, and Amanda being swept off her feet. "Not so much. However, she adamantly defended Dr. Wallace. She believes in him, which I find interesting, because Jen strikes me as a person with good instincts."

"She defended him, huh?"

"Adamantly."

"As it turns out, her instincts might be half right."

"What do you mean?"

He ignored her question. "How was she at the end of the night? Did she talk about me at all?"

"Okay, I think. No, we didn't talk about you. A couple of guys hit on us at the bar, which we found annoying." Amanda tried to divert the conversation.

"I'll bet. Guys hit on her all the time. She's used to it," he said, not realizing that he was insulting Amanda.

She smiled at him.

He caught himself and tried to recover. "I'm sure guys hit on you all the time, too, Amanda. But it's pretty widely known that you're gay. Good lookin' for sure, though."

Amanda laughed.

He moved on to business. "So, the reason I called you down here is to prepare a subpoena for the nursing home medical record of Maria Sangiolo, Dr. Wallace's mother-in-law."

"Why? What does she have to do with anything?"

"She might be the source of the Digoxin."

"Really? For Dr. Wallace or Susie Wallace, your ex-girlfriend?"

"Either. Apparently, I'm not the only one who thinks she has motive."

"Who else?"

"A Russian named Albert Petrov. I ran into him last night while he was tailing Susie at her gallery."

"Who's he?"

"He works for Dimitri Ivanov. His henchman. He told me he suspects Susie, so he's following her."

"Ivanov hired his own investigator?"

"Of course. That's what billionaires do. They have unlimited resources. I politely cautioned Mr. Petrov against interfering in this investigation, however."

"Good. I think I'll call Mr. Ivanov as well."

***

San Francisco Community Hospital

After fooling around with Amanda last night, Jen couldn't suppress her ridiculous smile. She'd never felt happier and was giddy with anticipation over meeting Amanda again. Emotions she hadn't experienced with Tommy sprang to life and swirled around her insides. She felt like she was on fire, her body needing to be fused to Amanda's, doing all the things that lovers do. She was smitten.

How am I going to tell Tommy? I thought I loved him once, and I still do, sort of. Will we still be friends? Can we? If I break up with Tommy, will Amanda really be there to catch me?

Feeling overwhelmed, she plopped down in a chair in the back doc room and clicked through her emails. Her brain was filled with too many thoughts, mulling over her old and new love interests.

I need a bike ride or a run. If it's windy when I leave work, I'm gonna run. If the air is calm, I'm gonna bike. Maybe I'll go across the Golden Gate—

Jen's phone beeped, interrupting her thoughts. It was a text.

Hey. Dinner? It was from Amanda. Un-fucking-canny. The woman's timing was scary.

Jen was torn. She needed exercise to clear her head, but she wanted to see Amanda in the worst way. She also had to break it off with Tommy. It was unfair—if not downright unfaithful—to spend one more second with Amanda before telling Tommy. She owed it to Tommy and their three-year relationship. She had to think. To clear her head.

I work til 5, then I need a bike ride. What time?

After ur ride?

If you're okay eating late

Yes. Can you meet me at my neighborhood place, Pacific Café on Geary and 34th?

What time?

You name it since ur biking

Seven or seven-thirty? It's on my way home. Can I wear my biking clothes?

Yes. Will you be sweaty?

Of course

Even better. See u out front

And there it was. Another meeting was scheduled. Or was it a date this time? Jen sat staring at the screen on her iPhone. She re-

read the entire exchange. Amanda needed to see Jen as much as Jen needed to see her. Amanda was even willing to bend her schedule and dine with a sweaty Jen to make it happen. She was less formal than Jen thought, which was a good sign. Hurray.

She silently vowed to talk to Tommy first thing tomorrow. Or maybe even tonight if dinner ended at a reasonable time.

Jen was dying to know if Amanda had reported to Tommy that she'd warned Jen about treating Dr. Wallace. That conversation wasn't appropriate for texting though. Jen had to hear Amanda's version in person.

***

Superior Court

"Are you kidding me?" Judge Grady yelled at Tommy in his chambers.

"No, your Honor, we'd never joke around about subpoenaing a neutral party's medical record," Amanda said. "As Detective Vietti's affidavit indicates, Mrs. Maria Sangiolo is the mother of Susie Sangiolo, and we believe Susie or her husband, Lane, obtained the Digoxin and opioids from Mrs. Sangiolo's medical supply at her nursing home room in Legacy Manor."

Tommy nodded for emphasis.

"Is this another one of your hunches, Vietti?" Judge Grady asked.

"Absolutely not. An informant, who must remain anonymous, but who is highly credible, told me that both Digoxin and fentanyl went missing from Mrs. Sangiolo's room a month ago. We need to confirm that by reading only the recent activity in her medical record."

"And, what are you hoping to prove if it's true?" Judge Grady asked.

"That Susie Sangiolo stole the meds to poison either her husband or Natasha Farber, or both, your Honor," Amanda answered.

"That sounds like a stretch to me, but maybe you have other evidence to corroborate an actual theft, in addition to a means for Susie Sangiolo to deliver the mixture to the deceased," Judge Grady said.

"We do, Judge," Tommy blurted. Amanda looked at him in surprise.

"Are you going to link it up for me, Vietti?" Judge Grady asked.

"Let's just say I'm pulling it together as we speak. You won't be disappointed."

"I'd better not be. I'm still limiting the language, so only entries of those medications can be obtained from Mrs. Sangiolo's medical record. This is a major invasion of her privacy. Why do I have this sinking suspicion that signing this subpoena is going to come back to bite me in the ass?" Judge Grady asked rhetorically, as he signed it.

Tommy and Amanda sat on their hands like two kids in the principal's office.

"Don't make me regret this." Judge Grady handed the subpoena to Amanda.

"Thank you, your Honor." Amanda tapped Tommy on the shoulder to leave.

They raced down the steps of the court to her waiting Jag. Once they were inside, Amanda let Tommy have it.

"What the fuck, Tommy?!" she screamed, setting her cell phone on the seat between them. "You're pulling it together as we speak? You told me you had incriminating text messages between Susie and Lane Wallace!"

"Well, they're getting there. I'll show them to you when we get back. If I keep poking at each one of them, I think the texts will get better."

Amanda rolled her eyes. "Do *not* embarrass me in front of Judge Grady. My reputation counts for something with the bench. If you can't prove that Susie stole her mother's Digoxin and fentanyl lozenges, then poisoned the bourbon, we can kiss a conviction goodbye."

"I don't disagree with you, but these things take time and creativity."

She lay her head back on the leather head rest and pressed her eyes shut. *Even if Susie stole the meds, how are we going to prove that she dumped them into the bottle of bourbon? Impossible!*

"Your phone is lighting up with texts." Tommy picked it up, looked at the screen and handed it to her.

Amanda's eyes flew open as she quickly grabbed it. She had a surge of anxiety, praying they weren't risqué texts from Jen. When she looked at her screen, though, it was only her Assistant District Attorney, Jeremy, who was asking for her reaction to a plea deal that opposing counsel offered during a break in his trial. She replied.

"Emergency?" Tommy asked, observing her dramatic reaction.

"No. I was expecting something like this from Jeremy during his trial. It's important to him."

***

San Francisco Community Hospital

Jen immersed herself in her work, relieved to be thinking about something other than the murder investigation or her feelings for Amanda.

She concentrated on what was in front of her, meticulously examining each patient, taking more time than she usually did to talk with the patient and family, then critically analyzing diagnostic results, methodically ruling out potential diseases or injuries, finally making her diagnosis. She was beyond thorough as she moved through her day, but still, the need to set things straight with Tommy ate at her conscience. No matter how hard she tried to concentrate on the complex tasks before her, she was hopelessly distracted by the wrecking ball that was swinging closer and closer to her head—saying goodbye to Tommy.

By five o'clock, Jen's nerves and muscles were twitching with the need for exercise and release. She changed out of her scrubs and into her jeans and sweatshirt for the drive back to her yellow row house in the Sunset District, no doubt awash in the intense west sun as it fell into the Pacific.

She walked into her place, dumped her gear, and dug her biking clothes out of her clean laundry basket. She put on her padded shorts, followed by insulated leggings and a couple of layers on top. The misty Bay air would seep into her skin when she rode, making her cold and tired before she met her twenty-mile goal. She tied her clip-on bike shoes and carried her ultra-light Specialized bike down the steps of her house, preparing herself to bike down the Great Highway, so she could hop up to the Golden Gate Bridge and bike across to the Marin Headlands.

As she pedaled, she visualized successfully completing the triathlon, daydreaming about how good it would feel to conquer the challenge. The course began with a one-point-five-mile swim from Alcatraz, across the Bay to a pier in the Marina District.

After the ice bath in the Bay, her body would be fighting to keep her core temperature up, in addition to burning calories on the bike ride. The next leg was a twelve-mile bike ride across the Golden Gate Bridge to Mill Valley. The bridge usually was covered in fog, which meant that biking through the droplets would chill her to the bone. Her packets of protein, in addition to liquid mixes of electrolytes in her water bottles, would have to fuel her.

At the end of the bike ride, she'd peel off her biking tights and change into her running shoes for fourteen miles of hell, known as

Dipsea Trail, which coursed through the Muir Woods up to Stinson Beach. Smelling of pungent eucalyptus and dappled with giant redwoods and sequoias, the trail was a testament to environmental preservation. For the runners, however, it would be an assault on their muscles, containing ominous inclines named *Dynamite, Cardiac* and *Insult Hill.*

She was hell-bent on a mission to finish the triathlon, though, hopefully placing in the top echelon.

***

Chapter 28

Hall of Justice

Tommy drove over to Legacy Manor with his court-signed subpoena and served it on Karen, the Director. He paced the small waiting area, waiting for the staff to copy the pages from Mrs. Sangiolo's medical record regarding the Digoxin and fentanyl lozenges. He hoped to hell that Susie wouldn't arrive and see him there. His presence would be difficult to explain without tipping her off.

As Tommy found himself again weighing the pros and cons of smoking to help pass the time during mundane detective work, an administrative assistant brought the photocopied record out to him. He raced down the steps, got into his Charger and drove back to his office.

He tore into the package once he was sitting at his desk, reading the pages about Mrs. Sangiolo's medications. When he finished, he IM'd Amanda to join him, and she arrived a few minutes later.

"What?" she asked, a cappuccino in her hand as she walked through his door.

"I'm reading Mrs. Sangiolo's nursing home record, and it clearly states in here that her Digoxin went missing. They had to order an entire month's prescription because no one could find it," Tommy said.

"When did *that* happen?"

"A few weeks before Natasha died."

"What about an opioid?"

"It doesn't say any were missing, only that Mrs. Sangiolo had been experiencing more pain, so the nurse caring for her asked for an increase in dosage for lozenges to make Mrs. S comfortable." Tommy handed Amanda the sheet of paper on which the nurse's note was written.

"Which makes sense," Amanda said. "If Susie stole the fentanyl lozenges out of her mother's mouth, after the nurse left the room, then they wouldn't be missing from the medical supply, but her mother would be deprived of the pain relief. Yuck. We should probably charge her with a crime against her mother, too."

"Of course, Susie would have to melt down the lozenges into a liquid, so she could pour them into the bourbon. You'd think it would taste funny."

"Maybe fentanyl lozenges are tasteless."

"I doubt it. I bet I could tell if someone dropped that shit into my whiskey."

"I think you should be on the lookout. How did Susie sneak into Natasha's apartment?"

"Who said she snuck? Knowing Susie, she probably waltzed right through the front door —"

"So you have her on security cam footage?"

Tommy slapped his forehead. "Fuck! No. I didn't ask the guys to look for her. I guess I air-balled that one. I need to email them a photo of her. I have the one of her with Dr. Wallace on their sailboat that I took from his bookshelf. I sent the original to evidence, but I took a pic of it with my cell. Let me just find it," he said, scrolling through his photos.

"If Susie turns up on the security cam footage of Natasha's apartment, I'd be very interested in hearing what her explanation is. And if she was there when Natasha was at work, then it would be incriminating."

"Found it," Tommy muttered, and he emailed it to the computer guys. "She was trying to poison her husband—that's what she was doing."

"Silly me, I was thinking she was trying to poison Natasha."

"Hell no. You came up with this theory in the first place. She was after her cheating husband, so she could live happily ever after with her new squeeze, Nick Nutini."

"Susie has a new squeeze?"

"Yeah. I met him at her gallery last night."

"Well played, Tommy."

"I'm not done yet."

"You're on a roll. We need to button up this investigation, so I can convince a jury that Susie was trying to kill either Dr. Wallace or Natasha, or both. I guess I owe you twenty bucks."

"I'll get what you need," he said, energized now. "You can buy me a drink after we make the arrest."

***

Later that day

Tommy was about to call Dr. Wallace when Lobby Security buzzed him, indicating Mr. and Mrs. Ivanov were present.

"Fuck me," he said under his breath, not expecting them. "Tell them I'll be right down." He quickly IM'd Amanda, asking her if he could bring them to her conference room.

She replied that he could, and she would meet them there.

Tommy collected the Ivanovs after they passed through security, shaking their hands and taking them to the elevator, where they rode it to the third floor.

He settled them in Amanda's conference room and went to find her.

She came down the hallway and walked in, taking control of the meeting. After shaking their hands, she saw that they looked worse than when she had seen them a few days ago.

"How are you holding up?" she asked.

Just this simple question brought them to tears. After wiping bloodshot eyes and blowing noses, Dimitri spoke. "Not very well. What have you discovered?"

"We're actively working the case, Mr. Ivanov, so we can't discuss it. We're ethically required to keep evidence and investigation matters confidential," Amanda said.

They looked shocked, then angry.

"What do you mean? We're her parents," Dimitri said.

"We know that. We're working this case very hard for you, and for Natasha. Detective

Vietti and I have been doing this job for over twenty years, and we know that keeping the investigation confidential is paramount to success."

"It's been four days since our daughter died, Ms. Hawthorne. "I think we're entitled to hear something. Like the autopsy report," Dimitri said.

Amanda didn't want to throw back that the last time they met, the Ivanovs left the building, spoke to a news reporter and ended up hitting the reporter in the face. Nor did she tell them that Kip Moynihan had filled out a police report and wanted the SFPD to file charges. Amanda had successfully quashed that attempt.

"Of course. You're absolutely entitled to go over the autopsy report. Tommy will get it, and we'll walk you through it."

"It's in my office. I'll be right back," Tommy said.

After Tommy left, Amanda looked Dimitri square in the eye. "I understand you have a Mr. Albert Petrov investigating this matter as well. He crossed paths with Detective Vietti last night."

Dimitri didn't confirm or deny.

"Running a separate investigation is your prerogative, but it's not necessary. We're very thorough here. I will tell you, Mr. Ivanov, that if Mr. Petrov obstructs this investigation or threatens to harm, or actually harms, any person in this investigation, we won't hesitate to arrest and charge him, which would, of course lead to you," Amanda said.

"So far, Mr. Petrov reported to me that Detective Vietti isn't as smart as you think he is. Petrov had this figured out in a day. Vietti is four days into it and still hasn't arrested anyone," Dimitri said.

"That's because we have rules of evidence and laws that we have to follow. I'm confident that our results will be solid. Just understand where we're coming from with respect to interference," she said, politely smiling.

"I understand your rules, Ms. Hawthorne. Now, you need to understand mine. If your way doesn't pan out, I'm taking matters into my own hands."

"I wouldn't do that if I were you. You're not above the law, Mr. Ivanov."

He looked at her wrist. "Is that an Omega watch?"

She blushed. "Yes. Why do you ask?"

"I know government officials can't afford such luxuries, so I'm curious how you came by it."

"I don't know what you're implying, but now isn't the time or place."

"Very well." He shrugged.

Tommy chose that moment to re-enter the conference room with the autopsy report.

He set a copy in front of the Ivanovs and explained the bruise on Natasha's head most likely was from the fall. He also pointed out the bruising on her arms, which they both attributed to Blake. Unfortunately, Tommy couldn't correct them, because that would open an ugly can of worms about her lover, Dr.

Wallace, and whether Tommy considered him a suspect. It was frustrating as hell, but Tommy had to restrain himself from telling them everything he knew, especially since his current plan was to lay a trap for Susie and Wallace.

"Do you know what you're doing?" Dimitri asked, openly angry.

"Yes," Tommy said. "Can you please just trust me that I'm working in your best interest and the best interests of Natasha's memory by keeping my investigative work confidential? I want to solve this investigation into her death as much as you do. It's not going to help if you hire your own investigator. I had a chat with Albert Petrov last night."

"The hell!" Dimitri thundered, pounding the table. "You can't possibly know what we're going through."

"That's true. I'm sorry. Likewise, neither you nor Mr. Petrov have the expertise that I do in these matters."

Mr. Ivanov glowered at Tommy.

Tommy held his stare.

The Ivanovs finally gathered their belongings and bolted out the door without even saying goodbye.

It hurt that they didn't trust Amanda and Tommy, but there was nothing they could do.

"Guess I should go call Mayor Woo," Amanda said, sighing.

"I'll tell Ryan," Tommy said.

"I think Ivanov was on the verge of trying to bribe me."

"What? How?"

"He noticed my watch and said people on a government salary couldn't afford it. I shut him down before he offered to buy me something. He probably thinks I'm on the take. Dumb shit."

"Want me to have a talk with him?"

"Not yet. Let's see where this goes."

***

Later

Tommy grabbed his blue blazer from the back of his chair and left the building. He drove down to the St. Francis Yacht Club, where Dr. Wallace had indicated he had a slip for his thirty-one-foot Beneteau.

Tommy walked the pier, admiring the variety of sailboats, smelling the fresh air and watching the seagulls swoop in for food. He loved walking the piers when he had time to kill and realized he hadn't been down here in a few months. It was mid-summer, the high season for sailing.

He reached Wallace's impressive boat, named *Sangiolo Sun,* and wasn't surprised to see Wallace on the deck, toolkit nearby, screwing some teak trim into place. The strip was freshly sanded and stained. Wallace looked comfortable in a pair of shorts, a U.S. Army t-shirt and his sentimental Giants cap.

"Hi Doc. Beautiful day, isn't it?" Tommy asked.

When Dr. Wallace looked up from his work and saw Tommy, his face fell. Tommy knew why. Anytime he paid a visit after a formal interview, the witness knew it was because Tommy had more questions. And Wallace was no dummy.

"Hello, Detective. Are you coming aboard?"

"Do I have your permission?"

"Of course. Just remove your shoes."

Tommy complied, removing his socks, too, so he wouldn't slip on the smooth boat surface. He shed his tie and blazer as well, since the temperature was in the mid-seventies and the sun was hot. He didn't have a cap, but he was grateful for his sunglasses as he crawled on the deck to sit by Wallace, watching him work.

He again found himself wishing he smoked. He could be preoccupied with lighting his cigarette and taking a few drags while Wallace squirmed, wondering what Tommy knew. Alas, he simply had to rely on silence to make Wallace uncomfortable.

"Did you come down here to get a tan, or are you going to talk to me?" Wallace asked.

"You're a smart man, Dr. Wallace. I think you know why I'm here."

"I agree with the first part of your question, but I'm not a mind reader."

Wallace wasn't the chatty type, and he sure as hell wasn't intimidated by authority.

"I just need you to answer one question for me, Doc."

"What's that?" Wallace asked, still concentrating on screwing in the teak piece.

"When did you figure out that your wife killed Natasha, when she was actually trying to kill you?"

Wallace stopped mid-turn with his screwdriver, but quickly recovered and began driving the screw in once again, this time with more force. "Really? You think I'm going to fall for the 'when did you quit beating your wife' question?"

Tommy could hear the strain in Wallace's voice. "Was it when you were lying in your hospital bed and learned your lab results?"

Wallace was silent.

"Was it when Susie visited you at the hospital and saw that she almost killed you? In addition to Natasha? Did she ever apologize for killing Natasha?"

Wallace stopped turning again and stared blankly at a seagull swimming on the water.

"Or, was it later, when you returned home? Maybe Susie confessed to you. Told you how pissed she was that you were still alive, but Natasha had died because she made the mistake of drinking your bourbon. *Your* bourbon. The bottle you bought for *yourself*, but Natasha dipped into."

"If you want to charge someone with murder, charge me," Wallace finally said.

"Why?"

"I killed Natasha to keep her from telling Susie about our affair. I purposefully drank some poisoned bourbon to make it look like Blake did it." Unfortunately, he was a shitty actor, so his delivery sounded hollow.

Tommy laughed in response to the pseudo-confession.

"Do you always laugh when someone confesses murder?"

"Only when the acting is that bad, and I know he's taking the rap for someone else."

"I did it, okay?" Wallace said, with more emotion this time.

"Nice try. Why are you covering up for her?"

There was a long silence as Wallace returned to his task, attempting to restore some reality to his current predicament. "Angelina needs a mother to raise her."

"Personally? I'd choose a father to raise me instead of a mother who committed murder."

Wallace remained silent, but his shoulders shook. Then, the sobs that he was trying so hard to contain let loose.

Tommy sat patiently, looking the other direction, so Wallace could cry like a man. He knew he wouldn't crack, his resolve demonstrated by his education and service in Iraq. Tommy wanted Wallace to think about a few things, though.

"Did you ever play that game in science class in junior high?" Tommy asked. "The one where everyone stands in a circle, holding hands, and lets an electrical current run through them? If one person breaks the handhold, then the last person gets shocked."

"No."

"That's what I have here. You and Susie holding hands, hoping the electrical current will run through your bodies, perhaps ending in a shock to Blake. I think you and Susie were simply biding your time, hoping I'd charge

Blake with murder. Well, I'm not going to. Instead, I'm going to charge *both* you and Susie, then split you up and interrogate each of you. When you're both facing life in prison for murder, and conspiracy to commit murder, we'll see who talks first. How would Angelina feel if you both went to prison?"

Wallace didn't reply.

"Do you think Susie is going to go to prison? I don't. I think she'll fight it, and it will become a huge trial. It will be all over the news, and the coverage will impact Angelina for the rest of her life. Your daughter will never know who did it. She'll think both of her parents are murderers," Tommy said, going in for the kill.

Wallace still didn't reply.

"Can you live with that, Dr. Wallace? Ruining your daughter's life? Her wondering whether you're a murderer, when you and I both know you're not?"

Wallace cried, burying his face in his hands.

"I have the proof I need," Tommy said, standing. "I was just hoping you'd work with me, so I could put in a good word for cooperation, and we could try to keep it from turning into a media circus."

Wallace abandoned his project and sobbed into his hands.

"I'll leave you alone with your thoughts. I put my name and phone number in your contacts list on your cell phone while it was in my possession, and you know where I work. I expect to hear from you later today."

Tommy got up and crawled to the edge of the boat, jumped down on the pier and put his socks and shoes on again. He left Wallace to his dilemma and returned to his car.

On his way back to the Hall of Justice, Tommy detoured to Mama Mia's Restaurant to eat an early dinner. There was a line at the front door, as per usual, so he entered through the kitchen, looking for Tina, but didn't see her. A few people in the kitchen did a double-take at his holster and gun, but the *sous* chef knew him and waved.

Tommy pushed through the swinging doors and found Tina and Cy, and a few of Cy's friends, laughing and talking in the family booth. Thank God for some normalcy in his life. He was grateful for family.

***

Chapter 29

That evening

Amanda joined a line of people that stretched half a block from Pacific Café toward Lincoln Park Golf Course. She had selected the establishment because it was only a fifteen-minute walk from her house on El Camino Del Mar in the Sea Cliff neighborhood, and it was her favorite seafood restaurant in the city. She had walked over with George, while the other security detail drove her car. They insisted she would want a ride home after dinner, even though she had protested.

She was in line for only a few minutes when Jen arrived on her bike. Jen quickly disengaged her feet from the toe clips and hopped off, rolling her bike next to Amanda on the sidewalk.

"Thanks for meeting me here," Amanda said, smiling.

"Yeah," Jen said, catching her breath and stretching her legs. She was fully clad from head-to-toe in biking armor. She steadied her bike between them and slowly peeled off her gear. They didn't even bother trying to hug through the bike.

Jen regarded Amanda as she removed her helmet, sunglasses and gloves, and experienced the same jolt of attraction she had the prior night.

"I'm excited to try your restaurant. I hope I'm not underdressed."

Amanda laughed, appraising Jen in her long biking tights and red jacket. "You look fantastic in your biking clothes. I feel honored to be seen with you."

Jen blushed as she hooked her helmet to the handle bar, then stashed her gloves in it. "Thanks."

"How was your ride? Where did you go?"

"It was terrific. Across the bridge, over to the Marin Headlands. I have a twenty-mile loop and it was perfect." Jen enjoyed a long drink from her water bottle.

"Tell me about your bike."

"It's my favorite."

"How many do you have?"

"A few. Four to be exact, but each is for a specific purpose. This is a road bike."

"Impressive. Four bikes? You really are a beast, aren't you?"

"I don't know about that, but I'll take it as a compliment. I sort of have to work out to clear my mind."

"Uh-huh."

"If I could deal with life and not work out, I would. But I can't. I need the release, so I take care of it."

Amanda inclined her head. "I understand."

Curiosity and desire stirred in Jen's chest. Did Amanda mean what Jen thought she meant? If Amanda were a guy, Jen would know what to say and do, but since Amanda was an incredibly beautiful and sexy woman, Jen was at a loss for how to respond. Fortunately, she was saved by the restaurant hostess offering them free wine to help them pass the time on the sidewalk.

"I'd love that right now, but I better finish my water bottle before I drink any alcohol."

"Do you mind if I have one?

"Please, go ahead. I'll catch up with you after I rehydrate."

Amanda accepted her glass from the hostess. "They've been doing this for forty years. Keeps the customers happy." She raised her glass to Jen's water bottle, and they drank.

"I hope you're not self-conscious, dining out with me. The gay DA—with security wherever I go." She tossed a look over to the guys leaning against her car, which was parked across the street.

"Never. Get over yourself."

Amanda laughed genuinely for the first time that day. "I love that you're sassy to me. And standing before me in tights—" Her eyes flashed with mischief.

Jen didn't have any trouble interpreting that message. "Did you have a busy day?"

"Too busy. There are always lots of twists and turns during an investigation. Things never go the way you think they will."

"Did Tommy ask about our meeting?" Jen asked, in reference to their conversation the night before at Boulevard.

"Of course. I gave him a neutral report that reflected favorably on you," Amanda said, touching Jen's forearm. "You know how I feel about him. We've worked together a long time."

"I don't want to hurt him."

"Neither do I."

"What are we going to do?"

"We should take the honorable route and tell him. It's your choice, but the sooner, the better, if you ask me."

"It's just so hard. I'm afraid he'll end up hating both of us. I've betrayed him."

"You've done no such thing! We didn't make love," Amanda stressed, maintaining her grasp on Jen's arm.

"Not valid, Amanda. I've been thinking about you, daydreaming about you, and kissing you. I think that's betrayal."

"Thank you, but I don't think it's technically betrayal yet."

"So, daydreaming about having sex with someone isn't a betrayal?"

"No. It has to be physical."

"Interesting. How about holding hands then?"

Amanda laughed, then raised her eyebrow, indicating she didn't think so.

"Okay, I can see you allow yourself quite a bit of latitude in this area. How about kissing?"

"Depends."

"On what?"

"The type."

"Explain that!"

"Well, a few pecks here and there aren't sexual. But, a deep, wet, sloppy kiss that goes on forever, driving you both wild? Yeah, now we're getting into betrayal."

"Fascinating. So, life outside the Halls of Justice isn't so black and white, huh?"

"What's that supposed to mean?"

"You struck me as a ruled-based person, but I'm discovering you have different boundaries for different situations."

"Am I supposed to take offense? Are you accusing me of situational ethics?"

"Not at all." Jen held up her hands. "I'm just getting to know you."

"Well, back to Tommy. I don't think you've betrayed him. We haven't made love."

Jen regarded Amanda, letting her statement hang in the air. "Breaking up with a guy, after you've found someone else, always seems like betrayal."

"You're right. He's going to explode. Should we wait until this investigation is over?"

"Yes," Jen blurted, then cleared her throat. "I mean, I think so. I predict he'll want some space—from both of us."

"Do you think he'll leave his job? The city even?"

"He could, but his family is here. He *proposed* to me, Amanda. He thinks we're getting married at some point. This," she said, gesturing between Amanda and her, "is going to come as a complete shock."

"I know, I know. He loves you"

"It's so confusing, because I still have feelings for him. I'll always care for him. But—now that I've—It doesn't compare—"

"Yes?" Amanda pressed.

"To what I feel with you."

"This has to be pretty emotional for you, too. It's turning into a whirlwind romance."

Jen opened her mouth to respond, but the hostess arrived, informing them she had a booth for two. They eagerly snapped it up, and Jen padlocked her bike to a lamp-post in front of the restaurant. They were seated in a dark, cozy booth, hidden in the far corner, away from prying eyes.

Since it was Amanda's restaurant, she was familiar with the wine list and ordered a bottle of chardonnay from Sonoma County. She also asked the waiter to bring fresh grilled snapper dinners in to-go boxes to the officers on the street.

Jen took in the décor, a sort of dark, burnt-orange color, with subdued lighting, including large, suspended globes throughout the restaurant that cast an orange glow. There was an open kitchen, which added a homey touch, instilling confidence in quality.

Jen unzipped her red biking jacket and lay it on the seat beside her. Next came her long-sleeved wool zip-up that she removed over her head, revealing a tight, long-sleeved compression shirt as her base layer. It accentuated every curve on her.

Amanda watched and admired as Jen removed her clothes, a crooked smile on her face. "What are you wearing under the black compression shirt?"

"A tank and a sports bra. I apologize if I stink."

Amanda laughed. "No one's ever said that to me. No, I cannot smell you from here. But I'm admiring your body."

Jen blushed.

"How are things at the hospital?" Amanda asked.

"Everyone is still freaked out, speculating on whether Dr. Wallace killed Natasha. He's not there to defend himself, so people assume things, you know?"

"How do you respond to them?"

"I mostly just listen. I know stuff that I can't share because I was his treating physician. So, I remind them that, no matter how thin the pancake, there are always two sides."

Amanda laughed.

"What?"

"I like that saying. Were you a trial attorney in your former life?"

"Stick with me. We'll go places."

The waiter appeared and uncorked the bottle, pouring them each a glass. He asked Amanda how she'd been, recognizing her from previous meals.

After the waiter departed, Amanda asked, "What do you secretly believe?"

"About what?"

"The case, of course." The edges of her mouth curled.

"It's a case of two angry lovers, isn't it? Lane didn't want Natasha to rat him out to his wife. Blake was psycho-jealous that Natasha dumped him. One of them poisoned her with prescription meds. Lane has access to the meds, so naturally became a suspect. Lane told me that he shared his lab results with Tommy, though, so you know what was in his system. The presence of those drugs in Lane's body isn't consistent with him trying to poison his lover. No physician would purposefully take those meds in combination. So, my money is on Blake."

Amanda leaned back against the dark wooden booth as she listened, extending her arms and resting her hands on the seat. Her V-neck wrap top stretched open with her arms, revealing black lace under the neckline. Jen's eyes followed the outline of the lace, hovering above Amanda's breasts, then followed the wrap down as it hugged her slender body. She watched Amanda breathe, the gentle rise and fall of her chest a hypnotic cadence, her curls falling over her collarbones, framing her face. She was positively gorgeous.

Jen's appreciative stare wasn't lost on Amanda, who found Jen's eyes as soon as she raised them past Amanda's breasts. It was as if they were already swept up in passion, the way their eyes drank in each other.

Jen felt herself blushing for the second time that evening, but not out of embarrassment. Out of desire.

Amanda returned Jen's smile slowly, knowingly, experienced in seducing a woman. "I like where you're going with your analysis. Please continue."

The double entendre of Amanda's prompt wasn't lost on Jen. She found herself reveling in the freedom to explore her true needs.

"Uh-huh. This is where the pieces don't fit. Blake would have to acquire Digoxin and an opioid without a prescription, then slip it to Natasha without a struggle or her knowledge. He no longer lives with her, so how would he administer the deadly mix? Those two possibilities are still open in my mind, so I'm hoping you and Tommy can turn up some evidence."

"We always do. No matter how hard they try, there's always a trail, especially since security cameras are everywhere these days. Incriminating evidence is easier to obtain."

The waiter arrived and topped off their wine glasses. "Are you ready to order."

"What do you recommend?" Jen asked.

"The salmon," Amanda and the waiter responded in unison.

"Okay, count me in."

"Two grilled salmon filets," Amanda said. They ordered their sides and the waiter disappeared.

Amanda held up her glass of wine. "To on-going friendship, no matter how the Farber case turns out."

"I'll drink to that." Jen raised her glass.

"I've come to admire your loyalty to your colleague. It's a character trait, the way you've stuck up for him."

"I never thought I'd hear you say that. Maybe he wasn't trying to deceive you after all, huh?"

"He's been cooperative and informative."

"Very guarded words, Amanda. Not sharing your theory with me?"

Amanda liked the way her name sounded when Jen said it. "It's important to keep the details confidential. Leaks can ruin an otherwise solid investigation."

"I'm confident I could pry it out of you—if I needed to." Jen swirled her wine.

"Whoa. Pretty bold statement for a newbie."

"Guilty as charged. Nonetheless, I bet I could get you to talk in thirty, no—*twenty*, minutes."

"Not unless you played dirty and drugged me."

"Ha. The invincible District Attorney. I'm not talking about drugging you. I have other tricks up my sleeve."

"Are they dangerous?" Amanda's right eyebrow shot up.

"Of course not."

"Are you going to tell me what they are?"

"No. Leaks could ruin the element of surprise."

"I could threaten to have you arrested."

"You could do it yourself if you had handcuffs."

Amanda laughed, running her finger around the rim of her glass, considering that very possibility as she stared at Jen.

"I really enjoyed myself at the Curtain Call," Jen finally said.

"So did I."

"Someone is blushing, even though you told me you never do."

"When did I tell you *that*?"

"In the booth at the Curtain Call—when we were, ah, fooling around and talking." Jen's heart was beating as loud as a timpani as she spoke about their last encounter.

"I can't remember half the stuff I said at the Curtain Call."

"Why? I thought you had a good memory."

"I do, when it's not impaired by alcohol or attraction."

"Attraction?" Jen fished.

"Admission. I was really into you, so I wasn't listening to what you were saying as closely as I should have been.

"Are you listening to what I'm saying right now?"

"Yes, even though I'm very distracted by your charisma."

"I'm flattered beyond belief."

"Come on. This can't be the first time you've heard that. You have a mirror at home, right?"

It was Jen's turn to laugh. "Of course. *Men* have hit on me. I've just never heard a woman say that to me. It's more flattering than a guy, because I think women are more critical of each other."

"Or, maybe it's more meaningful now that you've realized you're gay. As soon as I met you, I was awestruck."

"Thank you." Jen looked at Amanda, and saw her guarded veil drop, allowing Jen a peek into Amanda's soul, where heat simmered. Jen got the distinct feeling that Amanda rarely allowed anyone such a glimpse into her true feelings. She usually conveyed simple self-assurance. While Jen considered Amanda's confidence an attractive trait, she knew there had to be so much more to her. Their silent exchange was broken when the waiter arrived with the first course—salmon bisque soup.

"Sorry to interrupt ladies," he said, looking back and forth at the women who seemed locked in a trance. "I have your first course."

They both ate, and Jen was delighted with Amanda's choice. She broke off a slice of sourdough bread and swirled the end in her cup of soup. Starved from her twenty-mile bike ride, Jen ate with gusto. Not long after they finished their soup, the waiter arrived with their salmon plates. Jen focused on eating. Politely. But eating.

"I can't finish this. Would you like the rest of mine?" Amanda asked.

"Seriously? That'd be great. I'm starved."

Amanda transferred her salmon to Jen's plate and swirled her wine as she watched Jen eat. Jen chewed happily, in a food daze as she watched Amanda watch her.

"I love your healthy appetite. Too many women pick at their food, attempting to stay skinny. I don't understand it. Food was meant to be enjoyed."

"I agree," Jen said between bites. "I wish I could actually enjoy it, but I tend to be a person who eats more for the energy than taste. Maybe it's a factor of my job. I only get so much time to eat, so I have to make efficient use of it."

"Uh-huh," Amanda said, enjoying the moment.

"That was delicious. Thank you for inviting me here."

"I'm relieved you liked my secret spot."

Jen smiled. Her head was swimming, and she felt intoxicated in Amanda's presence.

"We should pay and give up our table. I'm in the mood for a walk."

"Me, too."

They settled the check, Jen picking it up, except for the security detail, which Amanda covered.

"Mind if I use the ladies' room first?" Jen asked.

"Not at all. Let me show you where it is. Lots of character in there."

They went to the opposite corner of the restaurant, and entered what Jen assumed would be a broom-closet bathroom. She was pleasantly surprised when they stepped into a cozy space with a low ceiling. It was freshly painted white with pink accents, including a small vanity and sink to their left. It was a single stall, so Jen went in first. The restaurant had painted over the graffiti, but had decided to frame the best quotes. The one staring Jen in the face was, "Women have many faults. Men only have two: everything they say, and everything they do!"

Jen burst into laughter.

"What?" Amanda inquired from the vanity.

"The framed graffiti quote in the restroom."

"Oh, forgot about that."

When they emerged, Amanda said goodbye to their server, and they exited into the damp evening air coming off the ocean. Jen unlocked her bike from the post, and they walked comfortably in silence, George several feet behind them, and the other security in the car.

"Let me show you my neighborhood," Amanda said.

"Okay."

"The guys will follow us."

"Do you think they suspect anything?" Jen nodded back to them.

"I doubt it. They know you're dating Tommy, so they probably think we're just becoming good friends." Amanda checked her Omega. "It's still early, so maybe you can see my place."

"I don't know. I have an early shift tomorrow. What will the guys think?"

"Don't overthink it. Women can be friends, too, you know."

"Okay. Maybe a quick tour."

"You'll like it. I promise," Amanda said, looping her hand through Jen's arm. As they passed Lincoln Golf Course, Amanda told Jen about the time she played golf there with the rock band Santana. Carlos wasn't there, but his band members were.

***

Chapter 30

Sea Cliff

Amanda led Jen down 30ᵗʰ Avenue, into the exclusive Sea Cliff neighborhood, where the multi-million-dollar homes each had a view of the Golden Gate. They angled down curved streets to El Camino Del Mar, where they turned right, appreciating a sweeping view of the gleaming bridge as the setting sun shone off it. The evening coastal fog would soon be crawling up the cliff, draping its cloak over the neighborhood.

"This is a swanky neighborhood. Waay out of my budget range," Jen said.

"I'm very fortunate to live here," Amanda replied, but didn't explain further.

"I'm glad the China Beach is public. I usually swim there, just down the road. I was there a few nights ago, after I got home from retrieving my car from the impound lot."

"You went alone?"

"Yes, but there were people walking the beach, and a few surfing and swimming."

"I'd be happy to be a lifeguard for you. There are rip currents and sharks out there, you know."

Jen laughed. "I've been in a rip current before. I know how to swim parallel to the beach to get out of it. But, you're always welcome to join."

"No swimming in the Pacific for me. It's fucking freezing."

"Wear a wetsuit. I do."

"Of course, you do. I'm not a jock, Jen. I just do yoga in my basement."

"You're in very good shape, though." Jen cast a sidelong glance at Amanda.

They reached Amanda's hedge row and gated front yard. Jen watched as Amanda pressed in a security code and opened the thick wooden door into a small front yard and cobblestone walkway to her front door.

"Thanks for following us home," Amanda said to George.

"Our pleasure. See you in the a.m.. Same time?" he asked.

"Yes, thanks. Have a good night."

George got in their unmarked police car, while the other officer returned Amanda's car to her garage.

Amanda's tan three-story was a classic Edwardian architecture—stucco siding white ornamental accents, a garage leading beneath the house. The house was taller than it was wide, tucked in fence-to-fence between close neighbors. Jen guessed that the upper stories had breathtaking views of the Golden Gate Bridge.

She rested her bike against the house and removed her panier from the back wheel. It contained a cosmetics bag and a change of clothes. "Will my bike be safe outside?"

"Ah, no. Bring it inside my foyer." Amanda opened her front door.

Jen easily lifted the bike and set it inside. Amanda flipped a few light switches, and they settled Jen's bike on the far wall. She took Jen by the hand and led her through the living room into her upscale kitchen. Everything was sleek and expensive, from the Wolf stove to the quartz countertops.

"Amanda, this is a beautiful house. How do you afford this on a government salary?"

"I don't. I have incredibly wealthy parents who don't know what to do with their money. They have trusts and corporations, and are slowly transferring their assets to my older brother and me during their lifetimes. I think one of my dad's corporations owns this house. He's very clever."

"Is he a businessman or a lawyer?"

"The latter, in Silicon Valley. My mother owns a tech company. They live in Hillsborough."

"Lucky you."

"I'm lucky in some respects. In others, not so much."

"Understood." Jen recalled their earlier conversation about Chloe being disappointed.

"Something to drink? Wine?" Amanda offered.

"Maybe water. I'm still rehydrating, and I have to bike home."

"I have extra bedrooms and bathrooms. You could always stay if you like. I'm going to have a glass of wine."

Jen looked at Amanda again. Her offer was very tempting, but Jen wanted to stay sharp. The last thing she needed was a drunken romp that she'd regret. As much as she wanted to pursue her feelings for Amanda, she had some self-respect in the dating department. And, tomorrow was another work day.

"Just water. And maybe a quick shower?"

"Of course. I'll show you to my guest bath. You'll love the shower. Follow me." She led Jen down a hall and turned on the lights to a sizeable marble-floored bath with a full shower and vanity. Jen immediately noticed a dragonfly decorating theme on the hand towels and other accents.

"This is gorgeous. I'll be quick. I just don't want to get a chill from having a sweaty body."

"Yes," Amanda said, checking out Jen again. "There are Aveda products in the shower. Help yourself. Do you need clothes. A robe maybe?"

"No. I have some in my panier." Jen set it on the floor.

"Quite the girl scout, aren't you?"

"Not so much."

"I'll leave you to it, then," Amanda said, reluctant to leave. She trailed her finger down Jen's arm and across her wrist.

Jen wanted to invite Amanda to shower with her, but it was too soon. She was teetering on the edge of seduction, but she couldn't close the deal—not with Tommy still on her mind. Amanda was vibrant and sexy, calling out to Jen, but her head hadn't caught up to her heart. Her head was struggling over saying goodbye to Tommy.

Jen twined her fingers in Amanda's and brought her hand to her mouth, kissing it. Their eyes met and Amanda's lips parted. Jen reluctantly dropped Amanda's hand, and Amanda left, closing the door behind her.

Once Jen was done showering, she retraced her steps down the hall in yoga pants, a tank and a sweatshirt. She followed the light, and found Amanda outside in an illuminated, lush garden, sitting in an overstuffed chair next to a large gas fireplace.

"How beautiful." Jen stepped out to Amanda's patio.

"I love it out here. It's a perfect place to relax and enjoy the fresh ocean air. Have a seat." Amanda motioned to a matching chair on the other side of a coffee table. She had changed into comfortable clothes, too.

Jen sat in the chair facing Amanda, sipping her water.

Soft music was floating over hidden speakers, adding to the tranquil ambiance. The fire was throwing warmth in a wide radius, casting a glow over Amanda's refined features.

Amanda dropped her Birkis on the patio bricks and tucked a foot under her. "My feet are sore from racing around all day."

"Here. Give one to me. I'm an expert at foot massage."

"That sounds inviting. Are you sure? I wasn't hinting."

"Yes. I'm sure." Jen set her glass on the table. She might be new to a femme romance, but she wasn't inexperienced in human contact, for God's sake.

Amanda obliged, setting her foot on Jen's lap and leaning back, resting her head against her chair. Once Jen touched Amanda, a sigh escaped and she closed her eyes.

"Of course, you would have beautiful feet, too," Jen muttered under her breath, admiring Amanda's soft skin and red pedicured nails. She worked her thumbs into Amanda's arch, eliciting a moan.

Even though Jen had examined women's feet many times, she had never massaged one. Thinking back, she couldn't remember massaging Tommy's feet either. She cringed at the thought. His feet were gross—calloused bottoms, thick nails and hairy toes. Yuck. Amanda's foot, on the other hand, was perfectly shaped, soft to the touch and very attractive.

Jen could do this all night, especially seeing the look of pleasure it brought to Amanda's face. She was content in her garden, black curls unfurling down her shoulders and resting above her yoga hoodie. Jen watched the rise and fall of Amanda's chest as she relaxed in her surroundings. Amanda was breathing faster than she had been at the restaurant, even though she was supposedly relaxing in her garden. Jen realized that Amanda was turned on by her touch. How empowering.

Jen stopped rubbing.

"Ready for the other one?" Amanda attempted unsuccessfully to remove her foot from Jen's lap, but Jen held Amanda by the ankle, smiling at her.

"What?" Amanda's eyes flitted open.

"Are you getting turned on?"

"That obvious? Is a vein popping in my forehead or something?"

"No. You're breathing harder than you were at the restaurant, even though we're sitting down, and you're supposedly relaxed."

"What? Were you watching my chest again?"

"Again? When was I watching your chest?" Jen rubbed circles on the bottom of Amanda's foot.

"At the restaurant, when I leaned back against the booth. You checked me out."

"I did, didn't I? Your diversion won't work, though. You're breathing harder, aren't you?"

"Yes, because your foot massage feels insanely good. It's as exciting as it is relaxing." Amanda's husky voice underscored her desire.

"Give me your other foot while we talk. I can't stand asymmetry."

Amanda leaned her head back on the chair, closed her eyes again and lifted her other foot to Jen's lap.

"We need to talk," Jen repeated.

"Do I have to open my eyes for this conversation?"

"No. You can lay there. It's easier to talk about sensitive topics when the other person's eyes are closed, anyway."

"I'm sitting, not lying. You'll know it when I'm lying down."

"Whatever. Just don't lie to me, okay?"

"Wouldn't dream of it. I pledge honesty." Amanda held up her hand, as if taking an oath.

"Likewise."

"What would you like to talk about?"

"I don't know how I'm going to tell Tommy, and it's really troubling me. The engagement ring is still on my nightstand."

"I know. He told me."

"See? That's how fucked up this is. He told you he set it there?"

"Yes. He was confused as to why you didn't accept his proposal after being together for three years. He told me he set it there to remind you that he still exists."

"He told you that?"

"Yes. We've worked together for more than ten years, you know. He was genuinely hurt and needed someone to talk to."

"What did you say?"

"That women don't understand each other in matters of the heart any better than men do."

"Is that true?"

"Sort of. I feel like I'm tuned into the way a woman *can* think, but that doesn't mean I can read her mind."

"Hmm. So true. Although, I think I've been able to guess what you've been thinking all night."

"Is that right?" Amanda asked, opening one eye and smiling.

"It's the same thing I've been thinking."

"Do you want me to be there when you tell Tommy?"

"Thank you for offering, but I think it would be best if I did it alone."

"I want to support you and accept blame in person if he's going to be angry."

"How noble of you. Of course, he's going to be angry, but I owe it to him, and our past intimacy, to do it alone."

When Jen finished rubbing Amanda's other foot, she held it on her lap while she sipped her water. She lay her head back on her chair and closed her eyes. Having Amanda's foot in her lap, and sitting on her patio in her private surroundings, felt warm and intimate. She liked this pace of getting to know each other. She felt more content than she had in months, realizing that she had never felt this comfortable with Tommy. Well, simultaneously comfortable and excited, that is.

"Where did you grow up?" Amanda asked.

"Wisconsin."

"Milwaukee?"

"Madison."

"Happy childhood?"

"Yes, in every respect. You?"

"Mixed. I love my parents, but they weren't home much when I was young. I was raised by a nanny. I wish they would've spent more time with me. But that's in the past. They've always been very good to me."

Jen's heart stirred. She hadn't realized that her hands had moved from Amanda's foot to her ankle, and she was now absentmindedly caressing Amanda's calf, under the leg of her yoga pants. "Do you see much of Jack and Chloe now?"

Amanda smiled at Jen's use of her parents' names. "Mostly just the holidays. I've built my own life in the city, and they're on the peninsula. Frankly, I don't want to see the look of disappointment in my mother's eyes."

"I'm sorry. That has to be painful." Jen caressed Amanda's silky shin now. She thought she could hear pain in Amanda's strained voice.

"I'll live. Rich kid problems, right? Feeling sorry for myself never got me anywhere."

"Are you crying?"

"No. It's just difficult to form words while you're doing that to me. You have no idea—" Heat blazed in Amanda's brown eyes, the golden flecks dancing in the firelight. Her mouth was open, and Jen could hear her breathing.

Jen focused on Amanda's parted lips. She hadn't noticed their shape until now. Heart-like. And very sexy. She found Amanda so attractive in that moment that she couldn't bring herself to stop caressing. She was familiar with carnal messaging, as Tommy had lusted after her many times. But, it was much more intriguing to be the recipient of Amanda's longing stare, burning hot with passion.

Amanda withdrew her leg from Jen's lap and slowly rose from her chair. She closed the gap between them and leaned into Jen, placing her hands on the armrests of her chair. They were so close that Jen could feel Amanda's warm breath on her face.

"Thank you." Amanda pressed her lips to Jen's forehead. It was a lingering, affectionate kiss that signaled she was there to stay.

Jen raised her hands to Amanda's arms and squeezed.

Amanda rested her chin on the top of Jen's head, which positioned Amanda's chest in front of Jen's face.

A vision of tasting the skin above Amanda's tank filled Jen's mind.

"What are you thinking?" Amanda whispered.

Jen cleared her throat. "Honestly?"

"Always."

"I'm thinking about tasting the top of your breast."

"Umm. I think you should."

Jen leaned forward and traced a line above Amanda's tank with her tongue, feeling Amanda shiver as she did it.

Amanda moaned softly and moved her hands to the back of Jen's head, lowering herself to Jen's face while straddling her lap.

Jen breathed in Amanda's lavender scent and brushed her lips over the top of her breast, where she had made a mark with her tongue.

Amanda's sharp intake of breath told Jen everything she needed to know.

She ran her tongue along the top of the tank on the other side, eliciting another moan. Not surprisingly, Amanda tasted delicious.

Jen moved her hands to the small of Amanda's back, resting them above her derrière. She immediately noticed how petite Amanda was, especially compared to Tommy. It had been a long time since she had touched a woman this way, but the thrill was returning at a meteoric rate.

She cupped Amanda and pulled her closer —onto her lap. She trailed kisses up Amanda's throat, then her jawline, and finally found her lips, full of heat and promise. She nibbled Amanda's lower lip and drew back, searching out Amanda's eyes. When she found them, she was sucked in even deeper to the dark passion she saw there.

"You taste so good," Jen said against Amanda's throat.

"Come here." Amanda lowered her mouth to Jen's.

Amanda brought her hands around Jen's head, holding her as she French-kissed her properly—deeply.

Jen learned that Amanda was a fantastic kisser, much better than she had realized at the Curtain Call. She submitted to Amanda's lead, letting the sensation of a leisurely encounter wash over her. Desire sprang from her inner core, causing sweet spasmodic ripples in her abs.

Amanda's moans, combined with her subtle writhing on Jen's lap, made Jen explode with lust. She explored Amanda's back with her hands, wanting to touch and taste all of her. There was a point where the carnal catch overtook Jen—that exquisite, sweet moment when she was seized with passion and committed to fulfilling her sexual desire without turning back. She no longer cared about Tommy, her prior sexual identity or where she was. She focused only on her nerve endings and the endorphins exploding in her brain.

They kissed by the fire, reveling in the feel of each other, wanting the evening to last forever. Jen was swept up, more so than she had ever been with Tommy. Merely kissing and touching, fully clothed, were rocking her world! She couldn't get enough of Amanda's mouth or skin. She tasted better than ice cream, and felt soft, yet firm. And the things Amanda was doing to Jen's tongue were amazing, setting her on fire.

A husky moan escaped Jen from down deep, a sound that she didn't even know she could make, unleashing her innermost desires. Somewhere in the background, she heard a remake of an old song, *I Want You to Want Me,* covered by Gary Jules. It reverberated through her soul. "...*I want you to want me... I need you to need me... I'd love you to love me... I'm begging you to beg me...*" It was slow and sultry, the singer stretching out the lyrics, so meaningful to Jen at this moment, her second official kiss with Amanda.

After a time, Amanda sat back on Jen's lap and looked at her, her hair mussed from Jen's hands threading through it.

"What do you think?" Amanda smoothed Jen's hair behind an ear.

"Of making out with you?"

"Yes. Do you like it?"

"I can't believe I've been missing this all these years. Missing you. I don't want to stop." Jen bit Amanda's chin then licked it.

"Maybe we should take it slow. You need to process your new feelings, and the last thing I want is for you to regret doing anything with me tonight."

"No regret here. Just fire." Jen trailed her tongue down Amanda's throat, then over her collarbone.

"Hmm. I can...work with that," Amanda barely enunciated, finding it difficult to form words while Jen was doing that to her. "But I think it would be best if we didn't take it any further tonight. I want all of you. And I want you when you're ready—body and soul—not just in the heat of passion."

"I thought the whole point of heated passion was to *get* ready!" Jen said, practically jumping out of her skin with lust.

"You're not going to listen to me, are you?"

"Do you always make the rules?"

"Yes."

"You're right, then. I'm not going to listen. Kiss me."

***

Chapter 31

Sea Cliff

Jen awoke at five to the smell of coffee and padded to the kitchen in her tank top and sweats. She poured herself a cup of coffee and looked for evidence of Amanda. None. Jen had slept in an extra bedroom—a few doors down from Amanda's suite. Amanda had insisted they not sleep together until things were resolved with Tommy, despite the overwhelming temptation for both, and Jen couldn't argue with Amanda's moral compass. She was right, but Jen hoped it wouldn't be a habit—Amanda being right all the time.

A black and white cat was pacing at the sliding door to the garden patio, meowing to come in. Amanda was nowhere to be seen, so Jen didn't know if the cat belonged to her or not.

"Who are you? Amanda didn't say she owned a cat." She glanced around the kitchen for a food and water bowl, spying two by the pantry, she let the cat in. It serpentined around her legs, twisting its tail and rubbing against her, practically growling at her. It quickly concluded that Jen didn't know where the cat food was, so it trotted off with its tail straight up, twitching at the tip, clearly on a mission for Amanda. Jen followed it down the hallway to the magnificent wooden staircase, and they wound down the tightly curved stair to the basement level.

They descended onto a wooden landing where a door was ajar a few feet away. Yoga music was wafting through it. The cat slipped inside the door, obviously having done it many times in the past. Jen cautiously followed. They entered a wood-floored room with a ballet bar, full-length mirrors and workout equipment, lighted by transom windows under the substantial wood moldings. Amanda was in the center of the room on a blue yoga mat, stretching. The cat marched over to her and rubbed against her, seeking its morning attention.

"Zumba. Did Jen let you in?" Amanda asked.

The cat meowed in response.

Amanda returned to stretching, her legs curled in a pretzel in front of her, her back straight to Jen. She was finished with her routine, small stains of sweat beading her bare shoulders, and forming a triangle at the top of her yoga pants, just above her cheeks.

Jen set down her coffee mug and quietly walked up behind Amanda, sitting on the mat behind her.

Amanda saw Jen in the mirror. "Oh, I didn't hear you come in. What a nice surprise."

Jen encircled Amanda with her arms and scooted up to her back, throwing her own legs wide in a V-shape around Amanda. She rested a hand on Amanda's tummy, sliding it to her ribs and back down, while moving her pony tail to the side with her other hand, so she could kiss the back of Amanda's moist neck.

Amanda shuddered in response, leaning into Jen.

Jen touched Amanda's breasts for the first time, amazed at how full and firm they felt. Every fiber of her being was stirring to life again. She rested her chin on Amanda's shoulder and looked into the full-length mirror at their reflection. They looked good together. Sleepy and disheveled, but natural. Like a couple should look. Their eyes met in the mirror, conveying more desire than words ever could.

Amanda caressed Jen's knees, her thumbs on the inside, sliding up to Jen's thighs. Jen loved the feel of Amanda's hands on her as she held her gaze in the mirror. They remained in their embrace for a time, ignoring the angry cat that paced impatiently around them. Jen's breasts were pressed against Amanda's back, and the warmth and electricity were palpable. She didn't want to move.

She was falling fast and hard, before she had even finished her morning coffee. She gently rubbed her thumbs across Amanda's nipples, heard Amanda's sharp intake of breath, then did it again, making them grow taut. As Amanda responded, so did Jen, aching to kiss her, too.

Amanda quickly flipped over to her knees and put her hands on Jen's shoulders, pushing her back onto the yoga mat. Smiling at the surprised look on Jen's face, Amanda lay on top of her, mashing her breasts into Jen's. She looked at her neck, her lips, then into her eyes, and smiled.

Jen's heart skipped a beat, as she was swept up in Amanda's advance. Amanda leaned in and kissed her with a renewed enthusiasm from the prior night, so Jen found Amanda's pony tail and removed her hair tie, letting her jet-black curls cascade around them. She felt like she was swimming in chocolate pudding, setting every cell in her body on fire. She involuntarily moved her hips into Amanda's, an instinctive reaction to having Amanda's body plastered to her. Amanda slid her hand down Jen's body to her sweats and cupped Jen's front, which just about undid Jen on the spot. Just Amanda's hand on her was electrifying. She longed for more, but Amanda kept her hand on the outside of Jen's pants.

"More," Jen moaned into Amanda's mouth, writhing her hips into Amanda's hand.

"You're not ready yet," Amanda said.

"How do you know? I *feel* ready," Jen whispered between kisses.

"Trust me. We have to go to work, and I don't want to rush with you—especially the first time."

"Why do you get to be in control all the time?" Jen nibbled Amanda's lower lip a little too hard.

"Ouch! You bit me!"

Jen smiled, and Amanda moved her fingers against Jen's sweats, provoking a gyration, followed by a whimper. "Not fair. You're really good at that."

Amanda kissed her hard, moving her hand back up to Jen's breast.

Turn about being fair play, Jen rolled Amanda onto her back, then kissed a trail down Amanda's flat tummy, causing Amanda to tremble with desire. Jen lifted Amanda's tank and circled her belly button with her tongue, when something on Amanda's skin caught her eye. She pushed herself up on one elbow and looked at Amanda's right hip, just above her pelvic bone. There was a small tattoo there, composed of intersecting female gender symbols, a rainbow placed neatly inside the overlapping space.

Jen traced the tat with her finger, a thousand questions on the tip of her tongue.

Amanda tangled her fingers in Jen's hair, as she gazed down at her. "Do you like it?"

"Love it." Jen saw goose bumps rise on Amanda's skin under her touch. She placed barely-there kisses on the tat and felt Amanda quake with anticipation.

"We have to get ready for work, or I'm gonna be late," Amanda rasped.

"Are you out of your mind? We can't stop now. I won't be able to concentrate today."

"It's getting late—for both of us, and I don't want to rush it."

"I can be a little late." Jen licked Amanda's pelvic bone.

"Whoa, that's—that's—" Amanda whispered, unable to verbalize her rules.

Jen lowered the top of Amanda's yoga pants and kissed her, but Amanda squirmed away, panting.

"Where are you going?" Jen asked, confused.

"To work, I hope," Amanda stood. She held out her hand to pull Jen from the floor.

"Can we at least shower together?" Jen asked, getting up.

Amanda raised her eyebrow in a no.

"Major tease!" Jen accused.

"Come on. Be a big girl. A lot has happened to you in the last few days. Get your house in order, then come and find me. I'll be waiting for you." Amanda grabbed Jen by the hand and led her out of her yoga studio.

***

Later

George had Amanda's car idling and ready to roll, parked outside her gate. She and Jen emerged, and he held the car door for them. Amanda went in first and slid all the way across the back seat, Jen joining her.

"You ride to work in this every day?" Jen asked.

"Yes. One of my few extravagances. You know how the parking is South of Market."

"I'm learning that you say that about each of your extravagances, which number more than one, you know. The rest of us just go in search of spots on the city streets."

Amanda smiled sympathetically. "Do you want me to drop you at work or your apartment?" She moved her hand to Jen's knee, out of sight from George's rear-view mirror.

"Work. It's late."

"I could pick you up after your shift." Amanda's eyes danced with promise.

"I should probably return to my apartment for some fresh clothes," Jen said, even though the prospect of her lonely apartment was dismal.

"Where to?" George asked.

"San Francisco Community Hospital," Amanda said.

Jen looked from Amanda's hand on her knee to Amanda's eyes. Amanda smiled, her perfect teeth contrasting against her red lips. Her skin was flawless in the morning light. So alluring. She looked radiant.

"I'm going to miss you today." Amanda absent-mindedly drew on Jen's knee.

"Me, too. More than you know." Jen picked up Amanda's hand and pressed it to her lips, despite George's presence. She planned to tell Tommy today or tomorrow. So, what difference did it make if George saw them kissing at this point?

Amanda shot her a look, signaling that George could see.

"Text me today?" Jen asked.

"Of course."

Jen dropped Amanda's hand, and they busied themselves by checking emails for the remainder of the commute.

When they arrived at the hospital, Amanda surprised Jen by grasping her arm and dragging her over. "Come here. I want to leave you with something to remember me by."

Amanda kissed Jen gently on the lips, tenderly running her tongue against the outside.

When Amanda tried to slide back, Jen stopped her, taking the initiative and placing her hands on Amanda's neck, hauling her back for a deeper kiss.

Jen found herself falling into Amanda's sultry mouth yet again, her thirst still not quenched. They restrained themselves from moaning, but the full-on kiss was enough to get George's attention.

"I hope you think about us today," Amanda said against Jen's lips.

"Trust me. I will. See you soon." She slid across the seat and opened the door.

Amanda and George waited for Jen to disappear into the hospital, then accelerated out of the circular drive. Once they were on Potrero Avenue, Amanda decided to tell George, who had faithfully served her for the last three years.

"George, you clearly saw that exchange. You'd be correct in assuming we commenced a relationship. She's going to tell Tommy in the next few days, so you don't have to."

"Thank you." His earnest gaze met hers in the rear-view mirror.

"I don't want to put you in a position of covering up for me or jeopardizing your relationship with a fellow officer. Jen and I will take care of it."

"Good plan." He kept his eyes on the road, as he continued driving.

Twenty minutes later, Amanda scanned her ID badge into the security pad on her floor and entered the DA's office suite. She dropped her bag in a desk drawer and powered up her computer.

Tommy had IM'd her a few minutes ago. *See me as soon as you get in.*

She took a deep breath and prepared herself to face the man she was deceiving. It was so difficult working with him, knowing that he would hate her in a few days, and possibly never work with her again. God forbid he would find out before Jen told him. She liked Tommy, having a fondness for him in her heart, but—well, she liked Jen more.

"Good morning, Tommy." Amanda entered his office. "What's new?"

"Hey. You look happy today. Come around this side of my desk and look at this video that the computer guys just emailed me."

Amanda did as he requested, rounding his desk and gazing down at the photo of Jen in her swimsuit. Amanda had undeniably fallen. Hard. She dragged her eyes away from Jen's scantily clad body—the one she had been lying on top of in her yoga studio—and stared at Tommy's flat screen as he punched a few buttons on his keyboard. She watched as the gritty security cam footage that she recognized as the lobby to Natasha's apartment building came into view.

A woman with big hair, swept up in a bun, flounced under the camera, her red ruana wrap breezing over her shoulders. She walked quickly through the lobby and into the elevator. As she turned around in the elevator, the camera captured a facial shot, which Tommy enlarged. The woman was wearing round, designer sunglasses, but was unmistakably Susie Sangiolo.

"Oh my God!" Amanda exclaimed. "We have her on video visiting Natasha's apartment building?"

"A week before Natasha died."

"Is it just this once?"

"That we know of. The apartment management saves the footage for only a few weeks."

"It doesn't matter. We have Susie in the apartment building right before Natasha died, and a week before Dr. Wallace was sick. We've established means and opportunity."

"My money says she was trying to kill her husband."

"You think? The bourbon drinker himself?"

"I'm sure of it. Susie wanted her cake and frosting, too. Wallace probably has a life insurance policy, and Susie already had Nick Nutini's balls in her purse. I wouldn't be surprised if she and Nutini concocted the entire scheme, possibly thinking they were framing Natasha to take the fall."

"Harsh."

"Oh, she's more than capable of it, Amanda. You didn't go to high school with her."

"Even so, we don't have any proof of Susie actually in Natasha's apartment. I hope I can convince a jury beyond a reasonable doubt with the stolen meds and this security cam footage. It would be a lock if we had proof that Susie was actually in Natasha's apartment."

"I figured you'd say that. Unfortunately, the lab doesn't think we'll find her fingerprints on the bourbon bottle. We were lucky to have found Natasha's, Blake's and Dr. Wallace's. Everything gets smudged, and there are prints on top of prints."

"What do you have in mind?"

"I sort of set the wheels in motion yesterday when I spoke to Dr. Wallace. I caught up with him on his sailboat."

"Really?" Amanda was interrupted by her phone buzzing. She looked at the screen. A text.

Still hot for you. It was Jen.

Amanda nodded like it was business, but she could feel the heat creeping up her neck and flushing her face. She squinted her eyes to disguise her guilt.

"Do you have to go? You look pissed."

"Ah...no. This can wait," she said, still squinting. She dropped her cell into her jacket pocket.

"I told Wallace that I'd arrest both him and Susie for murder and conspiracy to commit murder, depriving their daughter of her parents, if he didn't help me prove the truth."

"That works for me."

"We're tapping his phone, so I'm hoping something breaks soon."

"Let me know. Great work, Tommy. Listen, I should go."

"Okay, catch ya later."

I hope not, she thought.

After Amanda left, an email from the Computer Forensics guys popped into Tommy's Inbox. It had an attachment. They had worked with the hospital Information Systems department and found a string of emails between Natasha and Dr. Wallace. There weren't many. Just a few dozen, all in the attached file.

Tommy clicked it open. Most were logistics, like *meet in the ER Radiology room at 2:45.* One caught his attention, however. It was from Natasha to Lane, and it stated, *Please don't think I'm paranoid, but I think someone was in my apartment last night.*

Why? Lane replied

My lingerie drawer was messed up, not how I left it. And, the paperback I'm currently reading was in the center of my bed instead of under the pillow where I left it, Natasha wrote.

Are you sure? Those sound like things you could do and not remember doing, Lane replied.

Seriously! This gives me the creeps. Do you think it was Blake? she asked.

He doesn't have a key, does he? Lane replied.

No, but he could probably pick a lock, she wrote.

I'll stay with you tonight/tomorrow if you want me to, Lane offered.

That'd be great, she wrote.

Tommy looked at the date on the email chain. It was six days before Natasha died. He minimized the email chain and opened the security cam footage of Susie entering the building. It was dated one day earlier than Natasha's email, which would make sense, since Natasha noticed the changes when she got home from work, then emailed Lane about them when she returned to the hospital.

It was Susie who had been in Natasha's apartment, looking in her lingerie drawer and at her paperback, but Tommy had no way of proving it. He just knew it had to be her. And, it seemed like what a disgruntled wife would do when prowling around her husband's paramour's apartment—the lingerie drawer and the bed. Then, she walked out to the kitchen and poisoned the bourbon bottle, hoping to kill Wallace. *Maybe her prints are on the book or the drawer pull,* he thought.

***

Chapter 32

Hall of Justice

Amanda returned to her office as fast as possible, unable to withstand the guilt she felt in front of Tommy. *Still hot for you.* Just that phrase from Jen made Amanda's legs weak. If only Jen weren't Tommy's girl.

Amanda closed her office door and sank into her desk chair, despondent over their love triangle. Diamonds were sparkling off the Bay in the sunlight, but their beauty was lost on her. All she saw was Jen's face—piercing blue eyes, a perfect nose, full lips, a clean jawline, blonde hair that went on forever, so silky to Amanda's touch. She replayed their hurried, desperate tangle in her yoga studio that morning, and realized that she wanted Jen with every nerve ending in her body.

She was torn between her loyalty to Tommy and her attraction to Jen. Overcome with guilt, the timing of their consummation being paramount, she had to reply carefully to Jen's text.

Amanda stared at Jen's message. *Still hot for you.*

Amanda replied, *Likewise, more than u know. I feel guilty, tho. Pls break it off with Tommy and I'll be waiting for you.*

There wasn't an immediate reply, so Amanda turned to her endless parade of emails. Her ADAs were handling hundreds of cases and needed her guidance and approval on a variety of actions, so she had to be timely about answering them.

Her phone beeped several minutes later. Amanda pictured Jen between patients in the ER, replying on the fly. *Is that a prerequisite to us having sex? Me breaking up with Tommy?*

Amanda anticipated this question, so was quick to reply. *Yes. I can't betray him. I need to be able to look him in the eye and tell him we didn't have sex until you broke up. I've never been 'the other woman' in a relationship, and I don't intend to start now. Not even for you.*

Jen's immediate reply was, *Done.*

Amanda's desk phone rang. It was her assistant, informing her that Mayor Woo was pacing in the waiting area, insisting on a meeting.

"Show him in," Amanda said.

Mayor Woo swept into Amanda's office, a frustrated look on his face.

"Guess who was in my office, yelling at me yesterday?" he asked.

"The Ivanovs?" she ventured.

"How did you know?"

"They were here first. Detective Vietti and I met with them."

"You didn't do a very good job. They want to know how their daughter died, but you won't tell them!"

"You know how this process works," Amanda said, her voice rising despite her best effort at control.

"What process? I can't tell if anything is actually happening over here!"

Amanda gave him a disarming smile. "Trust me, a lot is happening here, but we can't discuss our investigation, because not only are we prohibited from doing so by ethical rules, but we also get better results when we keep it confidential. You know that."

"To the detriment of the victim's family? Do you know who these people are?"

"Of course, I do. This isn't about your political career, it's about an investigation. They're impatient, and I can't blame them. Everyone wants results in a matter of days. Some investigations take weeks, Mayor Woo, weeks. I'd say we're working pretty damn fast on this one."

"Is this a homicide investigation?"

"It's an investigation into the death of Natasha Farber. I'm not saying one way or the other."

"What am I supposed to tell the Ivanovs? The media?"

"It's your job as an elected official to provide leadership and support. You're supposed to tell the Ivanovs that you trust law enforcement to do its job. You're supposed to assure the citizens of San Francisco that we have a competent and effective police force and District Attorney's office," she suggested.

He snorted, threw his hands in the air, and stormed out the door.

Amanda rolled her eyes at his immature behavior and returned to her desk. She called Sylvia, her Press Secretary, and warned her that the Mayor's Office could very well release a statement that derided the District Attorney's Office.

She also IM'd Tommy to expect incoming fire about his work, but to stay the course and take the submarine approach—going low and silent.

***

Tommy received Amanda's message and smiled. He loved the way she ran interference for him. In all the years they'd worked together, she'd always had his back. He couldn't think of a better DA. She was a class act.

He IM'd her back: *Thanks. I won't disappoint.*

Tommy's desk phone rang, the screen display indicating it was one of the computer guys in Forensics.

"Hello?"

"You should come down here," he said.

Tommy leapt out of his chair and raced down a flight of stairs to the computer room.

"Whatya got?" he asked.

"A text conversation between Lane and Susie Wallace that just came in," the officer said, pulling it up on his screen.

Tommy wheeled a chair over and read the exchange between Lane and Susie.

We need to talk
Why?
Detective Vietti visited me. He knows
Knows what?
That you poisoned me and killed Natasha
Fuck you! Don't text lies

Stop it, Susie. He's gonna arrest both of us. Put us both on trial. Angelina won't have any parents. We'll both go to prison.

Vietti is bluffing. Grow a dick

Meet me at home now, or I'll go in and tell Vietti everything

"When did this come in?" Tommy asked.

"About ten minutes ago."

"Thanks, man." Tommy flew from the room.

He ran down to his Charger and sped over to North Beach to the address they had on file for the Wallace home, calling for backup on the way. This is what he'd hoped to accomplish by poking the hornet's nest, but he didn't want Lane or Susie to kill each other. He had to get there in time.

He turned on the flashing lights in his grill and had to chirp his siren a few times at intersections, making it to their upscale row house in a few minutes.

Two local patrol officers were standing at the ready on the sidewalk, at the bottom of the stairway. Tommy bounded up the stairs and rang the doorbell. He could hear yelling inside the house. He pressed the doorbell repeatedly, then tried the door knob. It was locked.

There was more yelling, then a gunshot. Tommy kicked open the front door, and he and the officers burst through, spilling into the living room, their guns drawn.

Dr. Wallace was lying on the floor in front of the fireplace, blood pouring out of a leg wound. Susie was standing at the entrance to the kitchen, a handgun wobbling horribly in her hand, causing it to sweep the entire room, randomly aiming at everyone.

"Put down the gun, Susie," Tommy yelled.

"I…can't…." Her eyes were crazed with fear and surprise.

"Put it down, or we'll have to shoot you," Tommy said.

Her wrist went limp, and the gun fell to the floor. One of the men pounced on it, picking it up. Tommy flew to Susie, grabbing her wrists and spinning her around so she faced the wall. He pushed her against it and patted her down.

The other officer attended to Dr. Wallace's leg wound, which was gushing blood. He tied a tourniquet on Wallace's thigh, above the wound, and called 911 for an ambulance.

"I'm charging you with the murder of Natasha Farber and the attempted murder of Lane Wallace. You have the right to remain silent…," Tommy continued, Mirandizing her as he cuffed her.

Susie broke down crying as Tommy led her out to his Charger. He asked one of the officers to accompany him while he drove Susie to the Hall of Justice to be processed.

Tommy listened on the car radio while an ambulance collected Dr. Wallace and brought him to San Francisco Community Hospital, where Jen was undoubtedly working a shift.

***

San Francisco Community Hospital

Jen and the trauma team stood in Trauma Bay Number 21, waiting for the ambulance to arrive with a male in his mid-forties and a gunshot wound to his right thigh. The ambulance drove into the designated garage and wheeled Lane on a gurney into the trauma bay.

On the count of three, they transferred him from the gurney to the hospital bed. The EMT's gave report and the trauma team swung into action, connecting monitoring equipment and assessing Lane's wound.

"Lane, we're gonna have to stop meeting like this." Jen nodded to the nurse to place an oxygen cannula on his nose.

"Susie...shot me," he said.

"Okay. Is this the same leg that was injured in Iraq?" Jen asked.

He nodded.

"What time was the tourniquet put on his leg?" Jen asked the EMT.

"The police tied it, so it was on when we arrived at the scene. We got there within ten minutes of the call, and it took us twenty minutes to get him here, so it's been on thirty minutes already," the EMT said.

"Make a note of the time and that we have approximately ninety more minutes of tourniquet time, starting now," she said to her scribe, who was standing in the corner, entering information into the electronic medical record.

"Go ahead and cut off his pants and shorts," Jen ordered the nurse. Jen's concern was whether the bullet hit an artery, or more likely, shattered a bone that splintered, hitting an artery. Lane's blood pressure was normal, however, which was a good sign.

She inspected the bullet entry and exit. It was mid-thigh and very close to his superficial femoral artery. She loosened the tourniquet to see how much the wound would bleed. It gushed as soon as the pressure was released, so she tightened the belt again.

"Let's get an x-ray, a second IV, and labs," she said. "Is the trauma surgeon here yet?"

"He's on his way," the circulating nurse reported.

They quickly took an x-ray with the portable machine in the room. It demonstrated an old shrapnel wound from his Iraq service, and a shattered femur from Susie's gunshot. Jen shook her head. It was a nasty-looking fragmented bone. Since he could bleed out from the damage to his femoral artery, however, he needed to go to the OR immediately to have it repaired. They could assess his femur during the artery repair.

The trauma surgeon entered the room on cue, and Jen reported her findings, including the tourniquet time. "I gave him a loading dose of antibiotics, interrogated the wound and loosened the belt. It hemorrhaged right away, so I'm sure the superficial femoral artery is damaged from a shattered femur."

"Let me see the x-ray," he said. A nurse swung the flat screen over for the surgeon to view. "You're right, Dr. Dawson. We can explore the bullet hole and get an angiogram in the OR to save tourniquet time. Let's go, everyone."

Without hesitation, the team began preparations to wheel Lane forty feet to the OR.

The surgeon went to the head of the bed and told Lane he was going to perform surgery to explore and repair the artery. Lane nodded.

Jen walked alongside the rolling bed with Lane until they reached the OR doors. She gave his hand a quick squeeze.

"I'll be here for you, Lane. Good luck."

He gave her hand a tight squeeze as they wheeled him through the doors.

Jen stood watching, letting reality sink in. Her colleague had been shot by his wife, presumably for fooling around on her. Considering the scar tissue and damage his leg suffered from the Iraq injury, Jen wasn't very hopeful that he'd walk again on that leg. The x-ray looked horrible. Not only would they have to repair his artery fast, but then, the orthopedic surgeon would have to attempt to piece together Lane's femur with a rod down the middle. It was a shitty prognosis.

She returned to the ER, distraught over Lane's predicament. Everyone in the ER was talking about the gravity of the situation they'd just seen, again speculating on who killed Natasha, in light of Susie shooting Lane.

Jen didn't want to be a part of it, so she went into the back doc room and pulled up Lane's electronic medical record, entering her notes of the care she had just provided.

Her phone beeped with an incoming text.

It was Tommy. *Susie shot Lane. He's on his way to you*

She replied. *We received him. He's in surgery*

That was it. Tommy didn't reply. He was probably busy dealing with Susie. *Why now? Why today?* Jen wondered. If Susie were shooting Lane out of anger that he had an affair, she would have shot him several days ago. It didn't make sense to Jen that Susie had shot Lane today.

***

Chapter 33

Jen was visiting Lane in his hospital room on the Medical Surgical Unit. He had undergone almost six hours of surgery to repair his femoral artery and shattered femur. His prognosis for full functional use of that leg was low. At least they hadn't needed to amputate it, Jen thought. Lane was asleep, but Jen held his hand and clicked on the television to see if there was anything on the local news.

The top story was: "Art Gallery owner Susie Sangiolo shoots husband, Dr. Lane Wallace, who is a suspect in the murder of Natasha Farber." *Good Lord,* Jen thought, *It doesn't get much worse than that. And, to have it splashed all over the local news.*

The station was replaying a video that accompanied the tagline. It was a press conference of District Attorney Amanda Hawthorne, flanked by Detective Thomas Vietti and the Chief of Police. Amanda was at the podium, speaking into multiple microphones set up by the media.

"I'm District Attorney Amanda Hawthorne. I can inform the residents of San Francisco that Detective Thomas Vietti of the San Francisco Police Department arrested Susan Sangiolo Wallace today. She has been charged with two counts of attempted murder of her husband, Dr. Lane Wallace, and one count of felony murder in the death of Natasha Farber. Mrs. Wallace was arrested at her home in North Beach, shortly after she shot Dr. Wallace. Dr. Wallace is in stable, but serious, condition at San Francisco Community Hospital. Earlier, the judge set bond at one million dollars for Mrs. Wallace."

"Any questions?" Amanda asked.

"Do Mrs. Farber's parents know?" a reporter shouted out.

"Yes. They've been informed," Amanda replied.

"How did Natasha Farber die?"

"Poisoning," Amanda said.

"How?"

"A mix of prescription drugs and alcohol."

"Did Mrs. Wallace confess to the felony murder?" a reporter asked.

"No," Amanda said.

"Will there be a trial?" the same reporter asked.

"The District Attorney's Office is prepared to go to trial on all counts, if necessary."

"Did Detective Vietti witness Mrs. Wallace shooting Dr. Wallace?" a reporter asked.

Tommy stepped forward to the microphones. "No, I did not."

"How is felony murder different from murder?" asked an astute reporter in the front row.

Amanda explained. "It's a type of murder charge. When the defendant commits a felony, such as attempted murder, and someone else dies during the commission of the first crime, the defendant is liable for the murder, whether it was intentional or accidental."

"So, are you saying Mrs. Wallace was trying to poison her husband, but Natasha Farber drank the poison instead, and died?" the reporter asked.

"Yes," Amanda said. "Mrs. Wallace is responsible for killing Mrs. Farber, regardless of her intent."

No more questions were shouted, so Amanda, Tommy and the Chief of Police exited through the side door.

Jen's chest swelled with pride as she watched both Amanda and Tommy in front of the cameras. They made a great team. Of course, Jen was more attracted to Amanda now, so was partial to her on-camera charisma. Amanda had deftly answered the media questions and came across as a force to be reckoned with. The press conference had taken place over an hour ago.

Jen texted her. *Nice job on T.V.* Jen's pager went off, so she picked up the desk phone and answered it. A nurse wanted new orders for pain medicine on a patient. Jen asked a few questions and gave the orders.

When she ended her call with the nurse, she looked at her cell phone. Amanda had replied.

Thanks. Not nearly as important as what you do every day.

Jen replied with an emoji of a young woman with her hands over her head making the "I can't believe it" gesture.

Her shift would end soon, so she texted Tommy. *Wanna meet for dinner after work?*

He replied right away. *Hey stranger, of course. Mama Mia's? Tina asked about you this week.*

Jen was touched. She liked Tina. Tommy must have returned to eating there this week since Jen refused to see him. However, she didn't want to break up with him at Tina's restaurant.

I miss Tina, too. But how about the Sushi place?

Five or six?

Six. I'm still at work.

Ok. Love u.

Jen closed her eyes. This was going to be rough. They had been together three years, and he had fallen hard. Rightly so. She would return his ring and do her best to explain, even though she knew her breakup would blindside him. At least he would have the satisfaction of just having solved his big case. She had to make it right with him. Make him understand that it wasn't his fault. There's nothing he could have done differently. It was about her realizing that she was attracted to Amanda. And if she was honest with herself, a part of her would always love Tommy. He had been good to her.

Can I even deliver this message? Will I sound phony?

When her shift ended, Jen changed into her street clothes in the women's locker room and left the hospital. It was always such a delight to step out into the cool, fresh air, especially if it was still light out. She drove to her apartment and changed into a dinner dress, grabbing the engagement ring box off her nightstand. She wasn't even tempted to open it and look at it again.

Her heart was heavy with facing Tommy. Not only was she experiencing a monumental change in her life, but breaking up with Tommy would devastate him. Would he even believe her? Would he make fun of her? Would he be vindictive and tell all her friends and family before she could? Should she be calling her family *before* she told Tommy?

What if she had an affair with Amanda and decided she didn't like women after all? That she wanted to return to men? She was certain Tommy wouldn't be there for her to come back to. Even knowing that, she was determined. The blood drained from her face. She never felt so ill-prepared for a discussion. It was heart-wrenching.

She texted Amanda. *Miss you. Having dinner with Tommy. Going to tell him.*

Amanda replied right away. *Good luck. Miss you, too. Going out for drinks with ADAs.*

Jen replied, *Proud of you. Have fun.*

Jen entered their favorite Sushi restaurant a few minutes after six. He was at the bar, where they had sat so many times, drinking beer, kissing and making plans between bites.

He saw her and slid out of his chair. "Hey, babe. You look hot," admiring her in the red wrap dress that he liked to unwrap.

"Thanks."

He kissed her on the lips and hugged her. She hugged him back, but it didn't feel like it used to. No zings in her tummy. No tingling in her nerve endings. There was warmth, but no electricity. The passion had left. Touching Tommy wasn't even close to what she felt when she mashed up against Amanda.

The absence of passion in their embrace confirmed that she had to break it off. It wouldn't be fair to go behind his back, beginning a love affair with Amanda while he thought they were still a couple.

"Would you like a beer?" he asked.

She thought his speech was a little slurred, and noticed an empty shot glass and almost-empty beer on the counter. *Good for him. He's celebrating solving his case.*

"A Sapporo would be great," she said.

He ordered one for her and another for himself.

"Congratulations on solving the case. Saw you on T.V.," she said.

"Thanks. It was fun to work with Amanda again. I'm sorry you had to get wrapped up in it. Are we still friends?"

"Of course." She placed her hand on his arm. "I want to be friends with you for the rest of my life."

He inclined his head, briefly considering her remark, then let it drop.

"Are you hungry?" he asked.

"No. You?"

"I just ordered a few California rolls. Had a few shots of Saki. My way of celebrating. That is, until later with you," he said, grinning.

She nodded and smiled.

Their beers arrived, and she took a healthy pull. *How to begin? Where to begin?*

He rubbed her knee and searched her face. "Is something wrong?"

Even through alcohol, the detective in Tommy could read her. "Yes. I'm sorry. We have to talk about something."

"What?"

"We...I'm...I'm sorry, but—" she stumbled.

"California roll," the sushi chef announced, setting Tommy's plate on the bar.

Tommy slid the plate toward himself and opened the chopsticks as Jen watched. He mixed a dollop of wasabi into his square dish of soy sauce, then added a few slices of fresh ginger. After stirring his mixture, like she had watched him do so many times, he dunked a slice of the roll into it and shoved it into his mouth.

Jen watched in amazement at how he could stuff his face, knowing she was trying to tell him something important. She drank more of her beer.

He chewed, watching her. "Well?" he asked, his mouth full.

"I'm so sorry, Tommy," she said, her voice catching, "but I have to break up with you."

There it was. Splat.

He stopped chewing for a second, focusing on what she had just said. "What?"

"I have to break up with you. I'm very sorry. Here's your ring." She removed the box from her bag and set it on the counter in front of him.

He reached for his beer and quickly washed down his bite. "You have to break up with me? As in, we're no longer a couple?"

"That's right. I'm sorry. If there's anything of mine at your place, feel free to throw it out. I'm sure you're going to be angry with me."

"What the hell are you talking about? Is this because I didn't agree with you about Lane Wallace being innocent? That I thought he whacked his lover?"

"No. It's not about that. It doesn't have anything to do with the murder investigation." She was frustrated, so she drank some more beer.

"Jen, what's going on? We've been together two years!"

"Three, actually, but that's not the point."

"Is it because I proposed too soon? Give me a second chance," he pleaded, placing his hands on her knees.

"No. It has nothing to do with you proposing. In fact, it has nothing to do with you at all."

He stared suspiciously at her. "There's another guy, isn't there? Who is he?"

She realized the alcohol he had consumed wasn't helping the situation. He couldn't listen worth a damn. "There isn't another guy. Stop thinking that. This is about me. I discovered something about myself that I didn't know. That you didn't know. It's as much of a surprise to me as it will be to you. Trust me."

"I'm really confused, Jen. Are you sick?" His voice rose with emotion.

"I'm not sick. I'm gay," she announced quietly.

"You're *what*?"

"I'm gay," she said, loud enough for others to hear.

"I don't believe you. You're just saying that to get rid of me." His voice cracked into a falsetto.

"That's not true. I wouldn't do that."

"Prove it, then," he slurred.

"How am I supposed to prove it to you?"

"Well. Ahh. Have you been with other women? How do you know?"

"Yes," she said, looking around at the other patrons.

He tried to focus on her, but his eyes were confused with shock and alcohol. "Another woman? When?"

"Recently."

"I don't believe you."

"Then don't. We didn't take it too far, because I couldn't handle the prospect of fooling around on you. Neither could she. We did enough for me to know though."

"How could you be so sure after fooling around a little?"

"I had a similar experience in college, but wrote it off to being bi-curious. I was in denial for the last decade, I suppose. But this recent encounter reignited all those same desires, and validated that I'm gay, Tommy."

"You're gay?" he slurred, shaking his head. "Well, fuck me!"

"I'm so sorry."

"Why couldn't you have figured this out *before* you broke my heart?"

Her eyes filled up with tears. "I know. Trust me, I know."

He downed his glass of beer and ordered another. "A *woman* stole you away from me?"

"Not exactly stole. I was a willing party."

"Whatever," he said, waving off her reply.

"There's more."

He turned to stare at her. "More? What else could there possibly be? Are you going to tell me you're pregnant with my baby, too?"

Other people looked at him.

"If you could just keep it down," she pleaded. "No. I'm not pregnant, but I need to tell you who my... my... the other woman is."

"Your lover, you mean?" he asked sarcastically.

"Yes. It's Amanda."

"What the fuck?!" He yelled loud enough for the entire restaurant to hear.

The host came over and asked Tommy to keep it down. He promised he would, then turned to Jen.

"My colleague Amanda? As in, Amanda Hawthorne?"

"Yes," she said, not blinking.

"Well, I'll be goddamned. Never would've guessed in a million years."

"Me either. I'm so sorry, Tommy."

"Are you sure? Did she seduce you?"

"No. If anything, she wanted to slow it down out of respect for you. She cares for you as much as I do. She'd do anything not to hurt you, as would I."

"So, you two have talked about me?"

"Yes, only briefly, to share how much we love you and don't want to hurt you. We're both very sorry. She wanted to be here, but I told her I wanted to tell you alone."

"How very noble of her."

"Don't be that way, Tommy. We didn't see this coming. We didn't prepare for it. It just happened, and we both care about you and want to be friends with you."

"Isn't that fucking nice," he sneered.

"Tommy—"

"If she were a guy, I'd beat the shit out of her," he spat, his face red with anger.

"I know. But if she were a guy, I wouldn't be interested in her."

Tommy stared at her, trying to figure her out. "I'm really pissed at both of you."

"I'm not surprised. I would be, too."

"I think you should leave now. Thanks for returning my ring." He turned and looked over the bar, shutting her out.

"Here's some money for my beer." She dug a few bills out of her bag and tossed them on the bar, then slipped out of her chair and pushed through the door onto the sidewalk. The fog was creeping in, right on cue.

After walking a few miles down Judah Street, she realized she had gone in the opposite direction of her apartment. Fueled by anger, she continued walking. Walking as far away as possible from Tommy. She walked and processed what had just happened, and how Tommy had responded.

Was she angry at Tommy for not embracing her decision? Applauding her? What had she expected? If the tables had been reversed, she certainly wouldn't have congratulated *him*. She, too, would have been mad as hell. She needed to cool down and give him a break. He had a right to be upset.

She felt sorry for him, and was beginning to grieve their relationship. It was a loss for her, too. She still loved him, but it didn't compare to what she felt for Amanda. After thirty more minutes of walking, she stopped to figure out where she was. She found herself standing in front of UCSF Medical Center, where she had done a rotation back in the day. She liked this hospital, but as far as she knew, they couldn't treat her current anguish or Tommy's broken heart.

She removed her phone from her pocket and texted Amanda, *Hey.*

Amanda replied right away. *How did it go? How r you?*

Horrible. I'm at UCSF. R u still out with your friends?

The Medical Center? Are you hurt? Should I come?

No. I just meant I started walking and ended up here.

I'll send George to collect you. We're in the bar at Zero Zero. Come join us.

R u sure? I feel weird about George coming to get me.

He's my driver and it's my car. Do you want me to come with him?

No. Stay with ur friends. I'll wait for George.

There was a pause while Jen watched her phone.

I just sent George. I'm waiting here for u. I promise.

Jen ducked into a covered bus stop as she waited for George. It gave her more time to think. She was worried about Tommy getting drunk tonight, but didn't feel like it was her place to interfere in his life. Was she supposed to stop texting him now? It all felt so cold.

George arrived, and Jen fell into the back seat. The expensive car felt too big without Amanda in it. Her scent lingered in the air, but it wasn't the same.

"There's a bottle of water back there if you want one." George glanced in the mirror at her.

"Thanks. You read my mind." She opened it and drank half.

"Not feeling well? You look pale."

Jen looked in the mirror and agreed with him. Having just picked her up at the Medical Center, he probably was curious.

"I feel like crap. Not because I'm sick, but because I just broke up with Tommy. I had to tell him I'm going to start a relationship with Amanda."

"I'm sorry. If it makes you feel any better, I think he'll receive an award for solving the Farber case. At least he had a banner work day."

"That's good, but I'm worried about him. He's probably drinking too much. He was pretty angry when I left him."

"No worries. As soon as we get to Zero Zero, I'll call some of the guys to take him out."

"Would you? That would make me feel a whole lot better. They could keep an eye on him."

"That's what we're here for."

"Thank you. I'm sorry Amanda and I put you in an awkward position of knowing about us before Tommy knew."

"Amanda spoke to me this morning after we dropped you off. I couldn't help but notice the kiss. She told me you were going to tell Tommy as soon as he concluded the Farber investigation."

"And I did."

"He'll survive."

"I hope the fact that I left Tommy for Amanda doesn't embarrass him at work."

"I'm sure it won't," George lied.

***

Chapter 34

SoMa

They arrived at Zero Zero, where George quickly exited the driver's side and hustled around the back of the car to open the curbside door for Jen.

Amanda was waiting for them in the cool night air outside the restaurant. When Jen stepped out of the car, Amanda threw her arms wide, inviting Jen to seek refuge in her embrace. Jen accepted, crashing into Amanda's body.

Amanda was stronger than Jen thought. Drawing her close, wrapping her arms around Jen's back, enveloping her in her comforting embrace. Jen nuzzled her face into Amanda's neck, elongating the contact and seeking the emotional reassurance she desperately needed.

After a minute, Jen retreated slightly, so she could rest her hands on each side of Amanda's face, tilting her head up for a kiss. There was nothing tentative or shy about Jen's need for Amanda's mouth. It was primal. Once their lips collided, Jen soared with the passion that was springing to life inside her. It was a frenzied affair, each greedy with the need to taste the other.

Overwhelmed with emotion, Jen's face contorted and she broke down—crying silently at first. She tore her lips from Amanda's and lay her forehead against her, her body convulsing with tears.

Amanda moved her hands from Jen's back to cradle her head, smoothing her hair, planting small kisses on her.

"It's okay. You've been through a lot," Amanda whispered.

"I can't believe I'm crying," Jen said, fighting for control.

"I'm here. Let it go."

"This week has undone me, seeing Lane with a bullet in his leg. He'll never use it again, you know. Kissing you, but feeling horrible that Tommy is drowning his sorrows, when he should be celebrating his success. I broke his heart, and I feel horrible about it. I've left a trail of heartbreak—"

"That's not true." Amanda ran her fingers through Jen's hair, placing soft kisses on the tip of her nose. "You've made me very happy." Amanda's attention was as sensuous as it was comforting to Jen.

"You might want to move inside, ladies," George said. "I think I see some high-powered businessmen coming down the street. And their cell phones are out."

Amanda snapped to attention, breaking away from Jen and grabbing her hand.

"Thanks, George. Follow me." Amanda pulled Jen inside the two-story bar and restaurant.

Jen absorbed the crowded bar and the open stair to the upper level, as Amanda guided her past the long bar into the ladies' room. Once inside, Amanda hugged Jen again.

"Do you want to leave? We can go back to my place right now if you want," Amanda offered.

"No. I just need a minute to gather myself. I want to be here with you—if you want me, that is."

"I do, I do. I want you to meet everyone in my office, but only if you're comfortable."

Jen looked at her reflection in the mirror and practically shrieked with fright. Her hair was frizzed from walking in the mist down Judah Street, and her makeup had run from her tears. "I look like shit."

Amanda laughed. "It's all relative. Your shit is another woman's best night. Here, let's put you back together." She removed a hairbrush and compact from her bag and set it on the counter. She brushed Jen's hair, and just that simple act gave Jen so much comfort. "That feels nice."

Amanda smoothed out Jen's long, golden strands and pulled them back into a pony at the nape of her neck. She hugged her from behind, just long enough to show Jen how much passion was burning underneath. "I love this dress on you."

"Thank you." Jen was about to toss in that it was Tommy's favorite, too, but decided against it. She didn't want to go there, reminding herself and her new lover of her old flame. Why bring him into the mix constantly?

Jen dug into her own bag and found some makeup brushes, then used a mixture of her and Amanda's products to cover the red blotches on her cheeks that were telltale signs of crying.

"Better," Jen said, after she finished.

"Beautiful. My colleagues will think you're stunning."

"Umm...I have a question for you about that."

"Anything."

"Would it be too much to ask that we not engage in a lot of PDA?"

"No problem. I usually don't. I've brought dates to work functions in the past, so, you know—"

"Dates, huh?"

"Yeah, well, that's a conversation for a later time. But, we are in a public place, and I'm still the DA, so we should probably be discreet. More importantly, though, how do you feel about being seen with me?"

"With you? Fantastic. Being gay in public? It will take some practice and time. I feel sort of insecure."

"We can leave if you want."

"No. Let's do this."

Amanda turned Jen to face her, then put her hands on the back of her head to pull her down for a kiss when the door opened and a few young women entered. Amanda broke their embrace and smiled. "Let's go meet my colleagues."

They walked through the first-floor bar, then climbed the stairs to the second level, where there was another bar in front of an open kitchen with fires blazing in two ovens. It was much warmer and cozier on the second level, and Jen realized she appreciated the heat after her walk in the mist.

Amanda led her over to her colleagues, who were congregating in front of the bar. "Everyone, I want you to meet my friend, Dr. Jen Dawson."

They all smiled and introduced themselves individually. Jen could tell they were checking her out, as they would any romantic interest of Amanda's. After all, Amanda was their boss.

"What can I get you to drink, Dr. Dawson," a young attorney named Jeremy asked.

"I'd love an Anchor Steam on tap, if they have it. And, please, call me Jen," she said. She opened her bag to look for money, but he insisted on buying.

"We're celebrating Jeremy's victory in a jury trial that ended this morning," Amanda said.

"Congratulations," Jen said.

"What type of medicine do you practice?" Jeremy asked.

"Emergency. I work at San Francisco Community Hospital."

"Oh, lots of action there, I'm sure."

"Never a dull moment. What type of trial did you win?"

"Homicide due to gang violence."

Jen's eyes widened. "Scary work. We treat gang members in the ER, and we constantly have to be on guard for enemy gang members storming in."

"No doubt. How long have you known Amanda?"

"Not very. Tell me what I need to know," she said flirtatiously.

Jeremy looked at Amanda, who was standing next to Jen.

"Only the good stuff," Amanda mouthed silently to Jeremy.

"She's smart and beautiful, but I'm sure you've already figured that out."

Jen laughed. "I'm just interested in her personality."

"I think you two will be good together." He handed her the beer. She raised her glass to him before taking a drink. The amber liquid felt so welcome after the emotional breakup.

Amanda leaned into Jen, looping her arm through Jen's and finding her hand, twining fingers. She smiled a ridiculously dreamy smile as she looked from Jeremy to Jen.

"I like you for *your* personality, too," Amanda said to Jen.

Jen leaned in and kissed Amanda's temple.

"You're a beautiful couple," Jeremy said, admiring them.

"Hey everyone," another lawyer shouted over the conversation, "do we want a table? The hostess just told me she has a table for ten ready." Everyone followed the hostess to a rectangular table in the middle of the second floor.

"Do you want to stay and eat?" Amanda asked Jen.

"If it's okay with you. I'm starved."

"When aren't you starved?"

"Valid." Jen caught Amanda by the hand and pulled her back to the bar.

Jen lowered her head for a quick kiss before they joined everyone at the table. Once their lips collided, however, Amanda was having none of it—a quick kiss, that is. Balancing her glass of wine in one hand, she guided Jen's head closer with the other, savoring Jen's full lips and exploring the liquid heat of her mouth. They were molten hot, the fire in the brick blazing behind them. Despite the raucous noise from the bar and restaurant, they could hear each other moaning.

"Hey you two, we're gonna order," Jeremy hollered, attempting to look out for Amanda's best interest in a public setting.

"God, so many people around—" she said against Jen's lips. "I suppose he's right."

"I'd say 'let's leave,' but I'm so hungry, I have to eat something."

Amanda smiled, her thumb on Jen's chin, affectionately wiping it off. "Let's eat."

They sat across from Jeremy and a female lawyer at the very end of the table. Jen had been introduced to her earlier, but couldn't remember her name. She had only two things on her mind—food and Amanda. Nothing else mattered.

They placed their orders, and Jen felt Amanda's left hand on the top of her thigh, possessively perched there, giving Jen a little squeeze. Jen experienced an involuntary shudder at Amanda's touch, making Amanda smile as she asked Jeremy a question about the judge who oversaw his trial. As far as Jen was concerned, Amanda could do anything she wanted to under the table. They were Amanda's work colleagues, not Jen's. She had nothing to hide or be embarrassed about.

She couldn't restrain herself, so she placed her hand on Amanda's neck, under her falling curls, and thumbed designs over her spine. Amanda's lips curled as she listened to Jeremy tell trial stories. At one point, Amanda looked at Jen and their eyes locked, both indicating they wanted so much more than what they could do with affectionate touches in front of colleagues.

Jen leaned into Amanda's ear and whispered, "I want you."

Amanda smiled, but kept her attention trained on Jeremy, who was content to entertain all within earshot with his heroics in the courtroom. After what seemed like an eternity, their food arrived. Jen ate with her usual enthusiasm, amazed at how Amanda could eat and still keep her hand on Jen's thigh.

"Amanda, I heard that you and Tommy Vietti wrapped up the investigation on the Farber homicide," Jeremy said. "Congrats."

"Thanks. Tommy did the heavy lifting. He's so clever, you know."

"Yeah, I've worked a few investigations with him and learned a lot. He intuits the criminal's motives. He's got a real, old-school talent."

Jen's heart swelled with pride. He was respected in his work, but she knew that all along.

"How true." Amanda glanced at Jen.

***

George was in the car, parked out front, eating the pasta dish that Amanda had sent to him. When he was finished, he called Ryan Delmastro, Tommy's supervising detective and second cousin.

"Hello?" Ryan answered.

"Hey. It's George. I'm on duty, so I need a favor."

"On a Friday night? This better be good."

"Can you call Tommy Vietti and meet up with him? I think he's wishing he had some company to celebrate with."

"Tommy? I thought he had a girl."

"He does, but they broke up."

"How the hell do you know?"

"I have ears and eyes. And, I look out for our own."

"I'll call him right away."

"Thanks." George hung up.

***

Chapter 35

North Beach

Tommy was laid out in the back of a cab, cruising down Columbus Avenue, the street lights and buildings a blur as they sped by. His phone rang. It was Ryan, his boss, but Tommy was drunk, so he answered it anyway.

"Hello?" he slurred.

"Hey Tommy! It's Ryan. How the hell are ya?"

"Hi, Ryan. Shitfaced."

"Ha-ha. You deserve it. I just wanted to tell you again, congratulations on cracking the Farber case today. Good job, man!"

"Thanks." Tommy was grateful for the attaboy.

"A few of the guys and I are at McCrery's Pub on Folsom. Wanna join us? We wanna hear all the details."

"Really?"

"That's right," Ryan encouraged.

"I'd love to, but I need food, so I'm on my way to my sister's restaurant. Maybe I'll catch up with you after I eat some dinner."

"That'd be great. Just call before you come over in case we leave, okay?"

"Yeah, thanks, man."

Ryan knew Tommy would never call. He was too far gone. At least his sister would look after him.

The taxi pulled up to Mama Mia's, and Tommy paid him what he thought was the fare, but he couldn't be sure because he felt fuzzy, and the driver had said the amount really fast. The display on the meter was no help because Tommy couldn't read it without his half-glasses.

He stumbled out of the car and made a zigzag for the kitchen door of Tina's restaurant. It was unlocked, so he threw it open and stepped into the loud, chaotic atmosphere of a busy restaurant kitchen.

He drew a few double-takes, given his inebriated state. Tina spied him and came rushing over. "Hey, Bro, congratulations on solving your case! I saw you on the news." She threw open her arms for a hug.

"Thanks, Sis," he slurred, falling into her with so much force that they stumbled back together against the stainless-steel counter.

"Whoa, Tommy. You been drinkin'?" she asked.

"Maybe." He looked at her and lost it. His face contorted, and he burst into tears, burying his head on her shoulder.

"What's wrong?" She hugged him tightly as he cried.

"Jen broke up with me," he said between sobs.

"I'm so sorry, Tommy." She would hold him as long as he needed.

***

Hall of Justice

County Jail

Susie sat in the lower bunk with her knees pulled up to her chin. Her roommate had made it very clear that she wanted quiet, and that Susie should stay on the bottom bunk, keeping still.

The metal hallway door unlocked, and Susie heard a guard enter. The guard stopped in front of Susie's cell. "Sangiolo, come with me."

"Me?" Susie asked.

"Is there anyone else in there named Sangiolo?"

Susie bolted off her bunk and lunged toward the door. She slid out, and the guard closed and relocked it.

"Where are we going?" Susie asked above the cat calls from the other cells as they walked past.

"To processing. Some dude met your million-dollar bail."

"I don't believe it."

After Susie signed the paperwork and changed into her street clothes, she was given her valuables, and the door to the free world opened into the waiting area. Nick Nutini was standing under the fluorescent light in a black leather jacket.

"Hi doll," he said.

"God! It's you." She rushed into his arms.

"It's me." He smoothed her hair.

"Thank you for making my bail. It's a nightmare in there."

"Been there; done that. Don't you worry about a thing. I hired the best defense lawyer in California. We're gonna beat this thing."

"You think so?"

"I know so." He kissed her forehead. "Let's get the hell outta here."

They walked down the steps and got into Nick's car.

As they drove away, Albert Petrov followed a few car lengths behind them.

***

San Francisco Community Hospital

Lane was on his beloved sailboat in the Bay, a few hundred yards off Alcatraz Island. Natasha was with him, but the mast struck her as it whipped the opposite direction when Lane tacked. She was thrown overboard, into the cold, churning waters. He saw her struggling behind the boat as he sped on, her bobbing head and flailing arms becoming smaller in the wake.

He tried to bring his boat about, but the wheel wouldn't turn. She yelled to him, "Lane..." as she flailed helplessly, going under with each wave crashing over her head. Lane watched in horror as he helplessly left her behind, her raised hand the last to sink as she went under.

He jolted awake, opening his eyes. He was in a hospital room. *Am I on the night shift? Did I just nap for a few minutes? Do they need me?* He moved to roll out of bed, thinking he should return to work, only to discover the guard rails were up and he had a heparin lock on the top of his hand with an IV attached to it. That was strange.

He also noticed that his right leg felt like a tree trunk when he tried to roll over. He seemed to leave it behind as his body struggled to the left, trying to get out of bed. Then, he felt a dull ache in it, accompanied by a searing jolt of pain.

He screamed out.

"Daddy?" he heard Angelina ask. "Are you awake?"

"What? Who's there?" he mumbled, searching the room for his girl.

She scurried to the side of his bed, laying her hand on his shoulder. "I'm right here, Daddy. Are you okay?"

"Hi, baby. Yes. Daddy is okay. How did you get here?"

"I brought her," their nanny, Mrs. Giacomo, said.

"Hi, Mrs. Giacomo. I didn't see you sitting over there." Lane squinted through the after-effects of his anesthesia. "Thank you for bringing Angie." His voice was gravelly from the endotracheal tube and dehydration. He struggled to bring his life into focus, searching for an explanation as to why he was lying in a hospital bed with his daughter and her nanny in the room.

He closed his eyes for a minute and saw Susie yelling at him. Threatening him. She had a gun. She had never owned a gun, so he asked her where she got it, but she wouldn't tell him. She was screaming that if he went to the police, she would kill him. Her hand was shaking so badly that she fired off a shot, hitting the wall behind him. He tried to reason with her, tell her about his last conversation with Detective Vietti, but she wouldn't listen.

She said she knew Vietti and had set things straight with him—that it was all Lane's fault. If he never would have had an affair, they wouldn't be in the situation they found themselves. Since she had been holding the gun, he decided not to argue with her, pointing out that they wouldn't be in their current predicament if she hadn't killed Natasha.

The doorbell rang, and they both heard Detective Vietti yelling to come in. It was too late. Her hand wobbled again, the weight of the gun challenging her narrow wrist. She yelled at Vietti to leave, but fired off another shot, this time hitting Lane in the leg. Lane had been so shocked, looking down to see the blood stain his khaki pants. He collapsed to the floor, writhing in pain as the familiar sear ran his nerve endings to his spine, then up to his brain. He was back in Iraq, lying in the desert, bullets flying over his head.

He remembered now. Susie had been arrested by Detective Vietti.

"Did Mama really shoot you in the leg?" Angie asked, as forthright as only an eight-year-old could be.

Lane looked at Mrs. Giacomo, who Angie called Nani. She shrugged, indicating she hadn't told Angie anything. "The news," she mouthed at him.

Susie had hired Mrs. Giacomo because she was an old family friend to the Sangiolos.

Tommy recalled Susie saying something about being related through marriage. It didn't make any difference. Angie loved her like a grandmother, and Mrs. Giacomo spoiled Angie. That's all that mattered.

"Ah. Yes. She did," Lane rasped. "Can you lift that water bottle with the straw to my lips?"

"Sure." Angie carefully held the bottle so Lane could sip water. "Why did Mama shoot you?"

"I think it was by mistake."

"Is she going to shoot anyone else?"

"Come here." He held his arm wide so she could hug him. "No. The police took the gun, and I don't think your mom wants to shoot anyone else. You don't have to be afraid, sweetie."

"I'm afraid she's going to jail, and I'll never see her again."

"You'll get to see her. And, you always have me, and I love you very much. So does your Nani."

"Thank you, daddy." She climbed onto the bed, then squeezed in beside him.

"I'm sorry, Lane," Mrs. Giacomo said, but the steely look in her piercing brown eyes didn't match her words.

"Thank you." He shrunk under the weight of her stare. He could only imagine what she and her friends in North Beach were saying about Susie going off the rail and shooting him. He had a vague recollection of police officers being there, and he wondered if she had been arrested, but he didn't want to ask in front of

Angie. He also vaguely recalled seeing Jen in scrubs, standing above him with her OSHA glasses on, wearing a hat and surgical mask. Was that a dream or had she taken care of him in the ER? He had a thousand questions, none of which he could ask right now.

***

Chapter 36

SoMa

Jen's first dinner with Amanda's colleagues was going smoothly. Jeremy was telling them that the T.V. reporter, Kip Moynihan, still wanted to press charges against Dimitri Ivanov for punching him in the face. Jeremy had met with Kip and tried to convince him that no one was going to send Mr. Ivanov to jail for clocking Kip after he told the Ivanovs their daughter was having an affair. Kip had been incensed, promising that he'd do a hatchet job on the DA's office if they didn't.

"I know the owner of the KPIX news station," Amanda said. "I'll call him. I'd be surprised if he doesn't know who Dimitri Ivanov is. They run in the same circles. There's no way anyone would cross Ivanov. Thanks for telling me about this, Jeremy."

"Your connections are amazing," he said.

Amanda was still stroking Jen's thigh—with very talented fingers. Amanda's touch was stirring all of Jen's senses. Stealing a glance at Amanda's profile, Jen saw what she thought was a sly smile, although it could have been in reaction to Jeremy's imitation of Kip Moynihan.

Nonetheless, Jen was on fucking-fire and either had to get out of the restaurant with Amanda *now,* or forcibly remove Amanda's hand from roaming dangerously close to her erogenous epicenter. For the shear sake of her own sanity, something had to give.

Jen leaned into Amanda's thick, curly hair and whispered in her ear. "Wanna get out of here?"

Amanda nodded, an inscrutable look on her face for the benefit of her team.

Amanda picked up her wallet and placed two one-hundred-dollar bills on the table. "This is for Jen and me. We're going to leave now. This was a great week. Congratulations, everyone. See you Monday."

Amanda pushed back her chair and stood, waiting for Jen to do the same.

I guess Amanda isn't into long goodbyes, Jen thought.

"Goodnight. It was a pleasure meeting you. Have a good weekend," Jen said. She planned on simply following Amanda, but Amanda stopped and looped her hand through Jen's arm as they walked down the stairway together and out the door. Amanda must have alerted George to their departure because the car was idling, and he was standing with the back door open and waiting. *Note to self: never underestimate Amanda's preparedness.*

As onlookers in line for the restaurant tried to catch a glimpse of who Amanda and Jen were, Amanda glided into her car, pulling Jen in behind her, allowing George to close the door. He did, then quickly circled the car to drop into the driver's seat.

"Where to?" he asked.

"My place. Thanks, George." Amanda hit the button for the privacy glass, blocking him from their audible world.

"Is it too controlling for me to say we're going to my place? I haven't even seen your place."

"No worries. It's you," Jen responded, then fell into Amanda, kissing her as George pulled into traffic. Jen swiped her lips across Amanda's, not staying long, but making heated contact. She traced the outline of Amanda's lower lip with her tongue, nibbling it until Amanda moaned.

Unable to endure the teasing, Amanda grabbed Jen's head and held her as she kissed her, pulling Jen into her mouth with a ferocity that surprised even Jen, especially in the presence of George's eyes in the rearview mirror, which didn't seem to bother Amanda.

Amanda's warm hands found Jen's breasts, and she gently held them, massaging, then drawing her thumb across Jen's nipples. Jen rewarded Amanda with a gasp, pressing her chest into Amanda's palms.

"I can't breathe—when you do that," Jen whispered.

"Wait until we get to my place."

"I might not know what I'm doing."

"I'm sure you're a quick learner." Amanda pulled Jen close and blew into her ear, then licked it.

Jen collapsed into Amanda's experienced tongue and hands. It seemed like it took forever to make it to her house, Jen struggling to keep her hands on the outside of Amanda's dress.

"I want the first time for you to be perfect," Amanda said, as they passed through the stone pillars marking the Sea Cliff neighborhood.

"It already is," Jen said.

As soon as George stopped, Jen opened the door and they rushed out of the car.

"Goodnight, George," Amanda threw over her shoulder.

***

Jen awoke sometime later. She was lying on top of Amanda's back, relishing the sensuous contact. She didn't know how long she had slept on top of her naked lover, but it was the most intimate experience she had ever had. She gently rolled off Amanda and tried to figure out where she was. *Amanda's bedroom.* She smiled as she faced Amanda, who sighed and scooted into Jen's arms. Jen smoothed Amanda's hair as she nestled into her neck.

Jen held her, experiencing for the first time sleeping with a woman, feeling Amanda's curves pressed up against her own, her steady breathing indicating she had fallen back asleep. Jen found herself too excited to sleep, but she didn't want to wake Amanda. She lay there, processing their relationship. It had begun only five nights ago, but felt like they had been together for a lifetime.

While elated, she worried about Tommy. She knew him, and despite his tough exterior, he was a very emotional man, who probably was taking their breakup hard. She loved him and would miss him. She was so confused, satisfying herself sexually with Amanda, diving into Amanda's world, but only a few days from sharing a world with Tommy. It had all happened so fast, her mind hadn't caught up with her body.

"What are you thinking about?" Amanda whispered against Jen's neck.

"How did you know I was awake?"

"I can feel your mind spinning," Amanda said, her voice thick with sleep.

"I'm sorry. I was thinking about Tommy, and what he's going through."

"Uh-huh. No second thoughts about us?"

"God no." Jen kissed the top of Amanda's head. "Don't even think that, much less say it. This has been fantastic."

"For me, too." Amanda kissed the indentation below Jen's throat.

"My jugular notch."

"What did you just call me?"

"I didn't call you anything. You kissed my jugular notch."

"Oh. This little indentation here that's so inviting?" Amanda pressed the tip of her tongue into it.

Jen shivered. "Yeah...that..."

***

Chapter 37

Amanda was in a deep sleep, curled in Jen's embrace. Her face was buried in Jen's blonde hair, her arm and leg thrown over Jen's body. Her dreamless sleep was interrupted, however, by the sound of her phone vibrating on the night stand. How many times had it gone off? She couldn't move her lips from Jen's supple neck, warm and pulsing with life. She was entwined in her new lover's embrace, and whoever was calling could wait. Whatever it was could wait...

Amanda returned to her sleep state, secure in Jen's arms, feeling the beat of Jen's heart against the inside of her arm, which was thrown wide over Jen's chest. She inhaled as she went deeper, Jen's amatory scent permeating her mind. She fell into the cadence of Jen's steady breathing, unified in sleep, their bodies warming each other, perfectly entwined. *I could fall in love with you...*

The persistent sound of her vibrating phone on the night stand invaded Amanda's bliss, however. Pernicious, this time it vibrated longer and stronger. She had to look. She opened one eye and realized the sun was up. Reluctantly, she rolled away from Jen and reached for her nightstand, her hand slamming down on the vibrating phone. She brought it to her face and saw that she had two missed calls, a voicemail and several texts.

"Shit," she mumbled, waking now. It was seven on a Saturday morning. This couldn't be good. She thumbed the screen to her voicemail and put it up to her ear as Jen rolled into her, sliding her arm across Amanda's chest. Jen nestled her head into the curve of Amanda's underarm and onto her chest. Amanda held her phone with one hand and placed her arm over Jen's shoulders, pulling her close. Jen sighed and fell back to sleep.

Amanda listened to her voicemail message. "Amanda, this is Ryan Delmastro. Look at your emails. Tommy Vietti resigned last night. I think we both know why. Can you fix this today? Let me know how I can help. Thanks."

Amanda pressed the end button. *Fuck, Tommy. You're retaliating? Against your boss? The department?*

She switched screens to her email and read Tommy's email to her and Ryan. It was sent at midnight last night.

Amanda and Ryan,

I love this depretment. I love a lot of things, but theyre gone now. Consider this my resignation. I'm leaving this job. This whole fucking town. Sitauation is ass. Fuck you Amanda!

Detective Vietti

A sigh escaped Amanda's lips. Great. Exactly what she had been afraid of. She let her arm drop to the bed with her phone in her hand and blew out a small sigh.

"Ummm..." Jen moaned against Amanda's chest. "What's wrong?"

Amanda considered how to respond. She kissed Jen on the top of her head and whispered, "I don't want to bother you with it, but I do have to make a call. You stay here and rest."

Amanda moved to leave, but Jen's arm tightened around her. "Can it wait?"

Amanda loved the possessiveness, but felt she had to try to reach Tommy. She set her phone on the nightstand and rolled to face Jen. "I'm sorry. I wish it could wait, but it can't. Promise me you'll be here when I return in a few minutes?" She kissed Jen's forehead and eyelids, while gently stroking her back.

Jen arched, pressing herself into Amanda, kissing the base of her neck and licking the indent in her collarbone.

Amanda shivered. "God, Jen, what you do to me."

Jen rose over Amanda, pushing her back into the soft sheets and lowering herself onto her, mashing their bodies into curves fusing into curves. She kissed her until they were overcome with heat, paroxysms of desire, their bodies seeking pleasure and release. In a matter of seconds, Amanda's work obligations were replaced by her carnal catch to have sex with Jen, whose hands were gliding over all the right places, driving Amanda insane with passion. She had no control over how her body responded. She set aside the thought of calling Tommy and concentrated on pleasing Jen in every possible way....

Later, as their panting subsided, and Jen again fell asleep, Amanda scooted out of bed and grabbed her cell phone. She dressed in her robe and padded out to her kitchen for coffee. She had to think about what she could say to Tommy, and more importantly, what she couldn't say to Tommy—like, "Isn't Jen great in bed? Has she ever done that thing with her tongue to you? Doesn't she taste heavenly?"

As Amanda waited for her coffee to brew, she opened the sliding door and Zumba entered, twitching his tail and meowing in protest at the late hour for breakfast.

"Simmer down," Amanda said. "I'll pour some food." She rehearsed a few potential messages for Tommy in her mind as she poured Zumba's cat food and got him some water. Nothing sounded appropriate, maybe because she had just had sex with the girl who broke Tommy's heart. *Fuck. I knew this would come back to haunt me. I'm paying the price... But it was worth it. No wonder he proposed to her.*

Amanda poured herself a cup, adding cream and sugar. Maybe some fresh air would help. She threw open the sliding door and walked out to her garden. The ocean fog hadn't burned off yet, so it was still cool and wet, smelling of the Sea Cliff environs—the milieu of oceanfront and eucalyptus— Amanda's favorite smell in the world. The outdoor furniture would still be damp, so she paced around her patio thinking about what to say to Tommy. Chances were that she'd get his voicemail, especially if he was sleeping off a hangover. She had to be smart, because she'd get only one chance.

After she emptied her cup, she returned to a kitchen barstool and found Tommy in her contacts. She hit the number for his phone. Just as she went into his voicemail, however, Jen entered the kitchen in search of the coffee maker. *Shit.* Timing was everything in life, and this wasn't the right time to leave a message for Tommy. *What if Jen said something that Tommy overheard?*

Amanda ended the call and set her phone on the counter.

Jen turned around. "Sorry. Am I interrupting something? You look worried."

"I am worried, and you're not interrupting. Before I make this call, though, I should probably tell you about it. You'll overhear my end of the conversation, so I want to tell you what it's about."

"This sounds serious." Jen rounded the counter and leaned into Amanda for a hug. She set down her mug and held Amanda's face up to her, kissing her. Amanda immediately responded, and they found themselves tangling tongues once again.

Amanda had to disengage before she was swept off her feet. "You're such a good kisser. I should take care of this issue, though, before you make me dizzy all over again. I can't think straight when I'm touching you, or after touching you, or really just around you..."

Jen smiled and straightened, raising her cup to her lips. "Good. That's the way I like it. What's so important?"

"Tommy emailed a couple of us at midnight, resigning. Here. Read it." Amanda held her phone for Jen to read.

"He's pissed. And, he was probably drunk. No, definitely drunk. I wouldn't take it personally, though."

"But it is personal."

"What are you gonna do?"

"I got a voicemail this morning from Ryan, asking me to reach out to Tommy. I was just going to call him. I'm guessing I'll get his voicemail, so I was practicing what I'm going to say."

"Ahh. I should check my own phone. I wonder if he left any messages for me."

"Would you mind? Maybe they'll help me."

"Let me find my phone. I think I dropped my bag in your hallway when we got home." She walked out to the foyer and found her bag, then rifled through it until she found her phone. There were multiple texts and a voicemail from Tommy. Jen's shoulders sank as she returned to the kitchen.

"Yes, he contacted me last night, too. Let me read the texts to you."

Thanks for returning the ring. Not all girls would do that. "That one was at seven, right after I left him at the bar."

Tell Amanda that I'm really pissed at her for stealing you. "That one is an hour later."

You two deserve each other. Ur both beautiful and smart. "That one was at nine-thirty."

"He's still being nice," Amanda said.

"His last one is at eleven-fifteen," Jen said. *I need a new life. I'm gonna move. You and Amanda have a good fucking life.*

"I see the anger is seeping in by then," Amanda said. "He sent his email to Ryan and me shortly afterward. He doesn't have to quit his job. Why the fuck does he want to quit?"

Jen inclined her head at Amanda. "Why do you think? He's embarrassed and humiliated. He probably told all the guys he was going to propose to me, and the next thing he knew, I told him I wanted to be your lover. Everyone at work will be talking about it."

"What's to talk about?" Amanda insisted.

"I know you're evolved, Amanda, but think about it. You have so much sex appeal that you converted a supposedly heterosexual woman, who was with a handsome detective, to become your lover. The prurient interest of the entire force will be ignited. You know those guys?! They'll wonder what *you* have that Tommy doesn't. It's the ultimate humiliation for a man."

"Well, when you put it *that* way…"

Jen grabbed the carafe and refilled their mugs.

"It's probably fruitless for me to try to convince him to stay," Amanda said.

"I think you should try." Jen trailed her finger over Amanda's shoulder and down her arm.

Amanda stared into Jen's vivid blue eyes. "How do you feel about this?"

Jen didn't waiver, her stare holding Amanda's heart. "I feel bad for Tommy, but ecstatic for us. I mean, just being honest here —I've never felt happier." Jen leaned in and brushed her lips across Amanda's.

"Thank you. I'm glad you don't have any regrets."

"Not a one. Why don't I go take a shower while you call Tommy? You need your privacy."

"That might be a good idea. It's awkward enough, and I can't think when you're near me."

Jen ran her hand through Amanda's hair and cupped her chin. "Thank you."

Amanda smiled, and Jen left to shower.

She picked up her phone and hit Tommy's contact number again. She went into his voicemail. "Tommy, got your drunk resignation. I miss you already. Take a few weeks off then call me. I need you to testify in this case. Don't even think about coming back to work, though, because there's only room for one of us at the Hall of Justice. PS – I owe you twenty bucks on the bet I lost." Amanda prayed her reverse psychology would work.

She left the kitchen and went to her front door and opened it, looking for the newspaper. It was reasonably close to the front stoop, lying on the cobblestone walkway. She returned to the kitchen and made a bowl of granola with kefir on it, slicing some bananas on top. Zumba practically climbed into the fridge when she opened it, twitching his tail and meowing for milk.

"Do you want milk this morning?"

He answered by biting her toe, not breaking the skin, but pricking it with his sharp incisors.

"Ouch! Zumba!"

He hissed at her.

"Fucking cat. You're lucky I'm nice to you." She poured some milk in his bowl.

Amanda rounded the kitchen island and scooted onto a barstool, sliding the paper toward her, then she remembered she needed her cheapy reading glasses. Thinking back, her best guess was that they were on her bedside table, lying on top of a book.

She slid off the stool and walked to her bedroom suite. As she passed through, she could hear Jen showering in the bathroom. She leaned down to collect her glasses and noticed a piece of scratch paper on the bed with a nubby pencil lying on top of it. She fell into bed and picked it up. The paper had *San Francisco Community Hospital* embossed at the top, and Jen's handwriting below. Amanda put on her half glasses and scanned it—the beginning phrases of a poem.

There were erasure marks and a few words were scratched out here and there, with others written above them, but a few lines were intact.

The everyday love we long to carry

Awakening daily to the soft sounds...
That love [____]
A confident allure
No guilt, no doubt
Soft, supple and secure
Fitting like your favorite jeans—holes
in [just] the right places

Everyday love
Confidently naked
No guessing required
Knowing exactly ...
No thongs desired
[Just] ... striptease
Imagining the ...

Everyday love
Mundane, uncomplicated simplicity
Present without summons
A boundless ...
Everyday love
Perceived in a glance
An interconnected soulful [dance]

Amanda leaned back against the pillow and closed her eyes. So, Jen wrote poetry. What a window into her feelings as well as her expression of them. She hoped Jen was planning on sharing it, otherwise she had just invaded her privacy.

At that moment, she heard the shower click off. She remained in bed, but set the poem back on the sheet, returning the pencil to rest on top of it.

In a few minutes, Jen came out of the bathroom with a towel around her.

"Hey," Jen said, surprised to see Amanda back in bed. Her eyes fell to her draft poem, then searched Amanda's face.

"Guilty as charged." Amanda threw up her hands. "I peeked. And, I loved it."

Jen unwrapped her towel and slid into bed, pulling up the covers. "Thanks. I'm sort of embarrassed because I just started it. I'm far from finished, but I was in the mood, so—"

"It's beautiful. And, so are you." Amanda rolled into Jen. "I can't wait to read the final product." Amanda kissed Jen's forehead, then her eyelids, then the tip of her nose...

***

North Beach

Tommy woke in a foreign bed, a foreign room and a foreign body. He didn't know where he was or who he was. The body in which he was swimming couldn't possibly be his own because his head and heart hurt in equal parts. *Where the fuck am I?*

He slid off the end of the bed, still dressed in what he wore to work the previous day, and lurched for the bedroom door. He recognized the hallway as his sister's house, so made a hard turn to the left, heading for her bathroom. He found it just in time to empty the contents of his stomach into her toilet.

He ran a shower and stripped down. Once he was in her spacious tiled shower, he sat down and let the hot water cascade over him, restoring his sense of self. Everything hurt. Not able to contain his emotions, he cried silently, letting the water pound him.

He stayed there for several minutes, ultimately working up the courage to shampoo his hair and body. When he was able, he rose and dried off with one of his sister's stark white bath sheets. He wrapped it around his waist and joined her in the kitchen.

"Hey," he said.

"Alive?" she asked.

"Barely."

"Eat these eggs and bacon. Here's a tomato juice with aspirin. You're welcome to go back to bed and sleep as long as you like. Danny and the kids are at soccer practice, and I have to open the restaurant."

"Thanks," he said, sitting on a barstool at her counter.

"I'm sorry Jen broke your heart. Do you want me to talk to her?"

"No. I will. In time."

"Okay. Don't rush it. Love you." She gathered her belongings and slipped on a raincoat.

"Love you, too," he said, sipping the tomato juice.

"It's okay if you spend the day. Eat and sleep."

"I might do that."

She blew him a kiss and left.

***

TO BE CONTINUED

***

ACKNOWLEDGEMENTS

Thank you to my husband, Todd Wright. Our experiences in San Francisco, twenty-five years ago, and more recently, laid the foundation for this book. Also note that the poetry is by Todd.

I thank Michelle Burgraff and Erin Skold, with whom I work every day, revealing my inabilities, faults and irreverence at the office. I know firsthand how busy they are, so thank you for taking the time.

I'm grateful to Dr. Sue Cullinan, Medical Director of the Emergency Department, wife and mother of three, and friend to many. Her boundless energy and good cheer energize all around her. Sue, thank you for bringing your energy to this project.

I also thank Dr. Amy Thorpe-Swenson, whose insights into drug interactions were very helpful.

Another lawyer I admire and respect is my colleague, Sherry Hubert. Sherry has been steadfast in her support of my books, so I cornered her in Arizona and inquired whether she would be interested in editing the next project. She brought her considerable writing talent and intellect to the table.

My friend Dennis Pope is an Italian from Chicago, so he paid special attention to Tommy Vietti. Thanks Pope.

There is a certain executive superstar within our hospital system who has shared her creative insights and time in editing the final draft of several of my books. She is a class act, and possesses many character attributes, not the least of which is her ability to stare down an opponent in a no-blinking contest.

I am grateful for the talents of Linda Pophal, my media relations guru.

Thank you to Melissa Levesque, Project Manager at eBookIt and Dawn Fisher, Designer at eBookIt.

I thank M.J. Rose for her advertising skill, among other talents.

Finally, Rob Bignell was very helpful and generous with his editing services.

It takes the efforts of numerous people to make any enterprise successful, and writing and selling books is no exception. I thank my friend, Pammy Jo Craker, for helping me at book signing events. She is generous with her time, positive attitude and supplies!

***

ABOUT THE AUTHOR

Photo by Lily Susan Anderson

Popular author Alexi Venice is best known for her Pepper McCallan series, featuring a corporate lawyer-turned counterterrorism consultant. Pepper travels the world on assignments, fighting both external and internal foes, avenging the death of her son at the hands of terrorists. Venice draws on her own experience as a corporate lawyer for 28 years, an avid adventurist, and a survivor of catastrophic loss for that series. Venice makes it a point to attempt the same activities as

Pepper, including flying the Eclipse jet and boxing.

In 2016, Venice surprised her readers by publishing a contemporary fantasy, AUSTRALIA'S STARR. She explored both religion and politics in a depraved, yet vindicating, story about a young Australian woman who reluctantly fulfills the prophecy communicated to her father on the night of her birth.

BOURBON CHASE is the first in a new mystery series that follows Dr. Jen Dawson, District Attorney Amanda Hawthorne and Detective Tommy Vietti.

Venice is married and lives in Wisconsin.

Learn more about Alexi Venice at www.alexivenice.com or www.facebook.com/alexivenicenovels.